TRESPASS

TRESPASS

D.J. Taylor

Duckworth

First published in 1998 by
Gerald Duckworth & Co. Ltd.
The Old Piano Factory
48 Hoxton Square, London N1 6PB
Tel: 0171 729 5986
Fax: 0171 729 0015

A catalogue record for this book is available
from the British Library

ISBN 0 7156 2825 9

Lyrics from 'Boredom' (Devoto/Shelley) reproduced
by kind permission of the author.

Typeset by Ray Davies
Printed in Great Britain by
Redwood Books Ltd, Trowbridge

I've taken this extravagant journey
so it seems to me
I just came from nowhere
and I'm going straight back there
Howard Devoto, 'Boredom'

Family likeness has often a deep sadness in it.
Nature, that great tragic dramatist, knits us together by bone and muscle, and divides us by the
subtler web of our brains; blends yearning and
repulsion; and ties us by our heart-strings to the
beings that jar us at every moment.
George Eliot, *The Mill on the Floss*

Dream not of other worlds, what creatures there
Live in what state, condition or degree.
John Milton, *Paradise Lost*

For my father, with love

(and thanks, H. G.)

Prologue

Waking at five, in near darkness, I often used to experience that feeling of complete detachment which is characteristic of the overstretched mind. The properties of this sensation were always the same: the noise of the sea boiling away in the distance, a faint glow of light from the street, the low and slightly sinister hum brought on by the Caradon's eccentric heating arrangements. Proof of identity lay everywhere around – in my reflection in the cracked mirror, a foot away on the bedside table, in the copy of *La Nausée* lying next to it – but for quite a long time I would literally not know who I was. In this disembodied state, the people and incidents I thought about – they were seldom contemporary events, usually from fifteen or twenty years before – seemed profoundly alarming. My uncle standing in the wide board room; the big house at Sunningdale with the French windows open to let in the air; older pictures from the Redbridge days and beyond – all were both recognisable and full of a kind of horror I had never associated with them in life. Perhaps half an hour would pass in this way, mounting languor always balanced by the sense of impending doom, until, like a fast-working anaesthetic, sleep would come again.

On this particular morning sleep did not come. It was about half-past six. Beyond a patch of uncurtained window, rain fell over the grey streets. From below, somewhere deep in the bowels of the hotel, there came a sound of odd and somehow furtive movement, as if the person making it feared detection in every step that he or she took. Nearer at hand, someone else – almost certainly Mr Archer – was singing in a high, sad voice:

> 'Beans won't get no keener reception
> In a beanery
> Bless our mountain greenery home
> Ta-ta, ta-ta ... '

Long-standing residents sometimes said that the Caradon looked at its best in the early morning. The front lobby, reached ten minutes later – you could never be sure of hot water at that hour – bore this out. Sunk in grey light, which bobbed and glinted off odd protrusions of glass and chrome, it looked vaguely welcoming: austere, maybe, but not despicable. Standing on the lower stairs, at the point furthest away from the reception area, it scarcely resembled a hotel – more an exceptionally badly furnished domestic house or antechamber to some public room. Nearer at hand the place's true identity was revealed in a high, formica-covered reception desk, a green baize square set into the wall and pinned with notices, and a blackboard covered with unclaimed envelopes. As I stood looking at all this – a scene inspected twenty times before but forever fascinating in its seediness – a light went on in the office behind reception and there was a furious scrabbling noise: boxes being thrown about, heavy feet wandering. Eventually Mr Archer's face and upper body appeared from behind the hatch.

'Up early?'

'That's right.'

'Off to get a newspaper?'

'Probably.'

'We can get them delivered, you know.'

People going out to buy newspapers was an old grievance of Mr Archer's. I looked at him while he pronounced this rebuke. In the yellow early morning light he seemed more ghastly than ever: livid, his face cut while shaving and dotted with tiny plugs of tissue paper. The clothes he wore – an infinitely old and battered dressing gown covering a lemon-coloured vest – reinforced this effect. Thinking perhaps that it was bad policy to criticise a guest at such an early hour of the morning, he said in a more conciliatory way:

'Another ashtray went last night.'

'Did it?'

'That's right. Seven in the last fortnight. I shall have to start chaining them to the tables if this goes on.'

I moved on towards the door, which was unlocked as usual. Someone had left a pail of water, half full, on the topmost step. Narrowly circumventing this, I stepped down into the street.

'Not bad for – ,' Mr Archer would sometimes say, naming whichever month the calendar had reached. It was not bad for February. In the eastern sky, where, far distant and invisible lay the Hook of Holland, crimson streaks were emerging out of a slate-grey surround. Nearer at hand there were gulls crowding over the rooftops and the lighthouse tower. A few cars chugged by.

A hundred yards down the street, at a crossroads within sight of the sea, there was a shop which sold newspapers, cigarettes, cream cakes of a kind I rather liked. Here a minor crisis presented itself. Owing to a mix-up in the delivery arrangements, the teenager at the counter proposed, nothing had so far arrived at the shop except the local papers – the *Eastern Daily Press* and the *Waveney Gazette* – and a single copy of the *Financial Times*. I chose the *Financial Times*.

It was still hardly seven o'clock. A few of the town's early risers – old women walking their dogs, a couple of men who worked at the brewery – straggled past, bodies angled against the wind. Imperceptibly, I felt another tug on the thread of memory: first the pre-dawn reverie about my uncle; now the purchase of a newspaper with which I would always associate him.

Beyond the headland, to the north of the town, the sun was rising over the wet grass and the endless fields of sedge. In the distance the sea boomed. The Caradon's foyer was deserted, except for a pile of post that had appeared on the lino inside the front door. I picked it up, thereby infringing another of Mr Archer's private ukases, and began flicking through it. There was a letter to Mr Archer from the bank: that would cause trouble; nothing else of interest. I moved off into the silent lounge, reached by way of a corridor that snaked off along the left-hand side of Mr Archer's office. Here it seemed even colder than the street, each exhaled breath rising dramatically to the ceiling like an orc's spout. I settled myself in a frayed armchair underneath a reproduction of Dürer's 'Praying Hands' and began to examine the paper.

Reading the *Financial Times* alone in the residents' lounge of the Caradon, raw Suffolk air seeping through the thin glass, raised mixed emotions. A feeling of pleasurable recognition – like finding a school magazine describing the doings of your contemporaries – was quickly cancelled out by regret that everything you read described a world from which you were eternally debarred and could only monitor from afar. I turned over a couple of pages and read a report about joint venture agreements in Vietnam and a column in which somebody worried about the effect of Finnish depredations on the Eurobond market. The lines of level, even print, broken up with their advertisements ('*as a matter of record only*') ran stiffly away on all sides. In these circumstances it was the merest chance that I saw the two paragraphs about Huntercombe Holdings, the merest chance, in fact, that those two paragraphs had ever been included by some dutiful company news editor, for they recorded only the barest information: the final disposal by an administrator of the assets held by a collapsed unit trust. There it was, though. There was no getting away from it. Huntercombe Holdings had been only the tiniest fragment of my uncle's empire – in its original form no more than a shell company through which he intended to channel various off-shore profits – but for some reason I remembered the day on which it came into being with vivid accuracy: my uncle in the great board room; the blue company proposal books; the lunch ('Let's have a lunch, George,' I could hear my uncle saying, 'Simpson's or the Ivy or somewhere.').

The smell of cooking was beginning to pervade the room. Somewhere in the distance someone was striking a gong. I sat back in the chair. There was more of this, I realised, a whole lot more. Laying the paper carefully down across my knees like a travelling rug, I began to brood over past time.

In the six years since the crash I had lived a vagrant existence. Did you ever know a time when you hadn't the faintest idea what to do with your life or where to live it? That was me since the day the DTI inspectors moved in on Chell Holdings, and my poor, browbeaten uncle embarked on what was to prove his final journey. At a stroke that old life, that spangled existence I'd somehow imagined would go on for ever, was blown into smithereens. Even then I knew that there would be no point lingering in the rubble. The world had changed, and all that remained was flight.

Some instinct took me east. Not to Norwich, where I'd grown up – which would have been a rather symbolic admission of defeat – but to the coast. Enough money had survived the bust-up to allow me a competence, and for a couple of years I lived a frugal, solitary kind of life in bed and breakfasts and cheap flats. The oddest things kept me in one place or sent me on my way again: the way a cat sauntered across a farmyard in the early sun; the slant of a line of trees down from a railway embankment. I couldn't explain these sensations, or the contradictions they produced – the wish to settle down countered by the need to be moving on; all I could do was to react to them. Predictably, I've scarcely any memory of those early months. What there is is queer fragments: smoking a cigarette at Lowestoft station; watching a dog stalk a hare once in a field outside Woodbridge (he did it in an odd, delinquent way as if he feared that at any moment an invisible hand might fall on his collar); a sunset somewhere near Orford that seemed to go on for hours, burning off the rock and the distant sea. I don't know if I enjoyed any of this: I think I was numb in a way. There was also a sense that I was entirely alone, what with my uncle gone and the business closed down, and somehow without the resources to find a new kind of life. And yet I didn't grieve for him, because I knew he was vanished and there was no chance of bringing him back.

After a while things improved. As the money held out – I rarely broke into the capital sum and aimed to live off interest – I gave up the bed and

10

breakfast shacks for small hotels: gaunt seaside premises along the Suffolk coast in Southwold, Felixstowe and Orford Ness. Here, curiously, there was society of a kind: grim old ladies abandoned by their families, wayfaring middle-aged men, 'travellers' in confectionery and fancy goods who survived on twenty pound orders from the corner shops. All the jetsam of English society comes to rest in a seaside hotel out of season. There were even women of a sort, and a series of tense, fugitive relationships conducted in badly painted rooms that echoed to the cry of seagulls, and an ominous third presence – the long grey arm of the sea, always visible from the window. It is impossible to convey the dreariness of those days – wind blowing in across the flat, the subdued chatter of the lounge, the stinking corridors – so much so that I think at an early stage they became external to me, routine appendages to a proper life lived out somewhere else, away from the sandy carpets, the bridge fours and the eternal reek of salt. At the same time I don't believe I was unhappy. I was treading water out here in the narrows, half-submerged, head bobbing above the surface, the big ships far away, grateful to have avoided the deep water below.

From time to time the older, bygone world intruded. Sometimes letters came: I threw them away unread. Outside the context in which I knew them, their writers seemed scarcely to exist. Once Kippax himself arrived unexpectedly at a hotel I was staying at in Great Yarmouth and we walked up and down the front for an hour or so: two courteous ex-businessmen, each of whom knew more about the other than he cared to let on. I never liked Kippax, and I was glad to see him go. All the same, he had revealed something to me, something that the paragraph in the *Financial Times* had brought home with greater force: that it was all still there, that life, still constant and enduring.

And now, I realised, I had a purpose. There was an attaché case in the back of a wardrobe at the Caradon that had lain unopened for years. That evening, greatly daring, I took a safety-pin – the key had long since disappeared – picked the lock and shook the contents out over the bedspread. There wasn't much – less than I remembered. A few press cuttings from the late '70s. A letter from the DTI people. Some salary chits. One photograph stood out. In it my uncle, dressed in an expensive suit but still contriving to look faintly shabby, ambled nonchalantly up the steps of a great building – the immediate resemblance was to the Bank of England, but this seemed unlikely – his expression somehow combining several, though not all, of the elements I associated with him: good humour; candour; puzzlement; mild enquiry. I stared at it for a long time as the wind blew in against the high windows and the bulb danced in its shade.

11

Later that night, tumbling in above the noise of the sea, the voices began:

Do you think, later, you could explain it somehow?
I might ... Yes, of course I will.
... All of it, I mean. Right from the beginning.
The beginning? Where's the beginning?
The very beginning. Do you think you could do that?
I could try.
I promised him, you see.

Part One

In those days the council houses stretched all over the western side of the city: row after row of huddled, dingy dwellings in orange half-brick or pale white stucco, exotic street names – Fairfax or George Borrow – that weren't at all suggestive of the people who lived in them. In summer the chemicals from the May & Baker factory two miles away came and hung round the doors and gardens with an indescribable smell of sulphur, and the most common sight in that part of Norwich early in the morning was a paperboy wrinkling his nose in disgust as he negotiated somebody's front path.

Most of this early life I've forgotten. But there is a memory of sitting, or perhaps balancing, at any rate precariously, on some vantage point near an upstairs window, and looking at the houses as they faded away into the distance, and my mother – a vague, hectic presence – sweeping me up and carrying me away. Later on there are other phantoms – faces that I can't put names too, my mother, again, ironing towels in the back room of a house that I don't think was ours, snow falling over the turrets of the great mansion at Earlham – but the houses remain, a vista of sagging blue walls and sandpapered outhouses, propped bicycles and scuffed-up lawns. The Norwich council tenants were proud or disdainful of their backyard plots by turns, and a bandbox Eden was generally followed by a cratered dustbowl.

Into these early memories my mother habitually intrudes. I remember her as a small, precise and nearly always angry woman, the source of whose anger I never quite understood, and consequently couldn't do anything to appease. Even as a child, though, accompanying her to the small shops in Bunnett Square or on longer excursions into the city, I'm sure that I had some notion of the oddity of her personality. She was, for instance, quite the most solitary person I have ever known, as alone in a room full of people as on a moor. To this solitariness was added a fanatic adhesion to a kind of propriety uncommon on the West Earlham estate, which occasionally broke out in furious spring-cleanings or handwashings and instructions to 'behave proper'. As a moral code this was completely beyond my comprehension: even now I'm not sure that I understand it. To particularise, behaving proper meant not straying into neighbours' gardens or jeopardising their rose bushes as you walked down the street; it meant sitting for long half-hours in a silent dining-room, with your hands folded across your chest, listening to radio programmes that my mother liked; it meant – oh, a hundred proscriptions and prohibitions and adult blindnesses, and I never could get on with it or believe in its prospectus or deal with the directors who offered its scrip.

In time other figures emerged onto these grey early landscapes. For all her aloofness and her tart disparagement of the gossip of the street corner or the garden gate, my mother wasn't without her cronies. There was an old, faded gentlewoman with hair that might have been made of patent leather who came silently to tea on Sunday afternoons, with whom my mother talked ambiguously about certain 'old days' – horribly ancient and remote they seemed to me – that I later discovered to be a time when my mother had worked in domestic service. There was a decayed and entirely honorary uncle named Jack Carstairs, who rode an antique bicycle and had something to do with a hire purchase firm, with whom she conducted faintly embarrassed transactions in the kitchen. But above all there were the women who came to the house on Friday evenings, and together formed a kind of sorority of the back-kitchen. There were three of these women: Mrs Buddery, who was fixated on the Royal Family; Mrs Winall, who said exactly nothing, except for grunts supporting the main speaker; and Mrs Laband – livelier than the others, and of whom they vaguely disapproved. To me – of whom these ladies took scarcely any notice – they seemed grave, awful people, unsparing in their censoriousness and ghastly in their obsessions. A specimen conversation might go:

MRS BUDDERY: They do say that Prince Charles is going to Gordon-stoun. I wonder what his mother's thinking of.

MRS WINALL (*thoughtfully regarding her teacup*): Ah … um.

MRS LABAND: Now girls, what about a go at cards. Canasta or gin rummy?

MRS BUDDERY: My *Daily Mirror* said that Her Majesty – the old Queen, that is – likes a game of Black Maria. Though I must say I never held with it myself.

MRS WINALL: Oo!

MRS LABAND: Alice! That chap I was telling you about as works in the post office. Not the chap as was being talked of with her from Stannard – you know, the one that serves Saturdays in the Romany Rye – the other one, well apparently …

14

MRS BUDDERY: And when I heard the news about that Rhodesia leaving the Commonwealth, I said to myself *the idea* ...

MRS WINALL (*with a satisfied air*): Ah ... hah!

MRS LABAND: ... married a black man from Birmingham, as I'm a sinful woman.

MY MOTHER: This tea's stewed. I'll put the kettle on.

It was only later that I comprehended how stupendously, how blissfully, how incorrigibly ignorant this triumvirate were. Poor Mrs Winall! She couldn't have told you whether the earth went round the sun or *vice versa*, the name of the current Prime Minister, what fid. def. meant on a penny, any of those inconsequential pieces of information that give pattern and substance to our lives. Once, when I was in my teens, I came across her reading a newspaper – lip-reading, that is – with a kind of baffled, bovine stare, watched her with a profound interest and contempt. As for the others, they formed a depressed and depressing sisterhood, a little dribble of inconsequent talk about bad legs, obstetric horrors and the perils of ingrate children, a category in which I nearly always felt myself included. Looking back, it was as if a giant paperweight, composed of the West Earlham houses, my mother and her cronies, the obligation to 'behave proper', lay across my shoulders, and that it was my duty immediately to grow up and start the work of prising it free.

Growing up in West Earlham at this time followed a well-regulated pattern. Until you were five you simply sat at home and got under your parents' feet (I can just remember awful trackless days, when I must have been about four, playing on a rug in the front room while my mother sat frostily in an armchair). Then, the September after your fifth birthday, you were packed off to Avenue Road infants' school, half a mile away in the direction of the city. If you were lucky your mother would have a rickety bike with a child seat – these were extraordinary contraptions in cast-iron with improvised safety-straps. As far as I recall, my mother consigned me to the care of other children in the street. At seven, unless you were exceptionally stupid (in which case there was a remedial school called the Clare) you stepped up to 'primary', which had a proper playing field and a school football team, and – so the rumour went – the teachers were allowed to hit you on the hand with a ruler if you misbehaved.

If I remember anything about these early years it's the summer holidays, and the endless days spent roaming the parks or lounging by the roadside in Lound or Stannard listening out for the ice-cream vans. A cornet cost threepence in those days, and a Sky-Ray lolly was even cheaper – twopence, maybe, or even a penny-ha'penny. It was in the holidays, too, that you caught occasional glimpses of the world that existed outside West Earlham, an horizon that wasn't bounded by your mother's disapproval or the gloomy Bunnett Square shopfronts: a vague old man who lived next door to Mrs Buddery in Stannard and told stories about his time in the Merchant Navy, who would have invited me to tea if my mother hadn't worried about my being 'interfered with', stepped in and snuffed out our intimacy; a charity fête, once, held at a house far away in Christchurch Road, where a motherly woman doled out lemonade and tried to get me interested in something called the League of Pity – a kind of junior version of the NSPCC, I think – only for my mother, to whom subsequent application was made, to dismiss the scheme on the grounds that its organisers were 'only after your money'.

Mercenary motives were a familiar theme of my mother's conversation. To hear her talk you would have thought that the entire administrative world existed merely to take pecuniary advantage. Education, though provided *gratis*, was a conspiracy to charge you money for supernumerary pairs of gym shoes. The church – there was a friendly curate from St Anne's who sometimes called at the house – 'never paid for itself'. Politicians my mother held in the deepest contempt. If she thought of the House of Commons – and I am not sure if her mind was capable of such an unprecedented leap of the imagination – it was as a kind of opulent *poste restante* where plutocrats ripped open letters stuffed with five pound notes sent in by a credulous public. No doubt I exaggerate my mother. No doubt I ignore her virtues and magnify her frailties. But I can remember when I first came across the Bible marking the appropriate passage with a glint of recognition. There was no milk of human kindness in my mother: it had all been sucked out of her, sucked out of her and thrown away.

Such a queer life! Hedged round and bound up with suspicion, like one of Houdini's packing crates that I saw once in a book, so criss-crossed with thongs and chains that it seemed a miracle that the prisoner could ever free himself. There was a cathedral in Norwich – you could see its spire from the top of Mousehold Heath, triumphing over the skyline – but I never went there; there was a university rising up across the golf course to the west of Earlham Park, in great tessellations of concrete breeze block, but it might as well have been a sewage works for all the notice my mother took of it. To do my mother justice she wasn't unconscious of her role as the guardian of my education. On Sundays occasionally, when the furious 'tidying' mood was on, she would hustle me into my 'good' clothes – tight little jackets and pairs of drooping flannel trousers – and take me on the 85 bus to the Norwich Castle Museum. Here, hand-in-hand, suspicious, but mindful of the free admission, we would parade through roomfuls of paintings by Watts and Alma-Tadema and the painters of the Norwich School. My mother wasn't, it must be known, altogether averse to this recreation, which she called 'doing the pictures', and eventually almost got to have opinions on the various subjects presented for her edification. I can remember her stopping once in front of a painting by Lord Leighton of a gauzily clad Greek girl reclining on a balcony to remark, 'Well, she must have been able to count her goosebumps.' I recall this as a solitary instance of my mother attempting to make a joke. At other times, her mood painfully resigned, she would go off to the museum's restaurant – where they served grey-coloured tea at threepence the cup – leaving me to traverse the empty galleries alone.

Of explanation – who we were, where we came from, what we were supposed to be doing – there was none. And yet it seemed to me that my early life, lived out in the confines of the West Earlham estate, in a dark little house in a fatally misnamed terrace called Bright Road, was crammed with mysteries that demanded explanation. There was, to take the most obvious, the question of my father: a supernatural being, presumably, as he was never referred to or otherwise mentioned. There was the grey-headed gentleman who glared at us from the wall of a back room my mother described reverently as the 'parlour' and who some vague presentiment of ancestry suggested was my grandparent. There were occasional letters, which my mother took from the postman with the most terrific gravity and sat over grimly for a moment or two, and whose by-product, I dimly understood, was a marzipan cake from Oelrich's, the bakers in Bunnett Square, the following Sunday, or an extra-long bus-ride. My mother sometimes imparted little confidences to Mrs Buddery about 'doing her duty by the boy', but I could never get her to divulge what that duty was, or how she came by it. Once in fact – emboldened by some children's book in which He Came Back After All These Years – I came straight out and asked her. It was in the kitchen at Bright Road, on a seething August forenoon, with flies buzzing sadly from the strip of flypaper hung in the topmost window, and damp clothes from the wash lying in baskets under the table. Occupied with the contents of the sink, straightening up from some negotiation with a tea-towel, my mother only half-heard me.

'What's that you're saying, George?'

'I suppose,' I proposed innocently – I was ten years old and thought of myself very much in the manner of those pattern juveniles in children's books – 'that father's coming back soon. Seeing he's been away so long. And I just wondered ... *when* exactly?'

My mother had a number of stock phrases designed to quell irruptions

17

of childish spirit. They included 'Don't give me any of your nonsense', 'Don't start' (pronounced with duosyllabic emphasis, so that the word sounded like *star-art*) and – conclusively – 'That's enough of that, *young man.*' On this occasion she simply gaped, so that as I had no other words in which I could frame the question there was no knowing how long we might have gone on staring at each other, until finally, hoping to move matters forward, I venture again:

'About father. And when he's coming back.'

'Don't give me any of your *non* ... ' my mother began mechanically, and then stopped, and I saw her looking at me, not unkindly, but with an air of quite dreadful foreboding. 'I may as well tell you,' she said, picking up a flat iron and beginning to apply it with huge, angry strokes, 'your father's dead.'

So that was it. Wondering a little, I imagined a pale and somehow melancholy-looking man supine on a hospital bed. 'What did he die of?'

'Die of?' By this stage my mother was thoroughly exasperated. 'What does it matter what he died of? The *idear*! He's dead and gone and we've got to make the best of it.'

At this distance I can't quite recollect the tone in which this information was conveyed to me. Annoyance, certainly – as if I'd disturbed long-dead ghosts which had been better kept in their vault; alarm perhaps, in that I might have asked questions which would have been altogether beyond my mother's ingenuity to deal with.

Curiously I received the news, which might have distressed a less sensitive child, with a certain amount of complacency. The divorce laws had got as far as West Earlham by the early '60s and there were other children at school, several of them, who had absent fathers. Not having a father at all seemed to place me in an exclusive category, and I can remember several pitying looks from my mother's cronies at around this time, or rather pitying looks that now bore some sort of explanation. It would be true to say, also, that the mere fact of my mother's unburdening of herself in this way lent a kind of complicity to our relationship, that each of us was aware in the last resort that there was a great deal more to be said. Even my mother, capable at other times of the most fantastic silences and duplicities, was prepared to acknowledge that. What precisely was said about my father on this occasion I don't recall, but the abiding photographic image I have of him – a small, faintly put upon figure with greying hair cut *en brosse* – dates from this time, as do the few odd talismans that my mother had preserved in commemoration of him: some postcards sent from Occupied Europe during the war; an RAF pay book; a carnation pressed into a music hall programme.

As relics, though, they were hugely unsatisfactory, if only because no imaginative life seemed ever to have attached to them. My mother, for instance, though she wasn't above displaying them to me on odd occasions, never talked about them or cared to be drawn on their ultimate significance to her life. The consequence was that I found them arbitrary and faintly inhuman, difficult to connect with the living entity of my father and better forgotten. I can remember once or twice putting some direct question – it may even have been about the postcards, which contained queer little ironic protests of affection – and despairing at my mother's absolute refusal to become involved. After which the mystery of my father simply took its place among the many mysteries that lay behind my childhood; something that I imagined I would come back to but knew that I didn't possess the immediate resources to make my own.

I've said that my mother was ignorant. This isn't completely true, as her knowledge of West Earlham lore – in particular its social demarcations – was encyclopaedic. Even at a distance of thirty years I can remember something of this litany. Bright Road was 'better' than the adjoining thoroughfare of Stannard, though neither matched, in terms of desirability and *éclat*, their near-neighbour George Borrow. Ideally one would eschew council accommodation altogether – everyone I knew, even Mr Hopkinson, whom my mother worshipped as a kind of god because he worked for the Norwich Union Life Insurance Society, lived in a council house – but you could mitigate this disgrace by renting one of the 'double bay fronts' along Earlham Road. As a small boy, to whom social hierarchies existed simply as 'poor people' and 'rich people', I consumed details of this kind like bread-and-butter. Then there was the vexed question of what one produced to eat at the Sunday afternoon high teas that were the high-point of neighbourhood social life. A few society hostesses provided crab meat, which my mother thought was ostentatious. She herself served tinned salmon, bought in two-shilling tins from Davies's, the grocer on the square, but there were families known to make do with sardines ('The idea,' my mother scoffed) and Mrs Winall, whose husband was unemployed and whose children sometimes hovered on the brink of raggedness, incurred lasting ignominy by regaling a select band of intimates with a tin of frankfurters. Most important of all, though, was what you did for a living. My mother liked the idea of a schoolteacher, could have tolerated a reader of electricity meters, but regarded the average motor mechanic as a Morlock from the depths. Several other talismanic phrases remain in my head: that such and such a person was 'no class'; that such and such a family's children 'had no backsides to their trousers' – which was social conservatism, if you like, but of a peculiar and contradictory kind, in which envy and humility came curiously blended together, certain hierarchies were

19

meekly accepted and others sharply resented, the whole thing bound up in mysterious wrappings of divinity, royalty and precedent, and never experienced again from the moment I left the place for good.

I'd like to think that in the course of this humdrum early life, those sequestered parlour Sundays, those prematurely shortened evenings, I was kind to my mother, I conciliated her, tolerated her, did my best to please her, but I don't think I did. It was all too far gone for that, too broken up and irreclaimable. And also because, in the intervals of wondering about the curious and insoluble position in which I found myself, I was too busy doing all the things that being a boy in West Earlham at this time involved: going after horse chestnuts in the woods near Blackdale School, joining the Cub Scouts (which my mother vaguely approved of until she found out about the weekly subscription), running Saturday night errands to the fish shop or the off-licence, saving up for bicycles and pairs of 'longs' and the first Beatles LP.

Curiously, I retain only half-a-dozen extended memories of these preliminary days, by which I mean memories that aren't simply fragments but follow some proper and didactic path. The incident engraved on my mind, as forming the quintessence of West Earlham and West Earlhamite prejudice, concerns a boy named Mark Farrier. Everything about this boy – a young god of eleven with a snub nose and a shock of tow-coloured hair – was wonderful: that he lived far away from West Earlham in the paradisal splendour of Unthank Road; that his father wore a white coat and performed surgical miracles at the Norfolk and Norwich Hospital; that somehow I'd come to know him; and that – the most wonderful thing of all – he invited me to his twelfth birthday party. My mother pooh-poohed the party. She suggested with the most awful lack of tact, that it 'wouldn't do'. To counter my enthusiasm she devised half-a-dozen little embarrassments and obstacles. There was the present, for example, which would no doubt be expected of any celebrant of Master Farrier's nativity: how were we going to afford that? There were, in addition, the other boys, whom I 'might not know' and 'might not get on with'. Above all there was the mile-long journey to Unthank Road (this was the reddest of red herrings – she sent me further on her own errands) which might be 'dangerous'.

In the end she forbade me to go. I went anyway – it was the first rebellion of my eleven-and-a-half years of existence – stepping boldly out of the house in my 'party clothes' – grey sweater, long black trousers and sandals – only to find that each of my mother's predictions had been accurate. I knew no one except the host, who seemed somehow amazed and a little discomfited by my presence, and who grinned at my present of a Matchbox police car. In the end, after an hour, I slunk home. At the gate in Bright Road I met Mrs Buddery. This lady, folding her mottled arms together across her chest, regarded me with distaste. 'I've heard about you and your disobeying,' she said as I approached. Then 'I'm surprised at you, considering the circumstances ...' Then 'Break your mother's heart one day, you will.' Finally, as I made no move to acknowledge her presence but continued head down along the path, 'Well then, I've no patience with you!' In fact Mrs Buddery was wrong. It was I who had no patience with her, and all the dismal, stifling orthodoxies that she and her kind and the whole dead weight of West Earlham represented, and from that day I began to plot and scheme and reassure myself that whatever happened, and whatever misfortunes I might be subject to, my future would lie elsewhere.

'You'd be surprised, sir, at some of the people who've stayed here in their time. Famous people, I mean. Actors and actresses and so forth. I've a number of letters of thanks that I keep together in a folder, if it would interest you to see them. Quite fulsome, some of them are.'

Outside rain fell smartly against the misted-over windows. In the distance gulls cried over the boom of the sea. It was still quite early in the morning, and the overhead lighting had a sickly, unnatural quality. At intervals above our heads the telephone rang.

'In fact on one occasion a whole television crew came and stayed a week to make a documentary. Naturally I was glad of the money, but in the end so many people complained of the electrical equipment they left in the lounge that we had to ask them to go.'

'I can see that being a problem.'

Sitting in the kitchen listening to Mr Archer as he peeled potatoes was a good way of spending time at the Caradon. All the same it was hard to establish how the definite feeling of relaxation came about. Cramped, airless, always bitterly cold, never seeming to contain any food, the Caradon's kitchens were horribly cheerless. Mr Archer, too, was not at his best within their gloomy confines. Early morning – the only time of the day when he could be run to earth in these freezing depths – found him irritable, preoccupied and liable to take offence. On this particular morning, though, he seemed strangely talkative.

'Look at that now,' he said, holding a pale white object out for inspection on his palm. 'Isn't that a beautiful thing? Don't you think that's a beautiful thing?'

'Beautiful.'

'That's right. It's a shame to eat them, you know. I've often said as much.'

Sometimes I tried to reckon up the elements of this tableau – the spirals of exhaled breath rising above our heads, Mr Archer's keen pleasure in his task, the delicate white globes on the marble table-top – but it was never any good. Deconstructed, the picture not surprisingly fell apart: the chill walls of our sunken cavern drew imperceptibly nearer.

'Of course,' Mr Archer said unexpectedly, 'being in the hotel trade,

22

you always find yourself thinking about the past. I don't know why it is. Many's the time I've been sitting down here working or upstairs making out a bill or something of that nature and the queerest things have come into my head. The queerest things. Don't you find that?'

'What kind of things?'

'People who've stayed here. Curious things that have happened. You won't perhaps credit it, sir, but odd things happen in hotels. Very odd things. It's something I always tell my staff: "Expect the unexpected. Plan for the unplanned." '

It was one of Mr Archer's habits to deal out the most banal observations as if they were Johnsonian epigrams. Here, though, I rather sympathised with him. It stood to reason that a life like Mr Archer's, lived out among two dozen other people, none of whom he was particularly intimate with, would contain its fair share of surprises.

'You mean police raids, things like that?'

Mr Archer bent over the large, upright freezer and tugged hard several times on the handle. At the third or fourth pull the door flew violently open, in the way that a door in a situation comedy might have been expected to. Breathing heavily, he said:

'I was thinking more of exorcism, sir. I'd be obliged if you'd keep the information to yourself, but when I first came here, after a month or so had gone by – just time to get ourselves settled and think about new furniture – I found the place was haunted. Footsteps on the stairs at night. All the lights suddenly going off. A woman's voice screaming sometimes. It upset the guests no end.'

'What did you do?'

'I started out trying to make light of it, sir. You know, used to say, "That'll be Mad Mary again" – we always called her Mad Mary – whenever the bulbs dimmed, but it was no good. People used to laugh, but I could see they didn't like it. In the end I had to get a clergyman to come from Lowestoft and cast it out.

'Cost me twenty pounds as well,' Mr Archer said.

The gulls swooped in at the windows once more. Upstairs the telephone rang again, and Mr Archer bent his head rather sorrowfully over the potato bucket.

In the afternoon I walked across the common to the harbour. Here, out of sight of the sea, a few cows huddled together in the briny fields. Passing cars threw up sheets of water from the heavily rutted road. At the harbour's edge an outcrop of small buildings – tiny houses, ships' chandlers – backed onto the river bank. A plaque at shoulder height on the nearest house recorded the level of the 1959 Eastwold flood. I thought about Mr Archer's assertion that keeping a hotel made you think about the past. Staying in a hotel, especially of the kind Mr Archer kept, did that too. There was a sense of having slipped backwards, ebbed away downstream on a slack, uneven tide. Such voices that called were far back in time.

The collapse and dismemberment of Chell Holdings – half a decade ago, now – had stirred prolonged media interest. Two national newspapers, half-a-dozen publishing houses, the London end of a Hollywood film company – all had made lavish offers for the story of my uncle's life. All had been repulsed. At the time I'd seen these emissaries of stage, screen and print as no more than intruders, dustmen arrived to rake through the ashes of a shot, spent world. There had been a queer, ineluctable pleasure in turning them down. Five years on, the trail had gone cold. From the publishing houses and the newspapers came printed intimations of regret. A letter sent to the London office of the film company was returned marked 'Address Unknown'. Finally a literary agent with whom my uncle had had vague and inconclusive dealings – one of his many unrealised schemes to produce an autobiography – wrote expressing an interest, and I travelled up to London to see him.

As the train rattled west towards Ipswich, the coast behind it turning grey in the uneven autumn light, I thought not about my uncle but about my destination. It was four years since I'd been in London, ordered to attend the final day of the DTI enquiry. Curiously, I remembered this only for its incidental detail: Kippax outside in the street afterwards looking as if he might be about to faint, someone who claimed to have lost money in the crash – there were always such people hanging about the building – shouting 'That's him, that's one of them!' as I walked through the thinning crowds. They were bitter memories. By Colchester, though, and later as the carriage rushed forward into the familiar hinterlands of Romford and Shenfield, my uncle's shade had risen up to displace these thin, insipid ghosts.

MacCready & Sergeant had premises in a nondescript building in New Oxford Street. Treading the polished corridors that led through the rows of offices, I remembered similar journeys made fifteen years before in a London that had seemed less subdued. Outside pedestrians walked between the skidding cars. Rain beat against the windows. I'd descended into an older world, I thought, sunless and subterranean, that bore no relation to the revels of my youth.

Mr MacCready received me in his private sanctum. Fat, sandy-haired, in late middle-age, he seemed remote from popular conceptions of the literary agent.

24

'Chell Holdings,' he said. 'Remember it well. In fact I don't mind telling you a cousin of mine lost money in it. Got badly stung. Wasn't there someone did it at the time?'

'That journalist Myerson. And then Kippax wrote something.'

'Kippax, was it? The confidential secretary? I think I remember it now you mention. Any good?'

'Not really.'

'No,' said Mr MacCready, 'I don't suppose it was. What'll your line be?'

'My line?'

'Your line. What makes you better than Kippax?'

It was a good question. What was my line on my uncle? That he'd been misrepresented? That there were sides to his character that had never been brought to the public notice? That he was much better than the popular conception of him or much worse? Somehow none of these statements seemed wholly true, or even particularly useful. In the end I settled on personal knowledge.

'I knew him better than anyone else, I think. We spent five years in the same office.'

Even that, I realised, posed all manner of unanswerable questions. Had I really known my uncle better than anyone else? Than Greta, for instance, who'd spent upwards of ten years living with him. Than my mother? Than Kippax even? While I thought about this Mr MacCready made notes on a jotting pad. Eventually he said:

'I need to think about this one. You've got documents, I suppose?'

'What kind of documents?'

'Old school reports. Wedding photos. Human interest stuff. That kind of thing.'

I thought about the box files under the bed at the Caradon. 'Oh yes,' I said, 'I've got documents.'

'And what about the writing? Could you do that?'

'Doesn't everybody?'

'I've had people in here,' Mr MacCready said savagely, 'wanting to do books about themselves who could barely write their name. If you wanted some help, I dare say we could find it.'

He made further desultory squiggles on the jotter pad. Behind the desk, ascending in rows almost to the ceiling, were shelves of books: old paperbacks wedged together in little clumps; squat, hardcover editions of filmstars' memoirs in powder-blue jackets with titles like *From Vermont to Vegas*. The vision they conjured up of literary endeavour was hugely dispiriting.

'Don't mind my asking,' Mr MacCready broke in, 'but were you wanting to make a lot out of this?'

'Not specially.'

'Depends whether there's a lot to be had, of course. Normally I'd say you were wasting your time. I mean, no disrespect, but old bankrupts are ten-a-penny, aren't they? But I remember old Chell in the papers. Wasn't he a bit of a lad? Nightclub hostesses, that kind of thing?'

'He had a colourful personality, if that's what you mean.'

'Going to take more than a colourful personality,' Mr MacCready suggested, 'to sell a book about him. Any of his associates still in business?'

I selected a couple of names at random from the Sunningdale guest lists. Mr MacCready's mouth made a small O of appreciation.

'Point taken,' he said. 'I'll see what I can do. Is there anything on paper yet?'

'Not really.'

'Publishers like a synopsis,' said Mr MacCready, as if he had just divulged some momentous trade secret. 'Just put down half-a-dozen paragraphs or so. Your uncle as you remember him, that sort of thing. Something I can send round. Now, is there anyone we could get to write a foreword? Some ex-Governor of the Bank of England or someone?'

'I wouldn't have thought so.'

'Maybe not then ... I'll get Angela to show you out.' But there was no sign of his secretary, or indeed of anyone else in the glass-panelled cage that backed onto his office, and so Mr MacCready escorted me down the empty corridor himself. Standing by the lift shaft, watching his ponderous figure in retreat, I felt a sudden sense of misgiving.

Outside the rain had diminished into a steady drizzle. There were a couple of hours to kill before the train. I headed east towards more familiar lands that my uncle and I had colonised years before: along New Oxford Street to High Holborn, down into Chancery Lane and Fleet Street, on past Blackfriars Bridge towards the City. Here, strangely enough, traces of my uncle's presence still lingered. The old premises in Carter Lane had been rebuilt and turned into a travel agent's parlour, but the office in Lothbury where Roper the fat commissionaire had stood loftily inspecting the passers-by were more or less unchanged. Round the corner in Throgmorton Street I found a pub which Kippax and I had sometimes patronised on summer evenings – evenings that seemed a long time ago, quite remote and vanishing – and sat outside watching the traffic.

Back at Liverpool Street, on the Ipswich train, I thought about the encounter with Mr MacCready. Only two hours gone, it seemed completely unreal. I wondered what my uncle would have made of Mr MacCready, whether he would have been overawed by his profession, or contemptuous of his lack of 'practical skills'. It was never very easy to judge how my uncle might behave to people of the MacCready type. The train rolled on through the Essex suburbs, and I realised I was no nearer to solving any of the problems the day had thrown up. Outside grey East Anglian dusk rolled up to the track, the cattle in the fields receded into wavy swirls of ectoplasm, and I thought about Carole and Helena, my mother and her cronies, the grey stone sweep of Bunnett Square and the serious faces of long ago.

The Caradon, reached at half-past six, was sunk in early evening torpor. The lights were on in the residents' lounge and there was a smell of stale cigarette smoke. Mr Archer, alone behind the reception desk, was making entries in one of the vast, red-backed ledgers that he habitually carried about with him. Hearing my footsteps in the hall, he looked up and nodded.

'Been away for the day?'

'To London.'

Mr Archer considered this information for a good half-minute, as if he were not quite sure whether he approved. Then he said: 'I'm always telling myself that I ought to have a proper day out in London. See the sights. Go places. The Tower. The Palace. Soho. Now there's a wonderful place. Have you ever been to Soho?'

'Occasionally.'

'I often think of the days I used to spend in Wardour Street. There really isn't anywhere else like it.'

I walked slowly upstairs over the broken stair-rods. Dinner that evening was fish and creamed artichokes. In the morning another ashtray was found to have disappeared.

Beyond Bright Road, the West Earlham streets spread out in a geometric pattern: Stannard to the south, Lound – not much more than a dog-leg of three or four houses – to the east. After Lound and the back of St Anne's Church came Colman Road, which if you crossed it took you to the branch library, and if you followed its course downhill for a hundred yards across The Avenues brought you as far as Bunnett Square which, with its dozen or so shops, post office and pub, was the centre of the West Earlham world.

Apart from her weekly bus-trip into Norwich, and an occasional Sunday afternoon stroll to hear the band playing in Eaton Park – another half-mile away down Colman Road – I don't suppose my mother ever went fifty yards beyond these narrow boundaries. Once, I remember, there was a terrific upset because she had to visit someone in Bungay, fifteen miles away on the Suffolk border: it could have been Borneo for the trepidation with which she approached the four bus-rides and the half-hour wait in Bungay market square that the journey involved. Another time she won a competition run by the local paper where the prize was a trip to Newmarket races. My mother flatly refused to go. It was 'too far'. There was 'no point'. What was she supposed to do when she got there? Even Mrs Buddery, who generally supported my mother in her vagaries, thought this was overdoing it.

Curiously, these anxieties, which extended to bank accounts, official forms of any kind, even unexpected letters, were symbolic of a much more fundamental timidity. Like most of the West Earlham housewives my mother kept her front door locked and bolted, on the principle that anyone she knew automatically went round the back; feet moving up the front path were simply ignored. Travelling salesmen, who infested the estate in the run-up to Christmas, were dealt with from out of an upstairs window. Even here, though, extraordinary gradations of social terror came into play. Gypsies, whom she called 'didakois', my mother wouldn't open the window to, and once when a negro – the first black man I had ever seen – came round selling clothes pegs she locked the back door and literally went and hid in the lavatory.

It was into this tight, circumscribed world that my uncle arrived.

28

For my mother not to give any warning of what was, practically speaking, an unprecedented visitation was to be expected. In fact in nearly any arrangement concerning my welfare she was – to use another analogy from later life – like the chairman of an ailing company who, to lessen the chance of anyone attending its annual meeting, stages the event on Boxing Day at a hotel in Cardiff. My mother justified these *faits accomplis* by maintaining that I 'wasn't old enough to know my own mind' and that I was in any case 'lucky to get' whatever it was she had arranged for me. And so, dawdling home from school one day, a scuffed satchel lofted over one shoulder, I realised that her first words, looking up from the *Eastern Evening News*, which she read each afternoon from cover to cover, were:

'I b'lieve your uncle's coming to see us tomorrow.'

'Uncle Jack?'

'Hah'. My mother sniffed disparagingly. 'Thinking Jack Carstairs was your real uncle. The *idear*. No, your Uncle Ted.'

I was thirteen years old by this time and, so it appeared to me, a person of some consequence. I had a paper round, three intimate friends of my own sex, and had taken part in a dare that involved shouting the word *fuck* very loudly late at night outside the house of the school music teacher. All the same, the idea of possessing an uncle, even an uncle who had blown in, so to speak, from nowhere and might just as easily blow out again, strongly appealed to me. I could have glorious times with an uncle, I thought – confidential and revealing times. My mother caught something of this anticipation and went on hurriedly:

'He won't be staying long. Just a flying visit, he said.'

The vision of an uncle who led such a vagrant and wayward existence that he could only pay flying visits was even more enticing.

'What does he do?'

'I b'lieve,' my mother said, bitterly, 'I b'lieve he sells toys.'

As it turned out, this was pretty near the truth. Once, a long time later, my uncle sketched for me the unenviable routine that brought him to Norwich in what would have been the winter of 1965. 'I was eastern area rep for Palitoy in them days, George. Model aircraft kits and soldiers and stuffed animals, *you know*. Devil of a job that was. Train out of Liverpool Street. Another train from Norwich out over the flat to Yarmouth, and stand in the shop while some sniffy little tobacconist gave you a ten bob order. Anyhow, happened that a department store at Lowestoft had gone broke all of a sudden. Left me with a spare afternoon, so I reckoned I'd look you up.'

In a locale where the employed male population worked in the boot and shoe trade, or at Jarrold's printworks, or for the electricity board, selling toys had a conspicuous air of novelty. Such was my absorption in this alluring figure, I remember, that I asked a question which no right-minded person who knew my mother's habits or temper would ever have dared.

'Will Uncle Ted be staying the night?'

'Stay the night?' my mother repeated. 'Certainly not. *The idear.*'

I cut the last hour of school next afternoon to be home early (nobody noticed) but he was already there. He sat with my mother in the two worn leather armchairs by the fireplace smoking cigarettes – everyone smoked in those days, even downtrodden Mrs Winall fished packets of Park Drive out of her handbag and consumed them while the others talked across her – a small and faintly nondescript man in a dim grey suit with a chalk pinstripe, the face above it disproportionately large and a bit humorous, surrounded by receding and strangely perky tufts of grey-brown hair. Any ideas of drabness and restraint suggested by the suit and the scuffed suede shoes, one of whose heels was about to part company with its sole, were somehow cancelled out by a canary-yellow waistcoat that protruded from the folds of my uncle's jacket. The waistcoat was obviously a source of pride to my uncle. He caressed it occasionally when it rose over the mound of his stomach, like a cat, and he was forever polishing its buttons with a scrap of handkerchief.

My mother, I noticed, followed the movement of the waistcoat with a suspicious eye.

'So this is George, is it?' said my uncle easily as I came into the room.

'Yes, that's him,' said my mother briskly, as if she were identifying a suspect in a police parade. 'Say hello to your uncle, George.'

My mother had been smoking too: inexpertly, so that four or five cigarette stubs in varying stages of decomposition smouldered on an ashtray at her side. She looked faintly embarrassed and, I thought, skittish, as if I had intruded on some intimacy she would have liked to keep from me. My uncle, meanwhile, was looking at me keenly.

'So this is George, is it?' he said again, and the canary waistcoat slid sinuously out of the fold of his jacket. 'I'm very pleased to meet you, George.'

'I'm very pleased to meet you too, Uncle Ted,' I ventured, quite sincerely.

'Goes to th' grammar school, does he?' he enquired of my mother.

'Didn't pass the exam,' my mother whipped back triumphantly. 'Anyhow, you know I don't hold with grammar schools.'

Oddly enough, I agreed with my mother about the grammar school. At thirteen, the idea of dressing up in a bright blue uniform and cap six mornings a week and walking a couple of miles to a scattered outcrop of

30

buildings near the cathedral seemed to me absurdly juvenile and meaningless (there was a solitary grammar school boy on the West Earlham
estate whom we occasionally chased home from the bus-stop and, if
caught, flung into hedgerows). My mother, on the other hand, seized on
the notion of caps and exams and masters in gowns and mortar boards
in a spirit of furious utilitarianism. The *idear* of teaching huge great boys
Latin and Greek when they could be doing something useful. The result
of the eleven plus exam, consequently, in which I meditated a story about
an Angevin crusader, lost the thread of it and sat staring at the page with
a kind of irritated complacency – there was a small part of me that had
wanted to make something of the crusader – was a joint relief.

'Grammar schools never mattered to a boy with brains,' said my uncle
unconvincingly. He was sitting back in his chair now, chewing at an unlit
cigarette with his lower lip and disclosing a row of variegated and
discoloured teeth. It was then, I think, that I got the first hint of the
chronic restlessness which seemed almost to inflame him, and which I
now believe to have been at the root of his troubles. Using the cigarette
as a phantom toothpick and massaging his scalp with his other hand he
threw a series of sharp glances around the room, at the brown holland
rug which covered the area of the floor in front of the gas-fire, at the
antiquated wireless that my mother kept in a cabinet under the window,
and a bookcase which contained miscellaneous volumes of Arthur Mee's
Children's Encyclopaedia and a work called *Spirit Hands Have Touched
Me* in which my mother sometimes impressionably browsed.

'Snug little place you got here,' he said eventually.

'It is and it isn't,' my mother said enigmatically.

'I mean,' said my uncle, suddenly becoming animated, 'you could
really make something of it if you liked. Get one of those hanging lamps
– what they are called? *You* know, kind the big department stores sell,
and put them in over the mirror. Then take out the sideboard – nasty
heavy piece of wood – and put in a *chaise-longue* ...

'Elegant,' my uncle said, coming to an unexpected halt. We regarded
him silently: myself with growing respect; my mother with an
astonishment bordering on exasperation. It was clear that nobody had
spoken to her like this for many years.

'And then ... ' my uncle began, waving the tip of his cigarette above
his head and somehow drawing the length of the shaky ceiling into a new
and original focus, but something in my mother's eye deterred him and
he subsided.

From outside the customary five o'clock West Earlham noises were
starting up: footsteps drumming down the street, a breathless voice or
two, a woman shouting, 'Jimmy, where '*ave* you gorn again?', at first

angrily, then with increasing plaintiveness, bicycles skidding from road to pavement.

'George,' my mother said decisively, 'why don't you take your uncle for a walk? Take him round and show him a bit. And then when you come back, p'raps we can give him his tea.'

For some reason I expected my uncle to jib at this, but instead he put the cigarette back into his coat-pocket – they were Woodbines, rather to my surprise, a cheap brand which people said were made of powdered horse dung – and rose meekly to his feet.

'*I* don't mind a walk, Jane,' he said. 'That's if this youngster doesn't mind accompanying me. What do you say, George?'

My mother mumbled something on my behalf, but I lost it in the wonder of hearing somebody address her by her Christian name. Indeed, I'm not entirely sure that I knew it myself until that moment. The sorority of the back-kitchen always called her Mrs Chell, and it was the same on the rent books and the hire purchase agreements. Thinking about this, and about my uncle's apparent dissociation from this kind of life, its evasions and its secrecies, thinking too about the cavalier way in which he proposed to redesign my mother's sitting-room, I stepped out into the street.

There were two principal walks that you could take in West Earlham: the picturesque, which led you along the wide, tree-lined thoroughfare of The Avenues towards a school and a glimpse of ragged countryside; and the prosaic, which went along the cemetery railings for half a mile or so before plunging downhill towards the Dereham Road. I chose the prosaic. As we threaded our way along Lound Road through the groups of children playing hopscotch at the kerbside – girls with their hair in bunches and stringy woollen cardigans, squinting, crop-headed boys – past the shunted-up cars and the worn grass and into the mournful highway of Colman Road he looked enquiringly about him.

'Lived here a long time, haven't you, George?'

'Thirteen years ...' and something prompted me to add a courteous 'uncle'.

'That's right. Just you and your mother, eh?'

The cemetery gates loomed above us. Here, instead of following the path northward, my uncle wandered diffidently inside and stood examining a painted notice-board offering details of crematorium opening hours. In the fading late afternoon light the place had an unbelievably dreary aspect, a vista of great, gloomy catafalques crumbling into uncut grass, unpruned trees which drooped and wept over the palings.

'Famous old place, ain't it, George?' my uncle remarked at length.

'Just imagine what it would be after dark, eh?' He paused. '*I* once spent a night in a cemetery when I was your age.

'For a dare,' he elaborated.

Something seemed to strike him and he said: 'Get along all right with your mother, do you, George?'

'Not really.'

'No, I didn't suppose you did … Bit of an item I should think, your mother …

'I could tell some tales … ' he went on.

And so we strolled around the cemetery as the light began to fade and a blood-red sun sank starkly in the western sky, my uncle commenting on little details that took his fancy: a cracked angel's wing fallen drunkenly over a gravestone, a stupendous family mausoleum in black granite, other things. So practised was this commentary that I suspected it was merely one of his idiosyncrasies, that long years of solitude had accustomed him to talking to himself, that he scarcely noticed I was there. Eventually we turned out of a side gate and plodded back along Colman Road.

The confusion that Uncle Ted's visit had brought on in my mother's mind was sharply apparent on our return. It was fairly obvious that she had been torn between the contending notions that a tea in his honour required lavish preparation or none at all, equally clear that she had compromised by choosing an elaborate menu and presenting it with maximum slovenliness. Luckily my uncle appeared not to notice the fraying bread and butter or the glint in my mother's eye as she dispensed it. He ate a huge amount of pickled herrings and boiled eggs in an abstracted way, occasionally cocking his head at me as if to acknowledge that we shared some exquisite private joke.

Finally, standing in the doorway buttoning up his overcoat, he produced a black attaché case, very battered and worn, and took out a long, rectangular parcel.

'Got a present for you, George. What do you say to that, then?'

Unwrapping the Action Man from its nest of tissue paper – such things were for children, as any self-respecting thirteen-year-old knew – I caught my mother's glance: half-censorious and yet half-gleeful, as if she wanted to rebuke my indifference while somehow exulting in the failure of my uncle's gesture to hit its target.

'Thanks very much, Uncle Ted.'

'Glad it's what you wanted,' my uncle said affably. 'G'bye now, you people.'

'Huh!' my mother said, after the door had closed and we heard the sound of him whistling – whistling with an odd and somehow laboured jauntiness – along the darkened street. 'Giving you something like that. The *idear*.'

And so, leaving only the memory of a dozen sentences or so of fugitive conversation, my uncle slipped out of my life for the next six years.

Early on these winter mornings, often before the light had properly come on, I used to walk along the beach. At dawn, the rows of beach chalets locked up and silent, empty even of the old women walking their dogs, the place had an attraction that it rarely regained at other hours of the day. Fog hung low over the sand and the escarpments of the sea defences, so that the cries of the gulls seemed curiously disconnected, lost somewhere in dense clouds of vapour; the sea was the colour of gravy. Coming back along the high street it was sometimes possible to buy a cup of coffee at the baker's shop in the square. At other times, though figures could be seen vaguely through the misted-up windows, the door mysteriously stayed shut.

Part of the interest of these excursions lay in what you might find on your return. Mr Archer was subject to early morning fits of restlessness. These bursts of energy sometimes prompted him to embark on lightning schemes of refurbishment, so that it wasn't unusual, entering the lounge at 7 a.m., say, to find the carpet up and trays of tools scattered over the bare floorboards. At other times, however, a peculiar sluggishness overcame him: on these days breakfast would be served by the maids or, very occasionally, not served at all. Mr Archer affected ignorance of the physical cause of this behaviour. He said: 'I've never been able to explain, sir, why my body should behave in the way it does. You wouldn't believe it. Sometimes I wake up at dawn just bursting to run a mile, and other times I feel as if I couldn't lift a teacup. Several doctors, sir, have commented on this peculiarity in me.'

Negotiations about the book dragged. Two or three encouraging letters, written by Mr MacCready at an early stage in the proceedings, were followed by a long period of silence. Then he telephoned out of the blue to say that a small imprint of a substantial Anglo-American firm had made an offer. 'Not very much money,' he explained cheerfully, 'but there might be a newspaper deal.'

'Is that likely?'

'You never know.'

In the course of the conversation Mr MacCready explained how books of this kind got written. 'Best thing to do,' he said, 'is to speak it all into a tape-recorder, and then tidy it up afterwards. You need to be careful, though. I had a bloke who'd known Ronnie Kray fill seventeen cassettes once. The other way is to do a collaboration. Get a journalist to come and ask you questions, and then work the raw material up into manuscript.'

'Can you arrange that?'

'I could try,' Mr MacCready said. 'Leave it with me.'

I left it with him. Several weeks passed. Mr Archer disappeared for three or four days, reappearing dressed in a checked suit and looking faintly pleased with himself. It was rumoured that he had been racing in the Midlands. More than once I took a pen and paper and tried to follow Mr MacCready's instructions about the synopsis. It was a futile exercise. Momentarily pinned down on the page, my uncle immediately took wing again; laid out in recognisable planes and angles he changed shape, metamorphosed into a completely different object. In the end I was reduced to choosing words that I somehow associated with him: *fat, generous, secretive, curious, irritable, tenacious,* and *overbearing* were some of them. I put the pieces of paper in the box file and left them there.

Then one afternoon towards the end of February as I sat in the residents' lounge brooding over *Quentin Durward,* Mr Archer summoned me to the telephone by the reception desk. It was Mr MacCready.

'That chat we were having the other day,' he said. 'I think I've got just the person.'

'A journalist?'

'*Writer* she calls herself on her CV,' Mr MacCready went on. 'Not that I mind that. Woman called Frances Eccles.'

The name meant nothing to me. 'Is she at all well known? Should I have heard of her?'

'Let's see.' From the pauses at the other end of the phone I deduced that Mr MacCready was reading from a handwritten sheet. 'Editorial assistant on *Vogue.* Along with half of London, I shouldn't wonder. Two years out of the profession travelling. Occasional book reviews for *Good Housekeeping* ... Editorial work for a variety of small publishing firms ...'

'Does she know anything about the City?'

'I dare say she could pick it up,' Mr MacCready said. There was an uneasy silence. On the other side of the desk Mr Archer was polishing wine glasses, blowing fiercely on their upturned rims and burnishing them with a hank of tissue paper. 'Look,' Mr MacCready went on, 'didn't you say you lived in a hotel? Why don't you book her in for a fortnight? As a trial arrangement. See how it goes.'

'All right.'

Later on, when Mr Archer had finished the wine glasses and begun on a row of filthy brass candlesticks, I made the arrangements for Frances Eccles' visit. Mr Archer recorded these details with absolute impassivity, his eye fixed on the barometer six feet behind my head. When we had finished he said:

'Will the young lady be wanting a cooked breakfast, do you suppose?'

'I've no idea.'

'Well, perhaps you could let me know nearer the time, sir. Only it will be more convenient from the catering point of view.'

'I'll try.'

Later that afternoon the wind blew in violently from the sea. It would be a wet spring, Mr Archer said, because winter storms usually meant weather of this kind.

To get to Eaton Park you went down Colman Road, turned right into South Park Avenue past the Esso garage and the row of shops and walked a hundred yards to the point where the railings began. Inside were two dozen acres of bowling greens, football pitches, a circular edifice of tea-huts and changing rooms put up by an unemployed workers' project in the 1930s, and an ornamental fish pond into which – this was a famous local legend – someone had once introduced a pike. In the winter of 1963 the snow lay over the fields for six weeks, and I helped to build an igloo that took half a ton and stayed there for a fortnight until a rival gang came and knocked it down ...

I'm sure that I must have forgotten a great deal of these old West Earlham days. Sometimes I can find myself remembering some odd particle or fragment – Bunnett Square at dusk, say, with the lights flaring up inside the shopfronts, or the bus-stop on Colman Road opposite the church and the Scout hut – but the rest somehow escapes me. Which is to say that I recognise its elements, its shapes and substances, but that the whole thing hangs a little way off, and beyond my power to call back. It seems to me, too, that this is simply the essence of West Earlham seeping in and stifling me, like a pillow held over my head, so that it was only many years later, with these scraps and oddments as materials, that I could begin to reconstruct this early life.

I don't recall that my schooldays were unhappy – in fact I recollect a good deal of undivided fun. At the same time I wouldn't care to live through them again, and I know I couldn't wait for them to stop. Education in Norwich at this point was divided into three. There was a superior grammar school of ancient foundation, whose pupils wore blue blazers and whose prize day was elaborately reported in the *Eastern Evening News*; two inferior grammar schools, less ancient and less elaborately reported; and several 'secondary' schools of a mixed and ambiguous character. I landed up at a school even more mixed and ambiguous than its rivals called Bowthorpe High. Later on, if I wanted to remember what Bowthorpe High was like, I could remind myself by walking through the corridors at Lothbury early in the morning, just after the cleaners had left, and smelling the disinfectant. Most memoirs

38

of schooldays go on about the smell of the food or the chalk-dust – with Bowthorpe High it was the disinfectant that hit you in the face whenever you walked through the main door.

Despite the purdah in which my mother had raised me, I got on well with the rest of my classmates – they were great, hulking louts from Northfields and the Larkman Estate, which had a bad reputation even by the standards of West Earlham – and if you were to show me a school photograph from those days I dare say I could identify most of the people in it. Apart from this, though, the place was a disgrace, just a kind of sink aimed at preparing teenagers for the local factories. Beyond a few implausible mathematical formulae and certain geographical suggestions, I don't recall that we were told anything that might have a bearing on our future lives. The masters who taught us – we called them 'sir' in a feeble imitation of 'good' schools – were practical people. They wanted us to be quiet, they were keen that we shouldn't fight each other or boys from other schools (West Earlham was famous for gang warfare of this type), nor plunge the place into public disgrace, and on the whole I think they just about succeeded.

Happily – for I wouldn't have wanted it otherwise – my education didn't diverge from this elemental pattern. At the age of fourteen I believe I knew that density equalled mass over volume; that there existed a startling and limitlessly divisible number called 'Pi'; and that the capital of Ecuador was Quito – that was the kind of thing they taught you at Bowthorpe High. Beyond this all was darkness. And yet at the same time I was conscious that something, some vague kind of interest and intent, had begun to point me in quite another direction. Where they came from, these faint glimmerings of sensibility, I can't imagine, and I can remember trying to ignore them, to batten them down, and yet always failing to suppress them. I remember discovering Norwich Central Library – no one took me there, the building simply presented itself to me one Saturday morning as I climbed back up the market steps from Jarrold's department store – and moving with a kind of sacramental awe along its miles of shelving. Even my mother could see the point of libraries, though she hardly ever set foot in one. She was intimidated by the stacks of books, still more by the birdlike middle-class ladies who presided over them, and I've an idea that she was slightly suspicious of reading in general. If she looked at a novel it was usually a gloomy family saga with a death in the first chapter and the heroine forced into an unhappy marriage by her scheming parents.

But books were only one of the odd yearnings I cultivated in these teenage years. It was the same when I discovered a copy of the Bible in the bookcase in my mother's room next to an illustrated edition of *Foxe's*

Book of Martyrs and some old copies of the *Friendship Book of Frances Gay*. Naturally we'd had pieces of scripture read out to us at school, but this was the first time I'd sat down and taken it in, and the effect was electric. For about a year I walked the streets of Norwich convinced that I was in communication with God, a God who looked something like the Almighty out of Blake's designs for Job, and had pronounced views about the length of my hair and my personal deportment. I even once, nodded at by the friendly curate, went to a service at St Anne's Church and sat expectantly in the front row, entertained by a baying elderly choir, until the mysteries of the communion rite drove me out.

It disappoints me sometimes that I gave up this association with God ...

The result of all this brooding was that I went through my adolescence in a kind of ceaseless ferment. I was forever picking up things and putting them down. I planned schemes of reading out of useless old books that I found in second-hand shops in St Benedict's and then discarded them. I wrote poems in the back of an exercise book – very bad poems they were – and tore them up. I cultivated a passion for a meek little English teacher at school who read to us once out of *The Lord of the Rings* and thought me 'promising' which only died when she invited me home to tea and I sat round a table with three adenoidal children and a husband who washed up in a flower-patterned apron and never said a word. The English teacher was thrown over for a brief flirtation with an archae-ological society, whose excursions involved much sieving of powdered Norfolk earth and a great deal of dark tea dispensed by elderly ladies, followed by a gang of West Earlham skinheads who lurked under the streetlamps at Bunnett Square, insulted park keepers and once murdered a cat by cornering it in the cemetery and pelting it with stones.

It turned out that this restlessness wasn't unique to me. Gradually I worked out – and the revelation was comforting but at the same time vaguely shocking – that an identical ferment had begun to excite the world beyond the Bright Road back-to-backs, that it had a tendency to break out in demonstrations and marches, its generating spirit endlessly dividing and redividing like a colony of amoebae under the lens. Some of its more innocent manifestations could even be witnessed in the humdrum backwaters of West Earlham. The first West Earlham mini-skirt, which appeared on Bunnett Square in the summer of 1966, was greeted very satirically by my mother and her cronies ('The *idear*' they pronounced, 'of those women showing off their legs like that.') but within a year the Colman Road bus-stops were full of bolster-shaped women displaying their thighs. My mother and her friends took mini-skirts very hard, as they did all the inventions of that era, from contraceptive pills to decimalisation, as a kind of personal snub. They saw them – and I suppose they were right to see them – as the death knell of all the things they valued and held dear. For years they'd gone on imagining that life would always be the same, that until the end of time vague, put-upon middle-aged women would take the bus into Norwich to do their shopping, read *Woman's Journal* for its cures for bad legs, and sit round their kitchen tables trading scandal – and now suddenly it was all gone in an explosion of strikes and love-ins and women's rights. I can remember Mrs Buddery, once, drowsing in an armchair in our front room while my mother fussed about infusing tea, and picking her way with a moistened forefinger through a newspaper report about some period freak – Lennon's 'Bed-in for Peace' perhaps – and finally declaiming, in a kind of incandescent fury, that 'it shouldn't be allowed'. By 'it' I was shrewd enough to realise that Mrs Buddery meant not merely John and Yoko but everything – kaftans and beads and long hair and Harold Wilson, the protests against Vietnam and all the rest of it.

The sorority of the back-kitchen was breaking up in any case. Mrs Laband had decamped to Wymondham and, it was rumoured, an interest in spiritualism. Mrs Winall, poor vacant Mrs Winall, was dead of a long undoctored stomach complaint (none of the West Earlhamites 'held' with doctors) belatedly diagnosed, after God knows what agonies, as abdominal cancer. My mother, too, seemed somehow less solid, less liable to take offence, more likely to stop whatever she was doing and stand staring out of the kitchen window or sit rather sorrowfully in the front room with her eye fixed on the complex imbrication of light and shadow thrown up by the window frame. In fact there were times when my mother became practically confidential. I can't remember much of what we talked about, not because I lacked interest, but because my mother had a trick of collecting up whatever lay in her head and depositing it in so many fragments around more general conversation. But if there was no narrative with my mother, only allusion, it sometimes seemed to me that she was on the brink of some startling communication that might radically transform the view that I took of her, and our life here in West Earlham, and perhaps of myself, something that might lead away from the dull Norwich skyline and the reek of the May & Baker factory. On these occasions I strained very hard to interpret the queer code in which my mother communicated, convinced that revelation lay only a sentence away, but it was never any good, and I might as well have been talking to a fence-post.

Sometimes the figure of my father was present in these conversations, or if not present then dimly visible on their margins. It wouldn't be true to say that my mother never talked about my father, as I got older, but

when she did it was bound up in extraordinary vagueness and impreci-
sion. Beneath these shutters of concealment a few fragments of pale light
seeped through. In particular, my mother had a habit of apostrophising
'a certain gentleman' who could only have been my father. 'A certain
gentleman liked mustard on his sausages ... ' 'A certain gentleman used
to say ... ' What a certain gentleman used to say had a hard, didactic edge.
Never a borrower or a lender be, for instance, or *Blessed are the peace-
makers*. I was depressed by these allusions, as they seemed to bestow on
my father a glaze of irretrievable banality. Only the novelty of hearing
him discussed kept the tediousness of the reportage at bay.

There were other fragments here and there: odd bits of china hoarded
over the years from which occasional shaky mosaics emerged. Books in
the front room turned out to contain his signature on the flyleaf. Once a
little bundle of photographs came tumbling unexpectedly out of a tea
caddy, and my mother looked at them impassively for a moment or two.
Another time she started talking about a holiday they'd taken in the
North of England – the only holiday she seemed to have taken in her
entire life – which could only have been her honeymoon. Mrs Buddery,
too, was not averse to mysterious confidences, whose import it took me
some time to appreciate, and I have a memory – not a very precise one –
of a conversation in the dark of an October evening, when my mother
was out somewhere, full of gloomy hints about rows and departures, at
the conclusion of which Mrs Buddery solemnly swore me to secrecy, like
a great black witch looming up in front of the grim fireplace.

The upshot of all this was that by my mid-teens I'd built up a
reasonable portrait of my parents' life together. Much of it was the purest
speculation – I had an idea that my father might have been some kind of
commission agent, though I've no idea where this suggestion came from
– but I knew they'd got married in the late 1940s. I'd been born in 1952,
and I think there'd been some sort of separation before my father's death,
which Mrs Buddery thought (and even she seemed slightly alarmed at
transmitting the information) might have been in 1953 or 1954. Having
assembled this data, though, there was nothing I could do with it.
Confronted with any direct question about my father, marriage, even her
own early life, my mother simply clammed up or resorted to evasions
that would have disgraced a child. What do you do in such circumstances? It was a kind of mental treasure trove, which I brooded over and
polished up all through my teenage years, but knew that I could never
bring out on public display.

At long intervals my uncle communicated. He had a habit of sending
comic postcards from holiday resorts on the east coast: Skegness, Scar-
borough, Whitby, Wells-next-the-Sea, each with a line or so of

corroborative detail. My mother read these effusions aloud, without comment. There was something about them, I thought – perhaps the flagrancy of their humour or the sparseness of their messages – that displeased her, though she would never confirm that this was the case. And so our lives dawdled on in what I had already come to recognise as the approved West Earlham pattern: incurious, sequestered and remote, with only one question hanging over my head, and that the entirely mundane and familiar one of what I was going to do for a living.

At sixteen I hadn't any pronounced view of my destiny, other than a desire to get out of Bowthorpe High at the earliest opportunity. In this it seems to me that I was perfectly imbued with the West Earlham spirit, which sent boys into factories and girls into corner shops and looked down on 'cleverness' as the moral equivalent of leprosy. My mother, as it turned out, had certain vague longings for clerkish respectability. I think she had an idea of me working for the Norwich Union or in one of the offices in Exchange Street: at any rate for some time the words 'collar and tie' had featured largely in our discussions, and I remember her lingering once over an advertisement in the *Eastern Evening News* in which an auctioneer offered £10 a week to a smart boy who could write a fair hand and didn't object to rail travel. In the end, though, it came to nothing and, application being made to Mrs Buddery – who had watched over the clerical plans with secret scorn – I found myself apprenticed to the latter's brother-in-law, who kept a newsagent-cum-tobacconist's shop in Bunnett Square.

I think my mother regretted the collar and tie and the other seductive appurtenances of clerkdom. She looked unconscionably wistful when Mrs Buddery produced the figure of her brother-in-law and further alleged that I was 'just the kind of lad that would do'. For my own part, I was perfectly indifferent. It was how things were done in West Earlham, how life was arranged. You don't believe me? In every house in Bright or Lound or Stannard where there was a teenage boy, a tribe of relatives would sit in judgement on his prospects in this way, before bundling him off into some frightful apprenticeship: picking up scraps of leather off the floor of one of the boot and shoe factories, say, or manhandling boxes at Jarrold's. Even at the time I used to marvel at the oddity of these attitudes. The West Earlham people voted Labour in their thousands, 'couldn't abide' privilege or pretension, but still allowed themselves to be quite thoroughly downtrodden, or, rather, allowed themselves to have all their decisions made for them by prosy little patriarchs who smoked pipes, looked knowing and were invincibly ignorant of every topic that was suggested to them. The inanities I imbibed in that dim backyard society! The barefaced untruths about science, religion and human feeling! All this I remember very clearly – the ineffable stupidities and complacencies, the unkindness that was actually a kind of fundamental, dimwitted incuriousness.

Mrs Buddery's brother-in-law, Mr Blessington, was quite wonderfully representative of these attitudes. I've never had a chance to correct the brief impression I received of him, and he exists in my mind as a kind of dreadful caricature of incompetent self-righteousness. His newsagent's shop, which lay in the farthest corner of Bunnett Square squeezed up against an off-licence and a vague emporium that sold bicycle 'spares', was a queer, dingy place: a gloomy rectangle of premises with a corridor behind, crammed with all kinds of insalubrious clutter: bales of newsprint never returned to the wholesalers, cheap plastic toys hanging in rows off the vending spindles. Mr Blessington dominated this unpromising landscape in the way that a goldfish dominates its bowl, endlessly digging into old cupboards at the back of the shop, hobnobbing with favourite customers or standing in the window with his hands in his pockets metaphorically preening himself. He was a small, grim, desiccated man, balding and slightly stooped, so that in peering upwards from behind the till with the light shining off his wrinkled forehead he bore a faint resemblance to a tortoise, and in the six months I worked for him I don't believe I ever heard him make an original remark. His conversation was of the most stupidly querulous type, a kind of perpetual lament about the Church Commissioners (who owned his freehold) and his fellow tradesmen in the square, with whom he enjoyed chronically strained relations. Poor Mr Blessington! I suppose I should have felt pity for him, for like my mother and Mrs Buddery he was simply another victim of the pressing modernist tide, but at the time I merely thought him ridiculous and dull, and longed for a chance to outwit him.

It was clear to me from an early stage that Mr Blessington and I would fall out.

Mr Blessington (Mrs Blessington, Mrs Buddery's sister, lived a strange, isolated life in the flat above the shop, in which eyrie she could occasionally be heard lumbering back and forth, and I don't suppose I saw her more than twice) ran his establishment on individual lines. Essentially it was an old-fashioned 'paper shop' that sold cigarettes and confectionery and other uncategorisable items like string and baking foil, but made its money out of delivering newspapers, morning and evening, to around five hundred households within a range of three square miles. The opportunities for upset which this presented to someone of Mr Blessington's limited organisational powers were immense. He was forever devising 'schemes' for the greater efficiency of the delivery boys – there were a dozen of them who assembled blearily in the shop's backyard at six every morning while Mr Blessington regaled himself with tea inside – forever changing his wholesalers, or forgetting to change them, so that on one memorable morning the entire day's supply of newspapers arrived in duplicate.

One of the most bizarre of Mr Blessington's 'schemes' entailed the display of material that was not actually for sale. And so, one afternoon early on in my tenure behind the antique gunmetal till, ducking to avoid the hoops of suspended bicycle tyres (the result of some mysterious 'arrangement' concluded with the shop next door), I looked up to find him advancing surreptitiously on the shelves – shelves filled with knitting pattern-books, women's magazines, odd partworks about photography and sailboat construction – with a peculiarly thoughtful and satisfied air.

'George?' (Everyone called me George these days, rather than the 'Georgie' of my childhood.) 'You sell that copy of *Homes and Gardens*?'

In fact I was rather proud of this sale, to an unknown woman whose ten shilling note formed a quarter of the afternoon's receipts.

'Yes, Mr Blessington.'

Mr Blessington prowled stealthily along the shelves for a moment more. 'Y'didn't ought to have done that, George,' he said mournfully. 'Didn't I ever tell you y'shouldn't be doing that?'

'No, Mr Blessington.'

I never could resist a smile at Mr Blessington's locution, with its blithe disregard of vowels and its utilitarian truncations. He had a habit of pronouncing his 'sh' sounds in a lazy, sibilant way that sounded like a bottle-cap being drawn.

Abruptly Mr Blessington changed tack. He picked up a copy of *The People's Friend*, leafed through it solemnly for a moment, and then straightened up. 'Let's get this straight then, George. There's this copy of *Homes and Gardens* gone missing, that you say you've been and sold.'

'That's right.'

'Well,' (impressively) *'that magazine was on special order.'*

Brooding over the episode years later – and it seemed so starkly revealing of a certain kind of human temperament that I often reflected on it – I decided that it grew out of a primordial wish to have one's cake and eat it, that Mr Blessington in the last resort could not bear to have a ten shilling magazine for which he had paid a wholesaler six shillings and twopence lying idle on the customer order shelf when it could be proudly displayed in his window. In fact Mr Blessington had countless idiosyncrasies of this kind – 'notions' about selling newspapers at half-price a day after their publication, and a devious scheme whereby customers got a third off if they brought their papers back in the evening, thereby allowing him to send them back the next day as 'returns'.

45

I decided to get back at Mr Blessington over the copy of *Homes and Gardens*. For a week, whenever anyone attempted to buy anything in the shop – even a packet of cigarettes or a fourpenny cigar – I'd sing out respectfully, 'Is it all right for me to sell this, Mr Blessington?' It seemed to me that the customers rather approved the joke – they said I was a 'scream' or a 'funny young feller' – but it mortified Mr Blessington as I think no other failing of mine had ever done.

In its own curious way Mr Blessington's shop was one of the hubs on which West Earlham society turned. People came to gossip there, and hold fierce little arguments while they turned over back numbers of *Cage Birds* and the *Angling Times* in the bargain box next to the window. Gangs of small boys came and stood staring at the display cases of toy soldiers, or 'cheeked' Mr Blessington until he lost his temper and drove them out. The highlight of the day in Bunnett Square, though, came at four o'clock in the afternoon when the delivery van arrived with its three hundred-or-so copies of the *Eastern Evening News*. Standing in the shop doorway sometimes, while Mr Blessington fussed over the delivery books or conducted laborious inventories of the contents of cardboard boxes. I used to watch the square preparing for this event. By twenty to four there would generally be two or three women with prams or shopping trolleys starting to congregate on the concrete esplanade, or outside the front of Oelrich's bakery, three doors down. By ten to, middle-aged men in collarless white shirts with unlit cigarettes stuck in their mouths would be tethered restlessly at vantage points near the pelican crossing or by the Romany Rye pub in the square's far corner, whole half-a-dozen paperboys crowded their bikes into a circle on the pavement. The sight of the van charging down Colman Road to veer left into the sliproad before the row of shops galvanised these disparate groups into action: the men shifting purposefully forward, the paperboys thronging round the shop door, Mr Blessington on his knees at the roadside hacking at the bundles of newsprint with a kitchen knife, people flinging sixpences at him as they swooped on the first copies. Even my mother used occasionally to stalk down to Bunnett Square to 'wait for the papers' as she put it, and march proudly home to brood over the flower show reports and the small ads offering second-hand trailers and cheap radios. The *Eastern Evening News* was a proper local paper. When Robert Kennedy was assassinated – something I particularly remember, as it happened just after I went to work for Mr Blessington – it was reported halfway down page three, next to a story about a cat that had been rescued from a tree in Christchurch Road and a picture of a prize-winning vegetable marrow.

To go back to the question of the delivery arrangements, which were my undoing and in some sense the reason for my departure from West Earlham and the close of this chapter of my life: Mr Blessington's connections, 'worked up' over a period of thirty years, were extensive. His delivery routes – there were about a dozen, some of them taking as much as two hours to complete – snaked out all over the western side of Norwich, inward as far as the top of Avenue Road, outward up to the gates of the University. To extend, refine and command this network was Mr Blessington's obsession. He had an enlarged Ordnance Survey map of the city on which the limits of his empire were picked out in red poster paint, and he was forever colonising extra streets, 'taking on' additional customers from rival newsagents and generally making himself objectionable to the Norwich paper trade – they had a poor, run-down trade organisation and were always sending him lawyers' letters accusing him of breaking some protocol or other. For a short time I shared this fascination. There was to me a magic in the way Mr Blessington deployed his battalions, rallied them and sent them out. Even today, passing a newsagent's shop with a fleet of big iron-panelled delivery bikes gathered up at the door, I get an indescribable feeling of youthfulness and purpose. But there was also – this being Mr Blessington and West Earlham – ineptitude that a child of ten would have cried over. For a start Mr Blessington had a habit of transporting his stock from the backyard, where it was delivered each morning by the wholesaler's lorry, to the interior of the shop, from which vantage point he parcelled up the rounds to be taken back again by the delivery boys to the yard where the bicycles were kept. For a long time I used to wonder what benefit Mr Blessington derived from this half-hour or so of superfluous labour, but it was no good, he *would* start his day in this way. Far more injurious, though, was the business of the delivery books. There were a dozen of these: fat red notebooks in which the details of the rounds were set down in Mr Blessington's crabbed and allusive hand (thus FR – 17 DT, 19 DM, 21 DE XS34, which meant *Fairfax Road, Number 17 Daily Telegraph, Number 19 Daily Mirror, Number 21 Daily Express third and fourth week of September only*). Mr Blessington's idiosyncrasy in the matter of the delivery books was a habit of recording each change to the round occasioned by a customer cancelling his order, going on holiday or taking a different newspaper, by hand the previous evening, thereby ignoring the delivery boys' habit of memorising the contents of the book and referring to it only in extremity. When, on my own initiative, I devised a system of supernumerary slips, enabling the delivery boys to note changes at a glance, Mr Blessington was simply furious. Sighing through his teeth – a curious sound, suggestive of cataracts, which I couldn't hope to reproduce – he submitted me to a long, fragmentary monologue of complaint.

'Ju see what I tryin' to tell y'George ... On'y way y'can manage these things is to have a *system* ... Dessay you're a bright enough lad in y'way but ... No cause to go *interfering* in what don't concern y'...'

Struck dumb by this tide of long pent-up exasperation, I could only stare at Mr Blessington – head peering up from his bowed shoulders, hands clenching and unclenching as he delivered it. He was, I could see, genuinely shocked by this minor intervention in his affairs, and alarmed by the implications for his business. So bewildered was I by this unexpected rebuke that I took the unprecedented step of taking the matter back to Bright Road. My mother, stirred from contemplation of *Coronation Street* – we had a television set now, on the instalment principle – was doubtful ('Telling that Mr Blessington how to manage his own shop, the *idear*.').

Among other things my mother confirmed that Mr Blessington had a 'hot temper'.

Matters came to a head one morning in November, the unexpected early return of Mr Blessington from a jamboree of the East Anglian Confectioners' and Newsagents' Guild revealing that this intrusion into his livelihood persisted. It was 7 a.m. An early customer or two stood at the far end of the shop browsing through the magazine racks. To the right of the till assorted newspapers lay in piles awaiting the delivery boys. On each, tell-tale pink slips protruding from their tops, lay a red delivery book. Mr Blessington came noisily into the shop through the front entrance, altogether failing to conceal the impression of a man who has driven seventy miles through the dawn to detect an employee in some minor act of disobedience. When he saw the notebooks he stopped dead, picked the nearest one up and brandished it furiously in front of him.

'You ...' he said. 'You ... *shithouse!*'

There was a recognised West Earlham expression for losing your temper. It was called 'putting your parts on'. Hitherto my experience of this irruption had been confined to juvenile acquaintances. The adult version, I divined, was infinitely more fascinating and dramatic.

''Nearth d'y think y'doing?' Mr Blessington shouted, advancing on the till.

In an instant the shop seemed full of people. A middle-aged lady with a dog who came in every morning to buy the *Guardian* stared at us from the doorway; a wide-eyed delivery boy flattened himself against the shelves as Mr Blessington rushed past. The customers by the magazine racks began saying things like 'Here!' and 'Now then!' and, more menacingly, 'Now *then!*' and something hard and flat (later identified as a black account book from the stationery shelf) flew past my head and shattered a glass display cabinet. There was a confused impression of screaming, feeble grasshopper fists beating at my chest, an astonishing rictus of scarlet skin, popping blue eyes and peg teeth that was Mr Blessington's face in close-up, and an almighty thump as his head suddenly fell out of view, descended rapidly onto a pile of *Daily Mirrors* and ceased to move.

Whereupon we all – myself, the lady with the dog, the delivery boy and the two customers from the magazine racks – came and crowded round him with very grave and proper expressions of alarm.

Though it was later agreed that I hadn't hit my employer, whose sudden collapse was attributed to his feet having given way beneath him, my disgrace was absolute. Mr Blessington, very shaky and querulous, his forehead bound up with strips of sticking plaster, pronounced my dismissal within the hour. Two policemen, summoned by the lady with the dog, were entertained with cups of tea but then discharged (nobody in West Earlham liked involving the police in anything) and my mother arrived grim-faced from Bright Road to take me away. There was no question, I was informed, of Mr Blessington taking me back, or of anyone else employing me, and I should sit in my room until it was decided what to do with me.

That night my mother and Mrs Buddery held a council of war. I could see that what I'd done had badly frightened them – it was so beyond their experience, so alien to all the dismal West Earlham precepts they had grown up on. Mrs Buddery, I gathered, was all for enlisting me into the army, or the navy, or the air force, or anything that might make me 'realise my responsibilities' (the frightened, stupid gravity of Mrs Buddery's expression as she said this!). As for my mother ... Even now I don't really know what my mother thought, although I have a suspicion, based on certain remarks made in Mrs Buddery's absence, and a vivid, picturesque framing of the incident in the shop ('The *idear* of him falling on the floor like that ... '), that the thought of Mr Blessington's discomfiture wasn't wholly distasteful to her.

It might be wondered why I put up with this – Mr Blessington, Mrs Buddery, my mother's meek acceptance that I should 'realise my responsibilities'. But it was what one did in those days, in that kind of life, and in fact I've subsequently wondered whether such attitudes may not have been central to the West Earlham mind. Together they constituted a kind of smug resignation, a sort of wistful stifling of talent or enterprise, a grainy levelling down of expectations. You were always coming across

49

'promising' seventeen-year-olds jerked out of their education and put to work in a bank or found sheepishly stacking trolleys at one of the city centre supermarkets. Now and again some surly individualist would break out of this strait-jacket, win a place at university, say, or take 'a funny kind of job' (i.e. non-clerical) in some alien city. The direst forebodings greeted these divagations from the eternal path, and the West Earlhamites went to extraordinary lengths to recapture their escapees. I once knew a family who were so concerned at the probable dissipation of their son, a student at Leicester University, that they made a habit of visiting him every second weekend.

And so it might have been with me, had Mrs Buddery not overplayed her hand, my mother not had her private doubts, and the whole affair not been complicated by an unlooked-for revelation. By the end of the week that began so memorably in Mr Blessington's shop parlour I'd started to hear about a sum of money 'left' to me by my father, hitherto kept 'in trust' (my mother was vague about this), to be put into my hands on my eighteenth birthday. It was about £300, perhaps a shade more. And though I can't reassemble the exact details, I recall that a day or so later there was a definite feeling in the air that I ought to be given the money to 'go away somewhere' (Mrs Buddery) and 'make something of myself' (my mother). I was all for the idea, particularly as to 'go away somewhere' could only mean one thing. Once as a fourteen-year-old on a school trip I had spent a day in London. It remained with me as a confused impression of crowded streets, policemen in white bands directing traffic, great bridges perched above grey-coloured water and smoke hanging over distant, endless rooftops. And by this stage I'd read enough literature – mostly novels out of the West Earlham circulating library – about wide-eyed young men who had set off from dull provincial towns towards the bright metropolitan grail to make the prospect of London seem not simply enticing but somehow necessary and inescapable.

And so, incredibly, the business was fixed. The £300 ceased to be a mysterious secret of my mother's and became an actual blue-grey building society account book made out in the name of G.R.E. Chell in a faint and unrecognisable hand. But even here it seemed to me that the limitations of the West Earlham scheme of things stood pitilessly exposed. My mother and Mrs Buddery (between whom and myself there now existed a kind of armed truce) had not the faintest idea of what I should do when I arrived in London. My mother, whom I suspected had never been there in her life, suggested that there were such places as a 'temperance hotel' or a 'Rowton House' where I might stay until I 'got myself settled'. Mrs Buddery, I remember, was full of vague but profuse recollections of relatives who had 'done well for themselves' in London, and at one point unbent sufficiently to make me a present of an A-Z guide to the capital printed in 1937.

West Earlham begins to fade from my mind now, become inconsequent and strange, merely a synthesis of drab little streets and asphalt. I spent the time which remained to me there in a condition of profound euphoria. It was late September, and I recall that I occupied myself in walks: back and forth across Eaton Park, where the dead leaves lay carpeted across the terrace, to the great house at Earlham, whose thoroughfares plunged this way and that through fantastically overgrown shrubbery, out into the byroads near Brooke and Poringland. I don't think that my motive was nostalgic, or even elegiac: I believe it was simple restlessness, an urgency to be off, to assert myself, among unknown circumstances and people. And finally there came a day when I placed myself and my belongings into a taxi – a measure of the journey's importance, as I'd never travelled in one before – and was driven away to Norwich station along roads lined with late-flowering lime trees, sunk in the shadow of an autumn sun. My mother declined to accompany me to the station. She was altogether quiet and good-humoured that morning, I remember, a morning in which I found myself noticing all sorts of odd little things about her: the movement of her jaw as she ate, the slightly distracted way in which she arranged her thin, straggling hair on top of her head, her lists and tabulations – all things I'd seen a thousand times before but had somehow never remembered or assimilated into the idea I had of her. At the gate, as the taxi driver nodded over the suitcase and flocks of children roamed past on their way home from school, she gave me a very odd look.

'You better kiss me, George,' she said at length. And so I dabbed my lips in a general way in the region of her cheek – something I hadn't done for ten or even a dozen years – which was cold and leathery and smelt somehow of face powder, although this wasn't something with which my mother ever adorned herself.

'That's right,' said the taxi driver, who had begun to take a fatherly interest in the proceedings, and by this time I was in the rear seat, looking back at my mother's small, impassive but still faintly forlorn figure, unable to work out if she was in the grip of some violent emotion or really wished me gone, until the cab moved away, the housefronts receded, and she disappeared.

To this day I wonder what my mother thought of my leaving Norwich.

That is all there is to say about West Earlham. I sometimes wonder whether I've been truthful about the place, whether there were things – kindnesses, sensations, warmth – which I missed, and that prejudiced me against it. But there is a way in which it has never left me – the reason, no doubt, why I have spent so long in describing it. It stands in my mind as the representation of everything that I fought against, all that blink-eredness and vague stupidity that propelled me and determined my course in life.

I went back there once years later, at the height of the Boom, and wandered round Bunnett Square calculating how the place had changed. Everything seemed smaller, as if the intervening years had somehow shrivelled and diminished it. Blessington's was long gone, of course, transformed into a big shop that sold videos and computer games as well as the rows of newspapers; the bicycle repairer was an Indian take-away, and the field outside the Scout hut had been colonised by a municipal office. I saw no one I knew, except a very old lady who might have been Mrs Blessington tottering on sticks across the square, and whom I studiously avoided. Eventually I took a bus into Norwich down the same green avenue of lime trees and sat in the bar of the Maid's Head Hotel – a place I wouldn't have dared to enter ten years before – drinking beer and watching the sky darken over the cathedral.

West Earlham! It seems odd to me that the place exists, so fantastically conceived was it, so warped and generally misshapen, so defiantly out of kilter with the quickening passage of time. But it launched me and is, I suppose, in some way responsible for all that followed, and if someone were to ask me, 'What began it all?' I could truthfully answer.

Well – that's all I have to say about West Earlham.

52

In the afternoons, when I was tired of reading or Mr Archer's presence became unusually wearing, I used to wander through the town centre. As well as the brewery there was a second hotel, more expensive than the Caradon, to the extent of displaying printed dinner menus, a bookshop that sold prints of old Suffolk and a teashop with unusual opening hours. All these premises were congregated around a small square on which market days sometimes took place, thronging the hotel entrance and occasionally giving rise to quite severe disturbances.

Mr Archer incubated a violent dislike of this rival establishment. He said: 'Of course, in a town this size you end up seeing rather a lot of your fellow businessmen, but nothing on earth would ever induce me to eat a meal in that place.'

Coming back from one of these walks I found Mr Archer waiting expectantly in the hall. He said: 'The young lady's arrived, sir.' Then, as if there might be some doubt over the visitor's identity, he continued: 'The young lady you said you were expecting.'

'She's a day early then.'

'Quite all right, sir,' Mr Archer said. He was obviously enjoying himself hugely. 'No trouble accommodating anyone at this time of the year.' He rubbed his hands together obsequiously. 'You'll find her in the lounge then.'

Frances Eccles sat in an armchair by the unlit fire. Further proof of Mr Archer's high good humour appeared in the pot of tea that lay on a small occasional table at her side. In the past week I had spun various fantasies around her appearance. These ranged from blonde of a certain age to the kind of harassed girl you saw presenting news reports on the local television channel. None was in the slightest degree accurate. She was a pale and faintly sullen woman of around thirty, with dark circles under her eyes and badly chewed fingernails.

'I know I wasn't meant to come until tomorrow,' she said stiffly, 'but there was a bit of a mix-up.'

'It doesn't matter.'

'Actually,' she went on, with a faint air of wanting to unburden herself,

'I got thrown out of my flat. It was either that or spending the night at my parents'.'

'How did you get here?'

'Train to Lowestoft and hitched. Had to walk the last mile carrying my bloody bag.'

There was a battered suitcase, tied together with a pair of elasticated grips, lying in the corner of the room.

'I'll leave you to get on with it then.'

'OK. But tell that goon on the desk I don't need any more tea. He's already given me two cups and both of them were foul.'

'I'll tell him.'

At dinner that evening, as the rain beat against the window and the candles waved in their saucers, she was more forthcoming.

'To be honest with you, I've never done this sort of thing before. Helping someone with a book, I mean.'

'What do you do?'

On the far side of the room, cut off from us by a solitary old lady and an exhausted-looking commercial traveller, Mr Archer was ostentatiously carving a chicken. He glanced at me for a second, his face radiating curiosity, and then went back to his work.

'All sorts of things. Book reviews. Features. Sex research for the women's mags.'

'What's that involve?'

'Oh, it's not as awful as it sounds. You know every month *Cosmo* or whatever has a piece on "Men fake orgasms too" or "Why bondage is back"? And there are always lots of quotes: "Alan, 31, a journalist, says 'I like my girlfriends to tie me up' " – that kind of thing. Well, I have to ring people I know up and get them to say things.'

'It doesn't sound very difficult.'

'So anyway, I thought, I needed a change from all that, and when Eddie said he'd got someone needed help writing his autobiography, naturally I jumped at it.'

There was a silence while Mr Archer served us plates of chicken, cut up into odd, square cubes. It was hard to know what to make of Frances Eccles, harder to know if the way she talked about her career should be interpreted as gauche or impossibly knowing. Hardest of all was to work out whether she would be any use in the project we contemplated. For a moment I wondered whether I'd simply made a mistake, whether the whole apparatus – Mr MacCready, the publisher's contract, Frances – would be better abandoned.

'Do you know much about my uncle?'

'A bit. No thanks, go away.' Abashed, Mr Archer hoisted the dish of

54

chicken off to another table. 'I mean, I remember it happening – when everything fell apart, that is. But I went to Hendon and looked at the newspaper files. It's quite interesting in a way.'

'In what way?'

'I'm sorry. I keep forgetting he's your uncle. You look terribly like him too. No, it's interesting because of what people said about him. I mean half the journalists who wrote about the enquiry obviously detested him, even when what happened couldn't possibly have been his personal responsibility. The other half are always making excuses for him. *Always*. Putting it down to naivety or foolishness, whatever.'

'What do you think about him?'

'I don't know. Does liking come into it with someone like that? I mean they're just there, and they do things, and someone has to work out the impact.'

By now the dining-room was nearly empty. Brenda, Mr Archer's maid of all work, was grimly spooning pieces of uneaten potato into a kind of funeral urn held tightly against her waist. From the residents' lounge, not far away, came the noise of a television switched up very loud. Frances said:

'Is there anything to do here? In the evenings I mean?'

'Not really. They sometimes play bridge at the Conservative club. The nearest cinema is Aldeburgh, but it shuts for the winter.'

'There must be some pubs or something.'

'I'll take you to one if you're desperate.'

There were three pubs in Eastwold: the Nelson, which was always full of crab-pots and fishermen in blue pullovers; the George, whose land-lord was notorious for having married a Nigerian woman; and the King's Head, which was nearly always empty. We went to the King's Head. Here a solitary barman stood polishing the horse brasses. Light from the fruit machine flickered erratically through the gloaming.

'Very quiet tonight,' the barman said.

'Very.'

'I'm afraid if you were wanting food this evening there isn't any.'

The barman at the King's Head, if not in Mr Archer's class, was thought to run him close at times. We took our drinks to a secluded area near the fireplace.

'Do you like living here?' Frances asked.

'Yes, of course.'

'But why?'

I thought about this for a moment. It was difficult to explain East-wold's attraction. And yet there was an attraction: something to do with

55

absolute predictability, solitude, opportunity for reflection, those kinds of things. In the end I said:

'There's something about a seaside town as the autumn comes on. First the tourists disappear. Then the lights start going on earlier. Then the Salvation Army mission shuts down, and then they close up the putting course. Then one morning you go out on the beach and you don't see a soul. Except that you know life is still going on all around you, the difference being that you can't see it.'

'It sounds awful. I don't think I'm going to like it. I don't think I should have come.'

'You said you didn't have a choice.'

'Did I? Well, there are choices and choices.'

There was still no one else in the pub. The barman had finished the horse brasses and moved on to rearranging the beer mats. Frances said:

'God, you wouldn't believe the day I've had. What with having the row with those bitches at the flat, and then getting down here. I think I'm going to bed. I suppose you'll want to start in the morning?'

'How long are you planning to stay?'

'I don't know. A fortnight? Three weeks? I've got nowhere else to go.'

'Are you sure you won't have another drink?'

'All right.'

After Frances had had some more gin she cheered up a little. She said: 'That man who runs the hotel, Mr Archer, he's a scream, isn't he? When I turned up at reception and asked for you he looked, well, almost shocked. As if I were a tart or something. And then when I'd explained everything he suddenly went all polite. I think he even called me madam.'

'You obviously made a good impression.'

'Did I? Well, it's a change for me to make a good impression, I must say.' She said this with an odd, self-conscious wistfulness, and then made a meditative little prod with her forefinger at the gin glass.

As we made our way out the barman had begun to polish the framed engraving of the Battle of Sole Bay that hung over the fireplace.

'Sure you won't have another?' he asked.

'No thanks.'

'All right then.'

Back at the Caradon Mr Archer was arranging the typed notices on the green baize notice-board. When one of the notices fell off he picked it up off the floor and replaced it with an expert twist of his index finger. He said:

'A gentleman rang for you, madam. He didn't leave a name.'

'Must have been Eddie wanting to know if I got here all right.'

56

'A most interesting-sounding gentleman. We had quite a long conversation.'

'Christ,' Frances said.

Imperceptibly over the next few days a routine established itself. In the mornings we sat in my room – the residents' lounge if there was no one else about – tape-recorder between us, and discussed my uncle's career. After lunch, eaten at the Caradon or one of the teashops in the High Street, we went for walks over the common towards Walberswick or inland to Blythburgh church. Sometimes it rained and we took shelter under the great beech trees or huddled in the lee of the dunes watching the silent landscape of reed and sedge. Occasionally during these interludes I asked Frances questions about herself and her life, never with much success. She had a habit – as in the story about being thrown out of her flat – of revealing some faintly lurid detail about herself and then refusing to elaborate, however much pressed. In this way I heard about a man she was supposed to have married, a house in Walthamstow of which she was supposed to have become part-owner, and a holiday that she was supposed to have taken in Goa – queer, subjunctive fragments, whose ultimate design lay out of reach.

Little of her life seemed to have followed her to Eastwold. Sometimes in the evenings Mr Archer would summon her to the telephone; a letter or two came in the morning post; nothing more. Once, going up to her room on the upper floor and finding the door open, I stood for a moment or two taking in the contents. A white, sprigged nightdress lay on the pillow, and there was a copy of *Mansfield Park* on the bedside table.

Twice in the first week Mr MacCready rang. 'He just wanted to know how we were getting on,' Frances reported, coming back from the phone. 'What did you tell him?' 'I said we were getting on fine.' 'And are we?' 'Are we what?' 'Getting on fine ?' 'Of course.' Most of my conversations with Frances had this odd, rudimentary quality, the sense of nothing more being given away than was absolutely necessary. Trying to draw her out about her life, health, opinions, anything, you met only an impenetrable wall of monosyllables. 'Do you know Suffolk at all?' 'A bit.' 'The Constable Country's not far away. We could go there if you like.' 'All right.' As a result of this exchange we did in fact, one bitter afternoon, pay a visit to Flatford Mill and Copdock: it wasn't a success. At the time I sometimes wondered why I made such an effort with Frances. I think it was because I sympathised with her. The solitude, the disagreeable task, the bleak surroundings of the Caradon – these were all factors to be taken into account. Frances divined something of this sympathy, but did not resent it. 'You don't have to feel sorry for me, you know,' she said once. 'You don't have to *make me feel at home*. I've had worse jobs than this.' 'Such as?' 'All right. Hat-check girl in a night-club.' 'Tell me about it.' 'I might, sometime.' But the night-club, like the husband, the house and the holiday, lay deep in the bran-tub of her conversation.

There was one subject, however, in which we were in complete agreement: this was the fascination of Mr Archer. If anything, Frances' interest in Mr Archer's more bizarre pronouncements exceeded my own. 'You were right,' she said on the afternoon of the third day after her arrival, 'Archer's a real find. I've never met a bore like him. I mean, they could make a radio programme about him: "Archer Talks" or "The World According to Archer". He could make a fortune.' In fact Frances' most animated moments tended to come at times when Mr Archer was in the room – presiding over the supper table, perhaps, or dilating on holidays he had taken in France.

Mr Archer reciprocated this interest. 'A very polite young lady,' he told me once. 'It was odd, wasn't it, how interested she seemed about the cathedral at Arles. Do you think it would amuse her to see the photographs I took? There are a great many, and I should be delighted to show them to her.'

Q: Why did you come here? To the seaside?

A: I always liked this part of the world. 'Silly Suffolk', Norfolk people used to say when I was a boy. I never thought so. Curiously, my mother once brought me here when I was a child – I say curiously because my mother hardly ever countenanced any kind of excursion or holiday. But I think she liked it here. It was all much livelier in those days, of course. I mean, there was more going on on the pier, the local church used to hold a beach mission – that kind of thing.

Q: Those days being?

A: 1963, 1964. I have a vivid memory of walking back along the front towards the High Street, where the buses left from, and hearing 'I Want To Hold Your Hand' being played on somebody's transistor radio. That would be 1963, wouldn't it?

Q: But you couldn't have stayed in London?

A: I don't know. I suppose I could have, though in the circumstances it would have been difficult to find work. Despite the unconditional discharge. People in the City have long memories. Also, you see, by that time it had all ended. I had no affiliations. There was just my uncle. One or two others, perhaps: Kippax, who was his main associate, a man named Grundy who ran the administrative side. So when it all fell apart, after the mess had been cleared away, there were no threads to pick up, if you see what I mean. Just an absence. Also, I think I probably wanted to distance myself from it all.

Q: And you like it here?

A: I don't dislike it. Wilson-Steer used to come here to paint because of the light. Unfortunately that doesn't mean anything to me. But I like the sea. And I like the contrast between public and private perceptions. The sense of nothing ever happening on the surface, but a great deal seething away below. It's not really a tourist resort any more, you see. Not since Dr Beeching took the railway away, and the sea started eroding the cliff. There are a few diehards, not many. So the local people mostly have the place to themselves. So yes, I like it.

Q: The solitude doesn't bother you?

A: I live in a hotel with an average of fifteen residents: I don't call that solitude. But, yes, I see what you mean in principle and, no, the solitude doesn't bother me. I led a very restricted childhood, literally seeing no one, certainly hardly anyone of my own age. My mother was one of those odd working-class people – there were many more of them in those days – who really did believe in keeping themselves to themselves. *My* self too. It was a kind of religion with her. I can remember, well, one could only call it the delight with which she turned down the very few invitations she received. I think a great deal of what followed stems from that.

Q: What exactly?

A: That sense of restriction, deliberate limitations. Actually I'm a great believer in restrictions. But that was restriction for its own sake, unconsidered, simply a kind of meaningless private treaty with oneself.

From Norwich station the tracks head south under a few blackened bridges, past the cattle market and the distant floodlights of the football ground, on through the back gardens and allotments of Trowse and Tuckswood towards open country. Five miles out in the direction of Diss the landscape settles into its characteristic pattern and you see only flat fields, the square hedgerows falling gently away across the horizon and the rooks circling in the empty air.

I came to live in London, as I'll tell you, a few weeks after my eighteenth birthday. Norwich grows very small now, very meagre and distant, and West Earlham altogether remote, like a fairy kingdom of legend rolling into view every so often through the mist: I don't suppose that during the next five years I thought about them consecutively for more than a few minutes. In any case the memories of these days are dominated and superimposed by the figure of my uncle – which is odd in a way, as I didn't fall under his spell until at least a year later – as well as being inextricably bound up with the experience of London. In fact in a strange way the two have grown inseparable, and when I think about a certain part of the south-western city – Fulham, perhaps, or the streets round Putney Bridge – it's always my uncle who rises up to paint the memory in his own idiosyncratic colours.

All this is anticipating things, though. I remember that, before I arrived there, I had ludicrously distinct ideas about London. I saw it, I believe, as a wide, interminable landscape of grey, angular squares and monuments, a little ragged, perhaps, at its edges but stretching away into enticing suburbia. Later on, when this vision had been blown away, I still tried very hard to understand London, to map it out in my mind and to establish how it grew and functioned. Did you know, for instance, that with the exception of the central zones, London postcodes run alphabetically by district? Think about it: SE2: Abbey Wood; SE3: Blackheath; SE5: Camberwell; SE6 Catford ... I was always coming across information like this and storing it away in my head with a kind of glee that I'd never dreamed of bringing to the West Earlham back streets.

For all that, I don't think I ever really understood London, or imag-

61

ined it to be anything more than a chaos of streets and people. At the same time there were definite paths that I carved out through the rock, and several tunnels that I constructed through the green and populous moss. South of the river was a foreign country, but I knew north London pretty well, and there was a point in my life when I could probably have gone from Canning Town to Ealing Broadway without the aid of an A-Z. And of course there were all the curious places that I stumbled upon by accident – queer old museums found down alleyways in the heart of the City, wild little gardens discovered in the middle of Chelsea. They were refashioning the place then and the bulldozers were out uprooting the old Victorian terraces, but the bones of the old city shone up out of the dirt. It was here, oddly enough, that I came upon occasional reminders of West Earlham and the West Earlham system: a newsagent's shop in a square in Islington run by a man who might have been Mr Blessington's brother; a patch of small stucco houses somewhere off the North Circular that I remember examining curiously for a time in the dark of a Saturday evening, so sharply did they conform to the Bright Road pattern.

All this, though, was in the future. The London glimpsed out of a railway carriage that November afternoon was a very different animal. It was raining gently, and this, added to the drifts of fallen leaves that lay about in the streets and the grim little parklands, gave everything a silent, smoky and beaten-down quality. Churches, patches of waste ground, serpentine red-brick terraces – everything ran off into the distance in the same undifferentiated way. And yet sitting at the back-end of a second-class carriage – the only other occupant was an old man with bad teeth browsing through the *Daily Mirror* – I was perfectly happy. I felt – I don't know to any degree of certainty what I did feel, apart from a pervading loneliness, a huge dissatisfaction with everything that had previously been given to me, and the thought that for the first time in my existence there might be things I could look forward to. In those days the journey from Thorpe station to Liverpool Street took a couple of hours, but everything had a profound novelty, and I looked out contentedly at the grey expanse of the Stour estuary outside Manningtree, read the graffiti that gleamed up from the ironwork bridges of the East End and even got up a conversation with the old man with bad teeth, until the light began to fail, the passing stations – Ingatestone, Romford and Shenfield – came bunched together and the train rolled into Liverpool Street.

It was six o'clock on a Friday evening, the height of the rush hour, when I descended to a great grey concourse thronged with all manner of human traffic: rushing middle-aged men in mackintoshes with briefcases clutched to their chests, gangs of dawdling girls, silent youths loitering under the lamps. I can remember being so intoxicated with the scene, so desperate somehow to become a part of it all, that I carried my suitcase into a pub on one of the upper levels and sat at an empty table drinking a pint of bitter while the crowd swarmed around me. It was, I realised, like nothing I had ever witnessed before, almost like being set down in another country. Later on I wandered east through Whitechapel and Stepney, along cramped roads strewn with rubbish and splintered packing cases, and eventually fetched up at a men's hostel in Bethnal Green where for the sum of £3 I was presented with a single room, a batteryless transistor radio and the promise of unlimited hot water.

And so, for the next three months, the pattern of my life was established.

It was the oddest kind of life. I lived all over east and north-east London: in Bethnal, Hackney, Shoreditch, Bow, as far east as Leyton, as far north as Stoke Newington; in lodging houses, 'commercial hotels', furnished rooms taken a week at a time. Once, I remember, I spent a week in a YMCA in the Kingsland Road populated entirely by Nigerian students and marvelled, on coming down to breakfast on the first morning, at hearing the tables resound to a language that wasn't English. It took me perhaps a month to discover how little I could survive on, even in London in 1970. You could live on £10 a week then if you were careful. Trying to piece together this time I find that all the intimate details have simply eluded me, and that I only remember the wayside oddities: sleeping on Hampstead Heath one winter night (it was the merest freak – I had the price of a bed in my hand), or a fantastically cheap café in Dalston where a plate of eggs and bacon cost two shillings and the old woman who helped with the washing-up claimed to have watched Queen Victoria's funeral procession.

Looking back, I can scarcely believe the loneliness of those first few months. I used to get into conversations with complete strangers sometimes just to hear the sound of another voice, spend money that I couldn't afford in pubs simply for the sense of company, and travel miles on the off-chance of free entertainment. One Sunday, I remember, I took a bus from Leyton to Hyde Park and ended up at Speakers' Corner, where I listened to a man in a battered morning coat explaining that his marriage to the Queen Mother was to be postponed 'for reasons of state'. Another time in a pub in Whitechapel late on a Saturday night a gang of Irish road builders took a fancy to me, stood me drinks and even held out the promise of a job if I turned up at their depot on the Monday morning. I never went – it would have been the easy way out, or rather the wrong solution to the problems I was setting myself. I wasn't, I regret, particularly chaste or particularly scrupulous. I have a recollection – an awful guilty recollection – of waking up in a dismal garret of a room with frameless windows and a bare boarded floor, that contained only myself, two piles of clothing, a bed and the woman with whom I had spent the night, and of silently leaving the building – it was an abandoned house, colonised by squatters – feeling half-ashamed and at the same time faintly satisfied at the thought of a difficult task finally accomplished.

I might have gone to the dogs altogether during that first winter in London, if it hadn't been for a kind of bedrock shrewdness, a certain awareness that the kind of life I saw practised around me, the busy brooding life of the cheap lodging houses and the squatters' encampments, wasn't indefinitely sustainable. I don't give myself any great credit for this. It was simply that I knew that there were other kinds of experience that I badly wanted to appreciate. I had a huge book jag when I first came to London. In some ways the thing I remember most about those early times is reading paperbacks out of the bargain bins in Farringdon Road, or illustrated nature books in the upstairs room of Holborn public library. I hardly ever bought a book in those days. I once read the whole of *The Grapes of Wrath* in a dozen half-hour instalments at Foyle's in the Charing Cross Road, and I can never look at a copy of *New Grub Street* without thinking of the musty second-hand shop in Cecil Court where I first came across it and the silhouettes of the people outside passing by the green glass windows. In fact all I have to do is look at the cover of the old Penguin edition – the one with Whistler's *Nocturne* on the front – and suddenly it's 1970 again, the newspapers are going on about England's chances in the World Cup and Harold Wilson's in the General Election, and I'm eighteen years old, standing on the pavement of Charing Cross Road staring at the crowd.

By a mixture of economy and mental discipline, I managed to keep the practical realities of life in London at bay for nearly four months. It was only when my father's money had dwindled into single figures that I steeled myself to take drastic action. Oddly enough, it wasn't that hard to find a job in London in those days – every café would have a 'help wanted' sign on the wall or a handwritten advert for builders' labourers. For a fortnight I washed up in a café on the Old Kent Road which opened at dawn to service the passing lorry trade. A bit later I helped deliver milk on a council estate in Holloway where the walkways were always scattered with glass and mad old women negotiated their requirements from behind locked doors. Curiously, despite my temperament and the hold that all the West Earlham nonsense about a fair day's work for a fair day's wage had on my mind, I found the business of earning money in this way unexpectedly satisfying, as well as being an absolute stop on the notions (what kind of notions they were I could still barely put into words) I'd begun to conceive for myself and my destiny. I knew, you see, that it was something of which my mother and Mrs Buddery would have broadly approved. They'd have hated the notion of working in a café ('Nasty, dirty places' I could hear my mother saying) but the idea of eight hours' back-breaking labour for starvation wages would have deeply appealed to them.

It was at this time, in the foothills of these great ideas, that I encountered Ekwall.

I can remember precisely where I met Ekwall: on a Saturday morning in April at a pavement café near Camden Lock where we'd both gone independently to read books and look at the people. I haven't seen him for ten years, and I haven't the least skill as an artist, but I think that if you gave me a pen and paper I could make a stab at drawing Ekwall. He had one of those long, thin, horsey faces that look down on you from immensely stooped shoulders – rather like Doré's illustration of Don Quixote or, nearer at home, an early photograph of George Orwell. In no other respect was Ekwall the least like Orwell – apart from a curious, drawling upper-class-cockney voice – but he liked having his attention drawn to this resemblance. He was a tall, pale, faintly ramshackle creature, a year or so older than me, with a permanently hang-dog look, who'd been thrown out of Oxford for some escapade that I never quite got to the bottom of, and was living in his parents' house near Regent's Park (again there was some mystery about his parents, who were hardly ever in London) while he, as he put it, 'looked around for some inoffensive way to exert myself'. Ekwall was always saying things like this.

I never properly established what Ekwall was doing that Saturday morning in Camden, but I suspect that he'd simply gone there on the off-chance of a pick-up. Up until then – I was coming up to my nineteenth birthday – I don't suppose I'd exchanged a word with a genuine homosexual. We'd had them in West Earlham, of course – faintly epicene middle-aged men who lived on their own or with doting mothers, whom my own mother referred to contemptuously as 'nancy boys' – but this was my first experience of one at close quarters. In ordinary circumstances, I suppose, all my mother's prejudices would have come into play, but Ekwall was so painfully inoffensive, so utterly unlike the accepted caricatures of inversion, that I never dreamed of mocking him. There was also the fact that he appeared to take no pleasure from the furtive, predatory kind of life he led. I got the feeling that he regarded it all as something routine and unavoidable, and appalling even to himself. Once or twice, later on in our relationship, I got to meet some of Ekwall's 'boys' – he called them that – and they were always waiters or shop assistants who stared at their drinks while Ekwall prosed on about Dickens or Eliot: he'd been studying English, you see, until they threw him out. I remember once asking him why he couldn't find someone of his own type (by which I meant someone who was well-off and knew about books) but he looked grimmer than ever. He'd tried all that, he said, and you simply stayed at home all night having supper and arguing about who did the washing-up.

If all this makes Ekwall sound like an object of pity, that wasn't the case at all. In fact I admired him unreservedly and relished the time I spent in his company. As for Ekwall, I think he was a bit amused – not just because he'd found someone who liked listening to his talk, but because I was so obviously such a different person from the kind he was used to. Used to socially, I mean – in other respects I could have been taken, in fact probably was, for one of his boys by anyone who saw us together. To do him justice he was quite unselfconscious about this, and when he drew attention to differences in the way we talked or behaved it was with a kind of disinterestedness, like an anthropologist. He used to walk round the house in Regent's Park – he had a couple of rooms on an upper floor which he'd converted into a pigsty of dirty clothes and scraps of paper – pointing out things he thought I might be interested in. As I remember they had a Landseer and a couple of Hockney prints, and that, Ekwall said, was ignoring the safe in the cellar which he didn't have access to. At the time I couldn't understand his attitude to the house or its contents – he used to tread mud deliberately into the carpets and look the other way if one of the 'boys' stole anything, which they were always doing (one of them walked off with half the silver once, but he hushed it up somehow), and I remember him saying once that he wouldn't have minded if the place burned down provided he wasn't in it at the time. Now I think I understand it a bit better and can comprehend something of the mixture of boredom, unhappiness and resignation with which he approached life. 'The problem with me,' he used to say sometimes – and he did it without a trace of irony, 'is that I've lost my way. As simple as that.'

He drank a huge amount, of course. On the day we met we hadn't been talking for more than a few minutes before he suggested that we go to a wine bar, and later on any arrangement to do something usually began with me dragging Ekwall out of a pub somewhere. Again I don't remember being censorious about this, but merely accepting it as one of the compromises you had to make to spend time with him. Looking back I think I've a great deal to be thankful to Ekwall for. I don't suppose, if you were to reckon it up, that our acquaintance amounted to much more than a succession of nights spent drinking or watching films – we must have seen every film that came on general release in London in those days – but at the time it seemed as if an extraordinary new world had opened up in front of me, full of books and pints of beer and vague talk about 'life'. Oddly enough it was Ekwall who got me the job at Chaffington's. Hopeless about disentangling his own affairs, he could be highly objective about other people's.

'What you need,' he told me, a few weeks after we'd met, 'is something to do. Gainful employment.' (Ekwall habitually talked in these finespun clichés.)

'I've had jobs. I'll have them again.'

'No, I mean a proper job. Not washing-up. Something steady.'

'I get by.'

'But you don't get by, do you?' Ekwall said. We were in a pub in Soho waiting for Ekwall's current 'boy' – an off-duty guardsman from the Knightsbridge barracks – to finish jamming a pile of shillings into the fruit machine. 'You see, it's all right for me. I've got money. I can work this kind of Bohemian racket.' He made a large gesture round a room that included a Dickensian barman, two withered old women wearing cloche hats and shapeless coats that reminded me of the garments my mother put on for Sunday afternoon excursions to Mrs Buddery's, and a group of fishy-eyed teenagers. 'You can't. Well, not for much longer. Regular money's what you need.'

'Any ideas?'

As it happened Ekwall did have an idea, in the form of an uncle who was a partner in an accountancy firm somewhere north of High Holborn: 'Fine old firm. Could have gone there myself only it didn't suit.' Introduced by Ekwall in the character of bright lad and personal friend (you could still get jobs like that in those days), I went to an office in Red Lion Square one morning and was interviewed by a diffident old man in a pinstripe suit who seemed to think it would be all right. Why did I do it? I suppose because I had boundless faith in Ekwall and his judgement, and also because I suspected he was right, that I couldn't go on living from hand to mouth for very much longer or continue with the vague, restless life of the past six months.

And so, not without certain private misgivings, I became an articled clerk at Chaffington's in Red Lion Square. It was odd, this transformation. One moment I'd been spending my days lounging in the Charing Cross Road, the next I was one of the tribe of grey-coated men and women who were borne via the Central Line to Chancery Lane each morning, to swarm thereafter in a mournful tide along High Holborn and its multitudinous alleyways and conduits. For some reason my progress becomes clearer now, and the thoroughfares and byways of old Bloomsbury are very vivid to me. There was a particular seat in the gardens of Red Lion Square, stuck between a hydrangea bush and a statue of George Lansbury, where I used to eat my lunch every day, and a bookshop nearby in Sicilian Avenue where the lunch hour could sometimes be prolonged until as late as half-past two. Chaffington's 'went in' for legal work. They audited law firms in Shepherd's Inn and Carey Street and did tax computations for rich barristers with chambers in the Gray's Inn Road, and a veil of antiquated respectability hung over their premises. There were still iron stanchions by the door where, it was suggested to visitors, the link-men of two centuries before had hung their torches, and the partners' offices were done out in mahogany with framed Victorian audit reports on the wall.

Mysteriously, and by degrees, I became habituated to the profession and its regimes. Auditing seemed to me a gigantic guessing-game, played with inadequate materials, in whose satisfactory outcome men of fanatical probity would shamelessly collude. Taxation looked far more pointed and rewarding. Insolvency and some of the more exotic branches of management accounting I never came near to: the firm looked down its nose at bankruptcy cases and an insolvent tobacconist was generally referred to a liquidator's shop in Bedford Row. Despite these limitations there was a logic and an exactitude about accountancy that rather impressed me. In my second year I took a prize for auditing in the Intermediate Examinations of the Institute of Chartered Accountants in England and Wales and was rewarded by the firm with a copy of *Bartholomew's Principles and Practice of Elementary Book-keeping.* I learned to perform reconciliations and deferred profit forecasting, and to enter figures in a ledger opened by the senior clerk with an expression of the most sacramental awe. A sense of propriety was firmly enjoined at Chaffington's here in the early 1970s. The senior partner – I looked him up in the Institute yearbook and found he'd first been admitted in the year of the General Strike – still wore a morning coat to work and the junior clerks – white-faced youngsters from Highgate and Holloway – were famous for the sobriety of their get-up. I've a photograph of myself taken around this time: grey-suited, briefcase under one arm, looking very pale and serious on the office steps.

In the meantime, and in the company of Ekwall, I continued to lead an energetic double life. Mostly this consisted of an activity that Ekwall called 'seeing a bit of things'.

'Look here, George,' he would say over the telephone – personal calls were discouraged, but everyone knew about Ekwall's uncle – as I stared at the leafless late-November trees. 'Friday night tonight. What do you say to Soho?'

'We've had all that before. No fleshpots. By agreement. You remember?'

'No. Not that. Not the delights of Frith Street. *Writers*.'

'What kind of writers?'

'Poets. Novelists. Corporation of the Goosequill. Genius renascent in Old Compton Street. Apparently there's this club called the Colony Room ...'

And so we went to Soho in pursuit of writers, where, having been refused admission to the Colony Room, we ended up in a room above a pub in Brewer Street talking to a dirty, elderly man who in return for half-a-dozen glasses of brandy and water consented to tell us about the homosexual relationship he'd had with Dylan Thomas or it might have been Julian Maclaren-Ross.

Other times we sprawled in armchairs listening to Ekwall's records and trying to work out their effect on our consciousness.

'Like feeling hot wax dripping over your forehead.'

'No, you're wrong there. Like being whipped *very slowly* with birch twigs.'

'By a man or a woman?'

'A man, of course ... And what he's singing isn't *Lady in a black dress*.'

'No?'

'No. It's *Layer deer anna black duress*.'

It was at about this time that Ekwall had a poem (entitled 'The Grinding Gears of My Love Forge Upward') accepted by *Encounter*.

And so time went on in that calm and endlessly inviting way that it does in your early twenties when everything is dawns and horizons and promise. I was twenty, twenty-one then, and London was still a source of fathomless interest and amusement to me. The strangest places drew me to them. There was a particular road – called Dombey Street, I think – near High Holborn where I used to loaf in the sun for no other reason than that I liked the look of the shabby Georgian houses and the thought of Dickens walking there with Forster and Maclise, and a particular pub next to some run-down gardens near Doughty Street that I used to drink in because it contained some extraordinary specimens of taxi driver and Billingsgate porter. 'Half-past seven and an empty street' is a phrase that sticks in my head from these days. Together with half-a-dozen freer spirits among the articled clerks I founded a society called the Chaffington Irregulars and went with it on evening excursions to odd pubs and wine bars between Fleet Street and the river, or to quasi-official celebrations of completed audits known as 'drink-ups' held in the up-

69

stairs room of a big old railway hotel near King's Cross station. Even now I could give you thumb-nail sketches of the Chaffington Irregulars: a red-faced boy called Martingale whom I afterwards knew as the magnificent director of an insurance company in Eastcheap; Savage who went into traded options and died a bankrupt; Jenkins whom I last saw getting out of a Daimler near the Bank of England. Sometimes if I think very hard I can imagine myself back there in Red Lion Square, with the sunlight falling across the ancient pavements and the statue of George Lansbury, back in the days before my uncle's hectic reappearance in my life, before the shadows closed in around us.

My mother died in 1972, suddenly and according to Mrs Buddery – it was she who telephoned Chaffington's to tell me – inconveniently. In a subsequent letter she enclosed a list of items purchased by her for 'the dear departed' in the days before her death. They included a transistor radio, several pounds of oranges and, oddly enough, a pair of shoes. I took a day off work and travelled down by train to the funeral.

In the years since I'd left Norwich I hadn't stopped thinking about my mother. I'd thought about my father too, but he was remote and unquantifiable. The grey-haired man in the photographs, the postcards from Dresden and Cologne; it was my mother who moved most sharply through my consciousness. She reared up at me in the most unlikely circumstances: late at night in Soho with Ekwall, hunched over my desk in Red Lion Square, in the tiny bed-sit I'd begun renting in Belsize Park. Now, as the train rolled through Chelmsford and Colchester and the sun hung low over the silent estuaries, I thought of her again: a lean and slightly exaggerated figure, her features sharper and more pronounced than I remembered. In particular, I cast about in my mind for my earliest recollection of her and emerged once again with the white houses streaming away from the window and the sudden apparition gathering me up in her arms. And I have a distinct memory of repeating the word 'dead' to myself several times.

I'd assumed the funeral would be held at St Anne's, a stone's throw away from the house in Bright Road. In fact it took place at another church out along Earlham Road where Mrs Buddery had some vague influence with the vicar. I remember taking a particular interest in a memorial tablet to the left of me recording the accomplishments and progency of a certain Josiah Garbutts Esq. and in the difficulties of the undertaker's men who knocked the coffin against a pew and ended up pushing it before them like a supermarket trolley. In the pew behind me

Mrs Buddery, swathed in black vestments, vigorously intoned the responses.

There was a black-crape bouquet stuck to the door-knocker of Mrs Buddery's house in Stannard. Inside, the dining table had been dragged into the centre of the front room and spread with what the sorority of the back-kitchen had liked to refer to as a 'cold collation'. Here various more or less recognisable people in badly fitting formal clothes introduced themselves to me. In their vanguard was a shabby and slightly worn-looking figure in a crumpled serge suit. It was my uncle.

'I'm glad to see you here, George,' he said, shaking my hand with an odd effusiveness. 'Sorry of course, in the circumstances, but glad. Very.'

'Were you at the service, Uncle Ted?'

'Couldn't get away in time,' said my uncle vaguely. 'Spent half an hour sitting in a train outside Diss. But I'm here *now* and I'm very glad to see you. We can go back together. Have a bit of a talk.'

There was something proprietorial and faintly ominous in the way he said this, and at the same time something reassuring in his large, humorous face – the tufts of hair not quite as pronounced as they had been, but still in some way efflorescent and perky. Together we became part of a circle attending on Mrs Buddery, now in a state of advanced emotion.

'I don't know what I *shall* do now Jane's gone. They say the Good Lord takes the best ones first and I'm sure that's right. There never was a one as helpful and considerate as her for errands or helping a body with shopping and such ... I'm sure I *shall* miss her,' Mrs Buddery ended defiantly and, I thought, a shade unnecessarily. Later I found myself in the centre of a small crowd made up of a diminutive man and woman, both looking extraordinarily like one another, and a brood of noisy, round-faced children, anxious to ply me with reminiscence and advice. 'Fred and Eileen Allman. You won't remember us, but your mum used to bring you to see us when you were a baby. Out Blofield way. And if I were you' – Mr Allman lowered his voice – 'I'd take a look in the cupboards to see what the old cat's walked away with.'

I've only the vaguest memory of what happened in the next hour or so. But I do recall collecting the key from a tearful and in some way reluctant Mrs Buddery and, my uncle accompanying me in the role of close and interested relative, walking the forty yards to Bright Road for a last look at the house. Something in its silence, broken only by the sound of dense Norfolk air rising against the windows, conveyed to me what I hadn't even in the train chosen to consider – that my mother was dead, that whatever I thought about her I should never see her again, and that she had indisputably and according to her lights cared for me – and I roamed around the place for a while and my uncle stood sympatheti-

71

cally and it seemed to me a bit oddly by the stairwell. My mother's bedroom was quite empty. Somebody had cleared the wardrobe that stood by the bedstead, and there was a little scattering of hairpins and disturbed dust on the carpet.

I went back downstairs to find my uncle grown animated in the way that I remembered from our first meeting. 'Rare old place this is, George,' he said, standing in the tiny room and rattling his fingers on the window casings. 'I remember when these houses were built. One. Two. *Pop*! Blink your eyes and another street would've gone up. They didn't waste time in them days.

'Or money,' he added.

Then, on the instant, his mood changed. 'Of course, y'could stay here if y'like. A word to the council'd settle it. What do y'say to that, George? Live in Norwich and get a job eh? – a job that'd pay.'

I shook my head. 'I already decided, Uncle Ted. I'm not coming back.'

But my uncle was by now looking at a featureless picture of a country lane in winter that my mother had hung from the wall next to the big gilt mirror. 'Now this, this is a piece you could do something with. If I were you, George, I'd take this back with me and no mistake.'

In a cupboard by the fireside my mother had left what she called her 'heirlooms': old brooches with damaged catches, a photograph or two, silver threepenny bits that had once decorated a Victorian watch-chain. These I scooped into a brown paper envelope.

'Things to remember her by,' said my uncle approvingly. 'That's right.'

A moment later I shut the door on the house in Bright Road for the last time.

As we wandered back along Stannard, where the guests had by now debouched into the street and Mr Allman stood agitatedly calling his children to order, and thence to Colman Road, where there were buses to the station, I found myself wondering again about my mother, not now in relation to my own distress but in terms that were exclusive to her. What, I wondered, had my mother wanted? Had she ever been ambitious? Happy? The fact that I couldn't come up with answers to any of these questions seemed shameful and inexcusable.

I began to wonder, too, about my uncle. Clearly his work now took him to London, as there was a return ticket sticking out of the breast pocket of his suit. In the train, despite the promise of 'a bit of a talk', he seemed forlorn and ill at ease. He had a battered and very rusty old umbrella that he placed point downward on the floor before him, the handle balanced in the groove of his chin, and in this attitude he passed the journey as far as Ipswich. Then, as the train picked up speed beyond

72

the Essex flats, he seemed ready for conversation, or if not for conversation then for the reflective and interruptive monologues which, I later came to realise, were his means of communicating to the world.

'A hard kind of a woman, your mother. I don't mean to criticise, I suppose we're all of us hard enough if you did but think about it, but ...

'It was all a long time ago,' he said conclusively.

'What was?'

My uncle appeared not to have heard. 'I can remember during the war buying her a hat, and her not liking it. Y'd be surprised, George, the fuss there was about that hat.'

This was interesting. In fact it suggested sides to my mother's life and temperament that I'd never stopped to consider. Wanting to tap this vein of reminiscence, I asked straightaway:

'Did you know my father at all well, Uncle Ted?'

My uncle looked uncomfortable. 'He was older than me, eight years older. That's a big difference when you're a kid. And then when I was growing up he was always away somewhere. But I remember him being good with his hands,' my uncle said cautiously. 'Remember him once making me a rabbit hutch out of a pair of old orange boxes. Extraordinary thing it was.'

Some odd fact about my father's family, remembered from the conversations with my mother years before, stole into view. 'Was that when you were living at Thorpe?'

But my uncle shook his head, a terse gesture that immediately established him, I realised, as my mother's confederate in any sortie in pursuit of my father's memory: unapproachable, evasive, shifty.

Grown suddenly restless once again, he began to ask me questions about myself. What was my job? Did I like it? Did I have a high opinion of my employers and they of me? Did I save money? Where did I live? There was a touch of shrewdness in these interrogations that I hadn't previously noticed in him, and his advice had an autobiographical flavour.

'Biggest mistake *I* made when I came to London, George, was to overdo things. 'Spensive lodgings. Three-course dinners. Football matches. Thing to do is to gather your resources and live cheap ...

'No one ever did any good by overdoing it.'

I had a sudden vision of my uncle a quarter of a century ago: spruce, dapper, hair slicked back, wearing black and white co-respondent's shoes, slipping along the thoroughfares of London.

'How's business, Uncle Ted?'

He looked thoughtful. 'Not so good as it might be ... In fact I'm thinking of making a change, young George.'

'A change?'

'That's right. Getting a bit tired of carrying boxes of toys round the country in the back of a car. Been thinking of setting up on my own,' my uncle announced proudly.

He paused. 'There's got to be more to life than selling toys,' he said.

'Not that I haven't done all right out of it,' he added hastily, as if I'd hazarded a career in the toy trade myself and this might be construed as dissuasion.

'... I might be talking to *you* about it one of these days,' he ended decisively.

More than this he wouldn't say. By this stage, tired, emotionally overstretched and in any case not specially interested in whatever commercial plans he had mapped out for himself, I didn't press him. It strikes me in retrospect, though, that perhaps the great Chell empire, with all its lustrous satrapies and satellite kingdoms, took root in this conversation, that in all probability its outline had never been put into words before, even in the few halting sentences that my uncle allowed himself here in a three-quarters empty train shuttling over the East Anglian fields in the twilight of a January afternoon. Looking back I can see that, far more than our later conversations – either in Putney or at the house in Sydenham – it had a prophetic quality, a sense of sharp, shrewd intelligence taking hold of itself in a way that it had perhaps never done before. At the time, though, I'm certain that I marked it down merely as another of my uncle's 'notions', sketchy day-dreams of the kind he'd already hinted at in the graveyard conversation of nearly a decade ago.

Liverpool Street, reached at five, looked even more like an ant-heap. My uncle stared at it from the train window, gravely but with a definite enthusiasm, as if in moving towards it he knew very well what he was about. We said goodbye on the steps of the underground station, after I'd refused his offer of 'a bite to eat'. Part of me was simply exhausted. Another part of me had had rather more of my uncle in the past four hours than it could decently take. But a third and much greater part had been struck, suddenly and inexorably, by a sensation that had nothing to do with the other two, though it may in a small way have been pushed to the surface by them. The sensation, which required silence and solitude, and couldn't have been approached in my uncle's company, was that I had fallen in love.

Q: Did your uncle ever talk about his early life?

A: About his private life, nothing. About his business career, a very little.

Q: Didn't this strike you as odd?

A: Not in the context of my family. The Chells are famously secretive. Even now, I don't know who my grandfather was. There was something disreputable about him that caused my mother never to mention his name. Obviously I inherited this tendency, because it never occurred to me to ask awkward questions – well, hardly ever. I think even when I was very young I respected these silences. *Especially* when I was very young. These hulking gaps in your family history weren't unusual in our part of the world. Nearly every family I knew as a child – and there weren't many – had some unexplained scandal fraying its edges, some delinquent brother or illegitimate child who was never mentioned. My family was an extreme example of this tendency.

Q: And your uncle began as a travelling salesman?

A: In toys, that's right. At least, that's what he was doing when we first met. Before that it may have been something else. I don't know. He always gave the impression that the travelling job was unimaginably awful – hanging around in tobacconists' shops on the off-chance of selling thirty shillingsworth of stock. And extraordinarily badly paid. A basic salary of a few pounds a week – this would have been the mid-60s – the same again in commission, maybe, if you were lucky.

Q: The register at Companies' House has two mentions of him in the late 1950s. The first as director of a toy-manufacturing concern in Harrogate; the second as director of a small printing firm, also in Harrogate.

A: Then the register at Companies' House knows more than I do! No, I was aware that he'd been involved in one or two business ventures before this. Very occasionally people would turn up at the office who'd known him from that time in his life, usually as a result of having seen his picture in the paper. It was all presented in a spirit of good fellowship, but inevitably they all wanted to touch him for money. My uncle had an absolute horror of these people – no, perhaps horror is the wrong word.

He was embarrassed by them and at the same time faintly sympathetic –
I mean, they could always be sure of getting something from him.

Q: Why embarrassed?

A: I think because all this represented a part of his life that he wanted
to forget. Both businesses failed, I think. He used to hate it when
newspapers ran 'profiles' that went in for this kind of sifting through his
earlier days. I remember him once nearly issuing a writ against the *Daily
Mirror* in that respect. In the end the lawyers advised against it. On very
good grounds.

Q: Which were?

A: That most of what the *Mirror* said was true. That he had been
appointed director of a certain company in 1950-whenever it was, that
two years later that company had failed, and that a dozen or so people
had lost their jobs. There might have been something odd about the
ensuing liquidation too – the directors managing to retrieve their goods
by way of third parties, something like that.

Q: Were you curious about this part of his life? Did you ever ask him
about it?

A: A little. Not much. If people don't want to talk about things, then
they don't want to talk about them, do they? *Won't* talk about them in
some cases. Certainly a quality I associated with my mother. As I say, I
collaborated to some extent in the air of mystery she put about, but at
the same time there were some things I did want to know very badly, and
she would never tell me. I spent a lot of time with my uncle, a great deal
of time, but that didn't mean he was approachable. He would *confide*
things sometimes, the oddest things, but there were great stretches of his
mind that I could never penetrate.

Q: What kind of things did he confide?

A: Financial things. What he thought about other people.

Q: What he thought about you?

A: We were both Chells. Chells don't tell other Chells what they think
about them. They leave them to find out.

In the evenings, when the sea could be heard in the distance beating against the esplanade, Mr Archer liked to talk about the things that had attracted his attention during the day: the peculiarities of the postal service, news heard on the radio, Brenda's inability to clean the upstairs corridors without leaving pools of water behind her. He delivered these observations in a high, breathless monotone, usually while carrying out some domestic chore – buffing up a caseful of fish knives, perhaps, or itemising a bill on scraps of paper torn from the margins of that morning's *Daily Telegraph*.

Occasionally this monologue became entirely personal.

For example, Mr Archer once said, 'I don't know if it would interest you to know, sir, but I once wrote a book.'

'Did you? What kind of a book was it?'

'A lot of people have asked me that question, sir – people who knew about my literary ambitions of course – and, do you know, I've never known what to say to them. It began as a kind of autobiography, but I always feel, at least when I read other people's books, that to write an autobiography you need to have had an interesting kind of life, and I don't believe that's something I could truthfully say that I've done.'

'What kind of a book was it then? A novel? A kind of memoir?'

'Oh there were no *characters* in it, sir, if that's what you mean. Just a lot of thought.'

It was impossible to draw Mr Archer out on the subject of his book, or indeed on any other topic to do with himself. I saw that his was the comparatively rare kind of egotism that takes its pleasure from concealment rather than revelation, offering up tantalising glimpses of some shadowy life which investigation would probably show to be duller than the listener supposed. At the same time Mr Archer specialised in rather lurid confidences. Once, when there was no one except ourselves in the silent lounge, he said unexpectedly:

'I believe you know Brenda, sir.'

'Of course I know Brenda.'

'The red-haired girl who cleans here in the mornings,' Mr Archer went on, ignoring my reply. 'The one I had occasion to complain of when she left the floor polish stuck all over the upstairs landing. Well, it's not something I like to ask one of my guests, but what would be your opinion of Brenda?'

This was a tricky question to answer, seeing that Mr Archer was thought to be obsessively interested in Brenda. Hinting that you liked her might be entirely the wrong thing to say – it might simply inflame Mr Archer's jealousy. On the other hand, saying that she fell short of whatever standard you or Mr Archer looked for in a chambermaid might be just as inflammatory.

'She seems fairly capable at what she does.'

Oddly enough, this answer seemed to throw Mr Archer altogether. He put down the pile of napkins he had been folding into neat isosceles triangles and stood for a moment rocking backwards and forwards on his feet. When he spoke at last it was in a lower and more subdued tone, as if what I'd said had been so unexpected that he needed to make a considerable effort to reply.

'Capable? I suppose you could call her capable … Do you want to know what I think of Brenda, sir?'

'Tell me.'

'I think' – there was no mistaking the absolute sincerity in Mr Archer's voice – 'I think she's the kind of girl *that will come to a bad end.*'

'What makes you say that?'

'Seen her type before, sir.' Mr Archer lowered his head. 'The way she scrimps on her work. Way she looks at me. Why, only the other day in her room … '

But the sentence was extinguished by the arrival of another resident in the lounge, and I never discovered what Mr Archer had found in Brenda's room, still less how he had come to be there in the first place. Frances, to whom I reported this conversation, had her own theories.

'I expect Archer lets himself into her room with the master-key and goes through her underwear. I can just see him sweating over her knicker drawer, can't you?'

'I don't know. I wonder if Archer has any sex-life at all.'

'Bound to. Those pale, red-haired types always do.'

'How would you know?'

'Bitter experience,' Frances said.

That evening the rain came in implacably. We heard it drumming on the windows in the small hours. By dawn the concrete yard visible from the bathroom was a brimming lake. An inspection of the breakfast room early the next morning revealed that a further three ashtrays had disappeared.

Part Two

It is odd that I can't remember when I first saw Carole, whom I was eventually to marry and to make more wretchedly unhappy than any other person I have ever met (I was made wretchedly unhappy myself, but then the fault was mostly mine). In fact I only noticed her at first as one among a number of familiar figures – the old gentleman in the Archie Rice pin-stripes, the ambling hippy in the kaftan – glimpsed on my journeys round Red Lion Square and the region of High Holborn. There was a small library set in a recessed courtyard off the Gray's Inn Road where I used to go in my lunch-hour, which she frequented with such regularity that for quite a long time I thought she was a student at the University of London. As it turned out she was interested in dressmaking and fabrics and used to use the library to hunt out 'patterns'.

She was a small, plump, blonde girl, but industrious and somehow indefatigable-looking: one of those girls who look as if they would be equally at home fell-walking in the Lake District or swimming the Channel. In those days my ideal of female beauty was somewhere between an Alma-Tadema portrait and a picture of Jane Asher I had taped to the wall of my bed-sit in Belsize Park. In the summer Carole played tennis on a court in one of the Bloomsbury squares and it was here, I suppose, that I first became aware of her. In those days she had very fine, long hair and it was this, bouncing off her back like the mane of a pony, that immediately distinguished her from the other players. There was a coffee shop, too, on the corner where High Holborn meets the Theobalds Road, where I used to see her after the tennis matches, pink-faced and animated between a brace of nondescript friends.

A piece of good fortune brought us together. Paying for her coffee once, as I sat a dozen feet away pretending to read a book, she began fumbling nervously in her handbag and then in the pocket of her coat: she had left her purse behind.

Luckily I had some money.

She accepted it with a minimum of fuss – at any rate nothing like the degree of relief I had wanted – and also with a kind of knowingness, as if the transaction was almost a private joke between us and she'd expected me to leap up from my seat and suggest it. After that we started seeing each other in a low-key and rather desultory way. There was another meeting at which the three or four shillings I'd lent her were restored (the money came concealed in a white envelope which seemed to me strange and utterly intriguing, revealing a social protocol I hadn't previously encountered) and a conversation in the library. We talked about books, I remember, and what we did for a living, and I discovered what I might have guessed if I'd thought very hard about it, that she was a legal secretary in one of the big offices on the Gray's Inn Road. Curiously I recall that first talk very well: the light from the open window shining off her hair in odd glints and softenings as she discoursed seriously about lunch-hours and overtime. We discovered, too, that her firm had some vague connection with Chaffington's – in fact most of the professional firms in the area were connected with each other and did little bits of business on one another's behalf – and rejoiced in what seemed to us a symbolic coincidence. Later, in what order I can't now recollect, we went to a cinema, an exhibition at an art gallery somewhere near the Tottenham Court Road, and – a tremendous excursion, this, that involved booking seats and chartering taxis – a musical in the West End.

The relationship was a source of frenzied excitement and bewilderment to me. Starting the day's work at nine, knowing that I would meet her at one, I used to divide the morning into sixteen quarter-hour phases, each one ruled onto a sheet of graph paper, and tick them off as the clock advanced (I still have some of these sheets, their backs scrawled over with calculations in my uncle's hand). And yet our conversation, squeezed out over sandwiches in a street café or seated next to each other in one of the Square gardens, was hugely unremarkable. If there was one characteristic I associate with her in these early days, it is determination. There were various little battles involving colleagues at work which she fought with the greatest persistence, and a woman called 'Collie', pointed out to me once or twice from a distance in the street, who I gathered did not treat her with complete cordiality.

I was very loyal on the subject of Collie, and hated her profoundly.

But I was excited and bewildered by Carole, and also hugely respectful, for it was clear to me that she knew a great deal more about the world than I did, and in fact was far more at home in it. She was, for instance, the first person I'd met of my own age who had any political opinions, who preferred Mr Heath to Mr Wilson and could explain the advantages of the Common Market, and she was very knowledgeable on such subjects as the tax registration of cars or who to complain to if a bus ran late. This feeling was only slightly lessened by a visit I paid to her parents' house one Sunday. The Bansteads – that was the family name – lived in

Redbridge, at the far end of the Central Line, in a road off one of those great thoroughfares that snake out of London to the Essex suburbs; the noise of the traffic was everywhere. Her parents were small and somehow dusty people, united and in my eyes distinguished by the pride they took in their daughter. Their house, halfway along a pre-war terrace of identikit semis, seemed the most perfect and conscious extension of their personalities: full of dark little rooms crammed with ancient furniture, the walls hung with pictures of Carole at various stages of her teenage life. But they were hospitable to 'Carole's friend', as they made a point of calling me, and disposed to be chatty. Mr Banstead, in particular, was greatly impressed by my apprenticeship at Chaffington's. He talked once or twice of his own business affairs in such a vague and disinterested way that it wasn't until long afterwards that I found out that he was a clerk at the Eagle Star Insurance office in Gants Hill.

For my own part, I was hugely fascinated by the Bansteads. Together with their house and their daughter, they were my first exposure to a kind of lower-middle-class suburban life which I hardly knew existed. My mother, I am sure, would have examined Mr Banstead, with his row of *Reader's Digest* condensed books and his *Radio Times* in its leather cover, and Mrs Banstead – she was a pale, straggling woman irresistibly like a goose who appeared to do nothing but sit at home all day – and said something highly disparaging. To me, though, they represented not so much culture – even I wasn't taken in by old Banstead's pose of 'knowing something about books' – but a peephole onto a kind of life, that intimate Redbridge suburban life, that I knew nothing about. The Bansteads, for instance, went to church on Sunday mornings (arriving there that first Sunday I found them, prayerbooks in hand, divesting themselves of their coats in the cramped vestibule that Mrs Banstead called the 'hall'); they went on summer holidays to resorts on the south coast. These were both activities that I regarded with a kind of wonder. Even more wonderful – their trump card, so to speak – was the fact that they were Carole's parents. They were talkative people, and consequently I learned from them more about Carole than she told me herself – how she'd turned down a place at teacher-training college (Mrs Banstead thought privately that this was a mistake, Mr B. wasn't so sure) and her broken engagement to a printer's representative living two streets away ('which I can't say I ever approved of', Mrs Banstead enigmatically pronounced). And at the same time I became aware, without ever making any strenuous effort to find out, of the sort of life they lived together as a family, and the oppositions that occasionally underlay it. The Bansteads deferred to their daughter in everything, but they sometimes declined to do it without a struggle and even on that first Sunday I

81

witnessed several bitter little engagements about the disposition of the tea-things or the scope of knitting patterns.

Oddly, the Bansteads were the subject of our first disagreement, a very minor one, but enough to rob the walk back to Redbridge station that night of its sheens and surfaces.

'You mustn't mind about mother and father.'

'I don't mind about them.'

'I mean ... They always take over everything.' She bit her lip.

'I don't mind. I like them.'

'You don't *understand*,' she said. 'The times they try and spoil everything ... As bad as Collie sometimes.'

Queerly, but not I think without all reason, the Bansteads liked me. At a time of student protests and long-haired dissent, they appreciated my deference and the way in which, as Carole informed them, I applied myself to my work. I think they thought, in their curious middle-class way, that I was a salutary influence on her. I took to spending weekends at Redbridge, interminable trackless wastes of time spent watching *The Morecambe and Wise Show* or eating fussily served but wonderfully indigestible meals. Once, I remember, I even took old Mr Banstead to a football match at Leyton Orient, where he smoked a pipe, commented knowledgeably on the game and, coming back on the bus, became highly confidential about the insurance office at Gants Hill.

And constantly, throughout all this, there was the thought of Carole springing up at the unlikeliest times and in the unlikeliest places. I used to think about her sometimes in the room at Belsize Park – a sparse, shabbily furnished room looking out over a row of perpetually weeping trees – as the night wore on, and the stock of shillings I kept for the gas meter dwindled away to nothing, and my face – glimpsed in the cracked shaving mirror – turned white and ghastly from want of sleep. At other times her presence became so tangible and unbearable that I took to leaving my desk, hurrying to a pay-phone on the corner of Red Lion Square and breaking an absolutely savage proscription on telephoning her at work. I don't know what I thought about her. I think even at this stage I'd worked out all the disadvantages that any kind of life with her would mean, and I'm certain that by then I'd already divined the glimmerings of everything about her that was later to exasperate me: her tendency to domineer, and her ineffable complacency about almost every aspect of her not very remarkable life. But it took no effort of will to ignore these conclusions: it was all, so to speak, part of the business. Mr Banstead and Mrs Banstead, *The Morecambe and Wise Show* and the endless traffic, it was all somehow inescapable and undeniable. I suppose I must have seemed particularly thoughtful at the time, because Ekwall swiftly established what was afoot. 'No doubt about it, my boy,' he said one night as we queued in the foyer at the Albert Hall, waiting to see a concert by Captain Beefheart, 'you're in love. Now is she – I'm presuming it's a she, you see – blonde or dark, eh? And are you going to tell me about it?' So I told him about it – not everything, which was perhaps an ominous sign – but with a fantastic cheerfulness that I'm confident was what I was experiencing at the time.

Curiously she never took to Ekwall, never quite saw the point of him or his function in my life. Quite early on in the affair I convened a grand meeting with the object of introducing them, of allowing Ekwall to bask in admiration of her and *vice versa*, but it hadn't the slightest effect. Afterwards she embarked on one of those brisk, impartial analyses which I remembered from the Redbridge supper table.

'I'm sure he's very clever and everything ... '

'He writes poetry,' I suggested. 'Very good poetry, some of it ... '

'I wonder how he lives,' she speculated. 'That is, what does he live *off*?'

'I think his parents give him a bit.'

'Still, it's not as if poetry was a job or anything.'

We were sleeping together by this time. In retrospect I don't know how we managed it. We did it at Belsize Park, in the house at Redbridge when her parents were away. They were joyless interludes: tense and furtive episodes which bore no relation to the feelings that I incubated about her. I don't think she enjoyed them much. Once, I remember, the Bansteads disappeared for a whole weekend to visit some relatives in Suffolk and we spent the time together. I recall waking up in her parents' bed, very late, with autumnal rain breaking against the window, as she snored gently beside me, and ghastly, embarrassed meals around the family table under the big old pictures in their frames.

Occasionally we had disagreements, intense, passionate disagreements that I could no more accurately reproduce than my childhood dreams. The following is a specimen:

'Do you love me?'

'Yes.'

'You shouldn't say things like that. After all, we hardly know each other.'

'Yes we do.'

'... Mother and Dad were engaged for three years before they got married. So she could be sure, she said. And then he took this woman at the office to a dance, and she nearly broke it off.'

For some reason I never believed the story about Mr Banstead and the woman at the office. I knew Mr Banstead wouldn't have had the guts.

83

'Anyway, I do love you.'

'There are some nice houses,' she said, 'out Wanstead way.'

And so you'll understand, perhaps, how the first great crisis of my young life came about. My mother dying, Ekwall, Carole and the queer, semi-genteel world of Redbridge – all played a part in the predicament in which I found myself. My work fell off, I shirked around the place at Red Lion Square and the various people who had congratulated me on my prize for auditing were heard to remark that none of the young men Chaffington's got these days were reliable any more. Worse than this, though, was the curious sense of listlessness that infected my life, and which had the effect of rendering the brightest experience pale and humdrum. I remember spending a whole long Sunday – my twenty-second birthday, as it happened – sitting in the room at Belsize Park staring first at the grey flock wallpaper, then at the rows of books on the shelves – a miscellaneous collection that included *Zen and the Art of Motorcycle Maintenance* and *Tolley's Tax Guide*, finally at the weeping trees in the street, and then going out to wander dejectedly through the twilight into Hampstead and Kilburn and a great stretch of north-west London.

All this finally became clear to me in a melancholy interview conducted with one of the Chaffington partners. He was a polite man (all the Chaffington partners were polite – they could sack an articled clerk without batting an eye) and the sedative effect of his smiles and peri-phrases was such that it wasn't until the very end of the interview that I began to understand his insinuations. I knew, didn't I, that my conduct was, well, not of a kind of which the firm could approve? I realised, didn't I, the implications for my future? I appreciated, didn't I, how greatly it pained Chaffington's to convey these kind of admonitions? (I remember nodding seriously at each of these suggestions.) Even then, the old gentleman diffidently proposed, they might have felt able to make an exception, had it not been … And here he produced a certain ledger which I vaguely remembered looking at in a fit of late afternoon depression two days before. I understood, didn't I, that Chaffington's prided itself on its professional standards, and that the ledger's inaccuracies had only by the merest chance been kept from reaching the eye of the client himself? Twenty minutes later I found myself sitting under the tree in the Square carrying my briefcase, a copy of *UK Generally Accepted Accounting Practice* and an envelope containing four weeks' wages in lieu of notice.

Oddly enough I didn't then – and don't now – bear the old gentleman any malice, for he was only acting according to what he imagined were the best interests of us both. Even more odd, perhaps, I wasn't at all cast down by this reverse. So far as I remember I walked airily into Soho, watched a film in one of the afternoon cinemas, ate a pound dinner at a wonderful restaurant called the Stockpot in Panton Street, and ended the evening in an advanced state of intoxication with Ekwall somewhere in Somers Town.

Carole, understandably, was aghast.

'You don't mean to say you've lost your job?' she said when I told her. 'What *are* you going to do?'

'Get another.'

'How? They'll want references, and who's going to give you one? How could you be so *stupid*?' She was genuinely distressed, far more so than I was. I didn't then know of the fear of 'the sack' that still hung over the sequestered world of Redbridge.

'But you said yourself that you were thinking of leaving Halperin's ... That you couldn't stand any more of Collie.'

'That's different. That would be my decision. You've just been thrown out into the street.'

There was a lot more of this. By the end of it I understood that I'd been shamefully negligent in allowing myself to be sacked, that the law required firms like Chaffington's to follow set procedures in these cases, and that I'd allowed myself to be made a fool of. I have a vision of Carole, very red-faced and tearful, lecturing me on this topic in a café near Chancery Lane, and ending rather lamely but perhaps ominously that 'mother and father will be so disappointed.'

I suppose I could have averted nearly everything that followed by giving up there and then – repudiating Carole, avoiding Ekwall, looking upon the old gentleman in Red Lion Square as a disguised saviour. Very likely if I'd been older or wiser I would have taken this sensible course, packed my bags and gone back to Norwich where at least there existed a world that I knew about and where I certainly wouldn't have starved. But I was twenty-two, and self-willed in a way that is now entirely beyond my comprehension. Worse, I felt that I'd by no means exhausted the pleasures that London, which continued to fascinate and startle me, could offer. And so rather than admit defeat, and with a kind of circum-spection that now rather alarms me, I put the four weeks' wages, together with various other small amounts that lay to hand, in a Post Office savings account and resolved to live modestly until such time as I could find another job. Feeling a need to tell someone other than Carole or Ekwall of this resolve, but finding that no name came immediately to mind, I wrote to my uncle at an ancient address that fell out of an old pocket book informing him of my intentions. It was 1974 and I had been in London four years.

In the event the Post Office money stayed untouched, as I found another job almost immediately. Travers & Peabody occupied four rooms of an upper storey in Hatton Garden, advertised incessantly in the trade press for 'part qualifieds' and were the kind of small accounting firm whose clients feel the need of someone to persuade the Inland Revenue of the legitimacy of spending four-fifths of your income on 'personal expenses'. They acted mainly on behalf of commission agents – weather-beaten middle-aged men who arrived on the premises bearing sample cases – and small jewellers, and maintained a fluctuating staff of five. There was no agitation about references.

I had been warned, on my departure from Chaffington's, about firms like Travers & Peabody.

Travers & Peabody I discovered on my arrival there that first Monday morning to be purely nominal. In their place I was inducted into the business by the firm's general manager, Mr Holroyd, a sad-looking middle-aged man who wore a pair of striped trousers so old that they shone, rather in the manner of black satin. He cheered up, though, on learning that I'd been articled to Chaffington's. 'Very superior firm, I b'lieve. Senior partner comes in at eleven and lunches out, I dare say. Accounts at twenty-eight days and that sort of thing. Well, you won't find much of that here, I can tell you.' He was right too: Travers & Peabody offered up their invoices at seven days' grace, and penalised defaulters by adding two per cent interest for each succeeding week. 'A highly equitable system,' Mr Holroyd proposed innocently. 'At any rate we always find that it works.'

What else to say about Travers & Peabody? The staff divided neatly into cheery and profoundly anonymous youths of about my own age and broken down old men superannuated from the big firms. There was a dreadful old wreck of about sixty, I remember, whose first act on arriving at the office was to remove his false teeth and place them on his desk, the better to drink his tea. Mr Holroyd looked benignly upon this person. 'Does us no end of good,' he would say, 'having someone like old Powell here. You see, *he worked at Coopers & Lybrand once*.' At times when Mr Holroyd was out of the office, and the rest of us grew boisterous, Powell would occasionally remonstrate that 'it wasn't quite the thing'. I had a desk looking out in an easterly direction along Hatton Garden, which afforded interesting prospects of sloping rooftops, gleaming frontages under striped awnings, and black-coated Jews going about their business.

In the middle of this induction my uncle telephoned, using the number of the pay-phone three flights down from the bed-sitting-room, and I was summoned by another lodger to speak to him. My uncle was mysterious, vague and allusive. Unprompted, he issued an open invitation to supper. The address was somewhere in Putney. On the next evening, having nothing better to do, I went to visit him.

It was about eight o'clock when I arrived at Putney Bridge and set off south across the river. At night the water was as sluggish and unparticularised as ink. Eastward towards Hurlingham and Chelsea Harbour a few small craft clanked together in the shadows. My uncle inhabited a dank little street by the river's edge, one of several dark and silent thoroughfares somehow giving an impression of recent inundation. The house, grave and remote beyond black shrubberies, lay sunk in shadow. Somewhere deep within, orange lights glowed and a radio was playing. Eventually, after a noise of plodding footsteps and a painful exhalation of breath, my uncle opened the door.

There was no light in the doorway and he looked at me with a kind of abstract moroseness – he was still champing his tea and held a pint glass full of beer in one hand – until faint recognition dawned and he opened the door a shade wider and grinned hugely.

'I b'lieve it's young George. Who'd have thought it, it *is* young George. You'd better come in. Greta, it's George! George, as I was telling you about.'

At the farther end of the passage in which he stood a light went on and I became aware of a plump, blonde woman of the type infallibly characterised by my mother as 'brassy' standing in an inner doorway. She, too, bore evidence of an uninterrupted meal, in this case the remnant of a sandwich clasped between the finger and thumb of one hand, but she was smoking a cigarette, negligently and almost insouciantly out of the corner of her mouth, and seemed highly amused by something.

'I told him, "Put your drink down before you open the door," ' she said equably. 'You never knew anyone like Ted for rushing about things. I've seen him go to the post office with a dinner plate in one hand.'

From the doorstep I made a vague, temporary stab at assimilating the aspects of my uncle's character and temperament which this tableau revealed. The house, I now saw, was substantial and not badly decorated: there were sporting prints on the wall and a coatstand draped over with an immense sable jacket. Greta, now revealed by the light to be about forty-five, with an extremely pink complexion and carmined fingernails, was further evidence of the way in which my uncle seemed to have moved up a gear, become in some mysterious way a more substantial figure. Something of these inferences seemed to have occurred to my uncle, as he transferred the pint glass from right hand to left and gripped my forearm in a savage grasp.

'I'blieve,' he said, 'as we've just about finished supper, why don't you come back here, into the office, and we can talk a bit?'

He led me off along the passage, past the open door from which the noise of the radio buzzed – I had a momentary vision of a flaming orange carpet, piled newspapers, Greta's face under the lamp – and towards another room, again in darkness, to whose centre he gently propelled me before switching on the light. The effect of this reversal of the ordinary processes of hospitality was bizarre: dazzled by the blinding light, I took several seconds to register anything of my surroundings. The first impression was of extreme untidiness: of papers stacked haphazardly over chairs and carpets, a filing cabinet disgorging its contents over the floor, and a pile of addressed but unstamped envelopes. The second, oddly enough, was of a photograph of my mother in a cracked gilt frame above the fireplace.

'Found that in Bright Road after the funeral and took it,' said my uncle easily. 'Didn't think you'd mind.'

It occurred to me that I'd never seen my uncle on his own territory, so to speak, and that previous encounters with him had always been in Norwich or on the neutral ground of trains or railway stations. Later on, in the big house at Sunningdale, or even in the hotel suites from which my uncle sometimes conducted his business, I didn't find anything to diminish this first assessment, which was of an overwhelming obsession with clutter, a complete inability to distinguish between the usefulness, or otherwise, of any item that came into his hands. Or, worse, an actual relish for huge quantities of junk and the problems of taxonomy that it posed. He was never so happy, I discovered, as when attempting to impose some order on the squalor of his abodes – inventing a new filing system, say, or storing things in a collection of plastic refuse sacks.

'Famous old place this is, isn't it, George?' my uncle exclaimed. 'Got it through an ad in the paper. As easy as that. Rang a man up, signed a piece of paper and we were in. Pictures. Furniture. You should see the bedrooms! Everything just as you'd like. And no expense spared on the fittings. Just look at this now.'

He picked up a flat, oblong canister which turned out to conceal a cigarette lighter and lit a cigar with it. The flame, held for a second close to his face and combined with the dark of the window, gave it an odd, Mephistophelian glint. I recognised immediately another side of my uncle's character, which I remembered from our graveyard interlude: that fusty, impressionable, antiquarian side, delighting in knick-knacks and trumpery rubbish that 'something could be done with'.

So many descriptions were written of my uncle in the period immediately after this time – the period when he began on his startling ascent through the social and commercial world – that it's important to me to set down an account of what he looked like at this early stage in his career, before photographers and public relations men and assistants took him up and worked on him and changed not a little of his external character. It seemed to me, looking at him then, that he'd shrunk somewhat since the day of my mother's funeral, grown even less tidy and presentable. The hair was mostly grey now, thinning over the peak of his scalp and forming a cluster of exiguous curls at the back of his neck. He wore an ancient shirt, devoid of buttons but reined in, if not wholly subdued, by a lavishly styled but extremely dirty waistcoat, out of whose pockets protruded items such as handkerchiefs, elastic bands and what looked like a packet of contraceptives. This impression of deep, residual shabbiness which no amount of tailoring or sprucing up could repair was heightened by a pair of faded trousers and the black gym shoes – a very shiny black, almost like ballet pumps – that my uncle wore on his feet. The overall effect was very close to absurdity – and I'm sure that if I'd come across my uncle in a shop or in Travers & Peabody's office I would have laughed – but at the same time there was something jaunty and confiding about him that redeemed this unpromising exterior. His face had grown more humorous, more droll and apparently animated by some private joke. His eyes ... I never did reach any satisfactory conclusion about my uncle's eyes. They were vague and impressionable and whether they concealed something else that was calculating or devious I never quite worked out. Nevertheless, I've set all this down as a corrective to some of the absurdities that were later printed about him.

'Here,' George,' he said. 'No need to stand on ceremony. Sit down now. I've bin wanting to talk to you. Sit down and have a chat.'

And so I sat in a small room at the back of the house on a wide, stiff-backed chair whose feet rose out of a carpeting of business papers, next to a window beyond which light glinted off the surface of the river and trains passed back and forth across the bridge, and we talked desultorily about my job and my prospects and all that happened in the year since we'd last met. It isn't an exaggeration to say that my uncle hardly listened. He was preoccupied, I saw, with something that clearly gave him deep personal pleasure but wasn't without its attendant cargo of anxiety. Wanting to uncork this reverie I asked:

'How's the toy trade, Uncle Ted?'

He looked up sharply. 'Oh, I've given all that up. Working on my own, so to speak. Doing my own thing, you might say.'

There was something in the way he said this – something resolute and nearly defiant and to a certain degree complacent – that made me pay more attention to him.

'That's right,' he said again. 'Doing my own thing now, I am. And b'lieve … I *b'lieve* … I'm going to make my fortune.'

God help me, I nearly laughed at this. Perhaps, in retrospect, I should have done – who knows what embarrassments and indignities might have been avoided? But again, there was something in his voice – conviction? assurance? – that stopped me. Instead I contented myself by saying, half-ironically:

'Going to make your fortune, uncle?'

'That's right. You ever hear of Sandy?'

I shook my head. My uncle rummaged enigmatically in a cardboard box that lay on a large, square desk towards the back of the room, brought out a couple of nondescript pieces of packaging, looked at them rather sorrowfully, in the manner of a conjurer who has been betrayed by some renegade assistant, plunged his hand in again and extracted a small, pink-limbed doll with a kind of straw hat angled down over her forehead.

'Seen one of these before?' my uncle enquired.

'No.'

'No? Well, it'd be surprising if you had. W'd be most surprising.' (In moments of excitement my uncle scalloped conditional clauses away to nothing.) 'Sandy. Came on the American market in summer 1973. Sandy doll. Accessory sets. Sandy at the beach. Sandy at the barbecue. Sandy's beauty parlour. They were thinking of making a boy doll too – called Randy, I b'lieve – but I haven't seen one yet. Anyhow, total sales so far are ten million units, going on ten million five.'

'What's the attraction? Why do people like it?'

'I don't know. The thing is, they do. D'y'know,' my uncle said, 'they got a Sandy club in New York, with a hundred thousand members. Plus the president's granddaughters have them.'

I listened to this efficient recitation of statistics – so practised that I imagined it to have been aired many times before – in silence. Outside a train rumbled noisily over the bridge; we waited for it to pass. At the same time it was difficult to work out what my uncle proposed to do about a doll favoured by American girldom.

'Will it come out over here?'

'Oh yes.' He looked thoughtful. 'Give it time. A year. Two years. Always takes time for people to pick up on things like this. Thing is, George, I've got a feeling about this. Don't quite know about it yet but I reckon someone could make a mint if they went about it in the right way.'

'But you're not a toy manufacturer.'

90

'Oh, that's all by the way,' my uncle pronounced loftily. 'Someone else can do all that. I'm talking about merchandising rights.'

'Merchandising?'

'Spin-offs. Authorisation. Think about it, George! Colouring books and chocolate bars, handkerchiefs maybe. Get in on the TV, I don't know – anything! But whatever you do you stick "Sandy" on the label – it's trademarked, by the way – and whoever does it pays you forty per cent. Look!'

He produced, out of the same cardboard box, a letter, typewritten on the gorgeous, embossed notepaper of some American conglomerate, announcing that in respect of monies paid to the above-named proprietor, Mr Edward Chell of London SW had been granted merchandising licences in the product styled 'Sandy' and registered etc. for a period not exceeding three years with the option of a two-year renewal, providing that etc., etc. My uncle watched me beadily as I read it. He was sweating, I noticed, and the cigar drooped out of his underlip.

'Cost me ... Well, I won't tell you how much it cost me, George, but I never felt safer about anything ...

'Only needs thinking about, and we can make business *hum* ...

'Can't think of a better proposition anyone could consider ...'

I realised dimly that my uncle was offering me a job. As he made these vague and in no way seductive comments, I went through a gamut of emotions: the sense of being flattered, gratitude at the thought of someone I barely knew offering to help me, and a deep assurance of my uncle's innate unreliability. To the temporising that seemed the only prudent response, he proved surprisingly amenable. Remarking that in any case he had 'sprung it on me' and that 'a thing like that needed thinking about' he announced that we should go into the other room where Greta might find us something to drink.

We went into the other room – the big 'family' room I had descried beyond the half-open door – to find Greta in the act of uncorking a bottle of wine. At close range she looked less like a barmaid and more like one of the women I remembered from the Norwich department stores – Jarrold's, say, or Debenhams – whose hankering after perfume and face powder was tolerated by captious onlookers such as my mother and Mrs Buddery as being an unavoidable part of the shop assistant's life.

'I didn't think you were ever going to finish that talk of yours, so I started opening this myself.'

Though I'd been brought up to be temperamentally suspicious of women in middle age whose hair stank of perfume I took an immediate liking to Greta, which persisted throughout the years that I knew her, although I never did succeed in finding out how my uncle had met her or the origins of their long association (I believe now that he simply picked her up in a pub or on a train somewhere in the course of his travels). In fact my uncle never spoke directly to me about her, and treated her merely as a fact of his existence which, like his job and his personal habits, anyone who came into contact with him should necessarily accept.

I don't remember what we talked about that first long evening, as the mist rolled up over the river and the lights from the Thames houseboats shone from the Middlesex side (the house's location appealed to my uncle and he spoke more than once of us watching the start of the Boat Race from the bridge). But I do recall my interest in the room, which was large, gaunt and crammed with an impenetrable confusion of objects, and in my uncle's treatment of Greta. They had an odd, noisy Box and Cox routine, which involved long silences and mock chastisings, but I got the feeling that Greta might be a tough customer in any serious disagreement.

She had a way of regarding my uncle (whom she addressed as 'Teddy') with a curious mixture of tenderness and exasperation. My uncle, for his part, darted back looks of unfeigned benevolence.

I came back from the house in Putney in a state of colossal perplexity. Part of this was to do with my uncle and his altered state – I wasn't then at all accustomed to the idea that the condition in which one first encounters a human being is not necessarily the condition in which he will remain. But far more of it concerned questions exclusive to myself – Carole, Travers & Peabody, destiny – all of them in some way knocked to the surface by my uncle's fervent chatter. It seemed to me that I had answers to none of them, nor to the wider generalities in which they reposed, and for the next week or so this knowledge tore and irked me.

'What do women want?' I asked Ekwall once. It was a Saturday afternoon and we were sitting in a pub in Covent Garden drinking brandy while Ekwall read the arts pages of the *New Statesman* and considered whether there was a film worth seeing.

'More than they get, that's for sure.'

'No, but what do they want? Not the obvious things. Rights and so on. But deep down?'

Ekwall turned down the corner of the page he was reading, put the magazine in his coat pocket and swivelled slightly in his chair.

'I don't know. What the rest of us want. Love. Security. A roof over their heads. Those are the big things. The rest is just temperament. I mean, wanting men to like you. Or wanting men not to like you.'

'But why would a woman want to get married? In this day and age?'

'Look at it the other way round. Why *wouldn't* a woman want to get married? I mean, most of them do. The odds are stacked against the single woman. Think about it. Sniffs in the queue at the grocer's. From the other women, that is.'

'What about from the men?'

'An offensive interest or complete indifference, depending on age and taste ... You must realise,' Ekwall went on, vaguely interested now, 'that I have no experience of this. Absolutely none.'

'Not ever?'

'There was a girl at college who thought we might go to bed together. And in fact we did – physically get into bed, I mean. But nothing actually happened ... '

'... Leaving aside children,' I went on.

'But you can't, can you? Leave aside children, that is. You can be as liberal-minded as you like, the biological clock will go on ticking.'

'I don't understand the maternal instinct ...'

'What man ever did? Look at it this way, George. You're living in a century that's witnessing the break-up of the nuclear family. At least the *Guardian* thinks it is – I never met anyone else who did. And then there's the pill and, I don't know, all kinds of things. But the trouble is, it's not going to make any difference to the way you live your life. Not now. I dare say in 2010 we'll all live in communes and no one will know who the children belong to. But for the time being ...'

Q: What do you think your uncle believed in?

A: That's rather a large question. I think, more than anything, he believed in stereotypes. No, *archetypes*. He genuinely did believe in the existence of entities like 'distinguished nobleman of large estates', 'starving poet', 'corrupt trade unionist'. Quiddity was quite beyond him: in fact his divisions of human society were almost medieval. Then, of course, there were class distinctions. He believed emphatically in those.

Q: In what way?

A: Oh, it was very odd. Or not odd. You have to remember that my uncle was a working-class conservative of a highly intransigent kind. But all this, curiously enough, was combined with a sort of personal rebelliousness. Perhaps you could define it by saying that he thought people ought to know their places, but he was damned if he was going to know his. This put him in a rather odd relation with the people he knocked up against. Anyone worse off than him was 'no class', as he put it, but he was always terrified that the City men he met were patronising him. He could be bitterly satirical about what might be called 'society'. I remember once going to Covent Garden with him and in the interval some well-bred lady was discussing – rather loudly – the relative advantages of ear-piercing. And for years after this, whenever he heard what he called a 'woff woff' – that is, an upper-class voice – he would do an absolutely brutal imitation of this woman: *Dahs wan have wan's years pee-arsed?* Like that.

Q: Social archetypes and social class. All very secular.

A: Oh, he believed in God of course. Absolutely. And he had fantastically bizarre notions of an afterlife. For example, he always believed that his mother was watching what he did, remonstrating with him when he did something she disapproved of. And he was very keen on what you or I would regard as the most laughable speculations. For instance, I once heard him ask a bishop whether he thought there would be cars in the next world.

Q: It sounds like a joke.

A: It may well have been. One of my uncle's characteristics – his distinguishing mark, if you like – was that you could never work out

94

whether he was being completely serious. It was the same when you came to race. Now, my uncle was fond of making little jokes about Blacks and Jews. For example, if he switched on the television to watch *Songs of Praise*, and they had a choir, and that choir contained a single black singer, he would *always* say, 'Seems to be able to follow the music,' something like that. But if you introduced him to a black person he would always be scrupulously – and, as far as I could make out, genuinely – polite.

Q: You don't make him sound – in this respect at least – a particularly nice person.

A: I don't? Well, I don't mean to. I can give you an example of how someone behaves, but I can't convey their essence. I enjoyed his company, luxuriated in it. I thought that in most respects what he did was admirable – how do I get that across? In Norwich, where I was brought up, he would have been known as a 'character'. And that meant, oh I don't know, eccentric, whimsical, slightly louche perhaps. But kindly, you know? I wouldn't want you to think that I didn't like him, or admire him, for all the stuff about cars and the next world.

It was Frances who put the sense of permanent unease which living at the Caradon entailed into some kind of context. 'Archer gives me the creeps,' she said, about a week after she had arrived. 'He reminds me of one of those serial killers you read about. The Stockwell Strangler or someone.'

'What makes you say that?'

'I don't know. Just the way he looks. I wouldn't be at all surprised if he picked up a carving knife at the dinner table one Sunday lunchtime and stuck it into somebody. Just to see what would happen.'

'Why a carving knife?'

'It would be just Archer's style. Dramatic but ineffectual. One of the things about carving knives is that you can hardly ever cut anything with them.'

Two incidents from around this time provided a revealing gloss on these insinuations. As it happened I was elsewhere in Eastwold for the first of them, known between us as 'the telephone incident'. That didn't matter: Frances described it as soon as I came back.

'It was about half-ten at night. Not later. There were still one or two people in the lounge. The old ladies watching *Newsnight*, you know. I'd just turned the light out when the phone started ringing. Quite near at hand. At first I thought it must be one of the ones in the residents' rooms. Then I realised it had to be the one in the office. That has a distinctive ring. Anyway, none of my business, I thought. Only it kept on ringing. At least four or five minutes, on and on relentlessly. You know how noise that continues at the same volume always sounds louder? Like the noise in that Kafka story? The one about the subterranean that goes mad from paranoia? By that time it was like an electric drill about a foot from my ear. In the end I got up, put on my dressing-gown and went downstairs.

'Quite a little crowd had gathered. The old girls that sit and knit in the foyer. That bloke who tried to borrow a tenner. One or two more. You could hear the phone ringing through the office door, but of course nobody would do anything. We had one of those absolutely archetypal English conversations about it. "That phone's been ringing for a long time now." "It has, hasn't it?" "Do you think one of us ought to answer it?" No sign of Archer of course, or any of the maids. In the end I simply marched into the office, where there was a dreadful smell of smoke but nobody about, and picked it up.'

'What happened?'

'That's the funny thing. A man's voice. At least I think it was a man's voice. The exact words were *Games are cancelled*. Just that. *Games are cancelled*. I said something fatuous about could he speak up or what did he want, but then the line went dead. The others were all standing in the doorway by this time, all very pleased at getting a sneak view of Archer's office, when suddenly along comes the man himself, wearing a kind of leather coat over his pyjamas, with his eyes rolling out of his head. Well, I was still pissed off about being dragged downstairs, and what with the Greek chorus hanging about in the background it was just too good to miss. So I put down the phone and simply said, "Mr Archer, Games are cancelled," just like that. And do you know, he started sweating? Uncontrollably. A split second later he'd absolutely grabbed the phone out of my hand and started shouting into it. "Who's there? How dare you disturb me at this time of night?" Blustering kinds of things like that.'

'What happened then?'

'Oh, the usual thing. People started filing away. Archer looked incredibly embarrassed and started muttering something about wrong numbers. But I could see all the time he was staring back over his shoulder just willing the phone not to ring again. Which it didn't, of course, but you had a dreadful feeling that it might ...'

The second and even more unnerving episode took place a night or two after this at dinner. Evening meals at the Caradon were strictly regimented, presided over by Mr Archer, who made a point of carving whatever meat was on offer, from a kind of wooden dais at the far end of the room while the waitresses handed round vegetables. Usually Mr Archer carved the meat on his own. On this particular evening, possibly because there was more than one joint available, he was allowing Brenda to help him. The two of them stood side by side at the dais, Mr Archer slightly in front, each armed with a carving knife and fork. From time to time Mr Archer would turn his head and say something in an undertone. Brenda, on the other hand, stayed impassive, head lowered above the serving dish.

I was halfway through the meal when I realised that this arrangement had broken down. In fact the tableau at the dais showed a striking juxtaposition of attitudes. Mr Archer, head bent a little forward, and therefore unable to see his assistant, was still carving industriously, while continuing to mutter instructions of some sort back over his shoulder. Brenda, alternatively, had stopped attending to the meat and was stand-

97

ing stock-still, eyes staring in front of her, the carving knife raised in one hand, like a mechanical toy that had reached the limits of its sphere of movement. As I watched she focused her gaze, which had been fixed on some unknown object in the middle distance, and directed it at Mr Archer. No one who saw it could have been in any doubt that Brenda loathed Mr Archer, had reached the end of her tether with him, and that there was even a kind of insanity about her. For a minute perhaps, or even two minutes, the figures stayed in this attitude – Mr Archer carving, Brenda brooding over him like Clytemnestra – the expression on Brenda's face reaching such a paroxysm of fury that I was about to shout a warning, when suddenly Mr Archer glanced back over his shoulder and rapped out a command. Instantly Brenda's face relaxed. She gave a little start, looked round wildly, and then went back to the task in hand.

Later I said to Frances, 'Did you see the look on Brenda's face when she was standing next to Archer?'

'Too busy eating. What was it like?'

'Murderous.'

'There you are,' Frances said. 'Archer's a man who arouses strong emotions. What did I tell you?'

In the end, against all the odds, we got married. To this day I still don't know why we did it. Did you ever do something – back a lame horse, maybe, or buy a badly fitting suit of clothes – in the certain knowledge that you were making a hopeless mistake? That was the spirit in which Carole and I approached the business of getting married. We'd known each other about two years – two years of television watching, endless journeys along the Central Line, snatched intimacy and bitter argument. Towards the end the rows began to turn on the question of marriage. I remember one extraordinary one in a teashop somewhere near Chancery Lane that reached such ludicrous heights that even now the words stick in my head.

'I want to get married,' I told her 'Don't you see? I want us to live together under the same roof.'

'I can't see why you're so set on it … I mean, I sometimes think you don't even like me.' During these disagreements, I noticed, she looked at me with an air of anxiety, a sort of subliminal worry that the world she'd picked out for herself was running dangerously out of kilter, sharpened by the feeling that she lacked the power to change it.

'Anyway,' she ended rather lamely, 'we don't earn enough. Not enough to buy anywhere. We'd have to rent.'

'There are always places.'

It was here, I suppose, that I betrayed my fundamental ignorance of what girls like Carole were like. Told that their daughter intended to get married and move into rented accommodation, the Bansteads would have been horrified – it would have been like having an illegitimate baby; worse, in that an illegitimate baby implied some element of chance or misfortune.

'If we could get a proper house, something out in Essex say, would you marry me?'

'I might.'

'What's the matter?'

'We can't go on like this,' she said.

'Why not?'

'We just can't. Sneaking upstairs after mother and dad have gone out

99

...' She brooded over the complexities of sex in a disapproving suburban household. 'You should see the look mother gives me sometimes when they come back in the evening. And then, thinking all the time you've made a mistake.'

'Well, let's get married then. Make it legal.'

'You don't *understand*,' she said. 'You just don't.'

It was late autumn, just beginning to turn sharp: outside the traffic was crowding down the wet streets into High Holborn. We sat there in silence while a waitress cleared the tea-things away and the door banged open and shut in the wind. The lights were going on in the law stationer's windows across the way, and I watched what had previously been grey silhouettes turn into the outlines of human figures.

'We're going to get married,' I said, 'so you'd better get that into your head.'

She gave me an odd look then – not exactly fear, but a kind of awe mingled with exasperation, as if by making it she surrendered up all responsibility for whatever future decisions I might take involving the two of us.

'Right then,' I said, almost jauntily. 'We've decided then. We're going to get married.'

'I suppose we are ... If that's what you want.'

We didn't go back together – she was meeting a friend from work somewhere. I remember going to look for Ekwall, not finding him, and then wandering the streets in an odd, half-exultant half-apprehensive state, exultant because I'd got what I wanted, apprehensive because I wondered if what I'd got was worth the having. Amid all this, I comforted myself with a series of complacent domestic visions: Carole sitting in a spacious, well-lit kitchen with floral wallpaper while I cooked her breakfast, the two of us doing unimaginable things like spending the day in bed or walking round the house naked. It was very late when I got back to Belsize Park, one or two in the morning perhaps, but I don't remember feeling tired. Amongst the stack of post piled up inside the front door there was a postcard from my uncle that said *Full steam ahead! Watch this space!*, but I didn't give it more than a glance. I was revolving all kinds of schemes in my head: Carole, house, promotion at work. Even now, writing this, I feel it again – that odd excitement of life somehow beginning afresh, those crenellations spun out of freezing north London air.

After this things happened very quickly. The Bansteads greeted the news of our engagement with a weary satisfaction. In the two years they'd

100

known me, the hundred or so Saturday nights I'd sat in their front room and watched *The Morecambe and Wise Show*, they'd been too polite, too tethered in the protocols of their class, to ask me outright how long this protracted courtship was going to go on, but I could see from an occasional glint in Mrs Banstead's eye across the teacups that the thought was in their minds. They used to leave property gazetteers around the place too – seriously. They genuinely believed that a good way of administering a hint to a man that he ought to marry their daughter was to decorate an armchair with copies of the *Redbridge Advertiser*. In the end, when there was a ring and talk of an engagement party, they came down very handsomely. Mr Banstead produced £300 for furniture and Mrs Banstead provided carrier bags full of confidential items hoarded across the years against 'Carole's bottom drawer'. At the time I fancied I could separate out the mixture of emotions they displayed: relief, at having measured up to some exacting social yardstick; satisfaction, at having found someone whose good opinion of their daughter confirmed their own; and faint condescension. Now I'm not so sure. I think they were simply proud, unassertive middle-class people who wanted to do their best by their family, even if it meant welcoming into it interlopers of whom they didn't really approve.

For some reason I'd assumed that the wedding itself would be the least troublesome part of the business. I couldn't have been more wrong. In fact the six months or so of our engagement were the first real eye-opener on the kind of life I'd stumbled upon out here in the east London suburbs, and in particular on the rituals around which people like the Bansteads conducted their lives. I saw that the skirmishes around the supper table, the bewildering ordinances about thank-you letters and 'seeing people', were only a preliminary to the really serious business that lay ahead. Almost from the start, for instance, there was a determination to emulate, if not surpass, something called 'the Harrison wedding', which turned out to have involved a cousin of Carole's some years back. Photographs of this event – its marquees, its dappled lawns, its morning suits and its charged glasses – were passed round by Mrs Banstead with a kind of reverential fervour. There was talk, too, of a 'carriage' to take us to the church, half a mile away in Redbridge, and 'favours', which I'd assumed to have died out sometime at the end of the nineteenth century. But no, they were all going strong here in Essex in the mid-1970s, and one of Mrs Banstead's first decisive acts on learning of our engagement was to send out for half-a-dozen caterers' catalogues.

Why did I go through with it? On the one hand, I suppose, because it was something I had brought into being and thought I ought to have the conviction to follow through; on the other because I genuinely had no

101

idea of the willed complexities in which I'd manage to entangle myself. Each stage of the preparations, I remember, involved an argument: about where we should hold the reception, about who should be invited, about what they should be given to eat, with Carole and Mrs Banstead goading each other to frenzied heights of expenditure. I remember above all a discussion about morning coats – there was a particular style then offered by Moss Bros called 'Mr Darren' that Carole wanted me to wear – but ... In any case, the details aren't important. It was the general air of being caught up in something immensely serious and profound and at the same time wholly inexplicable that frightened me, and which I could never quite subdue (Mr Banstead, I noticed, just kept quiet and looked miserable while these arguments were going on: he confided to me once that he thought 'the ladies were rather, h'm, overdoing it'). Something, more to the point, that only women could come to terms with. I watched Carole going about the preparations for the Great Day – it was called the Great Day, without a hint of irony – and she did so with the grimmest determination, brow perpetually furrowed, lost in some impenetrable world of bridesmaids and 'proper' orders of service. There was a particular moment once – it may have been during the argument about the morning coats – when she said, rather sorrowfully, 'You only get married once, you know' – and she said it with absolute seriousness: in fact I think it was the most seriously meant thing that she ever said to me. What do you do in such circumstances? I suppose that if I'd had any gumption I'd have given the whole thing up there and then, but I didn't. And in any case I could see the preparations going on around me, and the money being spent, and I believe that I was actually rather scared at the violent social forces that I'd nudged into being, and concerned to propitiate them as best I could. I don't think anyone suspected what I really thought, but I caught Mr Banstead looking at me once or twice – he was a shrewd old file in his way – and wondered if he had an inkling of what I was going through. Not that it would have mattered if he had. The Bansteads were decent enough people, but you couldn't talk to them, not about anything proper. I once asked Carole if either of her parents had ever volunteered information about sex or money and she said no, not ever. And that was the thing about them, really, the sense of a world governed by private codes, where nobody asked anybody a question because they knew the answer in advance. I went out for a stroll once with Mr Banstead, a week or two before the wedding, while the women were ensconced at Berkertex Bride, and there was a brief moment when he looked as if he was going to say something relevant to the topic of marriage, what you might expect from it, even his own experiences in the field, but then something else came up and the subject was dropped as quickly as it had arisen.

Of the day itself I don't remember very much, except that it rained and that I had a furious headache as a result of the previous night's carouse with the people from Travers & Peabody. In the event 'carriages' were unprocurable, and we went to the church in hired cars. Ekwall was best man. We hung about together in the porch smoking cigarettes, with rainwater dripping off the gables onto our silk hats, and even then I was still wondering whether I could get out of it in some way. I'd seen a film once where the bridegroom just disappeared, leaving a church full of guests, and went and spent the night in a pub. But the logistics were impossible. And I knew that even if I were to pursue this course somebody would find me out, track me down and punish me. I had a vision of Mrs Banstead coming upon me in Travers & Peabody's office with a raised umbrella, or Mr Banstead mowing me down on a pelican crossing in the family car. Something of this disquiet seemed to have occurred to Ekwall, because he said at one point:

'Do you seriously want to go through with this?'

'No option.'

'Seriously though. Have you thought about it? Really, I mean? The country cot and the pot of pink geraniums. The *wifey*.'

'Do you know her father's spent fifteen hundred pounds on this?'

'It's just money.'

'To you, maybe.' I remember being adamant about this as I said it. 'Not to him.'

'Well, have it your own way,' Ekwall said. And for perhaps the first time in our friendship he looked slightly pained.

'Car's coming,' somebody said as I stared back. 'Better get inside.'

After this I lose track. I remember my surprise at seeing Carole advance along the aisle of the church – surprise because her face, shining with make-up beneath the veil, bore no relation to the one I knew; Ekwall dropping the ring and an inglorious scramble to prevent it falling into a grating; grave middle-class voices singing 'Jerusalem'; fleeing through the porch in a hail of confetti. In the car, as the driver surveyed us tolerantly in the mirror, she became violently proprietorial: sprucing up a limp Moss Bros cravat, fastening an undone button. Slightly absent and certainly not pleased.

'Are you all right?'

'Of course I'm all right.'

'You look very nice.' This was a lie. She looked tired and harassed, and the make-up had robbed her features of any distinction.

'So do you.'

'I *did tell* mother about that hat,' she said bitterly, a moment later. 'That it wouldn't go with the green. But she never listens.'

'No need to worry about that,' I said, mock-jauntily.

'I suppose not ... It's just that I did tell her.'

The reception was at a hotel annexe somewhere near Gants Hill. There were two surprises. The first was the spectacle of my uncle, whom I hadn't remembered signifying his intentions of attending, sitting on his own at one of the side tables. The second was the presence of Collie, who turned out to be a meek, soberly dressed little woman of fifty and not at all the dragon of Carole's accounts. My uncle laughed uproariously during the speeches, which were facetious and feeble: he wore a pair of half-moon glasses now, I noticed, which made him look slightly owlish. Sweat coursed over his red, shiny forehead. Towards the end I found him lingering next to a sideboard littered with half-drunk cups of coffee, dirty plates and smoking ashtrays, and making vague little motioning signs with his forefinger. He seemed very knowing and confidential about the whole thing.

'Nice affair, George. Service. Reception. Hospitality. Everything.'

'I'm glad you could come, Uncle Ted.'

'Couldn't stand by and not see my own nephew get married. Wouldn't do at all.' He looked round the hall for a moment – at the wilting bundles of streamers and the knots of elderly ladies comforting themselves with tea, a general air of exhausted good fellowship – a shade critically, I thought, as if he felt that his initial summing-up might have been premature. 'Cost a fair bit, I shouldn't wonder?'

'I didn't ask.'

For some reason he was delighted by this. He gave a little whoop of amusement and had to rescue the glasses from the bridge of his nose with a whisk of his pudgy hand.

'You done well with the girl too, George. I was watching her earlier on. A big, *capable* kind of girl, I reckon?'

'I suppose so.' Something from the past grabbed at me, and I said: 'Do you remember my parents' wedding, Uncle Ted?'

He seemed a bit taken aback by this, took a sight on the throng of people and a clump of adenoidal bridesmaids – they were remote Banstead cousins, dredged up from God knows what tangle of ancestry, whom I never set eyes on again – and nodded. 'Quiet affair, George. Very quiet. I was best man. Made a speech and all, though I don't think your mother wanted me to ...'

'Why not?'

'Oh, I couldn't explain it in twenty minutes, George. Not in an hour.'

104

Mr Banstead, I noticed, was lurking a yard or so away, obviously on thorns to impart some confidence or other.

'I suppose so.'

'Ah well.' And here my uncle paused suddenly, lost in some peculiar reverie of wistfulness and bygone satisfaction. 'Anyway ... I got to be going now. Things to do. Business. I'll be in touch.'

I watched him go shambling off through the throng of guests towards the door and out into the dark Essex night.

And that is nearly it about the wedding. Several hours later we found ourselves in a hotel in Kent, *en route* for Calais. I remember looking out of the window to inspect a churchyard full of ghostly moonlit gravestones that abutted the hotel grounds, while Carole padded exhaustedly and resentfully around the room, and the sight of her fat, white haunches in the shadow.

'What do you think about being married?' I asked her at one point during the night.

'I don't know.'

'Are you happy?'

'I don't know. I'm very tired, George, and there were all sorts of things I thought I'd put in my case that I think I've forgotten, and ... *I didn't think it was going to be like this*. But perhaps it'll all look differently in the morning.'

'Perhaps it will.'

When I woke up it was a half-hour or so after dawn. For some reason I didn't feel like sleeping any more, so I put on my clothes and went downstairs through the dead, empty corridors, found a side door that was unlocked and wandered out into a tiny, overgrown sliproad – it was no more than a farm track – overhung by great drooping trees. In the distance fields ran uphill towards a line of woodland drenched in mist. A vague white snuffling presence grouped behind the hedge turned out to be cows huddled together in the wet grass. The air had a raw and curiously bitter taste, and I stood there for a moment breathing it in and wondering what to do. Even now, I supposed, there was nothing to prevent me leaving, no real force that could compel me to stay, to go back to that dreary hotel bedroom and pretend that I hadn't made the wrong decision. Reaching into my pocket I found the two tickets for the Channel ferry. I could simply throw them away if I wished. Suddenly and dramatically it began to rain. The cows bellowed dejectedly behind the hedge. Northwards, beyond the trees, mist was streaming down over the damp fields. Still clutching the tickets, I began to walk back.

And so we went off on our honeymoon, came back from it, began on our married life and were about as thoroughly unhappy as two people can be who have made a calamitous mistake and realise that it was in their power to prevent it. We lived in Redbridge at first, in a ghastly two-bedroom affair half a mile away from her parents which Carole thought had 'possibilities'. Mrs Banstead didn't visit more than three times a week. I used to come back in the evenings and find them sitting on either side of the fire like a couple of malignant sibyls. It was 1975 now, 1976. Amazing how quickly time passed, back then. One moment I'd been a boy of twenty boozing with Ekwall in Dean Street whose only problem was whether I could afford the bus fare back to Belsize Park; the next I was a married man with a Woolwich Building Society mortgage account an an obligation to eat Sunday lunch with my parents-in-law fifty weeks of the year. Sometimes, doing the washing-up in Redbridge or during one of our rows – mostly during the rows – I used to wonder where all that past life had gone, why I hadn't appreciated it while it was there, made better use of it, until something – a voice, a phone call, soft Essex rain on the window – recalled me to the aching present.

What went wrong? After we'd come back from the honeymoon – a fortnight of low-spirited sightseeing and dismal semi-intimacy – and my initial bad temper had subsided, I decided that I ought to make the best of it. I used to bring her back little presents from the City, spend weekends decorating rooms she thought 'needed seeing to', take her out for meals, but it was never any good. Somehow marriage had knocked all the wind out of her, left her spiritless and morose. I'd lie there at night watching her lying there next to me in a fat, bovine kind of way, and want to reach out and shake her, so acute was my distress at the great weight of inertia that seemed to sit upon her. Everything about her irked me: the grim determination with which she set about 'getting the house right', a systematic campaign of refurbishment in which there was no joy, simply a resolve to effect change for change's sake; the Bansteads, who monitored these developments with a pious satisfaction; the evening parties of work colleagues and their husbands which were her idea of entertainment. Fundamentally, I suppose, all our perceptions of life differed. I can still remember the patient, sedulous way in which she 'arranged' the front room in Redbridge, filling it up with pretentious knick-knacks and absurd little piles of pottery, the arguments we had about pictures or television, or fifty things that weren't important in themselves but betrayed the deeper malaise. She knew nothing, I realised, about books or art – just a few vague but tenaciously held opinions picked up at school and buttressed by her parents. As for Mr and Mrs Banstead, they haunted our house like a pair of ghouls. Once we began on the decorating, Mr Banstead took to coming round at odd hours with lengths of plywood and paint samplers: I think he saw me as a kind of surrogate crony that he could have man-to-man chats with, but I always fended him off. Oddly enough, his is the image that stays with me most from those days – fiddling about with a tape-measure in the kitchen or wandering from room to room with a hammer in one hand and a couple of rawlplugs sticking out of his mouth.

It was a queer kind of life, those old Redbridge days: sitting on my own late at night in the front room reading *Vanity Fair* or *Jude the Obscure*; hearing Carole roaming about in the bedroom above my head; taking her on dismal Sunday afternoon 'drives' to Ingatestone and Brentwood; staring out of the kitchen window on endless weekend afternoons at the backs of the adjoining houses; and it took only a few months or so to establish that it had all been a terrible mistake. In the end I simply took to spending as much time as I decently could out of the house – going to the football at Orient or West Ham on Saturdays or working late at Hatton Garden. I was still at Travers & Peabody, which was precarious if you like – the Institute was forever talking about closing them down or suspending one of the partners – but in a strange way I enjoyed it. At Chaffington's there'd been this great illusion of gentleman-liness, that 'commerce' was conducted by silver-haired chaps in pinstripes at desks in EC2 who'd all been at school with each other. Working for Travers & Peabody you saw business as it really was: shifty-eyed commission agents worried that the Revenue was chasing them for three years' unpaid tax; half-dead 'family' concerns in mori-bund parts of the East End where the profits were sliding, the leases were running out, but the old father still believed that some miracle would enable him to transfer everything to a layabout son just itching to squander the money on women and the dog track. I was an audit manager by this time, too, which meant that I had a couple of trainees to order about and a table of my own to sit at and smoke cigarettes while the junior brewed tea and looked out back numbers of *The Accountant*.

Most of this time, when I wasn't worrying or wandering around Redbridge, and quite a lot of the time when I *was* doing these things, I spent thinking about Carole. Her spectre visited me with unfailing regularity: swooping down over the steps at Chancery Lane station, looming up over the streetlamps at the day's end. At first I thought about her with a seething, irrational fury, later with a colder, more calculated anger, finally with a kind of intrigued neutrality, but she was always present, more present, in fact, than at the times when I was actually talking to her. What I suppose I wanted was some kind of explanation: to know how the person I'd been obsessed with had turned into the kind of woman who agonised over fabric patterns or marked down the night's TV viewing with a series of Xs in the *Radio Times*, but I supposed, too, that in trying to procure it I might simultaneously uncover the roots of my obsession. Well, I never found it, never really worked out why so many years' desperation had finally broken themselves here on this plump, cross-grained and imperious girl who in the end I could hardly bear to speak to. Curiously, the idea of being unfaithful to her scarcely occurred to me, not so much out of loyalty – though I did for a long time maintain that loyalty, if only because I knew it was all my fault – as from a feeling that all that side of my life was over, closed off and shut down. Whatever Carole thought about this I never found out. She used to look at me sometimes in that puzzled, faintly scared way that I remembered from the night I'd asked her to marry me, and once, right out of the blue, when we were out somewhere with her parents, she asked me, 'Did you get what you wanted?' – so matter-of-factly that I thought it was something to do with the afternoon's shopping. It was only later that I realised she'd probably raised a question – the only question – about marriage and what I expected from it. Oh, but I couldn't sketch it out for you if I tried: the silences, and the mean, shrivelled conversation.

Sometimes I'd get a brief, tantalising glimpse of the world I'd known before Carole, the Bansteads and Redbridge. The Sandy dolls were in the shops by this time: you saw knots of them grinning at you from supermarket windows, a bit later children marching down side streets with them tucked under their elbows. My uncle sent occasional postcards – old pictures that had taken his fancy or holiday resorts in the Mediterranean – with unintelligible messages crawled on the back. I never replied. I had a feeling that what I'd done would mark me down as a failure in his eyes; a suspicion, too, that my uncle, whom I'd always regarded with tolerant disdain, was drawing away from me, spiritually reinventing himself in a way that I could never hope to follow. And yet for some reason I kept the cards. Left in desks, propped up on dusty mantelpieces, they occasionally resurfaced to remind me of the life I'd left behind.

Time dragged. The hot summer of 1976 came, and the house turned into a sun-trap of boiling surfaces and dancing motes. Ekwall had gone off in a van on the hippy trail to Afghanistan or somewhere by this time, but in any case I'd hardly seen him since the wedding. I used to get up at dawn and sit in the lounge listening to the early traffic and riffling through old books while Carole slept on above me. In the evenings, when she disappeared to sports clubs or her parents, I'd drag a chair out into the dusty yard, where in the distance children scuffled and Alsatians barked, and drink my way through a six-pack of lager. Sometimes it would be gone eleven before I went in, with the din of the yard reduced to the hum of television sets behind curtained windows, the firefly lights of the Essex suburbs fading away into gloomy darkness. There were other people who did this, I noticed: baffled fathers of six who sat in deckchairs surrounded by their romping broods, who crawled and top-pled over them like swarming bees; morose younger men tethered to transistor radios while their wives washed up indoors – a whole commu-nity of silent, solitary husbands cast down by the destinies they'd fashioned for themselves.

The circumstances of my removal from this slough – or if not removal then the first glimmering of another life that might be lived out elsewhere – are still extraordinarily vivid to me. It was late on in that summer – very late on, as there were leaves blowing over the pavements in Hatton Garden and a breeze disturbing the distant pennants and garage bunting – about half-past twelve in the morning, and I was lounging in the outer offices of Travers & Peabody talking to a couple of the clerks when, from twenty feet below us at the foot of the staircase, came the sound of the street door being turned. This in itself wasn't unusual. Travers & Pea body suffered perpetually from 'callers' – travellers in office stationery with trays of paperclips, insurance salesmen who sat uninvited on the one easy-chair trying to wheedle an interview, clients who 'needed a word' with the senior partner. In fact, so determined was I not to have to deal with whichever representative of these species the footsteps now re-sounding on the wooden stair turned up that I was bending deviously over a filing cabinet when the door opened, and so heard rather than saw the person who entered.

'Name of Chell,' a breathless but companionable voice announced to the room at large. 'That's who I'm after … ' And then, as I straightened up, 'Why, there you are, George. Knew I'd find you!'

I hadn't seen my uncle for two years. Framed in Travers & Peabody's seedy vestibule, where shadows crept over the distempered wallpaper, he seemed an incongruous figure. Suit, carnation, black and white co-respondent's shoes – each gave notice of a visitant from an altogether grander commercial universe than the one which we inhabited. Some-thing of this discrepancy occurred to the younger of the two clerks, who immediately jumped up and demanded:

'Will you have a cup of tea, sir?'

'Eh?' My uncle looked vaguely round the room for a moment, taking in the guttering ashtrays, the cheap suppliers' calendars on the wall and the shelf of dusty reference manuals, and then turned back. 'No, no tea. It's George I want. You busy, George?'

There was no point in pretending otherwise. My uncle nodded. 'Got something I specially want to talk to you about, George. Thought about ringing you at the weekend, but reckoned it wouldn't keep. You free to have lunch with me, George?'

'Yes, Uncle Ted.'

'Right then.'

While I pulled on my jacket and combed my hair – Travers & Peabody inclined to informality about the office – I stole a closer look at him. My uncle, feet planted squarely before the glass-fronted bookcase, was evincing the greatest interest in a volume called *Taxation of Foreign Nationals in the UK*. Clothing apart, it took some time to work out the definite change that had come over him. The hair had mostly gone now, hands, face, stomach were fatter, but there was a kind of sheen about him, a self-possession even, that I hadn't noticed before. We descended the small flight of steps to the street in silence. Outside on the Hatton Garden pavement he immediately took charge of the situation.

'Lunch, George. Where do you like to lunch?'

'There's a place in Chancery Lane I usually go.' For some reason I said this with a kind of timidity.

'No, I didn't mean that ... Where do you *like* to lunch? Savoy Grill? Simpson's? Tremendous steak and kidney they have at Simpson's,' said my uncle reminiscently.

There was a taxi edging by that looked as if it might be about to pick up a fur-coated woman with a clutch of carrier bags, but which, seeing my uncle's raised hand, stopped suddenly alongside us. Wondering a little, I followed him into its interior and was borne away along High Holborn and towards the Strand.

'You're looking very well, Uncle Ted.'

'I am well, George. You'd be surprised. Want to know what I've been doing this morning? No? I'll tell you. Got up at five and read some prospectuses. Dull things they are, but you have to do it. Breakfast at six. Then I had Jarvis – Jarvis is my driver – bring me in. Early meeting over in Finsbury Square. Property company I've had a punt with in my time, but I'm not sure about this one. Left them at ten and went and took a walk. Do you ever go and walk round the City, George? It's the strangest place. Lothbury and Bucklersbury and those funny little streets near the Bank. Full of churches, too, that you'd never know were there. Got to the office around eleven and signed some letters. Then I thought I'd step round and look you up.'

'Where's your office?'

'Carter Lane, EC4. Know it? Handy for the trains, but it's a bit poky. We shall have to be moving soon.'

There was a briskness about the way he said 'moving soon', like a general giving orders to break camp, a tracker sniffing the air and

110

deciding that his quarry had gone. By this stage the taxi had halted. Still trying to come to terms with the idea of a travelling salesman who had himself chauffeured around London and attended meetings with property companies in Finsbury Square. I was carried into the depths of Simpson's, where black-liveried waiters stood in little knots beneath the winnowing fans. It was here in the tiled entrance hall, caught up in the lunch-hour traffic, that I think I understood the transformation that had come over my uncle. There was a polish in the way he dealt with the waiter, a kind of habituation of gesture, that the old, battered figure from the West Earlham days could never have brought off. My uncle seemed to have realised the effect of this new manifestation of his personality, for he said, almost naively:

'Bit of a change, isn't it, George? Coming to eat at a place like this? Do you know, when I first came in here and looked at the wine list I was *scared*? Frightened I'd make a fool of myself, I dare say.'

A waiter approached, bearing an ice bucket from which the neck of some unknown vintage protruded.

'Not that,' my uncle said affably. 'Not that old stuff … Now why don't you see if you can find something you fancy, George, while I deal with the wine?'

And so I sat in the wide, gleaming room, while the last of the summer sunlight spilled in through the high windows, and did as my uncle directed. Looking back, I remember the surroundings rather than the conversation that passed between us: the damask carpet and the rolling draperies, big, red-faced men brooding over solitary meals, a general sense of self-absorption and well-being and calm, unhurried time. While we ate, my uncle talked. He did so in a curious, rambling way, pulling out scraps of information that he thought might interest me, making queer little allusions that I altogether failed to understand, discussing his business affairs as if I were an associate who'd been with him from the first. I had a sense of numberless schemes and plans, at once vast and vaguely conceived.

'What happened about the dolls?' I asked at one point.

'Oh, I got out of them,' my uncle said. 'Asked for a price. *And* got it. There's no money in toys, not on this side of the Atlantic. Thought of going into model aircraft kits – you remember those Airfix models, George? – but it's not the coming thing. No, I'm putting my money to work, George. Speculation. 'Vestments. Who knows how it might turn out? You know anything about gilts?'

'A bit.' Travers & Peabody had once possessed a client who had dealt, with catastrophic lack of success, in gilts.

'Interesting things they are, George. I've been making a study of them.

All down to mathematics, you know. Working out what your profit's going to be. And when to realise it. Of course, I don't do that. But I can pay people to do it for me.'

Even at this stage I didn't know whether to believe everything my uncle told me. There was a moment, I'm afraid – somewhere during the speech about gilts – where I decided he was simply an impostor, one of the hundreds of people who in those days floated around the City on a tide of self-delusion and a smattering of technical jargon. But it was only a moment. Somewhere, I divined, my uncle had acquired knowledge, information, about the world he proposed to inhabit. This absorption in milieu became painfully apparent when the talk turned to my own affairs.

'Travers & Peabody ... Not a good reputation, George.'

'No?'

'I've been making enquiries. Oh, I dare say they're not a *bad* firm, but you're never going to get on if you stay there. Besides, I happen to know that the next time that senior partner of yours gets brought before the Institute he won't be let back into practice.'

There was a silence while my uncle lit a cigar, a great fat thing that quivered beneath his fingers like a miniature rolling pin.

'It won't do, George. Not now. Not when there's *opportunities*.' And here my uncle looked embarrassed, as if he'd revealed something that prudence counselled him not to reveal. 'What I mean is, George, I'm in a position where I could do something for you. Now I dare say you don't b'lieve the half of it. "Here's old Uncle Ted," you're saying to yourself, "dressed up in a pinstripe suit and talking about investments." Well, you can think what you like, George, but there's a job waiting for you if you want it. Least you could do is come to my office and take a look.'

'What kind of a job?'

My uncle made a cascading motion with his hands that suggested champagne bottles detonating, or doves taking flight. 'Bright lad like you. Accountancy training. You qualified yet? Well, that's worth an extra thousand for a start. Can be my right-hand man if you like, George.'

While I thought about this, my uncle brooded over a glass of red wine the colour of blood. Then he came suddenly to attention and examined his watch. 'I got to go, George. Meeting to attend. Anyway, you just think about it and let me know ... You remember that time in Putney when I said I was going to make my fortune?'

I nodded.

'I dare say you didn't believe me. Well, I never spoke a truer word. Never did.'

For all the incongruity – and even as he spoke I had a memory of the

112

toy salesman seated nervously in my mother's parlour – there was something irresistible about these words, something about their perky confidence, their self-assurance, that excited me. 'That's right,' my uncle said vaguely, and I realised that each of us was operating by means of some private vision that we had of the other: that my uncle perhaps thought of me as a combination of likely lad and unignorable connection; that I for my part regarded him as potentially unreliable, three-quarters comic but, above all, something known. And that, of all things, was something I knew myself to be profoundly in need of.

Afterwards we walked out into the street, where there were jacketless students loitering outside the gates of King's College and newspaper vendors selling the *Standard*. 'Start Monday fortnight,' my uncle said emphatically. I watched the taxi bear him away towards Fleet Street, aware that the world was not the same in his absence as it had been half an hour before, and that for the life of me I couldn't put my finger on the change.

There remained the business of telling Carole. I'm quite ready to admit that I was unkind about this, that I could have chosen a time when she might have been prepared to consider the idea, but did not, and that, when it came to it, I simply went home and told her. I'm not proud of it, but then I'm proud of scarcely any of my dealings with Carole. There was so much that I could have done, and so many ways that I could have mitigated the damage I caused her. Just to make matters worse, I made an extra mistake, which was to attempt to convey to her something of the romance of that lunchtime in Simpson's, my uncle and his cigar and the wine that looked like blood. It didn't work.

'What do you mean, he offered you a job?' she asked.

'What I said. In his business.'

'But doing what?'

And then it struck me that, apart from a few hints about investments and gilt-edged securities, I had no idea what my uncle wanted me to do for him.

'He said he wanted me to be his right-hand man.'

'How much is he going to pay you?'

For a moment I wondered about inventing a sum larger, but not improbably larger, than the £3,500 a year allowed me by Travers & Peabody, then realised that the consequences would be too grave.

'I don't know.'

She started crying after that, noisily and reproachfully, sitting on a chair by the kitchen window and refusing all attempts at consolation. I gathered that I'd done something unprecedentedly foolish and wilful, so wilful in fact that I could only have done it to spite her. A bit later she said in that decisive and impassioned way women have at these times:

'You must go and see Mr Holroyd first thing tomorrow and say that you've made a mistake. Say you want to withdraw your notice.'

'I won't do it.'

'I don't understand you,' she said. 'You have a perfectly good job. With *prospects*. And now you want to throw it all away for some, some ... With a man who sells toys ...

'... As if you were doing it deliberately.'

I'd stopped listening then, but that wasn't the end of it, not be a large measure. She had the Bansteads on the case within the first half-hour, of course, and over the next few days I had a series of exhortatory visits, singly and jointly, including one dreadful episode when the two of them simply harangued me for an hour in the front room. Funnily enough, of the two it was Mrs Banstead whom I couldn't tolerate. Mr Banstead was merely cross. He knew that I'd made a decision I wouldn't be talked out of, and he just wanted to tell me what he thought of me. Mrs Banstead, on the other hand, simply chipped away relentlessly, like water dripping on a stone: couldn't I *see* how foolish I was being; didn't I *realise* how upset her daughter was, etc., etc. What made it worse was that I don't think Mrs Banstead even knew what it was that I was doing – just being told that it was a bad idea gave her an excuse to whine on in that depressing lower-middle-class voice. It was an odd experience, because it showed me what people of the Bansteads' sort were really like when the chips were down: all the sham politeness went out of the window, and you weren't left in any doubt about what they thought of a jumped-up proletarian from a council estate who'd presumed to marry their daughter. There was one awful moment – following on from the argument in the front room, as it happened – when Mrs Banstead took me on one side and frostily informed me that she wouldn't have her husband spoken to like that 'by the likes of you'.

The Bansteads! I never think about them without remembering Mrs Banstead's piteous, complaining, *good* kind of voice, or Mr Banstead bristling up in that scandalised but still painfully inoffensive way he had. In the end, of course, they knew there was nothing they could do about it, and I can recall Mr Banstead shaking my hand on the hearthrug and announcing that he intended to 'let bygones by bygones' – whatever that meant – but I knew I'd disgraced myself irretrievably in their eyes. In any case it was all slipping away, that kind of life – the clatter of the Redbridge traffic, grim dawns at the tube station, Carole's face in the summer twilight – and while one part of me regretted its passing, another was

114

looking ahead to a new world in which my uncle appeared at the top of dusty staircases, cowed waiters with a flick of his hand, and was borne away by taxi into the heart of the mysterious City.

Q: Did you ever see her again?

A: Oddly enough, yes. Quite by chance. I was in one of the big West End stores around Christmas time, a year or two later, and literally walked into her.

Q: Did you speak?

A: Of course. After all, she had been my wife. Still was, in fact, at that point, as we hadn't been formally divorced. And I didn't feel any anger towards her. I was more afraid she'd feel anger towards me.

Q: And did she?

A: Not really. Some, perhaps. I remember she said she'd had trouble selling the house in Redbridge. I think that annoyed her.

Q: What did you talk about?

A: I don't know. What do people who haven't seen each other for years talk about? I remember her being interested in my uncle's business. We'd had a fair amount of publicity by this time, to the extent of getting our pictures in the paper fairly regularly, and I imagine she'd noticed this.

Q: Did she have any regrets about what had happened?

A: Again, I don't know. There may have been another man on the scene by this time. There certainly had been in the past. I think we swapped phone numbers and talked about meeting again, but I never tried to contact her. Or her me. Later I remember trying to get in touch about some legal thing, but she'd moved by this time and I had to send the letters care of her parents.

Q: What feelings do you have about her now?

A: Whatever feelings I have about her are coloured by the fact that it was all my fault. Well, mostly. (*Pause.*) Obviously it takes two people to contract a marriage, but it need only take one to ruin it (*laughs*). It was my fault because I stuck out for something I already knew it was foolish of me to want. That it could only end in tears. I think she was slightly stunned – and a bit anaesthetised – by my persistence.

That aside, I think I thought that she was rather complacent in the way that middle-class people of that kind sometimes are. She assumed that people like her parents and herself had a kind of God-given right to have comfortable jobs and live in comfortable suburban houses, and watch

116

ineffable TV programmes, and not really care about anything else. But I also thought that she was slightly angry, and that the anger was to do with all that not being enough. I suppose that was part of the attraction.

Q: The rest being?

A: You have to remember that, with the partial exception of my mother, she was the only woman who had ever taken an interest in me. I mean, taking an interest to the extent of wanting to know what I thought about things, and not seeming to mind spending time with me. You can put up with quite a lot on the strength of that.

Q: But it was all your fault?

A: Oh yes. Well, at least I think so. I mean, it would be very odd if it weren't.

Idling in the residents' lounge one evening, and prompted by a pack of playing cards that somebody had left lying about, Frances volunteered to tell my fortune. She did this in the most ingenuous and amateur way, simply taking cards at random from the two or three piles placed face-down on the table before and making plausible suggestions based on what she knew or suspected of my own life. Flattered by the exercise, I was also intrigued as I imagined – correctly as it turned out – that Frances would use it as a way of projecting various hypotheses or conclusions about my character that she would never have wanted openly to discuss.

Several unexciting cards were turned up, then the Queen of Diamonds. 'There have been many women in your life,' Frances proposed. 'You have liked some and hated others. Some have hated you.'

'I don't think that's very original.'

'You don't know whether you want them to like you. If they like you, you sometimes want them less.'

This was much more interesting. I was just about to suggest that the opposite could be the case, thinking of all the women I had very definitely liked and whose complete indifference had only made me want them more, when I noticed that Mr Archer had come into the room. Normally we would have ignored him: in fact life at the Caradon largely consisted of ignoring Mr Archer and the pervasive interest he took in his guests. However, it took no more than half a minute of his presence by the door – he began by making a feeble pretence at tidying some newspapers, then merely stared at us – to demonstrate that the gleam in his eye was more than simple curiosity. Eventually he said rather wistfully:

'I could do that for you, you know.'

'Tell fortunes?'

'If you like.'

Curiously, there was something enticing in the idea of having your fortune told by Mr Archer. Everything about him suggested that as an experience it would be out of the ordinary. I looked enquiringly at

118

Frances. The same thought had obviously occurred to her, as she winked back.

'Do you tell fortunes often?'

'It depends.' Seeing that he was being asked to perform, Mr Archer had cheered up immensely. 'Now and again. It depends who it is. Some people don't approach it in the right spirit.'

'What makes you think we will?'

'Instinct,' Mr Archer said, decisively. 'Always rely on instinct in my line of work. Now, do you want me to do you first or the young lady?'

Frances tapped her finger twice against her forehead. Mr Archer nodded. Seating himself next to me at the table he began to shuffle the cards in a practised manner.

'This is very exciting,' Frances said. 'I don't think I've had my fortune told since I was at school.'

'Ah,' said Mr Archer. 'But I expect that was a lot of silly girls, wasn't it? Wanting to know about boyfriends and exam marks?'

There was something definitely professional in the way he leaned forward over the table, gripping the pack lengthways between finger and thumb. Turning over the first card with a great flourish of his wrist and cuff, he produced the Jack of Hearts.

'What does that mean?' Frances asked. 'Something to do with love?'

By way of an answer Mr Archer raised his forefinger in front of his mouth. Taking up the cards had transformed him, I saw. Staring thoughtfully at the table he seemed a completely different person, wiser perhaps, more resourceful.

'I can see a tall man,' he intoned. 'No, two men. A tall one and a short one. The short one has gone away.'

'That must be Conrad,' Frances said. She was amused rather than animated, but I noticed that her hand shook slightly as she reached forward to light a cigarette.

There was quite a lot more of this: a dark man about whom Frances couldn't make up her mind; a sum of money that might be anticipated, possibly from abroad; nothing definite. Listening to these generalisations, I felt mildly disappointed. Somehow I'd expected something better from Mr Archer, something more idiosyncratic.

'That'll do nicely, thank you,' Frances said, a moment or two later. 'Lots to think about. You can do his now.'

We swapped places at the table. Mr Archer gathered up the cards again and divided them. Abruptly, I noticed, his mood seemed to have changed. With Frances he had been genial, even a bit patronising, obviously enjoying himself in doling out patter. Now he looked worried. The first card was the Ace of Spades.

119

'Don't worry,' Mr Archer said, without much conviction. 'Often starts like this ... I see a group of men, several men. You are one of them. There's money, but you are not happy. Another man comes ... It is very confusing. Somebody is warning you, warning you about something. The woman is not there.'

'Is it as bad as that?'

'Difficult to say.' Mr Archer didn't seem in the least put out by this catalogue of ill-fortune. 'You see, a warning could be anything. Could be an income tax demand. TV licence reminder, anything.'

'And the woman?'

'Anyone. Wife. Mother. Someone you came across.'

For some reason I was horribly depressed by this. The first part of Mr Archer's monologue had described so accurately the events of the previous few years that for a moment I wondered if he knew more about me than he wanted to say. Perhaps this whole episode was an elaborate act of revenge, the cards left out with the deliberate intention that Frances and I should come in and start telling our fortunes? This, I reasoned, was nonsense. The cards, I knew, belonged to another of the hotel's long-term residents, an old lady who amused herself on winter afternoons by playing patience. And Mr Archer's face was devoid of the irony that might have been expected in anyone who had manufactured a practical joke.

'It all seems a bit depressing.'

'It does.'

'Not a shade of hope anywhere?'

'It's only a pack of cards,' Mr Archer said, rather brusquely.

'Even so ...'

'Oh, for God's sake,' Frances broke in, 'will you shut up about those fucking cards? I wish I'd never suggested it.' Turning to look at her for the first time since Mr Archer had begun speaking, I discovered she was close to tears.

'Are you all right?'

'The young lady's a bit upset,' Mr Archer remarked sententiously. 'I think it's time for me to say goodnight. Dare say I've said more than I should have.' He left the room in a dignified way, while still managing to suggest that his feelings had been badly hurt. Frances and I sat and stared at each other.

'What's the matter?'

'Why do you have to take everything so bloody seriously? Why couldn't you just have treated it as a joke?'

'It didn't sound like a joke.'

'But that's the point, don't you see? Not letting things get to you.'

120

'I suppose so.'

Outside wind whipped sharply against the high windows. There was a storm brewing. You could always tell when a storm was brewing, Mr Archer maintained, from the way the wind came in from off the sea. I realised suddenly that he was a person of some consequence. First the business about the weather; now this. Perhaps Frances appreciated this expertise more than I had. It was hard to tell. In the distance the sea boomed. Frances was more composed now. She said:

'I think I'll go to bed. I've had enough excitement for one night.'

'So have I.'

As we passed through the foyer on our way to the staircase I stopped by the reception desk. The front door was open and a stream of cold air poured into the foyer. Outside rain was falling at an angle against the brickwork. I watched for a moment or two, wondering whether I ought to close the door or otherwise investigate, when a shadow loomed up suddenly from beneath the light and Mr Archer appeared in the doorway. His hair was plastered back across his scalp; rainwater fell in runnels over his face towards an already sodden jacket.

'Always like to go outside if there's a bit of a storm,' he explained. 'This time I got caught right in it.'

He shook himself vigorously, like a spaniel, so that water cascaded over the ochre linoleum. 'Very sorry about that business in the lounge, sir,' he went on. 'My fault entirely. Should have stopped when I had the chance.'

'It couldn't be helped.'

'I suppose not. Still.'

'I must go to bed.'

'That's right.'

Climbing the staircase, which was unlit and made hazardous by defective stair-rods, I wondered what my uncle would have made of Mr Archer. There was certainly an affinity between them, to do with self-possession, the sense of something hidden behind an unpromising facade. Whether my uncle would have welcomed his resemblance was something else. Like many people, he had a habit of disliking in other people the qualities that were his own.

'Something odd is going to happen,' Frances said when we met at breakfast the next morning. She looked curiously bedraggled, as if she had slept the night in her clothes. 'I know it is. I just know.'

I don't think I quite knew what to expect on the day I started working for my uncle. I suppose I thought I'd immediately be inducted into a gleaming universe of attentive secretaries and private sanctums, and I'm fairly certain that I imagined there would be a repeat of that ambrosial hour at Simpson's. In the end I spent the first three weeks in my uncle's employ in the basement of an office in the City Road itemising a packing case full of documents that he'd acquired as part of some queer transaction whose nature I never really determined. It was a damp, unheated room with a strip of glass at head height looking out through a dismal area towards the entrance to Old Street station, and the work would have been intolerable if it hadn't been for the company of an ancient clerk called Ridgebird whom I discovered already knee-deep in paper on the first morning I arrived.

For some reason I took to Ridgebird. He was a fantastically weather-beaten old man of about seventy, who claimed, among other exploits, to have witnessed Neville Chamberlain arriving at the Bank of England in a tailcoat for a meeting with the Governor, and to have fire-watched from a chimney stack on top of the Stock Exchange during the Blitz. The work was of the dreariest kind. The packing case mostly contained defunct share certificates, but here and there would be a discounted bill or a building society pass book dating from the 1950s, which Ridgebird seized upon like a boy pilfering eggs out of a bird's nest: he had a kind of genius for appraising the worth of a financial document in a couple of seconds. The packing case, according to Ridgebird, harboured the paper assets of a brace of liquidated companies that my uncle had bought in a fire sale, a purchase whose prudence depended on whatever we turned up. He was a talkative character, with a pair of striped trousers so old that they shone like the surface of oily water, and a passion for Victorian novels. We spent our lunch hours in companionable silence, drowsing over *Pendennis* or *Beauchamp's Career* while the rain fell over Old Street and pairs of legs, weirdly truncated at the knee, passed by the area steps.

Throughout this early and, I suspect, probationary period I saw my uncle several times. He had a habit of 'looking in', as he put it, late in the afternoon to see what the day's researches had amassed. On these

122

occasions I sat meekly at my desk in the corner of the room while he and Ridgebird – a galvanised Ridgebird, grown suddenly brisk and respectful – conferred over the lists of salvaged scrip. I was amused by Ridgebird's grave deference to my uncle – I can remember him once setting out a chair and then dusting it down with his handkerchief in a gesture straight out of drawing-room comedy – but also intrigued, for it confirmed the picture I had built up of my uncle as someone who had transcended his origins, established himself, through some mysterious and unguessable process, into a figure of consequence. I can recall him bending over a sheaf of foolscap that Ridgebird offered him and murmuring, 'United Textiles. Lemme see. Not paid a dividend in ten years, but there's no reason why they *oughtn't* ... ' and marvelling at the stock of lore he had acquired from somewhere.

His attitude towards me in these days was approving but distant. 'Getting on all right, George?' he would ask as he rolled into the room, or 'Found anything interestin' for me today?' but I could see that it was Ridgebird he was really interested in, Ridgebird and the contents of the packing case. By rights I suppose I should have been distressed by this indifference, but I fancied my uncle was applying what his curious and idiosyncratic mind conceived of as a test: if he were to employ me in his business, whatever that business might be – and I was wholly, shockingly ignorant of what it was that my uncle *did* – then it would be wise to know what I could do. That was how I reasoned, throughout these long, autumn days, yawning in the basement and watching Ridgebird unearth a Liverpool and District Coal Company share certificate from 1953 or poring over the Everyman edition of *The Return of the Native*.

And then on the Friday afternoon of the third week, when only a handful of documents remained to be docketed and filed, I received from a motor-bike messenger – a delivery channel that I later found to be characteristic of my uncle – a summons to meet him that night at an address in Sydenham.

Chronologically I suppose the Sydenham days are only an interim in my uncle's career, a brief resting space before he moved on to grander and finer things – and I don't imagine that he stayed more than a couple of years there – but somehow they are very vivid to me: much more vivid than my married life in Redbridge or the gloomy bed-sitter evenings in Belsize Park, though even those have a kind of retrospective charm that I wouldn't want to deny or minimise. At any rate I have a strong recollection of that first evening in the big dining-room with the parallelogram of garden descending to a little copse of trees, light splintering off a brace of cut-glass chandeliers, and the attitudes and complexions of the people with whom my uncle had populated the place. At a decade and a half's remove I realise that they were the dowdiest kind of suburban gentry – partners in accountancy firms with their desiccated wives, small solicitors and gold club loungers – but at the time I wandered through the wide rooms listening to their conversation (they talked about school fees and the Callaghan government) with an unmitigated respect. Without stating the fact in so many words, the house stank of money. There were flowers all around, in heart-shaped vases on top of a piano, piled up in baskets on the tables, and all manner of knick-knacks – miniatures and silver snuff boxes and cigarette cases – that I couldn't imagine my uncle buying on his own account. Dazzling white rugs stretched across the far end of the room and a couple of life-size stone leopards guarding the fireplace represented the limits of taste in this ornate but somehow slapdash and infinitely chilly setting.

What my uncle's guests made of all this I don't know. There was a kind of homogeneity about them, I now realise, that rather betrayed them and, though they talked knowledgeably enough about the latest West End play or exhibition, I doubt that many of them ever attended these entertainments. There was something unfeigned, too, in their interest in my uncle, the way that they appraised his house and its decorations. But to me, who had known only the middling stuffiness of Redbridge, they seemed very grand people indeed, and I was rather afraid of them. My uncle hovered in a little alcove apart from the main room, broaching bottles and directing a pair of waitresses in black cocktail dresses. He had picked a couple of cronies out of the throng, I noticed, demure little men of about his own age who called him Teddy and made what were to me incomprehensible remarks about the City. Outside rain fell over the neat, rolling garden, and I found myself, glass in hand, wandering through the rest of the house: into a wide hall where a personage in grey trousers and a dinner jacket was storing coats in a cavernous cloakroom, past a smaller apartment containing a desk, a row of box files and an engraving of the Cutty Sark, on again into a long, low kitchen, rather like a ship's galley, with a round glass table at the end. A plump, yellow-haired woman, discovered smoking a cigarette at the table, jumped up (half guiltily, I thought) when she saw me, and then gracefully subsided.

'Why, it's young George,' Greta said. 'Gone and got married, too, by all accounts, since we last met.'

'You should have come to the wedding. Uncle Ted did.'

'Oh, we were having one of our disagreements,' she went on. 'Would have stuck pins in each other, I dare say, if I'd come. Anyhow, what's she like, this young lady of yours?'

124

I explained as much as I decently could about Carole and our life in Redbridge, while Greta ate olives from a saucer positioned in her lap. Outwardly as jolly as ever, she seemed faintly irritated about something.

'Happy throng not to your taste, Greta?'

'Oh, him and his parties. "We ought to entertain, Greta," he says. "Ask people round and see them enjoying themselves." Well, I'm all for that when it's friends and suchlike. Where he gets this lot I don't know. Goes round to the golf club and asks anyone he finds there, I shouldn't wonder.'

'I didn't know Uncle Ted played golf.'

'He doesn't. Well, he does, but it's the funniest thing ... Oh, I don't *mind* if he enjoys himself. But I draw the line at asking them back to the house. If he wants to entertain them he's welcome to, but I'll just sit it out here, thanks very much.'

'I like the house,' I said, truthfully, and thinking to find a less controversial topic. It was obviously the right thing to have said, for Greta's face immediately broadened into an admiring grin.

'That's right. I've known him take trouble about things before, but never so much as he's taken over this. Do you know he had the decorating done twice because he didn't like the way the first lot had done it?' "No point in having something you don't like," he said, "even if it does cost money." Look, I'll show you.'

And for a quarter of an hour or so, with an immense gravity and seriousness that was delightful to watch, she conducted me round the house: its wide staircases and half-dozen bedrooms, its marble baths and box-rooms full of queer old lumber – dusty suitcases labelled *E. Chell* and old toy catalogues. From time to time we encountered other guests on the look-out for lavatories or cloakrooms. On these occasions Greta bristled up furiously.

'They probably think I'm one of the waitresses,' she said. 'Wouldn't surprise me. And the joke of it is five years ago it would have been true. Used to do waitressing work back in the old days before I met Ted.'

We were back in the kitchen now, seated at the glass table with a bottle of white wine Greta had produced out of the fridge. 'How is he?'

'Ted? He's all right. Always off on some scheme or other. Goes all over the place, too. Birmingham, Bristol, Manchester. Paris it was, last week,' she exclaimed as if it were incredible that anyone should travel to another country in pursuit of business.

'What kinds of schemes?'

'Oh, this and that. Sometimes he tells me about it, sometimes he doesn't. I don't mind. Been the same ever since he sold up the toy business. One long rush. And then coming here … It's a funny time, George.'

I didn't quite know what to make of this, whether it was a reference to my uncle or something more obscure. Greta went on:

'Reminds me of just after the war. Everybody terribly excited and tired at the same time, and with money they hadn't had before, but desperately worried about what was coming at them over the horizon. Anyway, that's enough of me. You'd better go and see your Uncle Ted, George. He'll be wondering where you've got to.'

'I like sitting talking to you.'

'I mean it, George. He was set on you coming. "We must have young George," he said. "There's things I want to say to him." You don't want to go and disappoint him.'

Looking back, I suppose that was one of the longest conversations I ever had with Greta, but it's surprising how many of the phrases that remain from those days turn out to be hers. *Fussing and fretting over nothing* (of some business anxiety of my uncle's). *Dressed up like a pox doctor's clerk* (a particularly lurid suit he persuaded me to buy at this time). Even then, I think, I knew there was more that I could have found out about Greta, and which might have done me good if I'd discovered it – and I don't mean things destructive of her privacy or our intimacy, such as it was, but things that might have helped me to understand myself.

I wandered back into the hall to find most of the guests gone, the grey-trousered butler drinking sherry at a green baize table, and the waitresses clearing up a dismal array of half-empty wineglasses, plates streaked with cigarette ash and dirty cutlery. The air was dense and smoky. My uncle stood slightly to one side, fidgeting his hands in his pockets and looking rather red and creased, with his chin low down in his collar.

'Wondered where you were, George. Thought you might have got lost somewhere. Hah!'

I explained about finding Greta, and the tour of the house. My uncle looked vaguely discomfited.

'Greta's not stuck on these occasions. Says they're a waste of time. Can't say that I blame her, I suppose.'

'I suppose not.'

'*You* know how it is, George,' said my uncle loftily, and I saw at once that I was being appealed to in a discreet way, so discreetly that anything I said would have been gathered up and trampled on as a rebuke to my own lack of discretion. 'Have to see your friends. Once in a while. Social duty. Do it in style. If you want. Why not?'

126

There was something faintly querulous about the way he said this, something remote and rather peevish. I saw him look me up and down once or twice, as if he couldn't quite work out whether I counted as Greta's ally in this argument, then thought better of it.

'Glad you're here anyhow. Sorry your young lady couldn't make it.' (There had been a polite fiction about Carole's absence from the gathering.) 'Wanted to talk to you, George. Did indeed.' In the outer reaches of the hall more waitresses were removing crockery, Greta a distinct, cynical presence in the background, and we moved through them like a couple of proud, confidential kings – not, as I'd supposed, to the room with the box files and the engraving of the Cutty Sark, but to a lofty sitting room at the very top of the house which I didn't recall Greta having shown me, strewn with books and newspapers, where a decanter and a pair of brandy glasses stood on a tray.

'Been doing a bit of reading,' my uncle apostrophised the books. 'Extraordinary thing, reading.' They were miscellaneous volumes. *Don Juan.* A manual of dairy farming. *Crockford's Clerical Directory.* As I watched he seized some of them in his arms and began slotting them at random into the long, low bookshelf. 'One of these days, George, we'll have a good long talk about books, you and me.'

Later it would become difficult to distinguish between the various conferences that my uncle held with me in the big house at Sydenham. They concertina'd into one another, blocking out the intervening days or weeks, so that what remained was a continuous stream of conversation – or rather monologue, as it was my uncle who did most of the talking. Sometimes they began in the evening and went on late into the night – I can remember once hearing a faint snatch of birdsong and glancing out of the window to find that dawn had come up over the grey Kentish gardens and there was pale sun shining over the distant weald. On other occasions, back early from the City, they started after lunch and continued into the afternoon, until Greta, exasperated, would knock on the door and ask if she should wait with tea any longer. As far as I can recall, the tea always waited. But for some reason I have a strong memory of that first night and its properties: the books spilled out over the Turkey carpet, the brandy, which was of a particularly old and fiery sort, owls out hunting in the dusk, and my uncle prowling the room as he talked. He was cagey but affable, congratulated me on the work I'd done with Ridgebird – apparently there'd been a couple of title deeds he'd been specially pleased with – digressed about a property concern he had some interest in, but always I could see that he was holding something back, some extra information that he wanted to surprise me with. At other times he launched on great commercial ruminations, all of which, I later

127

saw, were to have some bearing on what followed. I can see him as he did so – a short, squat man standing four-square on the rug with one hand anchored in his pocket, savouring his reflection in the brandy glass.

'What do people want, George? Money, of course. But they want security as well. Now, how do you get security?' And he paused for a moment to look reprovingly over the top of his spectacles. 'In my day it used to be savings. But what good's savings with all this inflation, eh? Say you're retired and such, with a few thousand in the bank, how are you going to get by on savings? No, that's what the politicians don't realise. They think if you're earning then you don't mind spending. But what if you're not earning? You want a guaranteed return on your money, that's what you want.'

It occurred to me that my uncle was talking about gilt-edged securities and the advantages of trading in them, also that he – or the people with whom he worked – had devised some exceptional way of performing this trade. And, though I don't make any claims for my intuition, this, curiously enough, was how it turned out.

'You ever hear about bond-washing, George?'

'A little. Not enough to tell you what it is.'

'Kippax'll tell you about bond-washing. He knows all about it. All to do with Capital Gains Tax. Say you buy a gilt just after it's paid a dividend? Well, the price'll be lower because there's just been the payment, don't you see? Now, say you hold the same stock until just before the next dividend payment. The price'll be higher, because it's going to take into account the money due. Now, what would you do if you wanted to get the maximum return?

'I don't know. Collect the dividend, I suppose.'

'No. There you're wrong, George.' And here my uncle looked very serious and knowing. ''Stead of keeping the stock and getting your divvy, you sell them at the higher price. That way you're not receiving a dividend payment – which is taxable – you're making a capital gain. And a capital gain up to the value of 5,000 isn't taxable.'

'I'm still not quite sure I understand it, Uncle Ted....'

'Let me spell it out, George. You're a pensioner, say, with a bit of money. A bit of money you want to make work for you. Well, this'll give you a guaranteed income *and* you won't have to pay tax.'

There was a great deal more of this, ebulliently dealt out as beneath us the noise of the house receded and fell away into silence, stuff about transfers, abstruse financial instruments that I couldn't comprehend without a copy of the Stock Exchange Handbook. Much of this, I suspected, my uncle had learned by rote at someone else's instruction,

128

but here and there a pet phrase would show how he'd taken the material to heart.

'It can't lose,' he said at one point. 'That's the thing about it, don't you see? It can't lose.'

Travers & Peabody had dealt with the aftermath of many a crazy scheme of this kind over the past three years: the man who claimed to have invented a 'scientific' method for predicting the movements of penny shares; the firm that worked out an infallible way of playing the Chicago Futures Exchange. Each of them Mr Holroyd had happily delivered to the bankruptcy court. I shook my head.

'What about the capital? What about the intermediaries? What about the banking regulations?'

'Don't need capital, George. This is clients' money we're handling. All we do is take commission. The intermediaries – those little chaps as call themselves independent financial advisers – they'll come quick enough when they see our ads. As for the banking regulations, no one quite knows if we need a licence, but Kippax says there's nothing in the rules that stops us commencing to trade.'

He had it all pat, of course. Clients. Business. Profit. And such was the pitch of his enthusiasm, such were the surroundings – that it was impossible not to be caught up in it, not to feel flown, exalted and expectant. In this spirit I learned that I was to become my uncle's personal assistant (at a salary to be agreed), that a glorious future awaited me, that my life – I remember these as my uncle's exact words – had just begun, and that there was no knowing, no knowing at all, where it might end. Later, I remember, we descended to the huge, empty drawing-room, where Greta sat soberly and pale-faced over the fire, and discussed what to do with me, it now being 1 a.m. and the last train long gone from Sydenham station.

'Can stay here if he likes,' my uncle ventured. 'Make up a bed for him upstairs.'

'Of course he can stay here,' Greta said sharply, and I got a sudden glimpse of the old days back in Putney to which I'd been a witness, back before the arrival of money and the trackless schemes which my uncle had devised, or had had devised for him, about bond-washing. We contrived a bed in a room on the first floor: I climbed into it to the sound of my uncle's footsteps rising in a series of crisp detonations to an upper storey.

And so began that unforgettable period when I laboured as my uncle's personal assistant, was party to his monetary secrets and his dearest wishes, lived cheek-by-jowl with him in the big house at Sydenham and half-a-dozen other places, and moved with him among great people in the great world. I suppose it must have lasted six years, but it seems both shorter and longer: hectic, indiscriminate, infinitely drawn out, but at the same time containing a number of dominating pictures, endlessly repeated – my uncle at his desk, outside his offices at Lothbury (formerly inhabited by a defunct metal-broker), consulting with Kippax and his henchmen. My uncle looms very large now, very bright and purposeful. When they wrote about him in the newspapers, which they did profusely and incessantly, he was always photographed at the big desk in Lothbury, cigar balanced in his thick fingers like a wand. The promotional literature issued by the firm was always in the end about him, and came in homely little paragraphs about security and the rainy day, tailed by his sprawling signature.

You mustn't think, through all of this, that I was merely a passive observer: even then, at the very beginning, I had my own ideas about things, and my solutions to the many problems with which my uncle was daily presented. In the days that followed the journalists sometimes gave the impression that I was only a tiny cog in the vast, imponderable machine that my uncle had set in motion, but I like to think that I helped him. It was I, for example, who conceived the preliminary set of advertisements, the giant ones that filled half a page of a broadsheet newspaper, in which my uncle demanded of his audience: did they want to lie awake at night agonising over an uncertain future, or sleep the sound sleep of those who knew that their money was prudently invested? It was I, too, who devised, and in the end administered, our commercial network. I spent nearly a year in the late 1970s travelling round the country from one provincial town to another meeting small accountants and financial people and urging them to recommend us to their clients. For some reason these meetings usually took place over lunch, in the back rooms of gloomy carvery restaurants, and if I try to piece together that time it dissolves instantly into a sea of pinched faces guzzling their way through plates of roast beef and potatoes. And yet I don't think, even amidst the endless plates of roast beef and the damp salt cellars, that I was unhappy. For one thing I'd never seen England before, never once in my life travelled through the place or thought that it had anything to offer me beyond the West Earlham back-to-backs or the Redbridge traffic. There was romance, consequently, in these train rides across the Lincolnshire wolds or the western marches and their endings in grey-brick termini and run-down Midlands stations. I remember once discovering Salisbury and spending a rapt half-hour between appointments looking over the cathedral and its precincts; another time riding through Suffolk very early on a November morning and watching a pair of eager grey horses come loping forward through the mist. English cities: Oxford, Cambridge, Lincoln, Gloucester. It took me until my twenty-fifth year to find them and the things they contained: cathedral closes and old stone, cobbled streets and shops selling prints and second-hand books. I used to wonder about living there when it was all over.

But I'm advancing matters, losing sight of the true march of time. Kippax belongs to this period, there are even glimpses of Helena and Lord Charlesworth and the lunch tables of Belgravia, and my uncle's manoeuvrings after the football club, when the great world lay before us, defenceless and inviting. Somehow, though, in my imagination all these things belong to the future, to another part of life, and all that remains is a confused mixture of cathedral spires, the stink of diesel and the grey horses moving silently through the fog.

Q: How well do you think your uncle handled money? I seem to remember a TV programme concentrating on, how shall I put it, conspicuous consumption?

A: I take it you mean the ITV documentary in the early '80s? Naturally I think that was regrettable.

Q: Regrettable?

A: A good opportunity gone to waste. I seem to remember that when the idea first came up – and the TV companies were always hugely keen on my uncle – we advised him not to do it. On the grounds that it would make him look foolish. And then when he wouldn't be talked out of it, we tried to get him to send it up ... You know, allow the camera in to one of his dinners and simply have baked beans and a glass of water. In the event, it didn't turn out like that.

Q: You mean that it made him look foolish?

A: Oh immensely. That kind of thing brought out the worst in my uncle. The very worst. If the producer suggested that he ought to do a particular scene drinking a glass of champagne and smoking an eight-inch cigar, then he'd do it. He couldn't see that he was being sent up. And this was a pity, because that was a side of my uncle that he indulged very rarely. It was almost as if it needed to be licensed by a TV producer or a newspaper.

Q: Like the 'America with Chell' thing?

A: Exactly. All dreamt up by a newspaper editor, and for some reason my uncle bit. As far as I can remember, it was some competition whereby the winners got a free flight, first class, to New York – with him actually on the plane – and a certain sum which they could invest with us. It was all very successful, but I don't think in the long run it did us any good.

Q: Why not?

A: It made him look like a spiv. Which, to do him justice, I don't think he was. Also it made him look as if he wanted money just to be able to spend it on rubbish. In fact my uncle was very serious about money. It was something that brought you security. Not to be thrown away on trash.

Q: Even so ...

A: As you say, even so. And I wouldn't attempt to deny any of the stuff the newspapers came up with afterwards. I mean, it was all *there*, wasn't it? The yacht and the debentures and everything else. But I think I'd want to stress that this wasn't a normal part of my uncle's life. There were just times when he couldn't stop himself.

Q: Such as?

A: Oh, at public functions. In restaurants sometimes. You know that photograph of him drinking champagne out of Cilla Black's slipper? I was there. I never knew why he did it. But so much of it was the child-in-a-toyshop mentality. I mean, I remember once being with him at, I don't know, perhaps it was the Connaught, when they brought the wine list. Normally he would simply have ordered a bottle of house red, or a medium claret. But somehow – it may have been that he'd pulled a particularly adept stroke of business that morning – he got it into his head that he'd like the most expensive bottle they had. Just to see what it tasted like. And of course they produced something that cost £175.

Q: What did it taste like?

A: Warm raspberryade, so far as I remember.

Q: Did he mind?

A: I don't suppose he noticed. As I say, the mentality was that of a child in a toyshop. And he had this quite naive idea that something was always worth what you paid for it. Also, at times like these, that all economies were false. I remember him once ordering two half-bottles of something when, inevitably, it would have been much less expensive to buy a single bottle. That kind of thing ...

A highlight of life at the Caradon was Mr Archer's periodic rebukes of his staff. These took place at unexpected moments. You might go downstairs late at night to fetch something from the residents' lounge and find him haranguing Alison, a girl who worked in the kitchen, as she made her way out of the foyer towards the hotel door. Alternatively, it was possible to come across him at unearthly hours of the morning upbraiding the chambermaid as the two of them moved in and out of empty bedrooms. Undoubtedly Mr Archer enjoyed these occasions. The oracular nature of what he had to say, and the length at which he said it, suggested that he had composed and memorised the words in advance. Comfortingly, there was no embarrassment in breaking in on one of these scenes, if only because none of the Caradon's employees gave the slightest sign that they listened to what Mr Archer was saying, much less intended to take any notice of it. It was as if both parties realised that allowing Mr Archer to let off steam in this way was a necessary part of employment in his hotel. Certainly nobody bore any malice about it. The exception, perhaps, was Mrs Bennidge, who 'helped out' in some un-specified way upstairs. Mr Archer's treatment of Mrs Bennidge showed an interesting side to his character. With the other members of his staff he was simply irritable: there were specific failings that he wanted to address. With Mrs Bennidge it was clear that these public rebukes had a kind of moral dimension, that it was Mrs Bennidge's whole attitude to her work, to the hotel and to life in general that upset him. For her part Mrs Bennidge made it just as clear that she resented these pep talks, but was too frightened of crossing Mr Archer to make a serious protest. This gave their dialogues a touch of unease that other disputes lacked.

Usually these arguments took place in the foyer. Mrs Bennidge, a burly, eternally put-upon woman who was said to 'give her husband a time', normally stood with her arms folded on one side of the reception desk, while Mr Archer prowled round her. His tone was exhortatory. In fact, in lecturing Mrs Bennidge Mr Archer served notice of a moral vocabulary that was absent from other aspects of his life.

'The thing is, Mrs Bennidge, I know you could try harder. I know you could really make something of the work you do for us. And yourself, of

134

course. That goes without saying. Surely you can see that it would be better for all of us if you pulled your weight? Surely you can?'

'Perhaps I can.' In answering Mr Archer, Mrs Bennidge gave nothing away.

'And I don't want you to think, Mrs Bennidge, that it's just me who thinks you could do better. Everyone thinks so. Geordie in the kitchen. Brenda and Alison ... '

'Nasty little tarts, they are.'

'No, we're all of us of the same mind. All of us. As I'm sure you are too, when you really think about it. So that's why I'm going to ask you, on behalf of us all, to make an effort. So that we don't have to go on having these conversations. Now, don't you think that's a good idea?'

'If you say so.'

The glance Mrs Bennidge gave Mr Archer at this point was one of the purest hatred. On several occasions I almost thought she was going to hit him. For his part, Mr Archer obviously found these conversations a strain. At the same time you could see that he thought them something he was morally obliged to go through.

'The only reason I don't give that Bennidge the sack, sir,' he once told me, 'is that I feel sorry for her.'

The idea of Mr Archer feeling sorry for anybody was a novel one. 'Why do you feel sorry for her?'

'Lives in a rubbish tip down by South Green. Husband's a waster. Two idiot sons. The kind' – Mr Archer paused savagely – 'that make you glad you never had children. But it doesn't matter what you do with people like that, sir. I know. I've tried. Treat them badly and they just accept it. Treat them well and they take advantage. What am I supposed to do?'

Curiously, my sympathies were with Mrs Bennidge. It was not that I liked her – for as far as I could see everything Mr Archer alleged about her was true – simply that I agreed with Mr Archer's diagnosis that it didn't matter what you did with people like that. If you dealt with Mrs Bennidge, it seemed to me, you accepted her on her own terms. Anything else would merely store up trouble.

Frances was interested by this aspect of Mr Archer's personality. 'Why doesn't he just get rid of her? If what I hear's true, she's already been sacked from half the hotels in Suffolk.'

'Maybe he sees her as a challenge.'

'That's what people always say about other people whose thought processes they couldn't begin to comprehend.'

'I feel sorry for Mrs Bennidge.'

'So do I. So would anyone ... It's her that takes the ashtrays, by the way. I came into the lounge one day and saw her stuffing one up her skirt.

135

What people like Archer never realise is that there'll always be other people like Mrs Bennidge. It wouldn't matter if you paid her £50,000 a year with ten weeks' holiday, she'd still come in and steal the ashtrays.'

'So what do you do about people like her?'

'Tolerate them, I suppose,' Frances said. 'And nail down the ashtrays. But the last thing you do, the very last thing, is to read them lectures on moral usefulness.'

I had always known I would find the second lot of photographs. It was one of those things to be counted on in advance, like a rotting tooth that would eventually have to be pulled. They came to light at the bottom of one of the box files, wedged between old bank statements, company prospectuses, odd bits of artwork that my uncle had commissioned on a whim and then forgotten. Finding these smudged black and white mementoes of past time was both comforting and the exact reverse, each warm association somehow cancelled out by the memory of what had followed. There was no getting away from this. These feelings were symbolised by a picture of my uncle, Kippax and myself standing outside the office in Lothbury in what must have been early 1983. In retrospect, knowing what had happened six months later, it was impossible not to translate our satisfied expressions – my uncle's peculiar gleeful gaiety – into the grimmest of grim jests. It had not seemed like that at the time. There was a photograph of Carole, taken outside her parents' house in Redbridge: plump, red-faced, mouth half-open, hair fanning out behind her in the breeze. This conjured up a bewildering range of sensations: memories of dense traffic heading east towards Essex; fields seen from a train; Carole's wedding dress thrown over a bed; a weekend spent decorating; odd remarks let fall by her father; evenings taken up playing cards with her parents. There was a lot more of this: painful, immediate, difficult to push aside.

Beneath the photographs there were other odd souvenirs: football programmes from the early 1970s; press cuttings; notes in a slanting feminine hand written on the headed paper of a City PR firm; queer fragments of my uncle's handwriting sprawling across scraps of card; dinner menus; even a paper napkin on which were inscribed the words *Mem: buy 25,000 pref. TTW, Consolidated to query?* It was impossible to work out what they meant. Why had I kept them, I wondered? Not for information. What then? My uncle had been keen on the talismanic aspects of business life – renting office space previously tenanted by a famous venture capitalist, engaging a chauffeur previously employed by the chairman of Lloyds. He felt that in some way the qualities of their

136

former owners rubbed off on him. More curiously, he may even have thought that material success depended on some magic wrought by the possession of symbolic artefacts of this kind.

All this was beside the point. Having found the pictures, it was difficult to know what to do with them. Keeping them would be painful. Somehow, not keeping them would be worse. I knew, for example, that if I tore up the photograph of Carole I should instantly regret it, would probably even try to retrieve the pieces from the wastepaper-basket half an hour later and reassemble them. What was to be done? In the end I thought of the strongbox Mr Archer kept welded to the floor of his office, and in which were stored his own items of value. The knowledge that the bag in which I had put the contents of the box file lay in a locked safe, and that someone else had the key, would be an adequate hedge against temptation. Mr Archer was intrigued by this transaction. 'Used fivers, I shouldn't wonder,' he remarked as he placed the bag inside the strongbox, which contained in addition a watch and, for some reason, a set of false teeth. 'And I hope, sir, that you've written down the serial numbers.'

Oddly, Mr Archer supplied a twist to the dilemma of the photographs. A couple of days later, entering the residents' lounge at a furious, headlong pace that suggested he was trying to retrieve a hat carried off by the wind, he said:

'I expect you've often wondered, sir, about the photograph that hangs on the wall to the left of the reception desk.'

As it happened, I had occasionally wondered about this photograph, if only because it was next to impossible to stand in the foyer for any length of time – usually kept there on some pretext of Mr Archer's – without your eye coming to rest on it. It was a black and white studio portrait of a youngish, not specially attractive woman – over-large nose, slightly protruding teeth – dressed in the fashions of the late 1960s.

'Who is it?'

Mr Archer seemed pleased by this interest. Baring his teeth obsequiously, pausing to give greater emphasis to what followed, he said:

'The lady in question was my wife.'

Given Mr Archer's habitual silence about his past, this was a startling revelation. I fought for something to say.

'I didn't know you'd been married.'

'It wasn't for very long, sir. All most unfortunate. Between you and me, I wouldn't want to go through that again.'

'Why? What happened?' By this stage I was seriously interested in Mr Archer's marriage. It seemed a subject of consuming importance.

'Not something I'd like to talk about.'

'Go on.'

What followed was an elaborate but disconnected monologue, which had clearly circulated in Mr Archer's head for many years but was only rarely brought out on public display. 'Difficult to say what I didn't like about her ... Dreadful habits she had, I may say ... When all's said and done, just a question of incompatibility ... The *personal* side I shouldn't care to go into ... Could have thrown the crockery at her sometimes, just sitting there at the dinner table ... All a terrible mistake ... Talking about it somehow makes it worse ... Misunderstandings ... Terrible sense of relief when it was all over ...'

This went on for some time. Once or twice Mr Archer seemed about to draw the proceedings to a close, only to rattle on at an even faster rate. In the end he wound things up with a final, dramatic flourish.

'To tell the truth, sir, it cast a blight over my young life.'

It was difficult to know what to say. Compliment Mr Archer on his altered state? Ask him for further details (it might be that he wanted to make further revelations but needed some kind of prompting)? Fortunately, the photograph itself offered an exit route.

'But why do you keep it on the wall?'

'Keep what on the wall?'

'The picture of your wife. If being married to her was such a hell on earth, why remind yourself of it every day? Every hour even?'

Mr Archer thought about this for a moment. He looked worried, more worried than I ever remembered seeing him. In the end he said:

'Well, the way I look at it, sir, is that it's a part of your life, isn't it? Something you can't get away from. Not even if you tried. I did do that for a time, you know. Pretended that I never had been married. Whenever I had to fill in a form that said "Marital status" I *always* put down single. It became quite a habit with me. But then I thought I ought to face facts. After all, you've got to face facts, haven't you?'

'Do you think your wife – your ex-wife – feels the same? I mean, does she have a picture of you on her wall?'

'I wouldn't know, sir,' Mr Archer said, a shade stiffly. 'The young woman's habits are of no interest to me.'

For the first time during my stay at the Caradon I wondered whether I had been entirely wrong, whether there wasn't something admirable about Mr Archer. The story about his wife cast him in an unexpected light: resolute, tenacious, obdurate. Some of us hid pictures of people we had loved and who had made us unhappy in locked safes; others placed

138

them in a position where they might see them a dozen times a day. Did this make Mr Archer a better man than me? I felt a powerful urge to find the ex-Mrs Archer and hear her side of the story.

'Do you want to hear what happened on the last day we were together?' Mr Archer asked, less formally than before.

'I'd like to very much.'

'It's harrowing stuff. Are you sure?'

'Go on.'

'It was about this time of the year. We were living in Frinton in those days, keeping a boarding-house. Quite a nice little business it was. Funnily enough we weren't getting along too badly. A few disagreements. The guests used to joke about it. And then one morning I came down to the dining-room and the guests were all sitting there complaining they'd had no breakfast. And about the smell, of course. She'd locked the kitchen door, but I broke in and found her.' Mr Archer paused impressively.

'Do you mean to say she …?'

'Oh yes. Those were the days when mains gas could kill you. But do you know what was worse than that? She'd left a note. Pinned up on the notice-board, too, so that everyone could read it. *You have ruined my life.* Just that. *You have ruined my life.* I often wonder,' Mr Archer said, 'what I did to deserve that. Wouldn't you?'

Frances refused to believe the story of Mr Archer and his wife.

'I don't think he was ever married. I think he just made the whole thing up.'

'What makes you say that?'

'I don't know. Yes, I do. He's too self-conscious about women ever to have been married to one. Have you ever seen the way he looks at me when he comes into the breakfast room? Now a married man might look at me – well, he might – but he wouldn't do it in the way Archer does.'

Frances was caustic that morning. There had been a letter from the magazine she wrote for, returning an article as in some way 'unsatisfactory'. But I was intrigued by this idea of the married man's unselfconsciousness about women.

'What about me? Where do I fit in?'

One of Frances' agreeable characteristics was her ability to discuss her own and other people's lives with something like objectivity. She said:

'I wouldn't say you were self-conscious about women. I just think you're the silent type. Most men who've been married – even when it was a long time ago – talk about their wives *all the time.* It doesn't matter

139

if they hated them. Then it becomes a war story, only the bullets are all plates, and the sentry duty the night you spent outside in the car.'

'But Archer talks about his wife. Where does that leave him?'

'Archer talks about a picture of a woman on the wall. It could be anyone. He could have had a wife who committed suicide – and I never knew anyone whose wife committed suicide who was prepared to talk about it – but the picture could be someone else. I just don't think you should believe everything Archer tells you just because he tells it to you.

'Anyway,' Frances went on, 'why are you so interested in Archer? He's just a dreary little man who owns a hotel. Not a very good hotel either, if it comes to that.'

Later, when Frances had retired upstairs to read a book called *Iris Murdoch: The Relativity of Guilt*, I thought about this. For a start, it seemed to me that Mr Archer was the reverse of dreary. Sinister, perhaps, overbearing in the way he pressed his company upon his guests, but not dreary. Fortune-telling, speculation about the lives of his staff, a wife who had killed herself: none of these qualifications might have shown Mr Archer in a favourable light, but he wasn't for that reason uninteresting. There was also the Caradon itself. Without seriously exerting himself, Mr Archer had managed to impress his personality on every aspect of the hotel. It flared up at you when you walked through the door; waited on the doorstep to usher you out. This was an achievement too. Then there was the question of the late Mrs Archer. Here Mr Archer had seemed to speak with absolute conviction. The story had a kind of practised quality. I thought about this for a long time as the sky darkened and rain broke in across the eastern sky. Later I went up to Frances' room. The door was open. *Iris Murdoch: The Relativity of Guilt* lay face up on the bed. I read a paragraph which began: 'Murdoch's characters aspire to freedom, but there are times when these aspirations are confounded by their very articulacy. In analysing their various predicaments to their own satisfaction, they are more likely to be constrained by the emotional patterns revealed than released. This reining in of temperament can sometimes have dramatic consequences.' There was no sign of Frances.

Coming back from my early morning stroll along the beach, I found the letter lying in a pile of envelopes recently delivered by the postman and stacked up inside the front door. Inside the buff rectangle, postmarked 'London W1' and with a typewritten address, a single sheet of paper had been folded into a tiny square the size of a small coin. Unravelled and smoothed down, it turned out to be a piece of lined foolscap on which, printed in letters of differing size cut from pages of a newspaper in the manner of ransom demands, ran the message GEORGE CHELL IS A SWINDLER.

There was no point in taking something like this in to breakfast. Instead I carried letter and envelope up to my room and sat down to examine them. There was no clue, though, as to provenance. The individual letters looked as if they might have been snipped from a copy of the *Daily Telegraph*. No other incriminating details emerged.

In the years since the crash I'd received a good many hostile letters. Some were anonymous. Far more, unhappily, had been signed by the former investors who had written them ('As a pensioner in my seventies, I wish to place on record my disgust … '). There had never been anything like this. I decided that I was intrigued rather than alarmed. Whoever had sent the message clearly knew where I was, even down to the final letter of the postcode. Anyone meditating violence would presumably have done something by now. You could only wait and see. I put the envelope in the box file and went downstairs.

At breakfast Mr Archer was particularly good-humoured. 'Do you know, sir,' he said as he offered toast from the Caradon's curiously elongated toast-racks, 'I'm sure I felt a touch of spring today. Of course, we never really get the decent weather here until May, but I must say it cheered me up no end.'

Part Three

For some reason I remembered that evening in the big house at Sydenham four or five years later in a board room high over EC3 as warm, late afternoon sun streamed in through uncurtained plate glass. In itself the memory was odd, because the Sydenham house was long gone by then, replaced by a grander and yet more luxurious mansion at Sunningdale, and the sensations it stirred up might have belonged to a previous era rather than a matter of a year or two since. What pushed it to the surface, I think, was the sound of my uncle's voice rambling on in that vague and faintly repetitive way he had as he talked to Kippax, the two of them craned earnestly over a sheaf of papers. Without warning, as I turned to look at them, the scene acquired a kind of mythical, eternal quality: light falling over the long, elliptical table, other people – a pale-faced clerk or two, a plump factotum from the firm on whose premises the meeting was taking place – reduced to the status of minor attendants, the two sharply contrasted figures absorbed in their discussion. Louder perhaps than the circumstances warranted, the voices – my uncle's bland and ruminative, Kippax's wholly deferential – came drifting across the room.

'Have to do something about that chap in the Midlands as wrote the piece in the *Post* ... Wouldn't do if any of the London papers picked it up. D'y' suppose we should talk to him? Ask him to lunch or something ... ? What is he anyway? You know I don't go much on them journalists ... But the people do read them, drat them.'

Kippax, as this monologue continued, made notes on a small, ring-bound jotter balanced on his knee and jealously guarded by an outstretched arm. He was a tallish, lean man with bristling russet-coloured hair that stood up straight on the top of his head like a sanitary brush, and an ability to project his voice into a variety of non-human personae. Dealing with a mislaid document, when his voice rose to a kind of strangulated bark, he could look distinctly foxy. Just now, inclining his head in a way that emphasised his over-large ears, and resting his protrusive front teeth on his lower lip, he resembled an exceptionally nervous rabbit.

'Of course, it's all part of communications generally ... Sure you think

142

that just as much as I do. In fact I don't wonder if it's time we had a proper PR campaign ... Y'know, something *understated* and that ... All very well advertising y'self in every blessed newspaper in every blessed town and then finding there's folk that's never heard of you ... '

Kippax, hand moving at speed across the page, looked slightly cross at this. As head of the firm's marketing department, in addition to his task of advising my uncle on investment strategies, he was ultimately responsible for any press coverage, favourable or unfavourable, that we did or did not get. Lowering his head still further, so that it was almost at the level of my uncle's knee, he spoke several muttered words in a tone of comparative urgency. If this was intended to stop or divert the flow of speech, it had exactly the opposite effect.

'In fact, what we ought to do, K, is to get up a circular ... Something we can send out to the chaps in the regions ... Perhaps you'll do me the kindness to investigate. And while we're doing that, *while* we're doing that, there's a whole heap of other things we ought to be considerin'. Treasury paper on capital gains and a statement expected. Now, what do we think about that, I wonder?'

My uncle sounded querulous, a bit exhausted. That was to be expected. Two years or so as a public figure had taken their toll of him. Physically enlarged – his stomach jutting out over the table, face lost in an accumulation of chins – he seemed at the same time slightly diminished, fallen away into some odd world of mental torpor, disinclination to act. Kippax, to do him justice, was usually the victim of my uncle's 'moods' as he called them. I watched the two of them for a moment longer, as the wide oak doors at the back of the room swung open, admitting another pair of functionaries, and someone else approached with what might have been a jug of Pimm's, wondering how long the afternoon would go on and whether it might be allowable to go and call Helena.

Outside, on a church tower a hundred yards away, clock hands moved towards five. The sound of the chimes, a few seconds later, seemed to galvanise the occupants of the room into action. The two functionaries – senior members of the merchant bank whose office we were attending – sat down abruptly at the table end. Kippax advanced on them sternly, his fountain pen held out in front of him like a duelling poniard. My uncle gave a sigh of weary resignation, flicked his spectacles up from their descent along the bridge of his nose, and swivelled round in his chair. In the two years spent attending gatherings of this kind I had become grossly over-familiar with these rituals: Kippax's nerves; my uncle's sulks; stalled negotiations kicked into gear. Here, as so often in his undertakings, my uncle wanted money: specifically several million pounds to fund expansion of the side of his business that targeted overseas investors. As security he was offering the lease of the building in Zurich where Chell Holdings carried out these transactions. Interested in principle, the bank was querying my uncle's ability to dispose of this lease under Swiss property law. Here the matter had stuck.

The clock finished striking. Ten storeys below, on the pavement beyond Threadneedle Street, shirt-sleeved hordes were already in flight. It was a Friday on the last day of July. Nearer at hand, sonorous, formal voices met, broke apart: Kippax, my uncle, a banker together. Then Kippax and my uncle. Finally Kippax alone.

'Think the bank may not have considered the true implications of such a scheme ... Collateral offered *in addition* to the extremely beneficial interest rate ... Can think of many similar arrangements concluded in the past ... Would like to draw the bank's attention to identical instances in its own recent history ... *Bona fides* not in doubt ... '

Fluent, grave, vaguely clerical, Kippax usually got his way on these occasions. For a moment I concentrated on what he had to say, half in admiration, half disapproving. If the truth is to be known, I never liked Kippax. His deference, which my uncle accepted at face value, I thought simply obsequious. But there was something worse than this. Kippax, in fact, in some distinct way, was sinister. I could never put this dissatisfaction into words, but it was always aroused at times like this: by the flat, accentless plod of his voice, the surreptitious glances at my uncle, his habit of appearing to read off what was actually a blank sheet of paper.

'A question of arriving at a *modus vivendi* ... Identical arrangements entered into by ourselves, both here and overseas ... National jurisdictions in no way an impediment ... Not at all disagreeing with the need for a full and frank exchange of views.'

Putting Kippax on to perform in this way was, I suspected, my uncle's idea. He had a theory that long draughts of undiluted Kippax induced a sense of panic or hopelessness – bitter despair at the tedium of time passing – in his auditors. My uncle, needless to say, revered Kippax, whom he called 'K' and consulted at every opportunity.

'A surveyor's report *not* necessary in the circumstances ... In fact surprised that the bank should think ... Elementary safeguards of property law ... Subterfuge ... '

There was no telling how long this would go on. I settled down to brood about my uncle and his affairs. We had been living this kind of life – Kippax, city board rooms, ever-increasing sums of money – for upwards of three years now. It showed no sign of diminishing, calming down. Newspaper journalists who wrote about my uncle sometimes stated that he had become a millionaire 'overnight' on the foundation of

Chell Holdings. This was hardly true. A good week's takings in the early days might have been £2 million, but this of course represented only the sum in which my uncle dealt, not the ultimate profit. All the same, this must have been a reasonable amount. There were bank statements piled up in the office at Lothbury to which only my uncle and Kippax had access ...

Was Kippax reaching the home straight now? He had a trick of repeating himself in the last stages of these exhortations, running through half-a-dozen pet phrases in an effort to round things off. Punched out of his mouth with an effort, the words seemed to bounce back from the opposite wall.

'... Lay this before you with confidence ... *Unreservedly* commend these details to your attention ... Clear that ... Urge you ... '

Nearer at hand my uncle was shifting his bulk uncomfortably from one area of his chair to another. Catching my eye, he winked. For all the veneration in which he held him, and the licence he allowed him in administering the affairs of Chell Holdings, my uncle wasn't above treating Kippax with a certain amount of irony: proposing some absolutely ludicrous business scheme, for instance, in an effort to see how far Kippax could be gulled into supporting it. What Kippax made of these jokes at his expense, which he received with indefatigable good humour, was anyone's guess.

There was a violent clashing of furniture as Kippax dried up, a kind of prolonged clanging of wood on metal, like a prison riot about to begin. My uncle said 'Yes' quite loudly to no one in particular. One of the City moguls leant back wearily in his chair and had to clutch at the table to regain his balance. Two or three people started speaking at once. It was too good an opportunity to miss. Nodding at my uncle, I wandered out through the swing doors into a corridor that backed onto a communal area where secretaries stood round gossiping or rifling through open handbags. Here I found a telephone and dialled Helena's number.

'Is that you?'

'We're practically finished. Kippax has been giving them the third degree.'

She laughed. 'Will he win, do you think?'

'Should do. If not, I'm sure they've got something else planned. Where can I meet you?'

'The train goes at 6.10. Say six o'clock at Paddington. Platform three.'

'OK.'

For a moment I wondered about returning to the meeting. Then I decided against it. Kippax would get his money. In any case I should be seeing my uncle that night, spending the weekend with him for that

145

matter. Standing by the lift I thought again about Kippax's slow smile, my uncle winking delightedly across the table, the dust motes hanging in the warm summer light.

If I've dramatised this scene it is because it is so vivid to me – infinitely more vivid than most of the events that preceded it. West Earlham seems very small now, very insignificant and meagre; the early London period is a forgotten glow, and even the Sydenham days appear somehow trivial and preparatory. I can't work out what caused this transformation, only mark its effects, and it's a fact that I can recall the conversations and the faces of this time in a way that still surprises me. Kippax's speeches to the money men, my uncle truffling his way through their ponderous dinners – all this is very real to me, and very poignant.

Imperceptibly, we had become great people. There was no doubt about this. I think it must have been about the time my uncle took the house at Sunningdale that I became aware of the fact of our greatness. He was on advertisement hoardings by now, asking worried investors if they thought they were getting the best rate of return on their money, and in newspapers waving a fat finger at a column of dubious figures. At the time we thought the advertisements were an inspired stroke – the mild, homely-looking man, the unanswerable demands – but looking back I don't think they were: they unsettled him, and they brought him too near to the people whose money he took. They may have raised the confidence of the public, but they lowered his own.

'Can't say as I like it, George,' he told me once. 'Why, it's like turning up in someone's front room and trying to sell them something.'

'It gives what we do a personal touch,' I explained. 'That's what Kippax says.'

'Too personal for me,' he said. 'Too personal by a long stretch.'

All the same, I think he liked the sensations of great persondom. If I've a predominating memory of the great house at Sunningdale, with its half-dozen reception rooms and endless conservatories, or of our final offices in Lothbury, it's of the sacks of correspondence – great shoals of letters addressed personally to my uncle and begging his assistance in the most unlikely matters. To settle a marital dispute, invest £100,000 in a lemonade bottling plant, stand for Parliament, present himself at a certain address in Bolton, Lancashire on a Thursday afternoon in November 'so that myself and a few friends can express our appreciation of your efforts' – all these demands it was assumed that my uncle would fulfil in the free-handed style that was thought to characterise his business dealings. In the wake of the letters came the visitors – fierce, moustachio'd men with trackless and unfeasible schemes in their heads for manufacturing cars that ran on electricity, or raising Spanish galleons and their trove from the Bristol Channel, or equipping polar expeditions. Some of them my uncle received in his sanctum at Lothbury, but he was rarely taken in. I think he listened to them – I was about to write 'spoke' – because he felt sorry for them, or recognised in them something of himself, or – less frequently – because their imaginings contained the kernel of something that could be put to his own use.

'George,' he would say ruminatively as I came upon him sometimes in the big office, where sacks of unopened post lay over the sideboard and a man in a baize apron might be seen hanging a painting on the farmost wall – buying 'pictures' was one of my uncle's passions at this time – 'George, got a chap in here this morning talking about a new distilling process. You ever hear anything about that kind of thing?'

'What sort of a chap?'

'Poor suit,' my uncle would say reminiscently. 'Looked as if he could do with a square meal. Damn it, I nearly asked him out to lunch only I had an appointment with them corporate finance people. Said he'd been in the loss adjusting trade. Think there's anything in it?'

'Could be.' (I had no idea.) 'Don't whisky manufacturers say the industry's fifty years out of date? Did he have any apparatus?'

'No. Just drawings. Such a sad-looking chap, too.'

Nonetheless, he made a number of shrewd speculations in this period. A couple of estate agencies in the suburbs that paid pretty well, a secretarial bureau in High Holborn and a Carshalton printing works found themselves shuffled into my uncle's grasp and placed under the notional control of Kippax and myself. Do you remember a literary paper called the *Monthly Bookman*? I still have one of the specimen covers they sent to Lothbury when the first approaches were made.

KINGSLEY AMIS – THE ENGLISH BREUGHEL?
THE STATE OF FICTION; A SYMPOSIUM
FLECKER'S DEBT TO HENLEY
MARGARET DRABBLE IN HER LIBRARY
A NEW POEM BY SIR JOHN BETJEMAN
THE DECLINE OF THE BELLES-LETTRIST
AN EXTRACT FROM THE LYTTELTON/HART-DAVIS LETTERS

'Extraordinary how these things carry on,' my uncle remarked as he signed the deed of purchase (I think he paid a sum in four figures) before relaunching the magazine with colour advertising and incendiary essays by Clive James and Anthony Burgess.

As I say, we became great people by degrees. Sometimes, lunching with my uncle in the City, I'd overhear people at adjoining tables considering his prospects. 'Isn't that Chell?' 'What, Chell Holdings?' 'Looks an ordinary little chap to me.' 'Well, he could have *my* money to lay out and welcome.' My uncle was unabashed by these salutations. 'Never does any harm to have people talking about you, George,' he remarked. 'You and me sitting down to eat in a restaurant, why it's as good as a free advertisement.' He was right, I suppose, but I never liked these occasions, never cared for the spectacle of my uncle blandly shovelling food to the accompaniment of these oblique murmurings. There was something shameless about it, I think, which he didn't quite appreciate, or perhaps I'm misjudging him, and the joke was really on the prurient throng that studied him.

But it was the house at Sunningdale that cemented our position as great people. I can remember my first sight of it, out of the nearside window of my uncle's Jaguar, as we motored down out of the Surrey hills towards the plains of Berkshire one hot summer forenoon: a little townscape of buildings and a rolling lawn like a billiard table, gravel moats, the infinite surround of gable and red-brick terrace. The spectacle was so extraordinary, so unlike anything that either of us had seen before, that my uncle stopped the car at the side of the road and stood silently on the kerb peering down through the heat haze. Later on as we prowled about the grounds, inspected the grottoes of funerary statuary and the spotless pathways, he seemed slightly shamefaced. 'I s'pose you think I'm a fool, George, buying a place like this, though you're too polite to say so.' 'No. Not at all.' 'I mean' – and I could see his mind working at the thought without reference to what I had said – 'who *lives* in places like this? Who lives in them, eh? Dukes? Duchesses?' 'Dukes and duchesses couldn't afford it,' I suggested. 'I s'pose not. No, they couldn't.' He looked worried for a time, as if the prospect of dukes and duchesses being unable to share in this good fortune troubled him somehow, but then he brightened up. 'We must find out who the neighbours are, George. Find out and invite 'em round.' Later still, as we sat in the biggest drawing-room and were served tea by a grave and awful butler, he revealed something of his purpose. 'This'll be good for us, George, a place like this. Make people take notice, you'll see.' He was right in a way. The newspapers pronounced him vulgar, hopelessly vulgar, but they were fascinated by the house, its regiment of staff, its platoon of gardeners, its heated swimming pool and its lustrous neighbours, who turned out to be a Lloyd's underwriter and an absentee Saudi prince. Myself, I never found its vulgarity annoying. In fact of all the places I associate my uncle with, I think I remember the fort at Sunningdale with the greatest fondness: not for its company days, but for the rainswept afternoons when Helena and I used to wander the great paths or watch the leaves falling on the virid lawns. At other times the house was full of people. My uncle entertained there: he had 'little dinners' for two dozen, served up by a chef poached – if you will excuse the pun – from the Dorchester, with wines sent up by the case from Berry & Rudd. And it was here, too, that, coming upon my uncle in conversation with a group of persons on the vast Turkey carpet – persons whom inspection revealed to be the Chief Financial Secretary to the Treasury and the editor of the *Daily Telegraph* – I realised just how far this frantic and overpowering progress had taken us.

I shared only intermittently in these social experiences. Often my uncle used to introduce me to the circle of grandees on the Turkey carpet, with an odd, knowing glint in his eye, as 'my nephew ... works with me in the business, y'know', but I disliked these occasions and tended to avoid them. If I've a memory of those evenings at Sunningdale it's of a dozen silent bald heads bent over the grand dining-table while I sat with Greta in an ante-room watching the dishes go in and listening to my uncle's laugh rising and falling in the distance. All the same I used to wonder about the kind of company we saw, here amid the Berkshire granges and the dappled lawns, here at the tail end of the 1970s, wonder where it came from and what our own part in it might be. Above all it seemed to me that there was a change in the way my uncle regarded the people who thronged his house, and whereas in the past he'd welcomed anyone who was prepared to be received by him, now he had begun to discriminate in a savage and yet subtle way. Characteristically, my uncle confirmed these observations.

'Always plenty of people want to know you, George,' he said. 'Question is, do you want to know them?'

'That depends. It depends what you want to know them for.'

'Right,' my uncle said thoughtfully. 'But we got to be thinking of the future. Moving the business forward ... Can't stand still for a moment, y'know, not in this day and age ...

'... They're nice fellers,' he said. 'Some of them, anyway ... '

At this distance I lose track of many of the celebrities he consorted with. Canforth the industrialist was there several times; Geoffrey Howe dined there once. If I ransack my impressions of this time I find a great uneasiness. I saw politicians outside the debating chamber, magnates detached from their board rooms, all sorts of eminent and significant people, and their shared characteristic was fear. They had no answers to

149

the problems that confronted them, and they assumed – with what now seems to me a startling naivety – that my uncle could help them. They had committees on which they wanted him to sit, funds that they wanted him to manage, even a parliamentary seat, once, that he could have had by lifting a hand, or rather writing a cheque. I can see him now, standing before that fireplace, a small, brisk, fat, figure crowded in by those heavy, distinguished faces, laughing at his jokes but not, I think, liking him or appreciating the fact of his dominance over them.

To do him justice, my uncle was quite aware of the position he filled in relation to those great people. 'Of course,' he told me once, 'we shouldn't really be here, George.'

We were standing in the big entrance hall at Sunningdale, and he made an expansive gesture around the swooning staircase and the glossed panelling to emphasise the remark.

'Why not?'

'Not our style. Not what we're used to,' said my uncle affably. 'Mind you, who's to say what a person's used to? But no, it isn't really our kind of thing, talking to big people ... ' His voice pattered off into silence. 'We're trespassers really. Found the gate left open and decided to walk inside.'

'Is that what you think?'

'Certain of it, George.' And then, 'Goodness gracious, look at the time. Due at Lothbury at three, we are.'

More than once in the months that followed I thought about that exchange, but I never reached any firm conclusion about it. For what the observation is worth, I think my uncle exaggerated his singularity. In fact it seemed to me, the more I examined the world in which we found ourselves, that England was full of trespassers, people who had come from nowhere to somewhere, and basked in the glow of their transit. There was Barnstaple the insurance broker, who had started life in a corner shop; Walsh the Barnado boy who floated his property company for £100 million. Curiously, there was no confraternity between these commercial meteors, and my uncle, who met them at dinner, was very scathing about Barnstaple's social peculiarities and Walsh's Devonshire accent. 'It's not where you come from, George,' he told me, coming back gloriously from one of these occasions, 'it's how you behave.' He was wearing a new suit, in elaborate pinstripe, and smoking a Havana cigar, and he looked like a little fat man whom the gods have suddenly decided to take pity on.

I am not mocking my uncle here: at least I don't think I am, for I continued to esteem him in all sorts of ways. He 'saved' a pre-Raphaelite painting for the nation at about this time, and he made legendary

150

contributions to charity. I suppose my anger wasn't directed at him, but at the people who surrounded him. I remember a conversation from this period that I had with a Tory MP met on the fringes of a Sunningdale party.

'So you're old Chell's nephew, are you?' he said. 'Delighted to meet you. There are people say that you and that chap what's-his-name Kippax are the real powers behind the throne. No, don't misunderstand me. It's just that people occasionally wonder how your uncle does it.'

'Does what?' He was a portly, twinkling character who sat for a farming seat in the south of England and was later supposed to have lost half a million pounds at Lloyd's in the '80s meltdown.

'Oh, keeps it all up. Do you know how much this place is worth? Of course you do. I had lunch the other day in Lothbury, a whole gang of us. Couldn't have been fewer than sixteen sat down. Champagne. Lobster. Hired waiters. Couldn't have cost under a thousand, that lunch. Does he do them often? I mean, I'd like to come again of course, but why *does* he do them?'

'We're gilts traders. We need to inspire confidence.'

It didn't sound very good, and I knew it didn't.

'Of course you do. Don't worry, I know all about it. But gilts traders put ads in the newspapers, don't they? They don't give thousand pound lunches to, well, anyone with a handle to their name. And those buildings your uncle goes after, those mansion blocks in South Ken, where's the money coming from, eh? It's all right, I know all about it, but you're not gilts traders, or not *just* gilts traders.'

We were standing, I remember, in a recessed window in the big drawing-room, looking out onto the teeming terrace. Scarlet-faced, dressed in a striped jacket and flannel trousers, my uncle wandered through the throng like some gorgeous, preening butterfly.

'Quite a phenomenon, isn't he, your uncle?' my companion went on. 'Shouldn't wonder if he does very well when we get back again. Herself approves, you know. All the same, nobody quite knows what to make of him, do they? And I'd be a lot happier if I knew where the money was coming from. Or where it was going to, just for the sake of argument.'

'We pay a fixed interest rate quarterly to all our clients,' I told him. 'Thirty days withdrawal notice for anyone who's not satisfied.'

'I don't doubt you do. All the same ... '

For quite a long time I wondered whether to tell my uncle about this conversation. In the end, though, I decided against. He had reached a period in his life when he fretted about trifles. If a financial journalist, writing in a daily newspaper, came out against one of our products he would write exasperated rebuttals. If a gossip columnist printed teasing

151

nonsense about him he would bombard the editor with endless letters of rebuke. The psychology of these irruptions quite escaped me. I don't think, in the last resort, that my uncle minded what people said about him, but I believe he resented the suspicion that he was being got at.

'There's people out there,' he told me once, with a kind of wonder that even then I couldn't wholly believe, ''ll write bad things about you just for the fun of it.'

'It's the first principle of journalism, uncle.'

'But it's not right,' he said. 'It's not right, do you hear me? They ought to be ashamed of themselves.' It was the most outraged I ever saw him.

It was odd how my uncle retained this touching, archaic naivety about people and things ...

And so our lives went on in this queer, irresistible way: a high and dizzying trajectory that there was no way of quantifying. I tried to keep a diary at odd times, but it was no use. The days spun away beneath my hand, went careering across the horizon and out of view. But I remember the night of the 1979 General Election, in front of the television at Sunningdale, in the company of a red-faced and exulting throng, and, a little later, the visit of a very grand and eminent person indeed (I recollect the exact words this lady spoke to me, as she turned a hard and stony blue eye, and they were 'Very hot, isn't it, for September?', and it *was* very hot). He was summoned to a Downing Street reception not long after, where he stood uncomfortably in a crowd of entrepreneurs who were supposed to represent the economic spirit of the age, but I don't think he was very happy. In fact I sometimes wonder whether he was very happy generally in these days. He would disappear for days on end to European capitals with Kippax and his advisers and come back tired and spiritless and somehow uneasy in himself. He became hypochondriacal, inflicted dull, insipid diets on himself and worried Greta with fish-oil and ginseng tablets. And while he talked all the time, he seemed to communicate less of himself. He was always, or so it seemed to me, hovering on the brink of some revelation, some mighty confidence that would astound me and bind me to him for ever, but the step was never taken.

Sometimes, quite unexpectedly, he used to talk about the old days, the very old days. We'd be lingering in the office at Lothbury, as the streetlamps flickered over the empty pavements, waiting for the car to bear us away, when I'd catch him looking at me – poised over his desk with a pen in one hand, say, or leaning back in his chair, hands behind his head, staring at the damask-coloured walls.

'George,' he would say – and he would say it in the tone of a man who is determined to inflict some damage on himself, whatever the con-

152

sequences – 'do you remember the old times? Norwich, I mean, and such?'

'A little. Different things at different times.'

'What kind of things? I mean, what comes into your head when you think about it?'

Curiously, I found these questions embarrassing: an old, tightly policed world of the imagination now penetrated by an intruder. 'I don't know. I remember my mother of course. All sorts of things. Norwich cathedral. Seeing the houses out of the upstairs window.'

He looked slightly disappointed at this, as if he'd fed me some obvious and unignorable clue which I'd failed to grasp.

'I'll go and see where the car is,' I said. 'Baker' – Baker was the chauffeur – 'may have gone round the side entrance by mistake.' I was half out of the chair, but he waved me back.

'No. 's all right. Nice to have a bit of a chat for once in a while. Don't worry about Baker. Now, where was I … ? I mean, Jane, your mother, what did she use to talk about?'

It was a good question. What had my mother talked about? I recalled a few censorious remarks about neighbours, stock phrases of one kind or another. Obviously my uncle had something more elevated in mind. It was difficult to know exactly what might satisfy him.

'It's hard to say, Uncle Ted … I can remember her being very upset when I went away to London.'

At this rather disingenuous account of my departure from West Earlham, his face brightened. Mystifyingly, I had said the right thing. 'Upset? Of course she would be. It's what any mother would feel.' For a moment he looked almost triumphant, as if a point had been proved to some invisible audience. 'Did she write at all … when you were in London, I mean?'

'Hardly ever.'

'Not much of a one for writing letters,' my uncle said, in a rather subdued way. For a second or two something hung in the air between us, something remote and quite unguessable. He opened his mouth and closed it once or twice, looked as if he might be about to speak, and then shook his head.

'Doesn't do to be harping on that kind of thing,' he said vaguely. 'Doesn't do at all.' A moment after that the car arrived.

I dare say I should have pursued my uncle on this topic – this mystery of his connection with my mother – drawn him out and established what he meant, but somehow I never did. It was all too remote, too far away, and in any case I was irretrievably caught up in my own concerns. I was leading a strange life then: intent days in the office at Lothbury, the long

153

evenings at Sunningdale (I had a flat in Kensington at this stage, but I don't suppose I went there more than one night in three), curious weekends at country houses where my uncle's celebrity had purchased us an entrée, solitary vacations in Continental towns where I wandered about without the faintest idea of how to conduct myself. I don't think I understood. No, let me be honest, I don't think I even tried to understand.

Q: How near before the crash to you think it was before he realised that things were going wrong?

A: Very near. Or maybe not at all.

Q: Not *at all*?

A: It's difficult to say. Have you studied the careers of the swindlers in Victorian novels? Merdle in *Little Dorrit*, Tigg in *Chuzzlewit*, Melmotte in *The Way We Live Now*. There's a tremendous inner conviction about them, an extraordinary sense of believing in their own myth, to the extent that they couldn't distinguish what was real from what was patently illusory. That feeling of carrying on in the face of overwhelming odds.

Q: You're suggesting that your uncle was like a character in a Victorian novel?

A: No, not really. Besides, they are bad men, I mean through and through bad men, which I don't think my uncle was. I think he just had a naive belief that if people could go on being paid, then everything would work out in the end. It's fair to say that people like Kippax encouraged him in this belief.

Q: The following is taken from the *Observer* special report on the collapse, dated 27 May 1985: 'A premeditated plot to defraud, in which it is hard to know whether the cupidity of the fraudster, the negligence of the regulatory authorities or the naivety of the investing public should take precedence.' Do you have any comment to make?

A: That's nonsense. Well, two thirds of it is. The 'naivety of the investing public' is simple patronage, as most of these investments were made under the auspices of independent advisers. 'Negligence of the regulatory authorities' is definitely right. None of this would have happened if they'd realised – and done something about it when they did realise – that we needed a licence to trade gilts in this way. Which, in fact, we never obtained.

Q: Going back to the first question, surely he must have had an inkling that everything was falling to pieces.

A: I think he had an inkling. But not much more than that. You see, we'd had these mini-crises before, and always managed to survive them.

155

Always the authorities' fault. Someone would ask a question in the House, or in the newspapers, as to whether we were trading legally, there'd be a few hostile articles and certain investors would ask for their money back, but the regulators would simply prevaricate. Make a few enquiries of the kind that a first-year audit trainee would have thought inadequate. It was only when the DTI was talking about outright closure that anyone became alarmed.

Q: You'd been investigated by independent auditors before this of course?

A: Twice. And very respectable firms they were too. But you see, an independent audit doesn't mean anything. An auditor just wants – or wanted at this stage – to see that the books balanced. Now anyone can make the books balance. You do it by shifting money from one bank account to another. If you're clever. And this is what Kippax did, I imagine. The account books showed that x million had been received from investors, so the auditors needed to find x million in a certain bank account. And they found it. Later it got more complicated.

Q: How?

A: In the end, as you know, the DTI sent insolvency specialists in, meaning that they thought the firm was insolvent and would need to be wound up. Even then Kippax had ways of throwing them off the scent. For example, there were several million pounds lying in a deposit account that hadn't come from gilts trading – they'd come from a property deal, which according to the letter of the law was illegal – so Kippax had to find some way of accounting for them. He did this by inventing and retrospectively recording in the books thousands of non-existent transactions. It very nearly worked.

Q: And your uncle remained ignorant of everything that was going on?

A: I think he could feel which way the wind was blowing. But he was able to dramatise it in terms of his personal myth – the little man up against the big battalions – and this comforted him. He got very broody, though, those last few months. He was always starting vague and faintly melancholy conversations about the future, which I now see to have been rather more ominous than I thought at the time. But there was never a sense that 'the shadows are drawing in' or 'the game's up', at least not until the very end.

That evening Mr Archer complained of a headache. Standing by the fire in the residents' lounge, one foot crossed over the other in an odd, balletic stance, he discussed his symptoms with hypochondriacal fervour.

'Of course, this is not what you might call a proper headache. Not on the general scale of things. If I were going to quantify it, I'd say three point five on a register of ten. Not like some of the headaches I've had in the past.'

'A kind of reminder, in fact, of past unpleasantness?'

'That's it. That's it exactly.' Mr Archer shifted the position of his feet slightly in an even more balletic shape, so that for a moment I thought he was about to spring up onto the mantelpiece. 'Many's the time I've been prostrate with pains in the head. Had to lie down in a darkened room with a wet flannel over my face.'

'But you don't feel like that now?'

'It's difficult to say. Of course, I'm not someone who complains about illness. I can't abide those people who go on endlessly about every ache and pain they have. But I should say that it felt like having something rustling inside your head, somebody walking on leaves a long way off. You understand what I'm saying?'

'Perfectly.'

It was clear that Mr Archer found the condition of minor illness gratifying not because it encouraged him to talk about himself but because it allowed him to ventilate various theories he had about illness in general. Later that same evening he said:

'I've always thought that being ill is all in the mind when you come to think about it. For example, I once had a great-aunt who was always taking sick. "Taking sick" – that's a good old-fashioned expression, isn't it? It became a regular thing with her. On high days and holidays, whenever anyone in the family wanted to go out anywhere, she'd lie there in bed. I used to go in and see her sometimes – I was only a small child, you understand, but I could see the truth of things – and I'd say, "Aunty, there's nothing wrong with you, you must get up." I was thought very forward for doing so.'

157

I had been reading the *Gesta Daemonorum* of Abbot Wulfric, which some long-departed guest had left in the Caradon's meagre bookcase. In those days – though written in the 1400s the book purported to describe events at the end of the ninth century – the Suffolk forests had stretched for thirty miles, from Newmarket to the sea's edge. Here the ancient kings of East Anglia had hunted lynx and bear. A wolf six feet high had been dragged out of a pit near Iken. At Rendlesham the royal hunt had brought down a fabulous wild boar in whose eye sockets red rubies glittered. Mr Archer, I now saw, was another of these mythical creatures, something set down arbitrarily in these bleak landscapes, ancient, elemental and rare.

Mr Archer's illness worsened by degrees. For some days he was not seen about the hotel, and was assumed to be keeping to his room. Then he rallied, and could be heard below stairs having a furious argument with the chef. People about the Caradon began to say that it was quite like old times, and that Mr Archer's having an argument with the chef was a sure sign of his return to health. All the same, he continued to look unwell, and could be seen sometimes examining himself in a large mirror that hung in the hotel foyer when he though no one else was looking. I found him doing this one evening on my way down to dinner.

'How are you?'

Mr Archer looked round rather furtively. He seemed absolutely wretched. Never at all healthy-looking, his face had the colour of putty. All the same, his reply was completely characteristic.

'I'm very well. A bit tired, but you have to expect that when you've spent a day or two in bed. It's what I always told my aunt when she complained of depression. I'm glad to say nothing of that kind ever affects me.'

'Pleased to hear it.'

'It's a funny thing, though, lying there on your own when you know you ought to be up and stirring. You have *premonitions*. For instance,' Mr Archer explained, 'I had this dream about a funeral. Big old-fashioned affair, like you see in picture books. Horses. A carriage and four. What do they call those black drapes that mourners used to wear?'

'Weepers.'

'That's right. Huge coffin inside the cart. The hearse, I suppose you'd call it. No idea whose it was, though. None at all. Do you ever get dreams like that?'

'No.'

'Now, my aunt, she was *always* having dreams like that.'

That night, browsing through Abbot Wulfric, I came upon an arresting paragraph. This described the character and habits of a thegn or associate of the East Anglian royal house named Eorpwald, in effect a tenant who paid tribute for his land and was obligated to provide military service when required: '... a very mournful, jealous knight. And if his liege should command that he doeth, or that he goeth, Eorpwald would wax great in his wrath, saying "I know more than the king knoweth" or "In that matter I have the advantage," so that his majesty did greatly wonder at the thegn's spirit ... His haunt was ever the chase: bear, wolf and beaver did he harry. And yet here his fancy knew no bounds, and he would beguile his majesty with tales of a hart that he had taken which dropt golden blood, or a wolf that spake to him, so that at length his majesty disbelieved his account, and put him from him ... ' There was no doubt about it. This, surely, in an earlier incarnation, was Mr Archer. The exaggerated humours. The wish to be affable contending with a hauteur that was manifestly unsuitable to his position in life. Above all, a complete inability to know where to stop. Eorpwald, I suspected, had spoiled a very good hand (royal favour, appreciative audience) simply by not knowing how far he could go. Mr Archer was the same. Or perhaps in both their cases, the line between fact and fancy had become irretrievably blurred. It was difficult to know.

Work on the book, which had slowed for a couple of days, mysteriously quickened its pace, only – just as mysteriously – to fall away again. Reporting this lack of progress to Mr MacCready over the telephone one afternoon, Frances came back shaking her head.

'He says there's no hurry. Apparently the editor's just been fired ...'

'What for?'

'Rationalisation or something. Eddie says he thinks they're going to be taken over again.'

'Will that make any difference? To the book, I mean.'

'Probably not. But you can never tell in publishing,' Frances said cheerfully. 'Ten to one they'll just forget about it until somebody finds the contract in a file in six months' time.'

Curiously, I refused to be dispirited about this. For some reason working out what I thought about my uncle and the pattern of our life together had taken on an independent existence, quite removed from its eventual appearance in print. Frances, though, seemed slightly depressed.

'I suppose I'd better stay for another fortnight.'

'If you want to.'

'If it comes to that,' Frances said, 'there isn't anywhere much else to go.'

Whether it was based on sympathy, appreciation of our joint predicament or the wish to make the best of a bad job, Frances' interest in me dated from about this time. She took to coming back from the town with little gifts: a bar of chocolate, a jar of home-made marmalade from the charity shop. These offerings were always handed over with utter nonchalance. Another time she said unexpectedly:

'You ought to do something about your room,'

'What in particular?'

'Make it look as if a human being lived in it. More welcoming.'

And so under her direction I bought a couple of pot plants which sat on the corners of the dressing table and a strip of yellow carpet that lay over the Caradon's regulation drugget like a rash.

'Much better,' Frances said, in the wake of these adjustments. 'It's never going to be cosy, but it might as well be habitable.'

She was especially interested in the anonymous letter.

'You mean to say you really have no idea who sent it?'

'Not a clue.'

'Nobody you can think of who'd know your address here?'

'No one.'

'So what are you going to do about it?'

'Nothing. If it was seriously meant I don't think whoever sent it would have stuck to letters, do you?'

'Maybe not.'

But there was something about the letter that vaguely impressed her. In some strange way, I could see that it gave our exchanges over the tape-recorder and the phone calls to Mr MacCready a seriousness that they hadn't previously possessed.

By degrees Frances became a fixture in the daily life of the Caradon. She could be seen writing her pieces of journalism at a table in the residents' lounge, or taking calls from the phone on the reception desk. At other times she stood in the foyer reading the notices on the green baize notice-boards, or hovered irresolutely in the doorway with her coat on, trying to judge if the weather was safe to go out in. For my own part, I never quite knew how far to involve myself in these extra-mural activities, had no idea whether she wanted to be taken out for a drink, invited to watch TV or otherwise entertained. The upshot was that we existed in a permanent state of silent semi-intimacy, forever bumping into each other on the main staircase or nodding across the foyer.

Mr Archer greeted the news that Frances would be staying at the Caradon for a further fortnight with huge enthusiasm. 'A highly intelligent young woman,' he told me once. 'It makes a nice change to have her about the place, sir, I can tell you.'

And so we became great people, and I met Helena.

I've some confused early impressions: a coil of blonde hair framed by a car window; strewn pairs of court shoes caught in sunlight; the entrance to her flat, one of those ornate mansion blocks in Earl's Court with a porter and double glass doors; effortful and unsatisfactory sex in a hotel along the Thames at – would it have been Goring?; a voice saying, 'And I really am leaving *this moment.*' I never did tie down that voice and work out just exactly what it was made up of: a hugely embellished upper-class drawl with flattened a's ('I wish you *hed*') and gross syllabic absurdities ('That would be *mah*vellous') but in the last resort idiosyncratic and unquantifiable.

Curiously enough, I have Kippax to thank for Helena. Towards the end, when the newspapers were getting to be a problem, he and my uncle grew obsessed with bringing in a high-class City PR outfit to represent us: 'raising our profile in the market-place' (Kippax); 'proper interviews *with pictures*' (my uncle). For some reason they settled on Egremont & Baker, where Helena worked, and consequently my first exact memory is of her sitting very primly half-way along a thronged elliptical table while Kippax prosed on about capital gains and my uncle ate boiled sweets surreptitiously out of a dirty paper bag. Three-quarters of the way through the meeting I stole a look at her jotter pad and it contained the words *Ravel, Rimsky-Korsakov, Rachmaninov* and *Rossini* ('Composers beginning with R, darling,' she explained subsequently, 'only I was so *bloody bored.*'). Later there was a dreadful lunch at Egremont & Baker's offices in Fetter Lane, culminating in an interview for the *Money Programme* somebody had managed to fix up for my uncle. Then an encounter at some Moorgate Place cocktail party. Then dinner. Then a whole range of absurd little meetings in pubs and theatre foyers in which neither side quite managed to articulate what it wanted from the other, climaxing in a series of guarded declarations and the weekend in Berkshire, whose other abiding memory is of Helena complaining about the sheets ('Nylon, darling, and none too freshly aired either.').

Already I'm conscious of somehow failing to do Helena justice, of making her too hard-boiled, which she wasn't, generic, *brittle*. I remember once making an inventory of her as she lay asleep on the sofa at Earl's Court, stark naked with one arm flung out behind her, and being quite unable to fathom the intensity of the attraction she had for me, how much greater the whole was than the sum of its parts. It was late on a Sunday afternoon, with long shadows already rising up the mulberry-coloured wallpaper and the answerphone blinking away in the corner of the room, but I sat there in a kind of trance, endlessly running my eye over her body – head, neck, breasts gathered up in shadow, pale thighs, feet – and then beginning again, like a big game hunter who can't quite believe in the existence of the felled tiger that lies in his path. Oddly it was the imperfections I liked best: a tiny cicatrix on the edge of her cheek, freckled shoulders, a tracery of shot veins on the back of one calf. She was – and how do I say this without exaggerating or diminishing the emphasis? – a big, tall, gay, smiling girl with one of those Lady Diana page-boy haircuts (it didn't suit her, but this was 1981 and everybody had them) who moved elegantly in and out of rooms, never seemed discomposed, and had an address book the size of a small bible.

Inevitably I compared her to Carole. There was something premeditated and cruel in the way I did this, even once writing down a list of their characteristics on opposite sides of a piece of paper, but I don't think it did me much harm. For one thing it taught me an immensely sobering lesson about my own shortcomings and reaffirmed to me how much I had been to blame. At the same time it taught me something valuable about Helena, which was that by the time you had reckoned up dim adjectives like *impulsive*, *generous*, and *spontaneous* you were left only with a boundless knowledge of environment and its possibilities. What separated Helena from Carole, it seemed to me, was really only a self-confidence born of superior information. I suppose what surprised me, in those early days, was how much she knew: the connections and inter-relationships of people in the City, ownership of land and property, the source of concert tickets. She was not a clever woman – I never saw her read a book, and any newspaper above the level of the *Daily Mail* was '*much* too brainy, darling' – it was merely that she possessed a stock of interior resources which she knew how to use.

I realise that in describing Helena in this way I shall sound like an anthropologist. All I can say is that I don't mean to, and yet she was so hugely unlike anybody I had ever met that I could only spend the moments in which I thought about her reflecting on this momentous divide. We used to talk about our respective childhoods with a show of reluctance that masked deep, implacable fascination.

'So tell me about a typical day at school.' (She'd been to some

163

extraordinary-sounding boarding establishment, staffed by vigilant nuns.) 'Describe it to me.'

'Oh, I don't know. Get up at six thirty. Breakfast at seven. See if Mummy and Daddy had written. Then lessons. Monday morning would have been Divinity. Domestic Science perhaps. But I don't know how you can be so interested, darling. Surely a school's a school, isn't it?'

I tried to tell her something about the educational arrangements prevailing in West Earlham in the early 1960s and she listened for a while.

'I'm sure it must have been absolutely ghastly. But you seem to have survived it pretty well.'

Or I would try to get her to talk about her home life.

'All absolutely conventional. I mean, I don't know if you know about those Surrey people, but take it from me, Mummy and Daddy are the last word in stuffiness.'

'But what did they do?'

'When we were little? Daddy was at Lloyd's then. Mummy had her charities. And, of course, there was the house to look after.'

There was a way in which these exchanges made her seem less shrewd than she actually was. All the same I sometimes suspected that the odd, complacent wonder with which she received the stories of my childhood really was no more than that, that for all her worldliness she couldn't believe that there were places like West Earlham and people like its inhabitants. 'After all,' she said to me once, and I never could work out if it was seriously meant, 'if you didn't like it you could always have moved somewhere else.'

I'm trying to be honest about Helena, to be honest, too, about the effect she had on me, and I know that even in the depths of my infatuation there were things about her I didn't like. She had scores of silly, aimless, talkative friends, all exactly like her save for the essential difference that I wasn't in love with them, who enveloped her waking life like a cloud of midgets: Henrietta, Sally-Ann, Lucinda – bold, confident women who communicated to each other what seemed to me the most inconsequential drivel. There were men too: short-haired ex-army officers working as trainee merchant bankers, hearty rugby-playing bores from Threadneedle Street and the Exchange with names like Gavin and Piers and Jonjo whom I disliked even more.

'You really mustn't mind Piers,' Helena said once at about this time. 'He really likes you, you know.'

'He's an idiot.'

'Actually, darling, he's *jolly bright*, and he went to Oxford. And you really shouldn't say those things about him.'

164

'And I suppose he'd have got the job at Lazards even if his father hadn't been on the board?'

'You don't understand, do you?' Helena said with unexpected seriousness. 'If you were the chairman of a merchant bank wouldn't you want your son to work there too? Come to that, if you had a milk round, wouldn't you want your son to inherit it? It's not our fault, darling, if we weren't born with your disadvantages.'

I note this exchange as a rare example of what I can only call class consciousness passing between us.

There was a dreadful irony about these preliminaries, as they coincided almost exactly with my attempts to separate myself legally from Carole. By this stage in the proceedings I hadn't set eyes on her for nearly three years, but queerly enough we hadn't altogether lost touch. Letters came occasionally from the old address at Redbridge: diffident but strangely rambling effusions retailing odd bits of Banstead gossip. By the time the legal hearings began I must have accumulated a dozen of these, and curious documents they were – not accusing, which perhaps I had a right to expect, but somehow doleful and resigned. They seemed to me wholly unbelievable, by which I don't mean that I thought Carole hadn't written them, or couldn't visualise the circumstances in which they'd been composed, merely that I couldn't believe in the world they conjured up: that fretful suburban world of traffic, gloomy evenings in the Essex twilight, Mrs Banstead's voice rising querulously from the sofa. It was all burnt up and gone, like so much firewood. In the end, most of the business was conducted by Mr Banstead, who began our transactions determined to hate me, but stopped when he saw that I was prepared to agree to practically anything, so that I saw Carole only once, when we were called in to sign papers. She seemed subdued but at the same time watchful and disappointed, as if she had come to make various dramatic statements but found them not worth saying. There was a moment towards the close out in the hallway of the solicitor's office – they were a biggish firm on the outskirts of Covent Garden who'd once advised my uncle on a property deal – when I found myself alone with Mr Banstead.

'Is she all right?'

He bristled up immediately, and I saw that all the credit I'd accumulated in our half-dozen meetings had vanished on the instant. 'No thanks to you if she is.'

'There's no need for that,' I told him. 'What does she do with herself?' For some reason we'd barely touched on this.

'Not a lot,' he said fiercely. 'She thought the world of you, you know.'

I was going to say something then, but I thought better of it. It was impossible to work out what Mr Banstead meant by this: whether he was being ironic, poking bitter fun, whether some extraordinary act of will had enjoined him to make the best of things, whether he seriously did believe that Carole had projected these emotions onto me. On balance, I concluded later, the truth was a combination of alternatives three and four: that whatever he might have thought of me privately Mr Banstead had decided that it was appropriate for his daughter to 'think the world of' whoever she married and once the fact was accomplished had managed to convince himself that this was the case. There could be no other explanation. All this occurred to me later. At the time I simply stared at him, there in the arid vestibule, conscious of Carole's bulky figure moving towards us through the double door, trying to think of something that would be simultaneously emollient, accurate, sparing of Carole's and his own feelings, but somehow conveying how dreadful and dispiriting life with his daughter had been.

'Perhaps she did.' It seemed absurdly inadequate to me, but Mr Banstead just shrugged, not unkindly, turned back to the doorway to gather Carole up as she passed (she glanced at me solemnly for a second) and shepherded her down into the street.

And so the Bansteads passed out of my life, perpetuated only in a photograph of the house at Redbridge with the two of us standing shyly in front of it, which I kept in a drawer somewhere, and the occasion on which, interviewed in one of the tabloids, Mr Banstead revealed that he'd always had the greatest respect for me personally but couldn't speak for the probity of my business affairs.

Meanwhile my uncle had contrived to find out, at an early stage, about Helena. At this point in his career – rather like Helena herself if it came to that – my uncle sat at the centre of a complex web of personal intelligence. Data of this kind enabled him to pull off what were to me astonishing strokes of connection and influence, but were, I suppose, only the way in which a resourceful businessman conducted his affairs. In the matter of Helena he was characteristically circumspect.

'Nice-lookin' girl I saw you with the other night, George. It was you, wasn't it? At Hennessy's or somewhere. So many blessed places I go to, I can't remember.'

'She's called Helena. Helena Charlesworth.'

'Know that name,' my uncle said. He was reading the business pages of the *Daily Telegraph*, held at an angle away from his face. 'Charlesworth. Tall feller sits on the board of Associated Life. Met him. Met him somewhere. Sure of it.'

I nodded.

'Now that, George,' my uncle went on, 'is a concern I'm interested in. More than interested. Next time you see that young lady, you ask her how her father is. Or bring her to dinner. That's right, bring her to dinner. Ask Greta and set a date.'

And so I took Helena to dinner at Sunningdale: an extraordinary meal eaten *al fresco* in gathering dusk on the terrace, now illuminated by strings of coloured lights, and Mortimer, my uncle's newly acquired butler, handing round ices on a tray and the smoke from my uncle's cigar rising evenly into the calm summer air. I wish I had a tape-recording of that night, something that could convey the full extent of my uncle's roguishness, his garrulity, Greta's ironising, Helena's laughter, my own silence. What did my uncle talk about? Racy City talk, mostly, anecdotes picked up on his travels around the Square Mile, society gossip that I marvelled he had access to.

'Nice girl that, George. Enjoyable evenin',' he said pompously when we met the next morning.

'You keep that up, d'y hear?'

I kept it up.

A great deal has been written about the zenith of my uncle's trajectory, the boom years and their traffic: my uncle's extravagance, the private jet he was supposed to have chartered for holidays in Tenerife and the Algarve, the lavish entertainments he sponsored, the matchless glamour of his ascent. You can read about it in the book Myerson the journalist wrote not long afterwards. 'A Fine Excess', 'The Shadows Lengthen', 'Countdown to Tragedy' – these are only the chapter titles: you can imagine the rest. For myself, I rather liked Myerson, whom my uncle took pains to cultivate at this time and whose account of his enormities, despite a certain tendency to exaggeration, was, I imagine, a more or less accurate *résumé* of what went on. So much of these last acts is in the public eye – how my uncle and Kippax tried to borrow the money to buy Associated Life, how they bargained with the regulatory authorities, the accumulations of capital piling up in Gibraltar and Grand Cayman – that the only gloss I can add is either corroborative or faintly mitigatory. And even this carries its cargo of doubt and speculation. My uncle's affairs had branched out now into all kinds of uncharted territory, much of which I neither penetrated nor understood. I never did comprehend the reason why we needed to buy Associated Life, although it was explained to me often enough, in the big room at Lothbury with my uncle's pudgy hand tapping at the sheaves of printed foolscap.

'It's capital we need, George. Capital and contacts. Get hold of Associated and we get both. Two hundred branch offices to bring in the business. Sell on the property portfolio when the market picks up.

Kippax has got it all planned. Respectable concern too. Two MPs and a baronet on the board. Just the thing to get the regulators off our backs and stop those blessed accountants asking questions.'

I don't know when exactly it was that my uncle began to lose my sympathy, but it must have been about this time. And again, I don't quite know what precipitated it. But I was aware that I thought he was behaving foolishly, and that sooner or later this foolishness would be flung back in his face. He gave silly, careless interviews full of little bits of indiscretion. He embarked on grandiloquent and unrealisable schemes: the Chell Award for Young Entrepreneurs, which ran for a year and was eventually bestowed on a hairdresser's shop in Brixton; a plan for bigger, purpose-built offices on a site in Docklands. He had vainglorious arguments with a newspaper proprietor that led to a series of incendiary exposures of the state of Chell Holdings and its finances. The offices at Lothbury had lost their air of quiet, sober efficiency and became a kind of caravanserai of human traffic. Those offices at Lothbury! Someone should have painted them towards the end – some modern-day Frith, I mean, not an interior decorator. Double doors leading down into the street, before which you could be pretty sure of finding a couple of mysterious old men in mackintoshes, a harassed commissionaire, a vestibule containing perhaps two dozen persons connected in one way or another with Chell Holdings: foreign investors talking in unknown mid-European languages; messenger boys from the City chatting together as they loafed by the marble pillars; a corporate finance team from one of the big accountancy practices seated proudly along a bench; fat, pompous men in pinstripes, with attaché cases under their arms, with appointments; nondescript characters in shabby serge suits without; clerks issuing all the while from interior rooms with messages for the receptionists, rebukes for the serge suits or merely to stand by the desk staring complacently at the throng. And my uncle arriving suddenly in the doorway, very red-faced and out of breath, with perhaps an attendant behind him or a factotum carrying a case of files, to be assailed on all sides by looks, salutations, even importunate figures clutching at his sleeve, before the commissionaire bore him away to his sanctum and the series of private audiences that followed. I cornered him in there once, on a morning when I'd been made furious by an interview he'd granted to the *Evening Standard*, thereby forcing an emissary from the Bank of England to kick his heels for twenty minutes on the bench outside. He was smoking a cigar and drinking a glass of tonic water in which a couple of dyspepsia pills clinked and fizzed.

'Hell of a stomach I've got this morning, George,' he said mildly as I strode in. 'Can't think what's caused it.'

'Have you seen this?' I demanded, throwing the paper down on his desk, where it came to rest amongst a pile of company prospectuses, several chocolate wrappers and a gilded invitation to drink cocktails with the Worshipful Company of Dyers.

'Read it first thing,' he nodded. 'Didn't seem too bad to me.'

'It's a disgrace,' I told him. 'Makes you look an idiot. And the firm look as if it doesn't know what to do with its money.'

'Now you look here, George ... '

'Just look at it. Did you really take him to Claridges? And give him oysters?'

'His idea, George,' my uncle wailed piteously. 'You know what those journalists are like.'

'Never mind that. All this business about a new building in Docklands. You know we can't afford it. And the two hundred extra staff. Where are they coming from?'

'Prospects, George. I was talking about prospects.'

'You're going round the City looking for money. You've got a corporate finance team from Price Waterhouse sitting out there *this minute* waiting to talk to you about venture capital. What do you think they're going to make of this?'

I was ready to carry on for another five minutes, but by this time my uncle had stopped trying to answer and simply sat staring rather vacantly in front of him. The cigar smouldered away against the invitation from the Worshipful Company of Dyers.

'I'm tired, George,' he said.

'Is that all?'

He blinked once or twice in a vague way. 'Well, that's the truth of it. I'm tired, George, and ... and I don't like you going *on* at me.'

'And the political stuff? The things about the unions and the benefit cheats. How do you think that's going to go down?'

'Twist things,' he went on. 'Twist things, those journalists. Just to make you look stupid ... You know how it is, George.'

There was an urgent knocking at the door then, and the voice of a factotum murmuring something about the Bank of England and kept waiting, and an ominous rattling of cutlery and tea trays, so I got up and left. That evening, though, I drove down to Sunningdale – he was dining in the City, I'd made sure of that – determined to see Greta. It was nearly dark when I arrived. Devoid of my uncle's presence, the big house took on an odd, sepulchral quality. There was a light burning in the courtyard but the rest of the place was plunged in darkness. In the wide hallway I fell over a henge of parcels, all propped up on their ends like standing stones. Further inside, pale half-light fell over the furniture in the giant

169

reception rooms and glowed off the great square mirrors. There were white invitation cards neatly drawn up across the mantelpiece and I took a look at them: *The chairman and directors request ... Lord and Lady FitzMaurice at home ... Sir Robin Charlesworth ...* Sir Robin Charlesworth was Helena's father. Higher up the wall numberless representations of my uncle stared out of their gilt frames: dazed and unhappy in a morning coat and striped trousers on a green lawn somewhere; leaning conspicuously over the rail of somebody's yacht; shrewd and interested in the Ascot paddock; at his desk in Lothbury, looking up sharply over the half-moons of his spectacles. I prowled on towards the back of the house, peering through doorways, negotiating the long track of bristling carpet. I found Greta in the kitchen, reading the evening paper by lamplight. She stared up vaguely as I came in.

'I knew it was you,' she said. 'Saw your car in the drive. Have a drink?'

Looking at Greta in the arc of light, yellow hair piled up on top of her head like candyfloss, I wondered how old she was. Fifty? Fifty-five? There were huge fissures down the side of her cheeks. She moved off purposefully to the cupboards and returned with a bottle of gin.

'Thought you'd be in the City still. At that dinner at wherever it is.'

'No one asked me.'

'I expect you could have gone if you'd wanted. Isn't that right?'

It occurred to me that Greta had perhaps had more than a little to drink. There was no visible evidence of this – no glasses, paraphernalia or physical manifestations – merely an odd sense of increased volubility.

'What do you do in the evenings, Greta? I mean, when Uncle Ted isn't here?'

'What do I do most evenings, you mean?' She smiled, but not fiercely. 'Oh, I look after myself, George. Mrs Cann the housekeeper lives in, you know, though she's off tonight visiting her sister, and we generally have supper together. And there's always the TV, only I don't really like it so much as most people. Sometimes I think I'll just sit down and write my memoirs.'

'What would you put in them?'

'Oh, you'd be surprised, George. Not things about *him*, perhaps. I had a life before that, you know. A good long one.'

'There was no doubt about it. Greta was emphatically drunk. I wondered how often she did this, and whether the information about Mrs Cann was accurate.

'Did you see those parcels in the hall?' she went on hastily. 'Expect you're wondering what they're for.'

'No idea.'

'Garden chairs. Seventy garden chairs. His idea. "Ought to have a

170

party in the summer, Greta," he says the other day. "People sitting out on the lawn and such." I told him there's dozens of chairs in the old summer house, but he won't listen. Goes off to Harrods the next morning and orders them.'

'You could send them back.'

'I could, couldn't I? I don't suppose he'd notice. It's in the head one minute and out of it the next with him.'

'How is he, do you think?'

Greta's features relaxed immediately. 'Says he's tired. Always. And he is tired. You should see him sometimes when he comes back here after one of those dinners. Face as white as chalk. But he doesn't sleep, not much. And then he worries all the time.'

'What about?'

'Business, stupid. He gets in a terrible state about Kippax and whether he'll leave the firm. Time last year when Kippax went on holiday, he was dreadful. Kept on sending telemessages to his hotel and got a car to fetch him at the airport. Never seen him so bad.

'I don't like that Kippax,' Greta went on. 'Don't know why, and I don't like to speak ill of anyone, but I just don't like him.'

After this she would say nothing more about my uncle's affairs: in fact there was a faint impression hanging in the air that she had said too much and regretted it. We went through into one of the smaller rooms off the big dining chamber, where there was a piano and sheet music lay scattered about on the floor.

'Been learning to play,' Greta said, with an odd, dreadful humility. 'Gives me something to do in the evenings. Afternoons too.'

I picked up one of the books. It was called *Mozart in Easy Steps*.

Half an hour later, turning into the asphalt drive that led to the main road, I saw headlights moving towards me. Pulled into the verge, I sat and watched a chauffeur-driven Jaguar glide by. My uncle sat in the back, face dropped into the shadow, presumably asleep. By rights I should have turned and followed the car back to the house. Instead I moved off again through the inky Berkshire night.

Q: What about Greta?

A: As I think I've tried to convey, Greta wasn't something my uncle talked about. As to how they met, your guess is as good as mine. It's perfectly possible that he simply picked her up in the street.

Q: Implying that ...

A: Implying nothing. Not the least shred of evidence. It was just that Greta seemed to know a great deal about a certain kind of life in which streetwalking formed a definite part. I remember once being with her in some quite respectable part of London – if not Belgravia then somewhere like Pimlico – when a modestly dressed but somehow conspicuous woman stalked past, and Greta said something like 'Cold day for it,' and I think I was rather startled that she'd been able to identify the woman as a tart. I don't think this was a reflection of her own previous life. But she'd certainly, I should say, worked behind a bar for a long time. Or maybe in a big hotel. Something like that.

Q: And she got on with your uncle?

A: Oh, invariably. They were like an old married couple. Except when she thought he was 'lording it' – that was her expression. Or perhaps that just made them more of an old married couple. I don't know. Actually Greta was kept very much in the background – never came out with him in public and so on. I don't think this was deliberate policy on my uncle's part: I think Greta preferred it like that. She had a kind of horror of being conspicuous, looked-at. It was a pity in many ways, because she would have been – was, when she was there – a good restraining influence.

Q: You make it sound as if your uncle badly needed a restraining influence.

A: Do I? Well, he did. Not always. Just occasionally. Greta was very good at that: don't have the extra glass; put your chequebook away; come home – that sort of thing.

Q: Do you think he was faithful to her?

A: Almost certainly. Yes, undoubtedly. If experience has taught me one thing it's that pronouncements on other people's emotional lives are completely valueless, but in so far as I can judge, yes.

Q: There was a certain amount of newspaper gossip ...

172

A: I'd never seen one of the girls who made the allegations, literally never heard of her. Also, the locations were – well, let's just say implausible. The other one was a secretary who got fired for petty theft, which I think answers your question.

Q: Nothing else?

A: My uncle had old-fashioned attitudes about women. Unreconstructed. I mean, he used to talk about 'bints' and 'bits of stuff' and 'hot tomaters'. Quite unselfconsciously. And he always had a dinner party list.

Q: Which was?

A: Oh, an elaborate fantasy of a dinner party at which he would be the only male guest, surrounded by the kind of women he found attractive. In the early days this meant people like Julie Andrews or Joanna Lumley. A bit later it extended to Mrs Thatcher and Joan Collins. But it was quite innocent. I mean, there was no harm in my uncle about women, certainly none that I could see. It was all done on a kind of music hall level. You know, jokes about newly married couples, and lodgers.

Two more messages came that week, both with typewritten addresses and W1 postmarks, both constructed from letters cut out of the *Daily Telegraph*. The first simply said JUSTICE WILL BE DONE. The second, a shade more elaborate, ran VICTIMS OF CHELL UNITE TO FIGHT.

'Doesn't this worry you?' Frances asked.

'A bit. Not very much.'

'You ought to try and find out who's doing it.'

'It could be anyone.'

'How many people in London know your address?'

I thought about this for a while. Kippax maybe. One or two of the Lothbury hangers-on. It was difficult to think of anyone else.

Mr Archer, I noticed, had developed an interest in these communications. He brought the third one to me on a plate – an archaic flourish that made him resemble a Victorian footman.

'Another letter, sir.'

'Thank you.'

'From London.'

'The correct postcode too.' (Inaccurate postcodes were one of Mr Archer's favourite grouses.)

'Wonders never cease.'

Mr Archer's expression, as I said this, was quite extraordinary – furtive, flushed and pop-eyed. Then, without warning, the light bulb above our heads – we were standing in the residents' lounge at the time – fizzed and went dead.

For some reason the effect on Mr Archer was electric. He went chalk-white and dropped the plate onto the floor, where it promptly cracked into several pieces.

'Are you OK?'

'You'll have to excuse me, sir.' With an abasing gesture, Mr Archer dropped to one knee and began to pick up the fragments. 'My nerves are something awful this morning. It could almost have been Mad Mary back to haunt us.'

'I hope not.'

'You've dropped your letter too, sir.'

174

'So I have. Thanks.'

I left him kneeling on the carpet, sweeping up the pieces of china with a wholly unnecessary fervour.

If I remember that weekend in Wiltshire so vividly, which began underneath the clock at Paddington on a Friday evening in July after a day spent in the board rooms of Threadneedle Street, it's because my uncle, too, was there. At this distance I don't properly recall what compulsion it was that forced him to descend on the big, manorial house a mile out of Westbury, where a driver delivered him with two suitcases and a parcel of wine late on the Friday night. I remember Helena explaining to me, with her habitual precision, the exact connections that drew him to our host and our host's acquaintance, but I was more interested by the spectacle of him, aloof and comfortable, in an armchair at the back of the drawing-room, or taking solitary rambles among the rose bushes. My uncle had a way of imposing his personality on a house, of being found in remote rooms where guests seldom penetrated, rooting through bookshelves, taking baths at odd times of the night. For a day or so our paths scarcely crossed, although I had half-a-dozen opportunities of watching him at a distance: playing croquet with fantastic ineptness on the lawn, reading the *Daily Mirror* in a chair after lunch, sitting up late with a couple of cronies (I remember coming into the room unobserved and seeing their three bald heads glinting together under the light). But on the Sunday morning he sought me out.

'Nice sort of place, George,' he said offhandedly as we moved towards one another in the garden.

'I like it. Helena likes it.'

'Often thought about it,' my uncle ventured. There was a weak sun shining over the chimney pots, and the eaves gleamed under the Wiltshire sky, and he shaded his eyes with his hand as he stared up vaguely towards the rooftops. 'But you'd miss London. Think about it in winter, too, with the roads frozen and everybody stuck waiting for a train.'

'I didn't know you were coming.'

'Neither did I. Last minute thing. Thought I'd talk about it here instead of on Monday morning.'

'Important then?'

My uncle looked mournful. 'There's something up, George. Don't quite know what it is, but there's something up. They're ganging up on

176

me, George. Out of *spite*. Associated Life. And some others. All quite above board, you know, but … ganging up.' He paused impressively. 'There's a question goin' to be asked in the House on Tuesday.'

'Who by?'

'Some Labour chap. Always a Labour chap asks questions like that. Ability to meet payments. Government licence. That kind of thing.'

'What does Kippax say?'

'Kippax? Kippax?' My uncle smacked his hand suddenly against his rib-cage. 'Kippax ought to take a holiday. Kippax is getting nervous. Starts seeing trouble when there isn't any. That's what I think of Kippax.'

We took another turn round the grass, my uncle blowing stertoriously as he came up to the gentle incline before the croquet lawn. There was something worrying him, I saw, that had nothing to do with people ganging up on him or Labour chaps in the House. Eventually he said:

'Come a long way, haven't we, George?'

'A very long way.'

'Where do you think it'll end?'

'I don't know.' I really didn't know, had no idea where my uncle's frantic, inexpressible ambitions might take him. 'Buckingham Palace. The Guildhall. Chairman of a building society. Who's to say?'

My uncle listened to this with absolute seriousness. 'Some of those chaps,' he went on – and I suppose he was referring to the kind of people who were knighted, became Lord Mayors of London, or sat on the boards of building societies – 'had to struggle a bit in their time. Not just up, I mean. Envy. People out to get them.'

'Bound to have.'

'That's right,' he said. 'Well, I'm not going to give up. They'll see.'

The lawn was becoming crowded now, with old gentlemen in striped jackets and red and yellow ties ('MCC,' my uncle had intimated proudly when he first saw these decorations) and freckled elderly ladies in sun-hats, and one of the cronies of the previous night loomed up and swept him away. An hour later I asked Helena:

'What's happening about the Associated Life deal?'

'I don't know. Daddy did say something the other day. Something about the money not being there.'

I related the conversation in the garden.

'I really don't know anything about it.'

'Nothing?'

'Nothing at all.'

At lunchtime my uncle had cheered up. He sat at the far end of the table and ate a Melton pie with gusto. 'Extraordinary good idea,' he was heard to say, 'putting all those things in it.' But there was a phone call

177

early in the afternoon, and by tea-time the Jaguar had come and gone and only the wine-parcel – my uncle's present to his host – lay on the broad windowsill next to the door as a reminder of his visit.

I think it was during that weekend that I first became aware of the peculiarity of my position in the world to which my uncle had introduced me. It was my first experience of living in, as opposed to watching or speculating on, an exclusive social group, and I don't think I much liked it. In fact my strongest impression is of a kind of confidence – of red-faced men sitting round a table laughing, cigars winking through the twilight, casual orders communicated to domestics – which I could never hope to reproduce. I don't want to emphasise this sense of apprehension, for I know that I was perfectly capable of holding my own with Helena and anyone else to whom I happened to be introduced, simply to say that I was always aware of it, and that it was constantly with me. At the same time, if I try to isolate the things that separated me from that world I can only come up with a kind of emphasis, a sort of self-asserting boosterism that disturbed me because I couldn't see its use. They were very kind, those people, but I was an attendant on the scene in which they moved and deliberated, and I knew there were great areas of their world that I could never hope to penetrate or understand, invisible doors and frontier gates that would always hold me back. Perhaps in the end it was collective memory that did this, the perpetual invocation of 'Do you remember?' and 'the time when', a bruising solidarity of schools and shared upbringings. I tried explaining this to Helena, without success.

'The odd thing,' I told her, 'is how well you all seem to know each other. I mean, right back to when you were children. The time Jonjo fell off the pony. When Hermione had to wear braces and what the other girls said.'

'It all seems very normal to me. You make friends, and they stay your friends. I know you grew up in a kind of leper colony somewhere in East Anglia.'

'You're missing the point. You all know *about* each other. Where you went to school. What your fathers do. You may live a hundred miles away from each other, but you're a real community. Shared assumptions. Shared ideals.'

'I dare say it's the same on any council estate.'

I have a feeling that Helena thought there was something rather regrettable about this curiosity, and wondered whether she ought to conciliate it. She said once:

'I think you have the wrong idea about people like me. Like Daddy. And the rest of them. You think, I don't know, some kind of oligarchy that runs everything and *decides* everything. But it's not like that at all.'

'You mean, if it was then I wouldn't be here?'

'Oh, I wouldn't put it quite like that. But I can see you bristling up every time you sit down to eat a meal. In case there's more than one fork and you don't know which comes first. Your uncle doesn't worry about that. He just gets on with whatever he's doing. You see, it's just how people behave, what they do. I mean, you must have had rituals of some kind when you lived with your mother?'

'I remember she always screamed if I put a milk bottle on the table instead of pouring the milk into a jug.'

'There you are … Would she have approved of me?'

It was a good question: would she have approved of Helena? For that matter, would she have approved of anyone? For a moment I imagined my mother appraising Helena's knee-length skirt, bobbed hair, heavy earrings.

'I expect,' Helena went on, 'she'd have thought I was a corrupting influence on her darling boy.'

In fact it was doubtful that my mother had ever thought of any relationship in these terms. I remembered her once disparaging the idea, apropos a piece of gossip conveyed to her by Mrs Buddery, that you could 'ever know what made some people like other people.'

'What about your uncle? Did she approve of him?'

Questions of this kind were unanswerable. 'Not really. At least, I don't think so.'

'Well, that surprises me,' Helena said. 'I think he's a sweet old man.'

Some highlights from Helena's vocabulary:

This chappie – any unknown man of working-class origin

Wet – variety of definitions, most consistently ineffectual but also obtuse or even ignorant ('It's very wet of you not to know.')

Civilised – expensive

Nice – all-purpose commendatory adjective, used ironically in descriptions of female acquaintances ('She's very *nice*, don't you think?')

Presentable – expensive

Oomski – dirt, mud, surface of a ploughed field, etc.

ETs – Essex tarts (of secretaries)

Clever – commendatory when used of clothing or other inanimate objects ('That's a clever tie/map, etc.'), deadly insult when applied to people ('They say Julian's very clever.')

SHAH – So Hurt and Humiliated (of minor inconvenience)

Solid – clever (of a weekly magazine, 'Is it solid, darling?')

Expensive – ostentatious, in poor taste ('You seem to be wearing a very expensive suit.')

What else is there to say about Helena? I met her parents once or twice, at weekends in a grim old house in Gloucestershire. They were polite, brittle, distant people whose affectation it was never to have heard of the most innocuous manifestations of popular culture. This pretence was elevated to such an awful level as to prohibit nearly any conversation. They even did it with Helena, I noticed. 'Is he an actor?' 'I'm afraid we don't read the *Daily* –.' 'Is that something on the television?' They had a TV set in the corner, neatly fenced off by a kind of embroidered screen, on which Lady Charlesworth occasionally watched nature programmes and afternoon racing, and pictures of horses lay all over the place: photographs in heavy gilt frames athwart mantelpieces and pianos, a great painting of a stallion in oils that hung over the fireplace. On Sunday afternoons we put on waxed jackets and Wellingtons and tramped laboriously around the country back roads or over the low Gloucester-shire hills, heads bowed against the wind. I don't know what the Charlesworths thought about it all, but I was conscious of them watching me: I remember once vaulting over a stile on whose further side the three of them clustered in an intent, staring huddle. In Gloucestershire Helena became an exaggerated and at the same time slightly ghostly version of her London self, trading gossip with her mother in an impenetrable shorthand. 'But didn't she marry old Newbridge in the end, post-Harry I mean?' 'Jonty had to sell Heveningham for DDs' (DD stood for 'death duties', I found out). My memories of this time are woefully thin and partial: Helena curled up beside her mother on the sofa, flicking through an illustrated magazine, in riding gear once on the gravel forecourt, exclaiming over the paperboard invitations on the mantelpiece.

But it was all falling away by now, all disappearing into some black hole from which I could never extricate it or check its descent. My uncle was fuddled by lunchtime these days, flushed and voluble, ready for a chat – a good old chat – give Kippax the slip – have something sent in on a tray hay? – anxious to talk – the weather in the Mediterranean – thinkin' of going there for a bit – the old days in Norwich, my mother, anything except the state of his business affairs. Kippax begins to fade a little from the picture now. No doubt he was still there, but I don't remember him. In the photographs which remain from that time it's always my uncle who dominates: shaking hands with a first division football side whose kit someone had induced him to sponsor; addressing a fringe meeting at the Conservative Party Conference; silk-hatted and stripe-trousered in the Ascot enclosure. In each of these representations he looks the same: petulant, preoccupied, defensive. There was a profile of him in the *Sunday Times* around this period that greatly upset him: not, I think, because it cast any doubt upon his business dealings, but because it depicted him as dull and stupid ('even his intimates recognise that Chell has no social sparkle ... '). I arrived at Lothbury on the Monday morning to find him deep in it, the cigar in his hand dangling two inches of ash.

'What is it about these fellers?' he asked. 'Now, if I'd written a book or something, that this chap didn't like, and he thought I was a fool for writing it, then I could understand. But why say I'm stupid? Why say I don't fit my clothes? Not as if I ever *met* the chap.'

'It's not worth bothering about,' I told him. 'Forget it. Burn it.'

'But you don't understand, George,' said my uncle slowly. 'It *is* worth bothering about. Never was anything more worth bothering about. Here I am, respected businessman, worked my way up, created employment – don't forget that, George, given people jobs – and now I'm to be abused for wearing a decent suit and liking a drink. It's not good enough.'

The upshot of this was an injurious episode in which, in the vicinity of a Press Association photographer, my uncle attempted to hit a journalist being presented to him by the President of the Institute of Chartered Accountants in England and Wales at a reception held at the Institute's premises in Moorgate Place. The picture – my uncle's wattled face, glasses slipping down the bridge of his nose, fist flapping weakly before him – made most of the next day's papers. There was talk of a court action, but my uncle's lawyers settled it behind his back.

One other incident from this time sticks in my head. It was late on a Friday afternoon, so late that the Lothbury receptionist had gone home, when the phone rang in the outer office. Picking it up I heard a woman's voice in which alarm, vexation and curiosity were uncomfortably blended.

'I need to speak to George Chell.'

'This is him.'

'Name of Edward Chell mean anything to you?'

'Uncle.'

'Thank fuck for that. You'd better come and get him then.'

'Where?'

With extreme gracelessness, as if it was exceptionally stupid of me not to know, she named an address in south-west London. I took a taxi through the dense, early evening traffic to a drab little street on the south side of Clapham Common where estate agents' boards jostled each other for space on the frontages of a cramped Victorian terrace. Half-way along, a woman standing in a doorway flagged us down. I left the taxi idling at the kerb.

Inside the house was a small hallway where coats hung on a row of stark metal hooks. Camphor pervaded the air. The woman stood at the foot of the stairs, passing one hand aggressively through a thatch of bleached yellow hair. She would have been about forty.

'Well, I'm fucking glad you got here,' she said. 'At least I'll say that.'

It was difficult to know how to respond to this, where to begin. The first task, obviously, was to establish my uncle's whereabouts. The woman looked me up and down once or twice, decided I was harmless, and half turned on the stair.

'Up here.'

At the top of the stairs the landing widened out into three or four bedrooms with their doors ajar. Each contained no furniture other than a bed, a chair and a side table. Outside the furthest was another chair on which lay a ball of wool, stabbed through with two knitting needles, and a half-finished pullover.

'Go *on*,' the woman said.

I have a fleeting memory of white-washed surrounds, a window looking out over the south London rooftops, a picture of a lachrymose Victorian child in a sailor suit fixed to the wall. My uncle lay on the bed, fully clothed, his arms drawn up over his chest, wallet and keys neatly stacked on the bedside cabinet. He was snoring loudly.

'Is he all right?'

Having got me into the house, and to a certain extent established that I was prepared to accept responsibility, the woman seemed slightly mollified. At any rate she lit a cigarette, leaned back against the door frame and looked at me thoughtfully.

'I don't know. He'd only just got here – been here five minutes maybe – when he says he's tired, can he have a bit of a rest? That was three, four hours ago. I got your number out of his diary.'

I saw immediately that there was no point in asking what my uncle was doing here, the identity of the woman or the nature of the premises: in any case all three answers were perfectly clear. The important thing was to remove him as quickly as possible.

'Have you tried waking him up?'

'A bit. He just goes back to sleep.'

There was a bathroom back along the corridor. Filling a tooth-mug with water, I threw it in his face. My uncle continued to snore. After a second application he opened his eyes. Of all the memories I have of my uncle, I remember particularly that look: resigned, hangdog, instantly aware of the position in which he found himself.

182

'I've been asleep, George,' he said, starting up from the pillow.

'Should think you fucking well have,' said the woman, not unkindly. 'Hours and hours.'

'Are you all right?'

'Tired,' said my uncle indistinctly. 'Heavy night. Lot on my mind. Glad to see you though, George.' I helped him down from the bed and he rested for a moment in my embrace, breathing deeply.

'George,' he whispered, 'I got to go to the *toilet*.'

'Are you sure you're all right?'

I watched him lumber off along the corridor. Some time later there was a sound of running water. Back in the bedroom the woman was smoothing down the disordered bedspread, cigarette twisted at an angle so that the smoke avoided her eyes.

'Does he often come here?'

The woman considered this with her head on one side, left hand pummelling the pillow. 'Now and again. Twice a month maybe. You his son?'

'Nephew.'

'Never said anything about a nephew.'

Any further revelations were silenced by the sound of footsteps proceeding back along the corridor, a door slamming. My uncle appeared in the doorway, breathing hard.

'I'm not feeling too good, George.'

'You want an aspirin, Ted. That's what you want,' said the woman, with faint animation. 'To pick you up. Put you on your feet.'

'I b'lieve you're right, Jennifer. I think that's what I do want.'

Watching from the doorway, I found these exchanges – the sudden use of Christian names, air of complicity, the hint of some fairly long-standing relationship – wholly sinister. What had he done in this room, I wondered, what had been said, and for how many years? If it came to that, what business was it of mine? Jennifer produced a couple of aspirin out of a packet concealed in the bedside cabinet, and my uncle crunched them up, looking round rather timidly but with a perceptible renewal of confidence.

'There any drink in the house?'

'Not that *you'd* want. Half a bottle of gin and some lager maybe.'

'Not gin,' my uncle demurred. 'Not that blessed rotgut. All right, George.' He stared at me for the first time since his reappearance. 'Better get off, I suppose.'

'You get an early night,' Jennifer instructed, almost affably. She was lighting a second cigarette off the stub of the first. 'No staying out now.'

Fetched up in the tiny hallway, briefcase clutched against his midriff, eyes red and blinking, he made an attempt at jauntiness, lifted his feet once or twice in an exaggerated military step, winked at me over his shoulder as Jennifer pulled open the door. As we trailed off towards the taxi, she stood watching us: expressionless, self-absorbed, mildly amused perhaps. Then the door slammed shut.

'I'm sorry, George,' my uncle said, as soon as we were seated in the cab. 'Truly sorry.'

'It doesn't matter.'

'Doesn't matter! All very well saying that,' my uncle went on. 'Doesn't help though. Can't think what came over me. Ought to have spared you that at least. And Jenny ringing you up like that! Can't think what got into her.'

'She thought you were ill. You wouldn't wake up.'

'I was tired, George.' His voice rose to a high, spiritless whine. 'You don't know what it's like. Being badgered from morning to night. Kippax always interferin'. Newspapers. I can't stand it, George, and I won't.'

'Where's the taxi to go?'

'Anywhere. The office. Sunningdale. No, better make it the office. I got an evening meeting.'

'You ought to go home.'

'Don't get *on* at me, George,' he said in exasperation. It was what the West Earlham women, leaning at gateposts, shouted at their husbands. But when I directed the driver to Sunningdale he raised no objection. By the time we reached outer London, where mid-evening sun drenched the lines of traffic queuing for the motorway, he was asleep again. For the rest of his life my uncle never referred to my rescue of him from the Clapham terrace, but I don't think he ever forgot it. I believe he thought that I never really forgave him for it. In some ways I believe he was right.

Q: When did you first think your uncle might be doing something illegal?

A: I don't know. I suppose when I found out about the gilts market, and the kind of returns it was capable of producing.

Q: Not before?

A (*giving the impression of having rehearsed the words*): I had a boundless confidence in my uncle. Limitless. When I'd first known him he'd been – well, I suppose the word is a very *humble* figure, living in very unassuming circumstances. And now ... he'd managed to reinvent himself in what was, to me, a startling way. He'd acquired this expertise, which I was greatly in awe of.

Q: But you are a qualified accountant. It can't have taken very long for this *expertise* to seem dubious.

A: It took long enough. For one thing, I wasn't working on the purely financial side, at any rate not on a daily basis. And then gilts accounting is extraordinarily complex – multiple transactions, staggered interest rates, floating commission to intermediaries. It's not really comprehensible, even to the financially literate.

Q: So when did you begin to suspect that something was wrong?

A: Not until late on. Very late on. And largely as a result of the allegations. That was when I sat down with the books – in so far as one could sit down with the books in a business like Chell Holdings – and did some serious investigation. But no, if I thought about it I suppose I'd have to say that I always had one or two doubts.

Q: Why?

A: Because I couldn't see how we could pay the interest rates we advertised and still make a profit. For example, a security might pay a thirteen per cent annual rate of interest. Now, we were offering thirteen per cent – sometimes even fourteen – to our investors. That would have meant paying no commission to our intermediaries – the people who recommended clients to us – and taking no profit ourselves. Yet we were declaring profits, *and* buying stakes in other companies. Corporate raiding. All that kind of thing.

Q: Did you express these anxieties to your uncle?

185

A: In the end. Up to a point. It was very difficult to pin him down. Essentially his position was that if we were paying the advertised rate of interest to our investors then our legal obligations were being met.

Q: But in fact you were paying the interest out of capital held on clients' behalf. Rather than investing that capital?

A: Absolutely. And effectively risking much of it in speculative stock market ventures. Robbing Peter to pay Paul.

Q: And what was your reaction when these facts were finally known to you?

A (*a long pause*): I don't know. A mixture of things. As I say, it was very late in the day. There was a definite sense that things were slipping away from us, that we'd lost whatever limited scope we had to amend matters, to set them to rights. But then again, I had boundless confidence in my uncle's abilities. Even at the end I thought he'd find some way out of the situation, that he'd manage to carry it off. I think a lot of other people in the financial community thought this too.

Q: Even though it was all illegal?

A: Even despite that.

Spring came slowly to these bleak hinterlands caught between the sea and the fields of sedge. In the afternoons fog rolled up from the marshlands and hung low over the town, so that a journey from the Caradon to the esplanade became a laborious trawl through twists of dense, unyielding vapour. A dead whale, washed up on the shore, lay and rotted there until the local fire brigade came and dragged away the remnant of its carcass with nets. Sitting in the residents' lounge in fading light as the mist rose outside the window, Mr Archer sometimes talked in a vague way of his troubled finances. He said:

'I'm a disappointed man, and I don't mind admitting it. All down to money of course. You wouldn't believe it, sir, the things that have gone wrong with me on account of money.'

'What kind of things?' I thought for a moment of all the ways in which money could make things go wrong. 'Legacies you expected not arriving? Losses on the stockmarket?'

Mr Archer shrugged. 'I sometimes think, sir,' he said, 'that it was all *fated*. Even when I was a child, you understand. I was always getting into trouble about money. I can remember my father telling me, in fact: "Money will be your undoing." I would have been ten or eleven at the time.'

'But how has money disappointed you?'

At these times Mr Archer sat at the head of the larger table, resting his hands on a small pile of items that he liked to carry with him around the hotel. They included a copy of that morning's *Daily Telegraph*, a pair of scissors, various pens and pencils. Moving these backwards and forwards with the tips of his fingers, he went on:

'Oh, it was all a long time ago. And it wasn't so much to do with the money itself. More the advice I was given.'

'Somebody gave you bad advice about money?'

'In a manner of speaking.'

More than this Mr Archer wouldn't say. But it was clear from the number of times he referred to the subject that money remained one of his deeper grievances.

Hurrying back to the hotel early one evening after a walk across the common, I came across Frances sitting on a chair in the foyer. There was no one else about: Mr Archer had gone to Lowestoft for the day. Seeing me at the door, she said unexpectedly:

'Are you doing anything tonight?'

'Not specially.'

'You can take me out to dinner if you like.'

'Now?'

'Half an hour. I'll meet you here.'

Standing in the reception area half an hour later, I wondered what Frances would wear for an evening meal outside the Caradon. It would be interesting to see if there were any variation on her usual dress of pullover and jeans. Seven o'clock came. I read the notices on the green baize notice-board, none of which had changed in the past fortnight. At ten past Mr Archer stalked in, swathed in an enormous greatcoat, the points of his ears sticking out from under the brim of a fedora hat. He looked rather wildly around for a second, saw me and said:

'As cold as charity out there, sir.'

'That's right.'

'I could drink a pint of brandy, I don't mind telling you.'

As Mr Archer disappeared into his office behind the reception desk, I saw Frances coming down the stairs. She had chosen a compromise between her usual get-up and its opposite. In fact she was wearing a kind of long skirt, so long that it reached nearly to her ankles, and a shapeless top.

'Where are we going then?' she asked briskly.

'Where would you like?'

Prospective diners-out in Eastwold between the months of October and May had a limited choice. Essentially it consisted of the rudimentary pub fare of the Nelson, the fish-and-chip shop or a restaurant staffed by harassed middle-aged women called Martha's Pantry. We chose Martha's Pantry. Here an enormous paraffin heater sat in the middle of the dining-room and two or three couples hunched close up to it effortfully conversed.

'Eddie rang this afternoon,' Frances said, as we ate eggs hollandaise. 'I meant, to tell you, but you were out.'

'What did he say?'

'Still nothing from the publishers. He sounded a bit gloomy.'

None of Mr MacCready's low spirits had rubbed off on Frances. In the month or so of her stay at the Caradon, I couldn't remember a time when I had seen her so animated. Wanting to keep the ball in motion, for some reason, I asked:

'Who was the person you were talking to earlier on?'

'When was that?'

'Ten, ten thirty this morning.'

'Oh, that. That must have been Conrad.'

'Conrad?'

'Oh, just some man.' Frances didn't seem put out by this enquiry. In fact the look on her face suggested that she was quite keen to be asked. 'Just some man you meet at a party and see for a month or two, and then can't work out why you bothered only they keep on ringing you up and there really isn't anything you can do about it. Actually, Conrad's something special. Do you know, he's been researching a thesis for eight years? That's right, *eight years*. Eight years in the British Library writing notes about some balls like the cult of the child in early Victorian literature.'

The reek of paraffin was almost overpowering. 'I thought you liked books. Literature.' For an instant I remembered how Carole had pronounced the word: *lit-ratcher*.

'Sure. Sure I do. But he just does it to look smug, I think. You know, here we are in the late twentieth century, in the middle of a technological revolution and a demographic nightmare, but no thanks, I think I'll just work out what Dickens thought of pre-teenage sexuality, and that's all that's important, Jack.' She brooded about this for a moment. 'Listen. Can I ask you something?'

'Whatever you like.'

'Something personal.'

'Go on then.'

'All right ... All that stuff about Carole. The Bansteads. Redbridge. *The Morecambe and Wise Show*. I mean, what did you think about her?'

'I don't know. Half of me was completely obsessed with her, while the other half always knew what the consequences of that obsession would be. But there wasn't any way of stopping it.'

'You see, I never felt like that about anybody,' Frances aid. 'Certainly not dreary Conrad with his special seat in the BM and his four-foot card index.'

It was here in the revelation about Conrad that I realised a certain kind of courtship ritual had moved into gear. Always, in any relationship with a woman, I'd been able to establish the precise point when some tiny spark of attraction ignited. With Carole it had come in an unexpected solicitousness about my health, instructions to put on my overcoat, things like that; with Helena a determination to finish a book I'd lent her.

I thought about other glances, other hints given and received. Frances said:

'This wine is completely disgusting. Let's go back.'

'All right.'

Outside, wind was careening down the high street, stirring the surface of the pools of water. In the distance the beam from the lighthouse broke into view and then disappeared. In an odd, flustered gesture, Frances took hold of my hand.

Half an hour later she said: 'I'm sorry. It's not going to work.'

'No?'

'I'm really sorry. I just don't think it's a good idea.'

Somewhere beneath us Mr Archer – it could only have been him – was singing along dejectedly to a radio playing 'When Your Old Wedding Ring Was New'. The room was dark except for the illuminated hands of the clock and orange light seeping in from beneath the door. Frances' pale shoulders gleamed through the dusk.

'Is it always like this?'

'Mostly. Look,' she said, 'if there's anything you want to do, why don't you just go ahead and do it?'

'Don't be silly.'

'Why not?' She was close to tears now. 'That's what Conrad used to do. Corpse fucking, he used to call it.'

'Will you shut up about Conrad?'

'I think I'm going back to my room,' Frances said. 'Don't come up, please.'

'All right.'

I watched for a second as she struggled into her clothes. Downstairs, now sounding even more melancholic, Mr Archer was accompanying 'You Can't Get A Man With A Gun'. The door slammed shut. I thought about the previous twenty minutes. It was difficult to get them into focus. Above my head footsteps pattered away into silence.

Next morning Frances sat at the breakfast table without speaking. The post brought another anonymous letter, this time an amateurish drawing of a gallows with the words JUST DESERTS assembled beneath it. In the corner of the room Mr Archer buttered toast with firm, decisive strokes.

Once around this time I asked her, 'Do you think this is going to be a good book?'

'Not really. No.'

'Why not?'

'It's hard to say. Sometimes I think you're not telling the truth. Other times I think you are telling the truth, but a bit selectively. Or that you're telling the truth but you're not really sure about the important things.'

'But isn't not being sure about the important things a point in my favour?'

'It might be. I don't know. But I think you could have worked it out a bit more in your head before you sat down and started this.'

'What do you suggest?'

'It's not really for me to advise. I suppose I'd say, stop trying to do everyone justice. If you didn't like someone or something they did, say so. I mean, what did you really think of Helena? She sounds like a dreadful upper-class bag.'

'Does she? What if I genuinely don't know?'

'This is *history*,' Frances said, quite sharply. 'Nobody ever got any-where with puzzled incomprehension.'

Mr MacCready's letter arrived a day or so later. It conveyed the news that owing to what Mr MacCready called a 'reassessment of priorities' arising from their recent take-over, the publishers no longer wished to continue with the book and were, in effect, cancelling the contract. In the circumstances they would not press for return of the advance. Mr MacCready added that he was prepared to approach other companies with the project, but that there was no guarantee of interest.

'Figures,' Frances said when I brought the letter to her. 'Happens all the time in publishing. Some American corporation moves in, pensions off the directors and starts writing off anything it doesn't like the look of.'

'Do you think there's a chance anyone else will want it?'

'You want me to be honest? Not really. For a start it's old news. And then your principal villain – here – whatever, isn't around any more. If he was in prison or on a Caribbean island somewhere it would be different. As it is, he's just in a cemetery in Oxford somewhere. I'm sorry,' Frances went on, seeing my expression, 'but these things happen.'

We sat in the dining-room for a while where a couple of waitresses – chivvied in Mr Archer's absence by Brenda – laboured sullenly over the rows of plates. Outside light was shining off the housefronts.

'What are you going to do?'

191

'Do?' She seemed surprised by the question. 'I'm going to pack up my things, climb into a taxi and head off for Halesworth station.'

'And when you get back to London?'

'Go and see whether I can get back into my flat. Ring up Eddie and see if he's got any more work for me. Go round to the *Guardian* and see if that balding swot who edits the books pages will give me a novel to review.'

'What about if I came with you?' I said desperately.

'No. I'm sorry, but it's just not going to happen, is it? I mean think about it. We can try and have a fuck for old time's sake if you like, but this is as far as it goes.'

I had a sense of things slipping away, of long-meditated plans suddenly snapped apart.

'Archer will miss you,' I said, half-joking.

'Oh *fuck* Archer. Look, why don't you leave Archer alone? I mean, interfering in his life, cooking up all those little fantasies about him. It's just a kind of trespassing, when you think about it. Feeding off someone else's world. A pretty sad world, if it comes to it.'

We sat there a while longer. I remembered similar scenes with Carole, Helena, other women, my complete inability to say anything that would mend the situation, relief even at the inevitable outcome.

'I'm sorry,' Frances said after a bit, 'but I don't think I can go through with the fuck for old time's sake. And I didn't mean what I said about Archer.'

'No?'

'There's a way in which people like Archer just lay themselves open. Like the fat girls at school. You must have known some. I mean, why *did* they look like that? Who was ever going to let them off?' She opened her mouth to say something and then stopped. 'We'd better just say goodbye, I think.'

She left half an hour later. I watched the taxi move slowly along the high street towards the bend in the road where it would take the Halesworth turn. Then it disappeared.

And so I come to that confused and inchoate period of my life which even now seems hedged about with uncertainty, the period of my uncle's final distress and abandonment. Often in the succeeding years I set out to reconstitute some of its fragments – my uncle's white face glimpsed through the car window, the newspaper headlines, the flight over the Indian Ocean – but the final mosaic always escapes me. I can remember sections – our conversations in the Cornish cottage in the rain, the path through the fields to the village, the fretful ascent of my uncle's breath above the bedclothes – never the whole. In fact there is a more prosaic explanation of my failure to distil the essence of this chain of events, for my imbrication in them began nearly four thousand miles away, in Sri Lanka of all places, and much of what I saw was at second hand. Other people have written accounts of that week: Kippax and several journalists. Reading them, I suppose I feel as Napoleon might have felt if shown a cartoon dramatisation of Waterloo: trivial things magnified, mighty episodes diminished, the whole somehow exaggerated and underplayed at the same time. And yet I've no reason to suppose that Kippax and the others didn't set out to tell the truth according to their lights, merely that, not having seen where our story had begun, they were incapable of imagining how it had ended.

What was I doing in Sri Lanka with Helena? You'll hardly believe me, perhaps, when I say that we were on holiday, and yet we were. Don't even business executives have holidays? And wasn't this a good time to take one, it being the slack summer season in Lothbury and elsewhere? It was mid-August and the Square Mile slept. People used to take month-long vacations in those days: the partners' offices in the big accountancy firms in Fetter Lane gathered dust in the sun and the secretaries sat and idled at their desks. Most of Chell Holdings' business, consequently, was in suspension, and while there were a brace of acquisitions pending and rumours of a government enquiry into the gilts trade, no one anticipated any movement until September. 'City's dead,' my uncle pronounced one morning early in the month as we met in the Lothbury entrance hall. There was no one about. The receptionists were fanning themselves with rolled-up magazines; the plump commissionaire stood uneasily fingering his collar in the sunlight, and a solitary messenger boy lounged in the vicinity of the marble pillars. 'If you and that young woman of yours were thinking of a holiday,' my uncle elaborated, 'you should get on and take it now.' He looked more cheerful than in recent weeks, redder-faced and with an immense stuttering cough that erupted out of him at unexpected moments. 'Summer cold,' he gasped as the final words ended in a paroxysm of wheezing. 'Don't seem to be able to get it off my chest. Go on. Take a fortnight. Kippax'll be back next week.'

I studied Helena's travel preparations with interest. A great family suitcase in scuffed leather, a gazetteer of pre-war Ceylon that had belonged to a colonial grandfather, a pair of ancient field-glasses that weighed nearly half a stone, half-a-dozen packets of digestive biscuits: all this accompanied us in the cab to Heathrow and the Air Lanka flight out over the Gulf. At Dubai, where we landed an hour or so before sunrise, it was 90 degrees in the shade and the water in the airport lavatories was boiling hot: I sat in the arrivals lounge talking to a couple of tea-brokers on their way to a tour of the plantations while Helena trawled the duty-free shop for perfume. Thirty minutes later we flew on into the purple dawn.

It was an immensely dull and pompous excursion, redeemed only by a few incongruities of scene: a decayed country club, like something out of Kipling, with leopard skins on the walls and elephant's foot waste-paper-baskets, where we ate roast beef and Yorkshire pudding in the midday glare; a beach hotel next to the ocean, populated by sun-cured old women who lay all day on the sun-loungers smoking cigarettes; a mongoose suddenly frisking over my feet in the botanical gardens at Kandy. I record these experiences if only because they are something hard and tangible to set against the accompanying silences and resentments.

From time to time, in amongst the queer, staring faces and the dusty roads, came glimpses of the life we had left behind. The island newspaper had a page each day devoted to English county cricket. On the wall of an old colonial hotel outside Colombo I found a framed photograph of some visiting American film stars, taken in 1940. Canny, amused, the face of the current American president stared out. Once, from a modern establishment near the airport, I tried to phone the office at Lothbury, but my uncle was away and the receptionist's voice was so faint as to be indecipherable. Two days later we went north to Kandy, to a hotel where there was only a single telephone, connected to the main exchange in the south of the country – or so it was said – for a bare three hours a day. Why I was so alarmed at the idea of losing contact with the outside world

194

I don't know, but I used to loiter about in the reception area. Helena, too, was forever making fruitless calls home, calls that never got beyond the Colombo exchange or perished somewhere in the ether above the sea. We used to discuss our predicament desultorily in the evenings, out on the terrace watching the firefly lights from the town below. 'Have you heard anything?' 'No, have you?' 'Daddy said he'd ring, but I expect the lines are down.' 'I expect they are, yes.' Neither of us could ever quite put into words the news we expected, but a sense of foreboding infected our conversation like a distemper.

Two days after this, Helena succeeded in getting through to her father. It was early evening in the hotel lounge, deserted except for a gaggle of German tourists, silent except for the occasional thud of a stag beetle hitting a window, and she glided back into the room like a thin, white ghost.

'What's the matter?'

'Daddy says there's something happened about your uncle.'

'What do you mean, "something"?'

'Something about an investigation. An official enquiry ... I couldn't quite get it all, but he says they've been forbidden to trade.'

'Is your father involved in any of this?'

She gave me a sharp look. 'What do you mean?'

'Only that the Associated deal was still pending. It's not inconceivable that he had something to do with it.'

'I don't know. What would I know about it?'

'Do you think we ought to go home?'

'I don't know.'

That night it rained. While Helena slept I flung open the shutters and sat staring out at the dense sheets of water, seeing my uncle's face through the downpour and the gloomy sky. Twenty-four hours later I saw it again – in a two-day-old copy of the *Daily Mail* bought at Colombo airport. The story took up most of page two. Helena wandered by my side as I read it, looking over the scarves in the tourist racks. Half an hour before the flight, from a telephone in an airport security room, watched by a wide-eyed functionary bribed with a twenty-dollar bill, I managed to get through to Lothbury and Kippax.

'It could be worse,' he reported. 'The DTI got here at nine the morning before last. Fortunately I'd got wind of it the night before and took the precaution of removing some of the files. They'll have to come back, of course, but for the moment everything's nicely confused. It's the full works. Independent investigating accountants – there's four Price Waterhouse partners shovelling print-outs in the basement *this minute*;

195

all trading suspended, balance account reconciliations in progress, that kind of thing.'

'What about the offshore accounts?'

'You tell me. They might find out about them, they might not. If they do, there's a chance we can claim the money's for – I don't know – software sales through a subsidiary, something like that.'

'How's he taking it?'

'Ted? Difficult to say.' (It struck me that this was the first time I had heard Kippax call my uncle by his Christian name.) 'He made a speech to the TV cameras when they caught him outside the office yesterday, that was on the lunchtime news. But the first Price Waterhouse meeting was a disaster.'

'Why especially?'

'Wouldn't talk. I was there. They asked him to comment on some discrepancy – just a few thousand, gone out of some holding account – and he sat back in his chair and said "I have been betrayed," just like that. He's gone back to Sunningdale now, gone back and switched the phone off, and I haven't seen him, but there's talk of a search warrant.'

There was a kind of jauntiness about Kippax, I realised, unexpected and yet wholly welcome. Confronted with the prospective loss of his livelihood and a great deal of unfortunate publicity, he was more animated than I'd ever heard him before.

'What did he mean by being betrayed?'

'He thinks someone at Associated tipped off the DTI. Someone who didn't fancy being taken over.'

'Is that likely?'

'Could be, could be not. When are you coming back?'

'Twelve hours' time.'

Kippax's voice faded away into the warm air. I put down the phone and walked out into the departure lounge where Helena sat appraising a batik print. 'I think,' she said, 'that this will be a bit much for mummy, but you can never tell ...' They were the last real words that she ever spoke to me.

These Sri Lanka memories stand by themselves: a little cranny of time whose deeper recesses contain a lot more that I've never cared to take out and examine: watching Helena stride towards me, once, through outcrops of rock on the outskirts of a ruined temple, and understanding the hopelessness of it all – realising, too, that I suspected her of something that I could barely put into words but was somehow central to my own and my uncle's existence.

We landed at Heathrow at dawn, to find the newspapers, the placards and the television screens of the duty-free shops full of my uncle's bankruptcy.

At Heathrow I took a taxi to the City, stepped out of it on the corner of Eastcheap and went to Lothbury on foot. Outside the office a scrum of people converged on the door – I could see Roper, the fat commissionaire, in the entrance hall feebly trying to repel them – monitored by a television crew encamped on the far side of the pavement. As I approached, somebody shouted, 'That's him, that's young Chell!' and there was a general movement of the crowd towards me. Someone took my arm. There was a dim sensation of someone else pulling at my legs, a woman's voice shrieking insults. Roper's face, white and exasperated, loomed up through the throng.

'Mr Chell's not here, sir. There's no one here at all.'

'Where is he, do you know?' I bawled back.

'At home, they say. Mr Kippax ...'

But whatever he was going to say about Kippax was cut short by a sudden surge and redistribution of the crowd. There was another taxi idling at the kerbside fifty yards away, and I ran to it pell-mell through an obstacle course of flapping raincoats, briefcases held up like shield walls to bar my path. It was raining hard by the time I reached Sunningdale, and the water ran in little rivulets over the gravel drive and the stone porch. The house looked infinitely gloomy and tragic: black creepers had grown round the marble porticos and two of the window panes were out. Inside Greta stood in the entrance hall folding and refolding a mournful black tablecloth. When she saw me she stepped back a little way and put her hands up to her face.

'We didn't think you'd be back. Kippax said ...'

'Where is he?'

She jerked a finger back over her shoulder. 'In the back room there. Unless he's gone upstairs somewhere out of the way. There was police here this morning.'

In the end I found him in the small room near the kitchen which I had once assumed to be his study. Shirt-sleeved, his face red and perplexed, he was opening box files and scattering their contents over the desk-top. When he saw me he stopped and stared sorrowfully at the mess, the sea of torn papers and the disarranged shelves. He looked tired, I thought, tired and bewildered, and the colour of his face was fearful.

'George! We thought you were abroad still, George. Ceylon or somewhere.'

As I explained the circumstances of my return, my uncle stood carefully drawing in his breath and letting it out again in great wheezy rasps. Long before I finished he said: 'I've been done, George. Done, by Christ! You seen the papers?'

'Some of them.'

'Associated Life. All those journalists. Not wanting our money and running to the Department. Independent auditors coming in and trying to reconcile the balances.'

'What do they say you've done?'

'One thing you've got to remember, George,' my uncle said heavily, 'is that we always paid our investors. Every penny of interest. Everyone always got paid.'

'But what do they say you've done?' I think in my heart I knew the answer to this question, but somehow I still had to ask it.

'It's bad, George. Oh, it's bad. I don't deny it. Fraud they're saying, misappropriation of funds. All the files gone from Lothbury ... '

'Kippax said he's saved some.'

'Kippax?' My uncle brooded savagely for a moment. 'It's my belief Kippax knows more about this than you'd want him to.'

What he told and insinuated and speculated to me over the next hour, as the rain rushed against the window and the telephone rang on unheeded in the distance, I can't begin to remember: about Kippax and Lord Charlesworth and anonymous letters and the three-hour grilling in the senior partner's office at Price Waterhouse, assurances received, accepted and then removed.

'I've been done,' he said again. 'By people I trusted. It's hard, you know.'

'Did you ...?'

'Oh yes. I rang Her. Quite early on. Wouldn't speak to me. Some dratted private secretary saying he'd pass on a message. Told *me* he'd pass on a message.'

After this he grew quiet. We sat down, the two of us, my uncle at the desk, myself on the floor with my back propped up against the wall, and he brooded again for a while as the rain fell. There was a cigar lying amongst the scrambled papers, a huge Havana like a small bludgeon, and he lit it, puffed uncomfortably for a moment and then lapsed into a fit of spluttering.

'Are you all right?'

'Chest infection,' my uncle gasped. He looked, I thought, much worse than when I'd arrived, shaky and unnatural, like an animated representation of himself. 'Got some antibiotics somewhere. Don't care for them.'

He wandered off vaguely into the hall and I heard him shouting for

Greta. In his absence I turned over some of the papers. They were bank statements: terse, uncommunicative documents concerning companies I had scarcely heard of. Some were addressed to my uncle, others to Kippax. He was gone a long while. When he came back he was carrying a mug of tea and a big accountant's briefcase, out of whose unfastened pockets more papers bulged.

'George,' he said absently, 'we got to go.'

'Go where?'

'I've been talking to Kippax. Got him on the phone just now, and there's a warrant out. They were at Lothbury twenty minutes ago, he says. So we got to go.'

I thought about this for a second or two, considering other possible courses of action, Helena, Kippax and betrayal, if that was what it was. There was a kind of congruity in what my uncle proposed, I realised. He wanted to flee, to remove himself from the mighty elements that oppressed him. What was wrong with that?

'All right,' I said. 'Where do you want to go to?'

'West Country,' my uncle hazarded. 'Devon, Cornwall someplace. Somewhere out of the way. Sit tight and weather the storm. Just you and me. Greta won't want to come, not her. Just you and me.'

He had it all planned, I realised. Even in his hour of extremity, his mind was still revolving in a way that was at once idiosyncratic, calculating and curiously naive.

'All right. The West Country then. Devon or Cornwall. How do we get there?'

'There's a car round the back,' my uncle said wheezily. 'The Jag. Can drive a Jag, can't you?'

'I can drive a Jag.'

And so, watched by a stern and quite unyielding Greta – who I think disapproved completely of what we were doing – I loaded a couple of suitcases into the back of the Jaguar, while my uncle hunched miserably under an umbrella. When this was done, he stood uncertainly by the open passenger door and tried vainly to release the umbrella's catch until Greta snatched it away from him. She was, I saw, hugely annoyed and at the same time deeply solicitous. Busying myself with the seat-belt and a road map I discovered in the glove compartment, I heard him say:

'You'll be all right, will you, Gret?'

'I dare say I shall.'

'I'll phone, you know,' he suggested. The water was splashing down his face now, and collecting on the point of his chin. 'Let you know about things.'

'That's right,' Greta said, giving him a strange look. 'You let me know.'

And so we moved off in a wide semicircle around the back of the house, silent and gloomy in the downpour, and along the side road that led to the front drive, past the great gates, out into the wider world.

Thinking about it now, I remember a considerable part of the first day of our flight, and while incidental vignettes occasionally supervene – eating lunch in a wayside restaurant near Stonehenge, with my uncle managing to interest himself in the weight of the stones ('Curious business how they must have got 'em there'), watching the sun rise up again as we entered a wide, sloping vale in Wiltshire – what remains is the memory of the road, like an endless conveyor belt, and the restless, unhappy figure beside me. For an hour or so, until we were well embarked on the A303, my uncle slept. Waking, he talked in a vague, jittery way, which suggested that his mind wasn't wholly in kilter.

'When you turned up at Sunningdale,' he said, 'could you see what I was doing?'

'Tearing up papers, it looked like.'

'That's right,' my uncle harangued. 'True enough. And what if I was?'

'It's illegal, for one thing.'

'Illegal,' he said. 'I'll thank you, George, not to tell me what is and what isn't illegal.'

A little later he said: 'That Lord Charlesworth, that chap whose daughter you were so friendly with. Come across him ever, did you?'

'Yes.'

'Queer chap. I'm not talking about business, George, not that. D'y'know, we once got talking about sport, and he'd never seen a game of football in his life? Not ever. Even when he was a kid …

'What d'y' do with people like that?' my uncle wondered seriously.

Once or twice I tried to draw him out on the subject of his shattered finances, but it was never any good. He had a number of pet phrases – 'I shall have my say in the end, George,' 'You'll find it'll all come out in the wash,' 'There'll be others that sink while I'm still swimming' – designed to plunge any enquiry into a fog of dissimulation. In the end I gave up.

It was mid-afternoon by the time we reached Exeter. At five, crossing the Tamar into Cornwall, the rain came on again and we sat in a lay-by listening to the radio news. The Chell Holdings story featured third on the roster, but there was no mention of my uncle's disappearance. Then we drove on towards Bodmin, as the moor rolled away dismally on either side of the road.

'I'm tired, George,' my uncle said. 'Want to sleep a bit.'

200

'We'd better put up somewhere for the night,' I suggested. 'Find somewhere proper to stay in the morning.'

In the end we got as far as Truro, and found a bed and breakfast hotel in the shadow of the cathedral. I had incubated the most absurd fears of our arrival, but the people weren't in the least bit interested in us. In the evening my uncle dozed while I walked nervously round the town: there was a picture of him on an advertising hoarding in the high street, a remnant of the old campaign six months back in which, forefinger extended, he demanded of the public if its money was safe.

We were sharing a bedroom. Still lagged from the flight, I was woken in the small hours by the sight of him lurching unsteadily over my bed. Behind him, moonlight streamed through the gaps in the curtains.

'What's the matter?'

'I don't feel well, George.' In his pyjamas he looked frail and wasted; his hands moved listlessly in the region of his chest. 'Got this *feeling* in my stomach. Cough's bad too.'

'Are there any of the pills left?'

'Disappeared somewhere. In the car maybe.'

I remember him standing by the window as I drifted back to sleep, while the light glowed around him, staring up at the cathedral spire.

It was in the morning that I first realised there was something badly wrong. Coming back to the hotel after a journey to enquire about holiday lets I found him sitting wretchedly in the front room beneath a faded poster advertising the Cornish Riviera and a bookcase filled entirely with back numbers of the *Reader's Digest*. Cheered by the sunlight, our remoteness from trouble and the ease with which I had managed to acquire a cottage near Falmouth, I was making light of this distress when he cut me short.

'George,' he said soberly. 'I'm not well, George.'

'You're exhausted. You said.'

'No, it's not just that. George, there's something I've got to tell you.'

'What is it?'

'I can't get up, George. I can't. I've been sitting here trying to since you went out and I can't seem to manage it somehow.'

'Do you want me to get you a doctor?'

'No. Just help me get up. Please. Just help me get up and get me into the car and I'll be all right.'

I did as he told me, and left him slumped against the window while I went to settle the bill. I suppose that if I'd taken him to a doctor then and there I might have saved his life: why didn't I choose to do so? I suppose because I still maintained the conviction that he was indomitable, that somehow he would survive these batterings, that everything, ultimately,

201

would fall away, leaving him exhausted but essentially the same. When I came back to the car he'd rallied a little, and was even conning over a copy of that morning's *Daily Mail* which I'd left on the driver's seat, but there was a film of sweat over his puffy, unshaven features and his hands shook as he turned the page.

'Hot today, George,' he said plaintively as I got into the car.

It was quite a cool morning. Then the last of his self-possession fell suddenly away and he beat the newspaper with his fist.

'I *can't* be bothered with this,' he whimpered.

The cottage was a mile out of Falmouth at the end of a farm track lost in clumps of rhododendrons. A farmer's wife living half-way up the hill gave us the keys and was helpful about bedding. While I made the beds and stowed away the food we'd brought from Truro my uncle sat blearily in an armchair rubbing his ribs with his hand.

'Got this pain,' he said thoughtfully, once or twice. And then: 'Would be all right if I could sleep.'

In the end I put him on the bed, fully clothed, and he slept through the afternoon, while the flies buzzed in the doorway and bored announcers – I had discovered an old transistor radio in the kitchen – unveiled thirty-minute theatres and afternoon stories. Later I went and walked in the woods, blundered through yards of tangled foliage and emerged into rising, verdant pasture, where a herd of cows regarded me wonderingly. In the distance yachts tacked back and forth across the wide estuary. When I returned my uncle was sitting bolt upright on the bed massaging his scalp with both hands.

'Just woke up, George,' he said. 'Such dreams I've been having. Actors and actresses. All kinds of people. Like being in a film ... '

I brought him a glass of water and he looked at it rather in the way that the cows had stared at me twenty minutes before. '*Such* dreams,' he said again.

Did he know that he was dying? Maybe. Maybe not. I remember him being bewildered rather than frightened; peevish, regretful. As his mind wandered it tracked steadily backward, moving rapidly beyond Kippax, Lord Charlesworth and the embarrassments of the last week to distant memories that were barely intelligible to me.

'Always served my country, George. Then and now. Wireless operator in the war, did you know that? Wanted to be air crew, to fly you know, 'stead of sitting on the ground ... Glad I never was ... Not that you were safe, mind. Once saw a man killed by a bullet from a Messerschmidt. Came straight through the side of the truck, through the wireless, through the operator, out the other side. Extraordinary thing.

'... Public works, that's what I started on, George. If you couldn't get a job fifty years back, that's what you did. Remember them buildings in Eaton Park – the changing rooms and the café? Spent three months working on them in 1937, with a barrow and shovel ... Nothing else to do, George, nothing else to do ... '

Occasionally his imagination soared to quite exalted flights. Where he'd got the information I don't know, but it poured out of him like water from a leaking reservoir.

'Napoleon, George. Did you ever hear about Napoleon? Saw a film once, all about him ... Years ago. "I shall ride a white horse. I shall ride at the head of my men." And Ney and the others. And the gates at Elba like a fairground show ... Would have been good to see him, George. Would have been good.'

Once something he said coincided so exactly with my own memories that I sat and stared at him.

'White houses, George, going down the hill ... Remember them ... Bright. Stannard. George Borrow. And then the fields running down to Earlham Road ... Old farmer who kept sheep. Came back after the war and they were gone ... Just houses going on to the roundabout ... Always wondered what happened to those sheep.'

I can't remember how long this went on for. A day? Two days? At intervals other people came and went from his bedside: a doctor, whom I summoned from the farmhouse telephone; the farmer's wife, intrigued and appalled at the prospect of death. By this time there was no doubt as to our identities. In fact I saw the doctor looking at my uncle with a kind of wonder, prior to taking his pulse. At noon on the second day a police car bumped down the farm track, idled by the gravel surround and then went away.

There was a general consensus that he was dying. A move to transfer him to hospital was shelved when his condition worsened. Three or four times I went back to the farmhouse to telephone Sunningdale, but the phone rang on endlessly. All this time my uncle lay barely moving on the bed, small grey head at an angle, wisps of hair flung out against the pillow. He had lucid moments. Once he said: 'Sorry to have given you all this trouble, George. Would have avoided it if I could.'

'I believe you.'

'And I'm grateful, George. Wanted you to know it.'

'Of course.'

There was something greatly animating him, I realised, something that disturbed him even more than the pain. Once or twice he tried to say something about money, but the thousands transformed themselves into millions and back again and it was impossible to construe. Then, on the evening of the second day, standing over the gas-ring in the kitchen, I heard him mumbling dejectedly to himself.

'What is it?'

'Something I want to tell you, George. Something you ought to know.' I sat down in the chair. 'Tell me.'

I have no means of reproducing exactly what he said. This is only the barest impression.

'You remember when you were a kid, George? Back in Norwich?'

'Some of it.'

'Times I used to come and see you' (with an effort). 'Time we walked round that cemetery.'

'I remember.'

'Well, the thing is … The thing is, *I'm your father, George.*'

I remember only an odd feeling of impersonality, a sense of looking into the room from above, staring interestedly at the figure on the bed and his attendant, but with a comfortable conviction that nothing there concerned me.

'It's true,' he said, after a half-minute or so had passed. 'Truer than true. Don't you believe me?'

Again, there was nothing to say. I sat and looked at him, thinking about the picture of my mother on the wall of the house at Putney and the years of surreptitious glances.

'Don't you believe me?'

'Why should I?'

'I'll prove it, George,' he said weakly. 'That case I brought with me. Full of old papers and stuff. You'll see.'

The big accountant's briefcase lay on a chair in the sitting-room. I went and fetched it, placed it on the floor at my feet and, following his directions, began to unpack quantities of folders and single sheets of paper.

'Look in there,' he directed. 'In the big envelope.'

Delving into it, I brought out a thin pile of ancient documents: old, flimsy paper that stuck to my fingers, some of it folded and refolded into grimy packages. There was an RAF identity card made out in the name of Leading Aircraftsman E. Chell, a book of W. & H.O. Wills cigarette cards depicting notables of stage and screen and beginning with Jack Buchanan, finally some bundled pieces of blue cartridge paper. Unfolded and smoothed down, these turned out to be letters – ten or a dozen of them – in my mother's handwriting. I glanced at them for a while, taking in their odd, forceful phrasings, their dramatic underscorings, occasional protestations of a kind that it was impossible to connect with the silent woman in the house at Bright Road.

204

'When were these written?'

'1952, 1953,' he said feebly. 'I was out on the road. Up north, travelling in confectionery. You were about by then, of course. She used to send me pictures sometimes.'

'And how did you …?'

'I don't know. I never could work it out. Ever. Me. Her. The two of them. They never did get on, her and Jack. Didn't matter what they did, what promises they made, couldn't get on. All news to me. I'd been away a year or so after they got married, came back to find Punch and Judy. And of course in those days you had to put up with it. No saying you'd made a mistake and trying for another go like they do now. Your grandad and grandma were dead by then, and I hadn't anywhere to go, so I used to stay with them a time or two. Not in Bright Road – the had a place over near the Fiveways roundabout then. And then I came back one day – he was out somewhere, he was always away in those days – and it just happened.'

I thought about this for a while: the house in West Earlham, my mother looking up, my uncle luminous in the doorway. What had he looked like then, I wondered? Fresh-faced? Knowing? Irresistible?

'Did he know?'

'No one ever said anything, but he was a sharp-eyed one, your dad. I reckon he guessed which way the wind blew. Then again, I never knew what your mother told him. Or didn't tell him. And she was a great one for not saying anything, your mother, for keeping things bottled up. But, whatever, he'd gone soon after that, and then he was dead, poor feller, in a cottage hospital out Attleborough way – just after the Coronation it was – with your mother and me coming over on the bus to see him.'

'But how can you be sure he wasn't my father?'

My uncle stirred himself slightly and clawed at his face with his hand. 'I can't. Nobody could. I'm just telling you what she told me, George. You can make what you like of it.'

'Why didn't you … I mean, after he'd died, what was to stop you …?'

'Often wondered that, George. Often wondered that. Then and now. But she wouldn't have it. Don't know whether she felt bad about your dad dying, or ashamed about it all, but it was never the same. Flaming rows we used to have. Not about anything in particular, just for the sake of arguing. I used to come home and stay a night once in a while – little chap you were, you wouldn't remember – but it never worked. In the end I took to putting up at the pub over the way, the Romany Rye. And pretty soon after that I stopped coming at all …

'… d'y think about it, George?' He was wandering again, in and out

205

of sense. 'Think about that for a temper? Goes to her grave, and ... and never tells you.'

'You never told me either. Not until now.'

'Tried to ... I was always going to, George. Times I was going to ... That night in Putney when you came over. Times at Lothbury, Sunningdale ... Used to mark dates on the calendar. *June the third, tell George* – that kind of thing. Christmas Day, birthdays ... So many things to tell you ... but you're an odd fish, George. Didn't know ... whether you'd be pleased.'

Was I pleased? I remember being intrigued, charmed, mournful, furiously angry. Other than experiencing these emotions, I had no idea how to behave, no idea of how he expected me to behave. Looking down at him, I saw that he was regarding me wonderingly, half affectionate, half curious.

I took his hand.

We talked a little more after that, mostly about my mother. Later, when he slept, I heard him murmuring phrases that could only have been about her. '... Time on Thorpe station ... In a blue dress ... Took the car and on up the hill, up the hill towards the sea, the bloody sea ... Waves in the distance ... Yarmouth and Lowestoft and the bloody waves ...'

It was getting dark. The doctor, who came again at ten, reported that a police car was on the track, and a television crew, the former keeping the latter at bay. As I was making him a cup of tea in the kitchen he said:

'Extraordinary thing him turning up here like this.'

'Oh yes.'

'My wife had a couple of thousand invested. It just goes to show.'

'It does. It goes to show.'

In the doctor's absence the cottage seemed bigger and more desolate. Outside I could see lights winking in the distance beyond the overhang of foliage. There was no sound except his breathing, rising and falling in the inner room like the ebb and flow of the tide. All night I sat in the chair compiling a list of questions I could ask him: questions about my mother, their relationship, his job, life, other particulars. When I woke it was dawn and he lay there huddled against the coverlet, the only proofs of our conversation the small stack of paper spilled over the floor, like spent cartridge cases, I thought, rising up to transform the innocuous Flanders mud.

I have written all this down because I thought it should be recorded.

Q: Do you believe that the allegations made against your uncle are true?

A: If you mean by that 'Do I think that he acted illegally and deployed his investors' money in ways that he was not entitled to?' then, obviously, yes. If you mean 'Did he know that he was acting wrongly?' then I'm not so sure.

Q: You think that distinction can be made?

A: It's very difficult to quantify. Especially at this distance. But I think a lot of the time my uncle didn't know what he was doing, whether he was breaking the law or not. Perhaps this gives an impression of incompetence, but in fact he was a very competent man, and so were the people he employed. You have to be in this kind of world.

Q: It's difficult to conceive of a chief executive of a firm of investment brokers 'not knowing what he was doing'.

A: I'm expressing it badly. For example, he always gave the impression of being utterly sincere. Sincere in what he thought was his duty to his investors, I mean. He genuinely had this vision of himself as a kind of saviour of elderly people on fixed incomes, whom he could help by making their money go a bit further. For instance, he used to love speaking engagements. An intermediary would fix up for him to go and talk to three dozen pensioners at a lunch-club somewhere. He relished anything like that.

Q: Why so much? Why pensioners?

A: I think because they were small people, not well off, making do. My uncle really believed in those clichés about 'struggled all our lives to get by', 'saving for a rainy day' and so forth. And he thought that people who had lived their lives according to these principles had suffered at the expense of big people. Corporations. Big business. As I say, I never found the smallest reason to doubt the sincerity of this. There was a moment, towards the end when the press were on the case, when some elderly people turned up at some function he was leaving, and an old lady shouted 'Swindler' at him, something like that, and he was hugely, deeply upset. He wanted to invite the whole lot of them to Lothbury, explain the situation to them, reassure them. I remember having to talk him out of it.

Q: Why?

A: I don't know ... Because I didn't think things were explicable by that stage. Because it wouldn't have helped, might have made things worse in fact.

Q: Small people and big people. Saving for a rainy day. It sounds – how shall I put it? – rather a simplistic view of life.

A: All I can say is that it made perfect sense to him. He was from the last generation who grew up before the war, you see. I think that made a big difference. He didn't understand inflation or asset-stripping or any of the financial things we take for granted. Or rather he did, but they annoyed him. He thought they were just wicked tricks, that's right, *wicked tricks*, designed to hurt the small man. I'm sure his business activities reflected this.

Q: And yet – you have acknowledged this, I believe – he was a corporate raider. I mean, there are several well-documented cases of him buying small concerns with a view to fattening them up and selling them off ...

A: There came a point, I think, when it became very difficult to distinguish between reality and its opposite. Buying a football club, or a shop, or a fashionable restaurant – these were all things that he wanted to do, with varying degrees of success. But he did them, I think, because it was what he thought people like himself ought to do. There were times when he really did see himself as a kind of commercial buccaneer, taking risks just to see what taking risks might be like.

Q: Did you approve of this?

A: I wonder how much my approval or disapproval meant to my uncle. Or anyone's for that matter. He could be very self-willed. All to do with the small man standpoint, I think. No one had ever helped or advised him – or at any rate done so disinterestedly – and so he thought he could do it all himself. *Think things out.* But perhaps this is an exaggeration, because sometimes he would buy really good advice, the best – get a firm of solicitors from London Wall to advise him on some legal point – and when he did this he could be very deferential ... But going back to the question proper, I don't know that I actually approved, but I remember being very excited about it, very disbelieving at first, but very excited. And this excitement persisted, even though I could see that in some very important respects his judgement was seriously flawed.

Q: His business judgement?

A: His business judgement, obviously. But there were personal things, ways in which he dealt with people that were inappropriate, *grand gestures* I suppose, which could sometimes be offensive. I can remember once – he used to support a great many charities, particularly those for the elderly, and he got invited to a Christmas party at an old people's home. Now my uncle was very concerned that he should give something away, distribute presents. He agonised over this. Nobody would have minded if he'd taken boxes of chocolates, bottles of wine even, but my uncle took it upon himself to bring a wad of ten pound notes and simply press them upon people. I can remember very vividly him going along this line of old people, sitting in their chairs, and giving them money … I thought that was horrible, distressing; I didn't want anything to do with it.

Part Four

And then Mr Archer died.

The news was communicated to the Caradon's guests at breakfast one morning by the younger of Eastwold's two doctors, a melancholy man who looked rather like the Prince of Wales. Though suitably euphemistic, the doctor did disclose that Mr Archer had been in a 'depressed state' and that 'things had become too much for him'. Close cross-questioning of Brenda revealed that Mr Archer had been discovered sitting up in bed, dressed in his pyjamas, one hand clutching an empty bottle of sleeping tablets. An incoherent note was found in the drawer of his bedside table.

Mr Archer's death was thought highly inconvenient by most of the Caradon's guests. 'That's all very well,' an old lady was heard to say after the doctor had left, 'but what about us? Are we simply going to be thrown out into the street? Somebody should say something.' For a while a number of people hung round the reception area in the hope that there would be an 'announcement' of some kind, but when it became clear that nobody knew what arrangements had been made to carry on the business in the event of Mr Archer's death, they slunk away.

It was difficult to know what to do in the circumstances. To stay in the hotel might seem prurient. An offer of help with the myriad arrangements necessitated by Mr Archer's death might be misunderstood. In the end I walked over the common to the creek, crossed over the Bailey bridge and sauntered round Walberswick for an hour. Here it was raining and none of the shops was open. Back at the Caradon I found Brenda standing by the reception desk. White-faced, with her hair fantastically disarranged, she had obviously borne the brunt of Mr Archer's death. Seeing me in the doorway she said:

'Could I have a word with you, sir?'

'What about?'

Brenda made a small, confidential movement with the fingers of one hand. 'It's a bit difficult to explain, sir. Perhaps you wouldn't mind coming into the office?'

I followed her round the desk and through the door of Mr Archer's private sanctum. Here some mysterious agency had been at work, for the papers which Mr Archer usually left over the floor and the mouldy

210

teacups had been taken away. As well as this the tear-off calendar on the wall now registered the correct date. Brenda shut the door with a terrific rattling noise. She said:

'It's about his room.'

'His room?'

'That's right.' Brenda looked as if she might be about to say something, thought better of it, and then began again. 'Did you know that it was me that found him?'

'No. That must have been a shock.'

'I've had worse. It's surprising how often people die in hotels. But it's not about that. The thing is, his sister's coming over in the morning, from Peterborough, to go through his things, and I just wondered, seeing how friendly you and he were – I just wondered whether you'd mind looking round the room.'

'You want me to look round the room?'

'That's right. Just to look round it.'

'Now?'

'If you wouldn't mind.'

I wasn't surprised that Brenda had brought this request to me. The idea seemed perfectly reasonable. Mr Archer, whatever you thought of him, had been a highly unusual person. It was on the cards that his living quarters would contain some unusual items. He and his sister could not have been close: in fact this was the first I had heard of his having a sister. For Brenda to want to prepare the way by sending in an advance party showed tact. All the same the task filled me with unease. For a second I wondered about making some excuse, but Brenda, I now saw, was looking at me with an expression of unutterable relief. Clearly some unimaginable burden had been lifted from her shoulders.

'I'll go up then.'

Brenda nodded. 'You'll find the door's open,' she said. 'I didn't see any point in locking it after the undertaker's men had been.'

Mr Archer's room was at the very top of the house, practically under the eaves. The corridor was sunk in gloom: cleaning materials – bottles of bleach, a bucket or two – lay scattered about. As Brenda had promised, the door was slightly ajar. There was a strong smell of ammonia. I grasped the handle and moved forward. Inside, the first sensation was of light falling gently over the surrounding furniture: a double bed with a thin white counterpane, a couple of chairs, wardrobe, Victorian dressing-table. The walls were bare except for a reproduction of an Alma-Tadema portrait that looked as if it had been torn out of a magazine. Beneath the window, which looked out over the common towards Walberswick, Mr Archer's shoes were drawn up in a long, wavy line. It was difficult to know what Brenda meant by 'looking around', for the whole air of the room was resolutely impersonal. Somehow this feeling of anonymity was symbolised by the wide double bed. It seemed impossible that anybody had ever made love in it, laughed in it, cried in it. Perhaps this was doing Mr Archer an injustice. I examined the drawer of the bedside table and found a packet of aspirins, a ball of cotton wool and a pair of false teeth. Downstairs someone was hoovering: the floor vibrated softly beneath my feet. It occurred to me that I ought to investigate the wardrobe. This was an immense wall of mahogany, six feet high and prevented from falling forward into the room by little plywood plinths. It was unlocked. Here at last some trace of Mr Archer's character displayed itself. There were rows of stiff, ancient suits, a striped boating blazer like a Neapolitan ice-cream, a dinner-jacket in a plastic dry-cleaner's carrier. Lower down, at knee-level, half-a-dozen cardboard boxes lay in a heap. Transported to the bed and drawn open they revealed a cache of boy's school stories from the early years of the century: *Shandy of the Shell*; *The Liveliest Term at Templeton*; *The White House Boys*. On their covers fresh-faced teenagers punted rugby balls back and forth or stood poised to dive into swimming pools. There were thirty or forty of these at least.

Nothing much else remained in the wardrobe except an unlocked Gladstone bag, much scuffed and dented. I hauled it out and inspected its contents. There were old letters tied up in bunches – Mr Archer's sister could look at them if she wanted to; a pile of miscellaneous papers, old tax demands, telephone bills, pages of notes in Mr Archer's thin, spidery hand. I examined a paragraph at random: ... *think that if you considered the position, you would appreciate the very real embarrassment to which ... Notwithstanding these efforts, I submit that this evidence entitles ...* Drafts of business letters? The ground-plan for an experimental novel? It was impossible to say. I got a sudden inkling of what must have been the awfulness of Mr Archer's life: the silent brooding in the Caradon's kitchen; the solitary letter-writing; reading Edwardian school stories. There were a few photographs wedged into the side-pocket of the bag: flyblown family groups; a picture of a small boy on which the vague hint of Mr Archer's adult features might just have been discerned. An envelope, on which these rested, turned out to contain six or seven pictures of Brenda. They were all shot from odd angles or distances: Brenda walking towards the Caradon's front door or bending over a table in the corner of the dining-room. It struck me that they had probably been taken without the subject's knowledge. I put the Brenda photographs in my pocket. At the very bottom of the bag there was a flat package of commercial documents bound together with elastic bands. Something

212

about the way these papers were arranged drew you towards them. I rolled off the bands and shook them out onto the bed. All at once there came over me that sensation sometimes induced by seeing a familiar object – an image from a well-known painting, say – out of context, a violent shake to the consciousness that immediately sends you searching for that broader framework. In this case the stimulus was a folded half-sheet of white cartridge paper hedged about with green scrolls. *Dear investor,* it began, *I should like to thank you for your very welcome enquiry. There has never been a better time to invest in gilt-edged stock. Why is this? Because the market conditions are such that gilts represent by far the most attractive proposition for the prospective investor. There has never been a better vehicle for your investment than Chell Holdings. Why is this? Because our analysis of the trading environment is unparalleled ...*

There was no point in reading any further. I knew the letter by heart, knew it because, ten years ago, in the office at Lothbury, while Kippax fussed over a Securities and Investment Board memorandum on advertising, I had written it. My uncle had signed thousands of them in his time, sitting in the big office, a fountain pen sticking out of his fat hand like a cudgel, looking out of the window at the crowded skyline and the dawdling traffic. Transfixed by this vision – my uncle seated in his room, the pile of documents, the signed letters being borne away – I went hastily through the rest of Mr Archer's papers. There was everything I might have expected – more letters from Chell Holdings, many more letters, some signed by Kippax, others with a great, sprawling facsimile of my uncle's signature in purple ink. Some of these listed dividends; others solicited Mr Archer's interest in other investment opportunities. A third category simply congratulated Mr Archer on his choice of investment ('Cheer-up stuff' my uncle had called this type of letter). Later came letters from the insolvency firm who had taken over the company, interspersed with copies of Mr Archer's replies. I read only the first of these before stuffing the whole bundle of papers back into the bag.

There was a small chest of drawers next to the wardrobe. For a time I went through one or two of the compartments, which revealed nothing more than that Mr Archer had possessed a lot of winter underwear. But this and a search in the wastepaper-basket proved fruitless. In any case, I was almost sure that Mr Archer had manufactured the anonymous letters.

Oddly, my uncle seemed very close to me then. I could see him, practically, alongside me in the room, and I could smell the distinctive combination of cigar smoke, sweat and expensive aftershave, could almost hear him coining one of his bland but curiously perky epigrams

213

about life or money. There was rain coming in against the window and I watched it for a while, thinking about all this – my uncle's unexpected presence, Mr Archer's unlooked-for embroilment in the story of my life. There was nothing to be done, I realised, nothing at all.

Downstairs the noise of the hoover stopped suddenly as I walked into the lobby. Brenda was coiling the flex into long, shiny hanks, like licorice. She looked up enquiringly.

'It's all right, Brenda,' I said. 'All perfectly in order. Nothing anyone could worry about.'

Brenda nodded. 'Always best to be on the safe side,' she said. It was clear that Mr Archer had confirmed her low opinion of him by not leaving something outrageous in his wardrobe to embarrass his executors.

There was something strange about the reception area, I realised. It took a moment or two to work out that the green baize notice-board had been taken down and replaced by a painting of some roses that had previously hung in an obscure corridor, also that the picture of Mr Archer's wife had disappeared. Brenda noted my interest.

'I never did see the point of that board,' she said. 'All the things on it people seem to know anyway.'

'I suppose you're right.'

The front door was open. I wondered what would happen to the Caradon. Brenda's enthusiasm suggested that perhaps she had a part to play. As in so many aspects of his behaviour, Mr Archer's posthumous intentions could only be guessed at. In any case I shouldn't be there to see. Outside the sky was growing dark. Eastwards, towards the common, the lights were going on. Wind blew in from across the tops of the houses. Head down, hands plunged into the pockets of my jacket, I set off towards the sea.

There was a recognised procedure for leaving West Earlham in times of crisis or extremity: it was called 'doing a flit'. Such departures happened literally overnight. Harassed by the hire-purchase collectors or chased by the council for rent arrears, it wasn't unusual for some families simply to disappear, leaving the neighbours to shake their heads and wilfully obstruct any official pursuit. At these times solidarity hung over Bright and Stannard like a fog, and people who hadn't spoken to their neighbours in years would cheerfully tell lies on each other's behalf. Once, as a teenager, I even witnessed one of these upheavals. It involved a family called the Kennedys, who lived two doors down from us and whom I don't think my mother ever spoke to during the three years they inhabited Bright Road, so far did they fall beneath bedrock local standards of decency and sobriety. My mother's dislike of the Kennedys, whose children she referred to as 'dirty little tykes', stemmed almost entirely from their previous address (they came from Cadge Road on the far side of the estate, which was popularly held to be the worst street in Norwich) rather than any outrageous personal characteristics. As far as I remember, Mr Kennedy was a thin, aimless-looking man who worked intermittently on building sites, and his wife a great vacant slattern who had flaming rows with him outside their house while the rest of the street affected not to notice.

Nobody knew what led to the Kennedys' departure, whether it was unpaid rent, trouble with the moneylenders, some more nebulous dissatisfaction with the milieu that my mother and her cronies wouldn't have been able to comprehend. Whatever the cause – and it may be that the Kennedys were simply the roaming, vagrant kind who arrive at places and leave them merely on a whim – I knew as soon as I turned into Bright Road and saw the van parked outside their house that something was afoot. It was quite late on a Friday night in summer and Mr Kennedy stood on the pavement directing members of his family – there were three or four lymphatic teenage children – as they carried boxes and brimming shopping bags out of the house. He looked slightly hangdog and furtive but not wholly embarrassed, as if a small part of him rather looked forward to the reputation for defiance, for not giving a damn about whole areas of civilised, mainstream life, that taking a step of this kind would retrospectively confer. I walked past head down – it was considered the height of bad manners to come out on the verge while these manoeuvres were going on – but he wandered over signalling for me to stop.

'It's George, isn't it?' he said. 'George Chell?' (Despite my mother's dislike of the Kennedys, and an absolute prohibition on having anything to do with them, I'd been out once or twice with one of the sons and even been round to the house. It was an indescribable tip – I think the first thing I saw was a dog-turd in the middle of the kitchen floor.)

'That's right, Mr Kennedy.'

'Well, you won't be seeing us again, George.' There was something almost impressive about Mr Kennedy as he said this, resigned but at the same time faintly impudent. 'Leaving in the morning, we are.'

'In the morning?' (Again, it would have been an unforgivable solecism to ask where the Kennedys were going.)

'That's right.'

We stood looking at each other for a bit, neither quite knowing what to do, until one of the children loped up to ask a question and Mr

Kennedy said, 'G'bye then,' as he turned away. Mrs Kennedy drifted out to watch the proceedings, and the last I saw of any of them was her standing at the kerb-side – she must have weighed twenty stone – staring stupidly at the pile of boxes.

But there was something else about the Kennedys, something else about this incident, that gave it an importance far beyond the admittedly dramatic severing of a casual acquaintance. It was the only occasion on which my mother, to whom I immediately went and related the episode, spontaneously mentioned my father's existence. Even more curious was the fact that she did it mostly by accident. Coming to the end of a string of remarks about the Kennedys and the foolishness of expecting anyone from Cadge Road ever to live respectably anywhere, she stopped suddenly, so suddenly that I see the memory flaring up within her, and said: 'The time your dad left he just took a suitcase with him.'

'Only a suitcase?' I was startled and alarmed, but at the same time determined to keep the ball rolling, to find out all there was to know.

'That's right. A suitcase. Walked off down the street with it under his arm as bold as brass in the middle of the afternoon so that everybody could see.'

'Couldn't you have stopped him?'

'Stopped him?' my mother repeated vaguely. And suddenly the realisation of what she had been saying dawned on her, her face turned scarlet and she began a great diversionary harangue about being seen with the Kennedys and the penalties that would await me if I repeated this sin – all of which was completely unnecessary as we never set eyes on them again and next morning the house was picked and empty.

Standing on the esplanade, as the rain whipped in from the sea, I thought about the Kennedys, West Earlham, my mother, my father stalking down Bright Road (if it had been Bright Road, which I rather doubted) with the suitcase under his arm. Behind, the locked doors of the beach chalets clanked in the wind. Above and slightly to the left a dull red beam pulsed from the lighthouse. There was something to be said for departures of this kind. I thought about my mother and my uncle. Both had loved or at any rate accepted me, but the one had held me at arm's length and the other sought me out on his own exclusive terms. Each had existed in a remote, inviolable world where, it seemed to me, I had barely penetrated, and whose conditions of entry I had hardly ever been able to fulfil. Whether you respected them for this, hated them, or veered somewhere between the two, nothing could be done. Meanwhile there was the question of myself. The rain was growing heavier now, and the flags warning against sea-bathing stuck out at right-angles from their posts. Presumably life at the Caradon would go on. Even without Mr Archer, Frances or the nagging stimulus of Chell Holdings, some sort of existence would be sustainable. For a moment or two I felt ashamed of the way I had patronised Mr Archer, amused myself at the expense of someone whose life I could be indirectly supposed to have upset. I considered Mr Kennedy and the transit van. The rain came again with redoubled fury. I began to walk back along the low greystone wall towards the high street.

Back at the Caradon the front door was open and pale yellow light gleamed from the ground floor windows. Brenda sat behind the reception desk, pencil poised over one of the thick black ledgers that Mr Archer had liked to carry about with him. She looked much better than she had done earlier that morning: the maid's uniform had given way to a kind of brown trouser-suit. When she saw me she looked up.

'Gracious, you must be wet through. There's a fire in the lounge, you know.'

'Thanks. I think I'll go up to my room.'

Brenda made a decisive tick in the ledger. 'I've just been going through some of the books,' she said, confidentially. 'You wouldn't believe the state they seem to have got into. Bookings that were never taken up. Beds you don't know were slept in or not. It's going to take me hours to sort out.'

There was a small pile of ashtrays, perhaps six or seven, lying on the edge of the desk. 'And then coming down after lunch I found these lying in the hall,' Brenda went on. 'Can't think where they all came from.'

I went upstairs. Unusually the bedroom was warm and a film of condensation stretched across the window-pane. The transcripts of the last month's conversations lay in a folder on the bedside table. After thinking about it for some time I tore them up and threw the fragments in the wastepaper bin.

Q: And afterwards. What happened afterwards?

A: What usually happens in cases like this. Some people stayed put and tried to brazen it out. Other people left in a hurry. As you know, I was acquitted. They brought Kippax back from Spain. I think he got a suspended sentence.

Q: And the business itself?

A: It took the insolvency experts nearly a year to sort it all out. Think of that! They had to trace every transaction back through the bank accounts and the ledgers, and this was before bespoke computer software. The only equivalent I can imagine is particle physics, where you can literally track a fragment of matter back through time, back to the Big Bang or whatever. Curiously, the shortfall wasn't that great in the end – about £10 million.

Q: Do you still see any of the protagonists? Hear about them?

A: Not at all. Not really. Greta disappeared. I think my uncle had settled some money on her, money that couldn't be got at or put against any of his debts. I saw Kippax's name in a newspaper a couple of years ago, quite respectably. I believe he'd been appointed finance director of a textile firm, something like that. I never liked Kippax, as you know.

Q: Why?

A: Oh, I suppose I felt that he was the one who was leading my uncle on, the one who was truly responsible for all this ... all this mess. And that's what it was in the end, certainly what offended me about it. It was almost an aesthetic thing. I remember being in the office a day or so before things got really serious – Kippax had already shredded half a ton of paper by this stage, and there were rows of split-open box files all over the floor – and thinking what one would think if one saw the compartments of a vandalised train: here is a mess that someone has got to sort out. Which it was, I mean. The receivers ended up billing the DTI for £2 million over Chell Holdings, which is an enormous amount for an insolvency.

Q: What do you remember about the aftermath?

A: Chiefly bafflement. In that the press reports of the case seemed to bear no relation to the life I'd been leading in the past five years. Also a

218

profound disorientation. In that all the people one had lived this life with were no longer there. Not only no longer there, but quite uncontactable. I remember once, for some quite innocent reason, having to track Kippax down in Malaga – a labyrinthine process that took about six phone calls – and it was like something out of an espionage novel.

Q: You were compelled to attend the trial of course. And I believe you were also present at the DTI enquiry?

A: That's right. I suppose because I was interested to see what the due and proper processes of public investigation would make of it all, whether they would be able to unravel something I'd certainly never come anywhere near being able to unravel. Going back to the remarks about particle physics, I seriously do have this image in my head of a tiny nugget marked 'truth' being dredged out of a primeval swamp, somewhere back in my uncle's early life, back in West Earlham even, certainly somewhere which I could conceive of. But in the end it was all highly unreal, tuppence coloured, *glamorous*, which it wasn't, really.

What I really remember in all this is the funeral. At some tiny church in Oxfordshire which he'd been to once and liked, and written into his will on a whim. They'd kept the press away for some reason, and what with the mass disappearances there was hardly anyone there. One of those bright, cold days when the wind scrapes you like a blunt razor, though it was only early September. The church was on a hill, and I remember coming out and seeing the mist disappearing into trees across the valley, and nearer at hand the undertaker's men with the coffin moving across the churchyard like a huge black beetle. Just that. The mist and the trees. Greta crying somewhere behind me. Turning away because it was all over, quite beyond the power of calling back, and walking away, towards the trees. And the rest of life, I suppose.

I've tried throughout all this story to tell things as they happened. Looking back on it, through the cracked glass of memory, I can only say that most of it astonishes me. Not so much the part played by my uncle – which is verifiable in books and newspaper libraries – as the more anonymous role cast for myself. Why did I do these things, I wonder – leave Norwich, marry Carole, roll through those hectic years in the big house at Sunningdale and elsewhere? All I can say is that I was impelled to do them, swept up by a series of personal and social forces that I couldn't comprehend at the time and am even less certain of now. I don't even believe that there was any pattern, any fundamental tethering in class and outlook. To particularise, I think that in leaving West Earlham I was trying to get away from a distinct and distinctly limiting kind of life, that in marrying Carole I was trying to grasp at what I imagined was a roseate version of that life, that in knowing Helena I was launched in pursuit of something altogether different whose real nature appalled me when I came to understand it. But I doubt whether any of this has any sociological force or validity. And I doubt even more that it comes anywhere near to solving the problem of my uncle.

Even now, I have no idea whether what he'd told me was true. Later, after the fuss had subsided, in the aftermath of the enquiry and Kippax's newspaper interviews and our general vilification, I went back to Norwich and looked into it all. I suppose at bottom I had an idea that even then, forty years on, some of it might be soluble, but there was nothing there. Bright Road had been dug up and rebuilt – even the stink of sulphur had disappeared, I noticed – and the people who'd lived there had vanished, gone nobody quite knew where, to the new estates at Tuckswood or Thorpe Marriot, and were quite beyond the power of tracking down. At the same time it occurred to me that even if I had found them, there would have been very little they could have told me. In the end, by dint of advertising in the *Eastern Evening News*, I turned up an old woman who'd lived in the same street as my parents and attended their wedding. She remembered my uncle as 'a fat chap' who 'made a speech'. That was all: nothing tangible, no indication of how my uncle and my mother had lived together, acted towards each other, fallen apart. Still less was there any explanation of the great wall of silence that descended after my uncle's departure. For some reason, out of shame, embarrassment, some inconsolable antagonism, they'd decided – or rather my mother had decided and made my uncle go along with it – that, their relationship having ended, it should be treated as if it had never been. I don't comment on this: I simply state it as the conclusion of my researches.

Curiously though, being told about the real nature of our relationship – and even now I can't be *certain*, who could? – didn't cause me to revise my opinion of my uncle. The things that I admired about him were still admirable, the annoyances still annoying. And I tried very hard not to colour our life together in a layer of retrospective pathos, because I knew it hadn't been like that, and that any kind of shift in perspective would devalue what I felt for him at the time.

So much of it, too, is quite impenetrable. My uncle's silence after my mother's death, for instance, I don't begin to understand. Did he not want to upset me? Fear the consequences of exchanging one elaborately developed persona for another? In some perverse way enjoy the long – and presumably agonising – years of procrastination? I could never answer any of these questions. And though there was probably other information I could have uncovered if I'd cared to – it struck me that Mrs Buddery, had she still been alive, must have known something – in the end I decided not to pursue it. There was something deeply purposeful in the way my parents – my real parents – had covered up their respective tracks, something ominously deliberate, and I recoiled from the prospect of following them any further. It was only after he'd left my mother, in fact, that my uncle's trail became at all decipherable. I shadowed it for a while through some vague and rather unsatisfactory business ventures in the late 1950s up to the repping for the toy companies. I got an impression of a solitary, faintly aimless life lived out in rented rooms and bed and breakfast hotels. Like father like son, you could say. Nothing in it suggested the remorseless trajectory that was to come.

My mother is gone from me now – it's all too long ago, and my attempts to conjure her into existence are useless – but my uncle is still very vivid in my mind. Scheming with him in the office at Lothbury, those endless nights at Sunningdale with the owls swooping over the silent garden: his voice still rises up at me when I least expect it. Of all this strange accumulation of people there is no one left but me. The rest is old newsprint, dead faces, ashes and dust.

Waking at five, as pale spring light glowed faintly behind the curtains, I

221

often used to reflect on the changes that had come over the Caradon in recent weeks. It was now over a month since Mr Archer's death. The funeral, held in Eastwold parish church, had been poorly attended: half-a-dozen local tradesmen, the president of the town's Conservative Association, a few staff and guests from the hotel and Mr Archer's sister, a tall woman in black who bore an uncanny resemblance to a figure from the *Commedia dell' arte*. Whatever this lady had said to Brenda after the service had ended was never made public. At the same time it was clear that some kind of accommodation had been reached, for the life of the hotel went on unimpeded. Unimpeded but not unaltered. A van came from Lowestoft to remove the contents of Mr Archer's room and clear the store-cupboards in the basement, and a painter was hired to redecorate the residents' lounge.

'There's nothing improves the look of a room like a nice coat of paint,' Brenda was heard to remark.

Lying in bed, sleep kept at bay by the gradual accretion of early morning noises – the faint hum of the central heating, footsteps sounding in a corridor nearby – I thought about all this. It was surprising how quickly Mr Archer's personality had been effaced from the premises. Going down to the kitchen the day before, for some reason that I couldn't quite put into words, I had been taken aback to find an electric heater installed beneath the streaming window and a sack of frozen, ready-peeled caterer's potatoes lying on the table.

From below, perhaps on the main staircase or in the reception area, someone – almost certainly Brenda – was singing in a high, relentless voice:

> 'I'm just a girl that men forget
> – Just a toy to enjoy for a while.'

Brenda had odd tastes in music.

Three days ago a letter had come from Frances. It contained an article she had written for the *Independent*, entitled 'Why motherhood is back', and a postcard that read *Sorry it didn't work out. Life goes on.* Well, that was certainly true. The noise of Brenda's singing was beginning to die away. I remembered a conversation I'd had with her two mornings ago as we met in the entrance hall.

'Up early?'

'That's right.'

'Off to get a newspaper?'

'Probably.'

'We can get them delivered, you know.'

222

'Rotten weather for April,' Brenda had added as I moved past. Coming out of my room the next morning at seven fifteen I had found a neatly folded copy of the *Guardian* propped up against the door.

The noise of the footsteps and the hum of the central heating were now moving in counterpoint. For some reason I wondered what my father would have thought about Brenda. He would have called her 'an attractive young woman', perhaps, or even 'a hot tomater'. Sleep came at last.